W9-BUV-580

Dear Reader,

I don't know about you, but I *love* a great reunion story where two lovers from the past find each other again. Inevitably, emotions are still raw, and the wounds of their past relationship and breakup not quite scarred over. So the sparks really fly when they meet again!

I'm over the moon that HQN has put two of my reunion stories into one larger volume, *Stormy Nights*. This book is comprised of "Summer Rain" and "Hurricane Force," two of my favorite tales of reunited lovers.

In "Summer Rain," Ainsley Hughes, a widow, returns to Wyoming and comes face-to-face with the one man who has the ability to turn her emotions inside out: rough and tumble cowboy, Trent McCullough, the man she thought she'd left behind. Not so, it seems, and boy, is she in for an emotional roller-coaster ride!

In "Hurricane Force," Alison Banning believes that her lover Cord Donahue, who proved to be an embezzler, drowned in the icy waters of Puget Sound. She married his brother and had a child, only to lose her husband as well. Now a widow, the last person Alison ever thought she'd see again was Cord, but here he is, big as life and mad as hell. Talk about a perfect storm of emotions!

Yeah, the sparks really fly in *Stormy Nights,* so look out!

There's a lot more information about this book and others at www.lisajackson.com, so come and visit me there! I'm also on Facebook, MySpace and Twitter! Please look me up and let me know what you think of *Stormy Nights* and any of my other books!

Keep reading!

Lisa Jackson

**Praise for *New York Times* and *USA TODAY*
bestselling author**

LISA JACKSON

"Lisa Jackson's books are compelling, her characters
intriguing and her plots ingenious."
—#1 *New York Times* bestselling author
Debbie Macomber

"When it comes to providing gritty and sexy
stories, Ms. Jackson certainly knows how to deliver."
—*RT Book Reviews*

"Lisa Jackson takes my breath away."
—*New York Times* bestselling author
Linda Lael Miller

"Jackson cranks up the suspense to almost
unbearable heights."
—*Booklist*

"Lisa Jackson sets her own standards [in] women's
fiction today, weaving her magic and providing us
with literary works of art."
—*The Road to Romance*

"Expect the unexpected."
—*The Clarion-Ledger*

"Queen of the modern-day suspense thriller."
—*The Providence Journal*

LISA JACKSON

STORMY NIGHTS

HQN™

If you purchased this book without a cover you should be aware that this book is stolen property. It was reported as "unsold and destroyed" to the publisher, and neither the author nor the publisher has received any payment for this "stripped book."

Recycling programs
for this product may
not exist in your area.

ISBN-13: 978-0-373-77489-0

STORMY NIGHTS

Copyright © 2010 by Harlequin Books S.A.

The publisher acknowledges the copyright holder of the individual works as follows:

SUMMER RAIN
Copyright © 1987 by Lisa Jackson

HURRICANE FORCE
Copyright © 1988 by Lisa Jackson

All rights reserved. Except for use in any review, the reproduction or utilization of this work in whole or in part in any form by any electronic, mechanical or other means, now known or hereafter invented, including xerography, photocopying and recording, or in any information storage or retrieval system, is forbidden without the written permission of the publisher, Harlequin Enterprises Limited, 225 Duncan Mill Road, Don Mills, Ontario, Canada M3B 3K9.

This is a work of fiction. Names, characters, places and incidents are either the product of the author's imagination or are used fictitiously, and any resemblance to actual persons, living or dead, business establishments, events or locales is entirely coincidental.

This edition published by arrangement with Harlequin Books S.A.

For questions and comments about the quality of this book, please contact us at Customer_eCare@Harlequin.ca.

® and TM are trademarks of the publisher. Trademarks indicated with ® are registered in the United States Patent and Trademark Office, the Canadian Trade Marks Office and in other countries.

www.HQNBooks.com

Printed in U.S.A.

CONTENTS

SUMMER RAIN

CHAPTER ONE

TRENT MCCULLOUGH STARED across the dry acres of Wyoming ranch land and slapped at a wasp that had been hovering near his face.

"Don't mind him, he's just thirsty. Smells the sweat on ya," Jefferson Smith, owner of the Circle S, said with a raspy laugh. The older man leaned over the top rail of the fence and frowned at the cracked earth and dust. "Everything's thirsty this year." Cattle still grazed on the stubble in the field, but the grass had already turned from green to harvest gold and summer had barely begun.

"Can't argue with that." Pushing up the brim of his Stetson, Trent studied the horizon. In the distance, past the rolling foothills of the ranch, stood the sheer Tetons, the mountains' stone-gray spires knifing upward through the clear blue sky. "Not much snow in the mountains," he observed, squinting against the bright afternoon sun.

"Yep. It's gonna be a dry year."

"So what did you want to talk to me about? Couldn't be the weather."

"Nope." The older man took off his hat and wiped away the sweat beading around his head. His silvered hair stuck up in odd angled spikes and he smoothed the wayward strands with the flat of his hand. "I've got a deal to offer you."

"What kind of deal?"

"The kind that needs a drink to seal it. Come on inside."

They walked through the dust and gravel to the back door of the house.

"You leave them boots outside!" a voice called from the kitchen as Sarah Martin stuck her head around the door and eyed the men's dusty feet.

With a growl, Jefferson kicked off his boots and walked through the kitchen. "Whose place is this, anyway?"

"And who keeps it clean?"

A smile twisting his lips, Trent followed Jefferson into his den. While the rest of the house was spotless, Jefferson's study was a pigsty. Sarah never set foot within the hallowed walls of Jefferson Smith's private sanctuary, and the thick layer of dust covering papers and magazines scattered all over the desk and tables proved it.

"Okay, what kind of a deal have you got in mind?" Trent repeated as Smith found a couple of clean glasses and filled them with bourbon.

"It's simple, really," Jefferson said, handing Trent a glass and settling into his favorite chair. He motioned for Trent to do the same. "It's no secret that things haven't been going very well here. I've got bankers breathing down my neck and threatening to foreclose on the ranch."

Trent leaned against the window sill and felt a twinge of guilt. "I'd heard."

"Okay. And part of the problem stems from investing in that damned oil company of yours."

"Not just mine. It belongs to my entire family."

"Well, yeah, Jonah did talk me into it. But you and Lila are his partners."

"Can't deny it," Trent said, sipping his drink. Jefferson had finally come around, nearly begging to invest in McCullough Oil several years before and then, just after the old man had put money into McCullough oil wells on his land, the market had gone bust.

"So, I figure maybe you can help me."

"Because you think McCullough Oil owes you."

"Not necessarily. I invested by my own choice. But it wouldn't do none of us any good if I lost the ranch. Oh, sure, you'd *probably* retain the lease to the mineral rights, but the land your wells are on would be owned by someone else. I don't think you, or your brother or your sister would be too thrilled about that."

"So what're you getting at?"

"I just thought maybe the tables had turned. It's time you invested in *my* operation."

"This ranch?"

"That's right. For fifty thousand dollars, you can be a quarter owner and that includes the land where your wells are sitting."

Trent rubbed his jaw and his eyes narrowed. "Will that get you out of the red?"

"Not by a long shot. But it'll give me six months."

"So then we still have a chance of losing it all."

"I always thought you were a gambling man, McCullough." His old blue eyes sparked. "Besides, I know you've been itchin' to get out from under your brother's thumb."

Trent's shoulders flexed. "So that's why you came to me instead of Jonah?"

"One reason," the older man said, rubbing his jaw.

"I'll have to think about it. See the figures." He finished his drink and set the empty glass on the corner of the old battered desk.

"Got 'em all here." Jefferson reached into a drawer, pulled out a stack of papers and handed them to Trent. "Take them with you. I've got copies."

"You're really counting on this, aren't you?"

The older man's shoulders slumped. "I've got no choice."

Trent scanned the documents and frowned. The Circle S was tied up so tight he couldn't find one loophole in the mortgages and second trust deeds. "So what's my collateral?" he asked, studying Smith.

"You get the plane." Jefferson's chin thrust forward.

"The Cessna?"

"That's right. But when we turn this thing around I'll expect her back."

"For the money."

"Of course."

"And that's it?"

"Not quite. I expect you to stay on as foreman. You know, run the place."

"I don't know about that—"

"Why not? Jonah practically runs the oil company by himself. And Lila, she don't care."

"Not much," Trent agreed, his lips twisting wryly.

"And you've been handling your ranch—you still can. I just want you to put in a few hours over here. You'd be paid, of course."

Trent doubted it. The Circle S was already drowning in red ink. "I'll think about it," he said, walking to the door. He hated to see the wiry old man so beaten. Always a scrapper, Jefferson Smith had managed to hold on to his ranch in good times and in bad.

"Do." Jefferson took a long swallow of his drink and then wiped his mouth with the back of his hand.

"There's something else you might be interested in."
His old eyes glinted.

"And what's that?"

"Ainsley's coming home for the summer."

The muscles in Trent's back tightened and his teeth
clamped together so hard they ached. Looking over his
shoulder, he studied the old man and wondered what,
exactly, Jefferson's game was. "So?"

"I know how fond you were of her."

"That was years ago."

Jefferson sighed and pretended to study his hands.
"I know, but if you would've spent that last summer
here instead of down in Houston, things might have
been different."

"I had to work."

"But you came back. And it wasn't too late. If you
hadn't let your pride stand in your way, maybe you would
have turned out to be her husband."

A corner of Trent's lips curved cynically upward and
his eyes grew hard. *Ainsley.* Just the thought of her did
dangerous things to his mind. "You think so?"

"Yep, if I recollect right. And I do. You let Robert
Hughes slip in the back door when you weren't lookin'."

"It was too late," Trent said, remembering all too
vividly the last time he'd seen her. "And it really doesn't
matter one way or the other, does it? She married Hughes."

"And now he's dead, and she's havin' trouble raisin'
my grandson alone."

"Too bad."

Jefferson stood and stretched as he studied the
younger man. "Yeah, well, it doesn't have to be. Like I
said, Ainsley's comin' back for the summer. But I was
hopin' you might help me find a way to get her to stay."

"Why?"

Jefferson looked away, out the window to the shaded porch and the sun-parched acres beyond. "I'm gettin' older, Trent. And I'm alone. All I got in the world is this miserable patch of ground, some oil wells that aren't worth the money I paid for them and a headstrong daughter with a rebellious son."

"Some people might say you were rich."

"Well, they'd be wrong, wouldn't they? The bank's ready to take back the ranch, my only daughter lives in San Francisco, for God's sake, and I don't have all that many years left."

"You talk like you're dying."

"We all are."

"So what does Ainsley coming back have to do with me?"

Jefferson frowned. "I may as well be straight with you."

"I'd appreciate it."

"Good. Because I think you should marry my daughter."

Trent's gray eyes flashed and his jaw tightened as he stared incredulously into the older man's serious gaze. Then he laughed. "You're out of your mind! You can't be serious."

"As serious as I've been about anything in my life."

"No way—"

"Just hear me out."

"Look, Jeff, I can't stand here and listen to this." He shoved his hat back onto his head. "I don't even know why you thought I'd be interested."

"That's simple enough. You're a good man, a damned sight better than that husband of hers was, and she needs help raising Korey. From what I hear, the kid's a regular hellion. That's my grandson we're talking about. My *only* grandchild."

"And *Ainsley's* son. Don't you think she should have any say in this?"

"Of course. Of course," Jefferson agreed, walking up to the younger man and tilting his head back to look Trent straight in the eye. "But I figure all she needs is a little push. From you."

"Is this part of your 'deal'?" Trent asked, holding up the papers.

"It could be," Jefferson said.

"No, thanks."

"Think about it, Trent. In the end you'd inherit this ranch—you and Ainsley. You and I both know there's more oil here; it's practically running in rivers under the ground. But right now it's not worthwhile to drill it. That'll all change someday. Depending on the market and what happens in the Middle East, this ranch could be worth millions in a few years."

"Or nothing," Trent said, his eyes narrowing. "Remember, the bank still owns it."

"More incentive for you to get it into the black."

"Just remember that I haven't agreed to anything yet."

"But you will."

"Maybe." His face muscles grew taut. "But let's get one thing straight, okay?"

"What?"

"You'd better leave Ainsley out of this."

"Can't do it. She and Korey will be here in the next couple of weeks." His face relaxed at the thought of his grandson. "I'm gonna have Ainsley send the boy along first—so we can spend some time together alone." He stretched his arms over his head. "The way I see it, Ainsley's back for good."

"Whether she wants to stay or not?"

"I'm just suggesting that maybe you can make her want to stay."

Trent snorted. "Why do you think I'd care?"

"'Cause you used to be in love with her—"

"That was years ago."

"You never married."

"Right woman never came along."

"Well, she's comin' along now."

"Forget it, Jeff. I'm not interested."

"Why not? You've spent your life raising your sister's kid while she's off gallivantin' in New York, and you work like a slave for your brother."

"My choice." He tugged open the door and strode angrily through the halls to the screened-in back porch. Jerking on his boots, he watched a fly buzzing on the screen, trying to find an escape route through the tattered mesh.

"Don't get your dander up," Jefferson suggested, following him.

Trent strode into the midday sun without saying anything.

But the older man wasn't through. "Think about it, son," he said, cursing as he stomped on a boot and hurried after Trent. "When I die, this place could be yours."

"Yeah. Mine and Ainsley's and First Federal Bank's!" He jumped into his pickup and slid into the sun-baked seat. "No thanks, Jeff."

"You'd better think about it."

"And you'd better quit meddlin' in your daughter's life. I remember Ainsley's temper, and neither one of us wants to be around when she finds out that you're trying to fix her up with a husband." He started the engine and slammed the pickup into gear.

"Not just any husband, Trent. You! How many men get

a second chance?" Jefferson shouted as Trent roared away, gravel spinning out from under the old Dodge truck's tires.

His blood boiling, Trent roared out of the lane and headed toward the offices of McCullough Oil. This entire "deal" with Jefferson smelled of one of Jonah's plans and he was going to get to the bottom of it.

AINSLEY HUGHES STRETCHED and looked through the open French doors of her third-floor studio. Pale rays of morning light were streaming through the panes, giving the old attic a warm glow.

Through the open doors, she could see the city of San Francisco stretching out to the Bay. A few lingering wisps of fog still clung to the dark water and ships slipped in and out of the mist.

She set her brush on the easel and ignored her cold cup of tea. Walking out onto the balcony, she lifted long, chestnut hair off her neck and took a few deep breaths of salty air. The wind was brisk but warm against her face, and she wished she could ignore the restlessness deep inside her. It was a perfect day. So why was she so uneasy?

As she watched a sea gull swoop from the blue-gray sky, she heard the front door open and slam shut.

"Oh, no," she said, recognizing the pounding of Korey's feet as he climbed the stairs to the second floor. Her son was home early. *Trouble again.*

With a sigh she hurried back inside the house and climbed down the steep stairs to the second floor. Then, softly, she knocked on Korey's door.

"What?" he demanded, sounding defensive already.

Ainsley's shoulders slumped. "I just want to talk to you," she said, cracking the door open and poking her head inside.

"Well, I don't want to!" He flopped onto his unmade bed, put his hands behind his head and stared up at the ceiling.

"Maybe you should tell me—"

"No! You'd just get mad!"

"Would that be any worse?" she asked walking into the room and receiving a hard glare from her son.

His dark eyes cut right through her. "Probably."

Ainsley sat on a corner of his bed and frowned. Comic books and boxes of crackers and cookies were strewn across the wrinkled quilt that draped to the carpet. Toys, books and records were cast in every direction. In one corner of the small room an aquarium gurgled and a long-forgotten rock collection gathered dust.

"What're you doing home so early?" she asked, ignoring the mess.

"I got sent home. There. You satisfied?" Crossing his arms over his chest, he met her gaze. His brown eyes were brightly belligerent.

"No." She hooked her hands under her knee and pursed her lips together. "You've been getting into a lot of trouble lately—"

"So who cares?"

"I do."

"But school's almost out."

"I know. So, maybe it would be smart to play by the rules for a while. At least until summer."

"Why? So we can go to Wyoming? Mom, that's *nowhere!*"

Give me patience, she thought, looking at the ceiling. "Just tell me what happened, okay?"

"Nothing." He lifted a shoulder, as if to dismiss the subject.

"The school sent you home because nothing happened?"

"Yeah." But some of his bravado had slipped.

"So tell me." She leaned closer and stared at him with her clear, blue eyes. "How dumb do I look?"

He couldn't help but grin. "Not too dumb—"

"Then let me know what really went on today."

"You won't like it."

"I've already figured that out."

"Okay." He shrugged. "I, uh, let the rats out of their cages in the science department."

"You did *what?*"

"I told you you wouldn't like it."

"Go on."

"Well, they got out of the room and scared old lady Buxton out of her wits! She even jumped up on one of the library tables right in the middle of showing a film on the Dewey decimal system."

Ainsley groaned and rubbed her temple. "Why, Korey?"

He looked away. "Some older kids dared me. And, well, it seemed like a good idea at the time."

"A good idea?" Ainsley repeated, incredulous. A headache had begun to form behind her eyes. "I'd hate to see what you'd call a bad one." She began picking up the empty cookie and cracker boxes, then sighed. Handling Korey was getting tougher by the minute. If only Robert were still alive…. Looking up she caught her son's worried gaze. "I think you're grounded, my boy," she said, "and as for this stuff—" she held up the crumpled packages "—off-limits except for the kitchen. Got it?"

"Got it," he mumbled.

She walked to the door, but paused. "And don't forget to clean up this mess." She looked at the littered room and leaned against the door frame. "So, after you let the rats out and Mrs. Buxton climbed off the table, then what happened?"

"The custodian found 'em. All of them except one."

"Great." She sighed quietly. "But I wasn't talking about the rats, I want to know what happened *to you*."

"Oh."

"Yeah, 'oh.'"

"Nothin' much."

"How much?"

He avoided looking her in the eye. "I guess I'm suspended for a week."

"There's barely a week left," she whispered.

"I know." Korey dropped his eyes and fumbled with a torn magazine. "I'm sorry, Mom."

"I don't think that quite covers it."

He stuck out his lower lip and glanced up at her. "And there's somethin' else."

Here it comes, she thought, bracing herself. "What's that?"

"You're supposed to call Mr. Gorman."

"The principal?"

"Yeah. He wants to talk to you—have a meetin' or something. Right away."

"I'll bet," she muttered, her stomach twisting as she walked downstairs. Back in the kitchen, she gathered her courage then reached for the phone. *No time like the present,* she thought, as she dialed the number of Korey's school and was connected with Maxwell Gorman.

TWO DAYS LATER she was cradling a cup of cold coffee and sitting at a battered table in a conference room at Johnson Elementary School. Maxwell Gorman was seated across from her.

"It's not that Korey's a bad boy," Gorman said, settling into his chair. "He's just taken the wrong direction."

"I see." Ainsley's gaze drifted around the bland-looking conference room, finally coming to rest on the thick manila folder spread open in front of Gorman. Korey's school records.

"It's just since he lost his father," the big man said, a kind smile twitching below his gray mustache.

"But you're recommending passing him on to the fourth grade?"

"No reason not to. Academically, Korey's right where he should be. His grades have dropped, but—" Gorman shrugged "—he's had a lot to deal with. It's not easy for a child to lose a father—that's just plain tough, for anyone, at any age."

"So what do you suggest I do?"

"Spend as much time with him as possible. And try to find a father figure for the boy to latch onto. Maybe an uncle or someone close to you."

"I don't have a brother," she murmured. "And… neither did Robert."

"Well, there are several big-brother type organizations in town," he suggested.

"I'll…I'll see what I can do," she said, her brows knitting. "But we're planning on visiting my father's ranch in Wyoming this summer. We won't be in San Francisco."

"Maybe that's just what your son needs," Gorman said, taking off his glasses and rubbing his eyes. "A change of scenery and some good hard work. And your father…maybe he can provide the male influence Korey needs."

"He's almost seventy."

"But he was a boy once, too." Gorman checked his

watch and stood, offering Ainsley his hand. "Thank you for coming in, Mrs. Hughes."

"Thank you." More worried than ever, she walked out of the building. Shoving her sunglasses up onto her nose, she slid into the warm interior of her Mustang and drove out of the rutted parking lot, maneuvering the little car down the hilly streets toward the heart of downtown San Francisco. She'd decided to stop by the Worthington Art Gallery, where some of her pieces were on display.

After parking the car around the corner from the building, she pushed her hands into the pockets of her skirt and shouldered her way through the tall glass doors. The two-storied rooms were filled with intent customers and objets d'art of all shapes and sizes. Soft jazz music filtered through and around the dangling mobiles, tall sculptures and impressionist paintings.

As she stopped to observe a white mannequin dressed in splashes of neon, Charlotte "Charlie" Worthington, a friend from college, looked up from behind the desk. "Ainsley!" she cried. A small grin spread from one side of Charlie's face to the other, exposing just the hint of a dimple. Her dark eyes danced as she hurried forward. "It's been ages! What're you doing down here?"

In a swish of magenta silk, Charlie slipped through the carousel horses, metal sculptures, mannequins and paintings. "About time you showed your face around here. I've got someone interested in your night seascape."

"That's good news. And I could use some," Ainsley admitted.

Charlie looked at her with a practiced eye, apparently not liking what she saw. "Okay—what's up?"

"I thought I'd better tell you that I'm spending the summer with my dad in Wyoming."

"I thought you said you'd never go back!" Charlie said, surprised.

"*Robert* said that."

"He would have," Charlie said dryly. "He seemed to have some phobia about it. So why are you going?" she asked, pulling a face. "I thought you liked it here."

"I do…but there are a lot of reasons."

"Well, come on, tell me about all of them!" Charlie waved at a red-haired clerk in the back of the gallery. "Angela—can you handle things for a few minutes?"

"Sure thing," the girl replied.

"Good. Now, come on." Weaving through the maze of sculptures, she shooed Ainsley up a circular staircase to the upper balcony, then led her into the employees' coffee room. After pouring them each a cup of coffee, she sat at the table and motioned Ainsley to do the same.

"No espresso?" Ainsley teased.

"Only for *important* clients," Charlie replied with a grin. "Now, tell me, what's all this nonsense about Wyoming?"

"It's not nonsense. I'm going. In a couple of weeks. I just wanted to leave you my address and phone number in case you needed to get in touch with me."

"Why now?" Charlie asked, then leveled her dark eyes at her friend. "It's because of Robert, isn't it?"

"Indirectly," Ainsley admitted, leaning back in her chair and blowing a wayward strand of hair from her eyes. "But really, it's Korey. He's having problems at school." She launched into her story, explaining about Korey's behavior since Robert's death and ending with her meeting with the principal.

"So he misses his dad, huh?"

"Yes…at least sometimes."

"And you?" she asked.

"I'm doing okay."

"Hmm." Charlie arched a skeptical brow. "Well, Korey'll be just fine," she predicted. "I pulled some of those same stunts when I was in school."

"I remember."

"And I turned out all right."

"You were a twenty-year-old college student. Korey's nine."

"I think you're blowing this all out of proportion."

"That's because he's not your son."

"Well, then," Charlie said, winking slyly, "it sounds like no problem at all."

"No problem?"

"Maybe you should take that principal's advice. All you have to do is find yourself a man!"

Ainsley made a face. "Easier said than done."

"Oh, come on. I bet that Wyoming oil country is absolutely oozing with rugged, good-looking men just waiting for the perfect woman to stroll into their lives."

Ainsley pursed her lips. "Hardly."

Charlie finished her coffee. "The least you could do is look!"

"Oh?"

"But not because of Korey." She leaned forward, her elbows on the table, her dark eyes piercing Ainsley's. "Because of you."

"Me?"

"Yep. You've been moping around ever since Robert died."

"I have not!"

Charlie arched a perfect brow. "Okay. How many dates have you had?"

"It's been less than a year—"

"How many?"

"None," Ainsley admitted.

"I thought so." Charlie crossed her arms over her chest. "Now, the first thing you do when you get to Wyoming is to find yourself a rich rancher or oil man or whatever it is they do there!"

Ainsley laughed. Charlie always had a way of making her feel better. "Look, I've got to go, but here—" She handed Charlie a card with her father's address and phone number on it.

They walked across the balcony and down the steps to the main floor of the gallery. Charlie winked as she waved goodbye. "Let me know if you find any extra outdoorsman types for me."

"Will do," Ainsley said, as she headed out of the building and onto the crowded sidewalk. The wind was blowing off the bay. It pushed her dress against her legs and the afternoon sun warmed her crown as she climbed into her old Mustang convertible.

Men in Wyoming, she thought wryly as she slipped on her sunglasses. There were only two that she cared about. "Yeah, and one is your father," she told herself as she turned on the radio. "And the other one…well, he's off-limits."

Trent McCullough.

She could still picture his taut, rugged features and furious gray eyes when she'd told him that she was marrying his best friend, Robert Hughes. Until that evening, eleven years before, she'd had no idea that he'd been in love with her.

Now, driving through the winding narrow streets of the city, she could remember that lazy August afternoon as if it had been yesterday….

CHAPTER TWO

AINSLEY HAD BEEN eighteen that summer and Trent had taken a job away from Wyoming. She hadn't missed him all that much because she'd thought of him as an older brother and a friend. Nothing more.

But now he'd returned from Texas and she was fairly bursting with her secret! She was anxious to tell him just what she'd done, but she couldn't. She'd promised. And besides, there was something in Trent's eyes that bothered her—something she'd never seen before.

They'd been riding through the fields for hours, looking for stray cattle that might have slipped through a broken section of fence and wandered from the McCulloughs' property to the Circle S. The dust and insects were thick, as purple twilight began to cover the land.

Ainsley's shoulders were beginning to ache. She rode her father's gray gelding, and the horse plodded slowly, continually switching his tail against flies, slapping Ainsley's thighs as it walked the dusty fields.

"We must have found them all," Trent said, reining his horse closer to Ainsley's, his eyes sweeping the fields before returning to her.

She glanced up and caught him staring at her. Just as he had been all afternoon. His face was handsome, no longer boyish, his skin stretched tight across high cheekbones. His jaw had squared and was dark from a day's growth of beard. Thick, coffee-colored hair fell over his penetrating, slate-colored eyes.

"So far..." Her eyes strained as she turned in the saddle, looking for any strays that might be hiding in the shadows creeping across the land. *If only she could tell Trent her news!*

"I think that's it. At least for me. I'm not used to this kind of manual labor," he teased, reining in his horse near a stand of blue-green pine bordering the stream that cut from the Circle S and wound a silvery swath under the fence to the McCullough property.

"So what did you do in Houston?" she asked.

"Nothing as interesting as this." He laughed, pushing his unruly dark hair from his eyes. "Believe me, working in a refinery just isn't what it's cracked up to be."

"Maybe you'd better leave the oil business to Jonah—he's the one who's interested, isn't he?"

"Yep. He and Lila." At the mention of his sister's name, his lips thinned and he slid a glance at Ainsley. "Maybe I'd better stick to ranchin'."

"Your pa would probably have wanted you to."

"I s'pose."

He'd been brooding all day, giving her long looks that made her heart flutter crazily. Stupidly. She couldn't think of Trent as anything more than a good friend. Especially now.

She dropped the reins and let the gray drink from the creek. Bridle jangling, the gelding swallowed eagerly and flicked at flies with his ears and tail.

"Good boy," she murmured, patting the horse's neck and surreptitiously watching as Trent lifted his hands high overhead, stretching the fabric of his faded cotton shirt and lifting it out of his jeans.

Ainsley had to look away. Groaning and stretching she slid to the hard ground. Every muscle in her body ached and she kicked off her boots to dangle her feet in the ice-cold water. She was tired of the hard life and the ranch, and now, at eighteen, she was old enough to leave. Finally, she had the means.

Sluicing water over his face, Trent washed away the day's grime, then stripped off his shirt, using it for a towel. His tanned skin was smooth across his back and the corded muscles of his chest. Dark hair arrowed down below the waistband of his faded, low-slung Levi's.

Ainsley couldn't help but stare again. She'd never thought of Trent as anything but the boy next door—an older brother type. But three years of college had aged him, and in the late afternoon shadows of early September, he looked all male; intriguing and dangerous.

Her breath caught in her throat and her heart fluttered a little when he glanced up and caught her watching him.

Blushing, she studied the ground. "There's, uh, something I was meaning to talk to you about," she said, picking up a handful of dirt and letting it sift between her fingers.

"Shoot." He leaned against a pine tree and slanted a grin in her direction. It slashed across his face and touched a special part of her.

Her stomach knotted, and suddenly, she couldn't tell Trent that last night she'd married his best friend, Robert Hughes. She hadn't even told her parents that while she and Robert were supposedly at a dance, they had been secretly married, and that they were planning to leave for California as soon as they could.

"Ainsley?" he prodded, his voice deep as he watched the emotions on her young face. "What happened?"

"Nothing," she lied.

"Come on, Ainsley. Something's on your mind. I can tell."

"Can you?" She looked up again. Her gaze met his and froze. Behind the deep-set eyes was the same mocking stare she'd always known—but something else, too, as if in this single summer everything had somehow changed between them.

"Sure. You've been quiet all day. Not like the magpie I'm used to."

"Magpie?" she repeated and gave him a frail smile.

He sat down beside her and studied the arch of her brow, the curls that had escaped from the long braid down her back, the nervous way she licked her lips. "Can't we trust each other?"

"I guess so."

"We always have." He placed a finger under her chin and forced her eyes upward to meet his. His eyes were clear and gray and direct, and the intensity of his gaze made her heart slam against her chest. "It has to do with Robert, doesn't it?"

"Yes," she admitted, wondering if Robert had broken his promise and told their secret. "He's…talked to you?"

Trent nodded, his lips thinning a little, his eyes narrowing. Every muscle in his body grew taut. "I'm sorry if he hurt you," he whispered. "I didn't know you two were so serious."

"Hurt me?" she repeated, not understanding. At last, she could confide in Trent, but suddenly it was the most difficult thing in the world. "He hasn't hurt me."

Trent inhaled sharply. He saw the brilliance in her

clear blue eyes, the lift of her mouth as she glanced at him.

Then playfully, to defuse the tension between them, Ainsley kicked some cold water from the creek in his direction.

His stomach muscles tensed when the ice-cold drops peppered his chest.

"You should be happy for me, too!" she insisted.

"About what?"

"About the fact that I'm an old married lady now!" she said, wondering why her voice sounded so breathless.

He didn't move. His eyes fixed, cold and hard, on her face. "What did you say?"

"Robert and I got married last night!" she repeated, laughing nervously and tossing her head back, her cinnamon-colored braid almost touching the ground.

"What!"

She tried to comprehend the sudden blaze of anger in his eyes and the way he paled under his tan. "But…but you knew that already. You said you talked to him."

"Ainsley—if this is one of your jokes," he warned, his voice low and threatening as he took hold of her arm and pulled her to him, balancing her on the edge of the creek.

"It's no joke."

"But you couldn't have married him—"

"I did. Last night!" She felt his fingers digging into her arms, saw the hard angle of his jaw and the tension in the cords of his neck.

"Don't play games with me!" he ground out.

"I'm not! Trent, you're hurting me. What's wrong?" she asked, her lips starting to tremble, her arms aching. She'd never seen him so furious. His nostrils flared and white lines hardened around his mouth.

"What about Lila?" he asked.

"Lila? Your sister?" she repeated, dazedly. "What's she got to do with anything?" Her eyes were round with wonder. What had gotten into Trent?

"I hope to God that you're lying to me!" he ground out.

"Why?" She inched her chin upward, stared deep into the gray depths of his eyes, noticing the strain of his rigid muscles as he gripped her shoulders. "You said you talked with Robert…I thought he told you—"

Trent's gaze lowered suddenly to her lips and he sucked in his breath, pulling her tight against him. Her jean-clad thighs pressed against the rigid muscles of his legs. "Oh, hell," he muttered, mesmerized. His hands tangled in her hair and quickly untied the ribbon holding the thick curls away from her face. Breathing hard, he glanced down to the quivering, frightened line of her lips, and before she had time to react, he'd placed his mouth over hers.

She could feel the pulse of his heart in his kiss, hear her own, beating a rapid counterpoint.

Dear God, no! This can't be happening! Ainsley tried to back away, but couldn't. His arms were too strong as they wrapped around her. Powerful hands splayed over her dusty blouse and his body crushed against hers as his weight slowly pushed them both to the hard, sun-baked earth.

"Please, Trent, don't…"

His breath was hot against her skin, his hands surprisingly gentle. She tried to fight but couldn't as he pressed her into the dry bank, his naked chest crushing her breasts, his lips claiming hers in a kiss that stole the breath from her lungs. Though the heels of her hands were pushing against his shoulders, she was aware of the hard feel of him, the fibers of his muscles under her fingers, the thudding of his heart as he lay across her. Her heart beat wildly, crazily, and she couldn't think as he kissed her full on the mouth, his hard lean body straining against hers.

"Tell me you're lying, Ainsley, that this is one of your crazy games," he rasped, when he pulled his head from hers. A sick look of disgust contorted his features.

"I'm not!" Tears had begun to build behind her eyes. *How could she kiss him when she was married to Robert? How could she feel this way? Why was she aching for a man she'd always thought of as a brother?* Loathing herself, she closed her eyes and turned her head away from him.

"Oh, God," he murmured, his face registering the sudden shock as it struck him that she wasn't teasing. Rolling away from her he groaned, squeezing his eyes shut tight.

"How could you?" she demanded, her voice hoarse, tears beginning to stream down her face. She lifted her hand to her lips, realized they were still swollen and felt shame burning deep in her stomach. *She'd wanted him. When she was already married to Robert, she'd wanted Trent.* Sick with herself, she brushed her tears aside.

"When did you have time to—" he whispered.

"When we were supposed to be at the dance. Last night."

"That bastard!" He slammed his fist into the ground and a vein throbbed in his temple. "That miserable son of a bitch!"

"What're you talking about?" she asked, her voice echoing over the hills. He wasn't making any sense at all.

He didn't look at her but continued to stare up at the

darkening sky. "Last night," he said, his voice hoarse, his lips drawn tight over his teeth, "after you were married…you and he…made love," he said flatly.

"No!" She wrapped her arms around her legs and he looked up, pinning her with cold gray eyes. "I…I had to come home. We haven't told Mom and Dad yet."

"This just gets better and better," he mocked.

"They would never have let me go to school in California—"

He paled and took in a quick breath, steadying himself. "You could still get the marriage annulled," he said, his gaze fixed stonily on the first stars winking from the lavender sky.

"But why?"

"Because he doesn't love you," he said simply.

"He does! Why else would he have married me?" she threw back at him.

"Figure it out."

"I don't know what you're talking about."

"For the Circle S."

"You're out of your mind! He doesn't want this ranch. He hates ranching—"

"But not the money it's worth," he said, his guts twisting inside.

"He's my husband," she said, as if that fact alone would make all the difference in the world. She tried to stand, but he reached forward and caught her wrist. "Let go of me."

"I don't care what you think of me, Ainsley," he said slowly, as if the effort cost him. "But for God's sake, use your head. Robert doesn't love you—he doesn't know the meaning of the word."

"He's your best friend!" she said, horrified.

"Was."

Swallowing hard, she backed away. "But not any more?"

"No."

"Why not?" she asked, dreading the answer, a chill of premonition skittering up her spine.

"I've got my reasons."

"Then spit 'em out!" she cried, frustrated and ashamed.

His throat worked and he saw the pain in her eyes. "There are things—"

"*What* things?"

"Things about Robert. I don't think he's been completely honest with you," he said, a muscle throbbing in his jaw.

"About *what*? Good Lord, Trent, quit talking in circles and get to the point!" she screamed, shaking.

"If only you weren't married to him."

"But I am, dammit!"

His eyes became slits and he wiped his mouth, as if to get rid of the taste of her. "Then there's nothing I can say," he whispered. "It's over and done. You love him, don't you?"

"Yes…no…yes! He's my husband!" she whispered, wondering why she sounded so breathless and felt so unsure. Her throat was cotton dry, her eyes fixed on the slant of his mouth.

His jaw tightened and his nostrils flared. "Then you're a fool," he whispered, muscles rigid. "And I've thought of you as lots of things, Ainsley. But never a fool."

"What're you trying to tell me?" she asked.

"That he's gonna hurt you."

"I don't believe it," she said. The warmth and feel of him had left her trembling inside, aching as she'd never ached, thinking dark, dangerous thoughts that should never have entered her mind.

He stood and walked to the creek. "Maybe you'd better go home," he whispered.

"I will!" she claimed, her face red, her lips swollen. With as much pride as she could muster she jerked on her boots, ran to the rangy old gray, swung into the saddle and gave the horse his head. Galloping as fast as it could, the horse raced away, leaving a plume of dust in its wake.

Ainsley took deep breaths of the cool evening air, feeling the wind tangle in her long, brown-red hair as it streamed behind her.

She only dared to look back once. Trent was still standing near the creek, feet spread wide apart, fists planted firmly on his hips, the ribbon from her hair fluttering from his curled fingers as the shadows of the coming night grew long around him....

NOW, FIGHTING THE traffic in downtown San Francisco, she sighed. "That was a lifetime ago." She drove the old Mustang through Union Square and fought the urge to feel sorry for herself. She wasn't a headstrong eighteen-year-old any longer. She was a twenty-nine-year-old widow with a strong-willed son who needed help. Though Trent's prediction had come true and Robert had hurt her time and time again, it didn't matter. Korey had adored his father.

Ainsley rubbed her neck. It was a tragedy that Robert had been killed in a freak accident at a construction site. Even though their marriage had suffered some blows, she could have put up with just about anything as long as Korey had stayed happy.

"Too late now," she murmured, frowning. She had to find a way to get through to her son!

Rolling down the window, she let the warm May air

fill the interior of the car. It caught in her hair and blew against her face as she guided the Mustang through the steep hills. Far below the winding road, the shimmering waters of the Bay reflected the bright afternoon sun. Sailboats and fishing vessels, tankers and tugs drifted on the calm water.

Ainsley had come to think of San Francisco as her home and she hated to leave. "It's just for the summer," she reminded herself.

After stopping at a local art supply store, Ainsley drove home and parked on the street. Then, shading her eyes from the sun, she sat in the Mustang and stared at the townhouse she and Robert had shared, the narrow, three-storied Victoria structure that she'd loved as much as she'd loved the whimsical city itself.

Painted gray, with white trim and accents of burgundy around the windows, the townhouse was a perfect place to raise a son as well as to sculpt and paint. Or it had been. Before she'd learned about Robert's string of affairs and before he'd been killed.

Wondering if she should sell the townhouse, get rid of all the unhappy memories and start over with her son, she got out of her car and climbed up the stairs to the front porch.

And do what? her mind taunted. *Go back to Wyoming— and Trent?*

"Idiot," she muttered to herself, before looking expectantly up the stairs. "Korey! I'm home!" she called.

She heard his feet hit the floor and then the scurry of footsteps as he raced into the hall.

Leaning over the banister, looking down the steep flight to where she was standing in the foyer, he asked, "Well?"

"Well, you're back in school on Thursday, and Mr.

Gorman recommended that you be promoted to the fourth grade."

"Radical!"

"Hardly," she murmured dryly. "You made it by the skin of your teeth and you've got a lot of work cut out for you this summer."

"Work?"

"Uh-huh." She held up the sheaf of papers Korey's teacher had given her. "Why don't you come down here and we'll talk about it?"

"Now?"

"Now."

Wearing a put-upon expression with his tattered jeans and wrinkled undershirt, he sauntered downstairs and followed his mother into the kitchen. She spread all of the math papers and reading projects on the kitchen table. "This is work you had trouble finishing," she said. "But we're going to do it—every last bit of it—before school starts in the fall."

"But it's almost summer—"

"And if you don't do it at home, you'll have to go to summer school."

Korey pulled a face and slumped into one of the maple chairs surrounding the table. "I don't want to spend the summer doing this junk!" he said, kicking at one of the table legs with the toe of a high-topped basketball shoe.

"Neither do I," she assured him with a crooked smile. "But we're going to do it. Think of it as a mother-son project."

"Great," he mumbled. "Homework and Wyoming. I'm thrilled," he mocked, looking as if the whole world had turned against him.

She took a chair across from him and pushed the hair out of his eyes.

He jerked away at the tender gesture. "Aw, Mom, cut it out. I'm not a baby anymore. And...I don't want to go to Wyoming."

"Why not?"

"'Cause all my friends are here! Besides we were s'posed to go with Dad. It won't be the same." He pouted, his lower lip protruding rebelliously.

"I know it won't, but we're going to make the best of it."

"I won't go—"

"Oh, yes you will," she said firmly. "And you're going to take all of this work with you. You're just lucky Mrs. Hayes didn't include the science and history lessons you ignored."

Seeing no point in arguing, he demanded, "So why do you want to go back there, anyway?"

"Lots of reasons," she admitted, thinking of the enigmatic calls she'd received from her father. She'd gotten the feeling that something at the Circle S wasn't quite right.

"Such as?"

"I haven't seen Grandpa in a while."

"He was here last Christmas," Korey mumbled.

"And I'd like to see the ranch."

"I thought you hated it."

"No—"

"That's what Dad said."

Ainsley had to fight to keep her voice calm. Robert had refused, time and time again, to return to Pine Corners, the nearest town to the Circle S. "Your dad hated it, and when I was younger—" she looked out the window and sighed "—I thought I had to get away. You know, see the world. California sounded like paradise."

"And now you miss Wyoming," he said, disbelieving.

"Yeah. I do."

"Well, I don't."

"It's not for the rest of your life, you know," she teased. "So go on upstairs and pack. I'll make a plane reservation for you for the day that school's out...unless you'd rather wait for me."

"I'd rather not go at all."

"Sorry. Not an option."

"Great," he mumbled, pushing his chair away from the table. "Just great."

She watched him stalk up the stairs, stomping rebelliously as he climbed. "Oh, Korey," she said to herself as she straightened the homework. "All I want is for you to be happy."

SOMEHOW, KOREY FINISHED the third grade and climbed on a plane bound for Denver all by himself. As Ainsley watched him walk down the ramp to the huge jet, she had the urge to run after him and make him wait another week until she could close up the house and go with him.

But her father had been insistent that Korey fly ahead and it was too late to change plans now. She watched the 727 take off and felt tears in the corners of her eyes. The next week would be quiet...and lonely.

In the next few days, she managed to tie up all the loose ends with the local galleries and her townhouse, and within the week, she'd flown from San Francisco to Denver and the madhouse that was Stapleton International Airport. Travelers from all over the country seemed to have converged in Denver, waiting for connecting flights.

Ainsley battled through the throng and waited impatiently at the baggage claim area, her eyes alternately searching the carousel for her suitcase and the terminal area for Korey's brown hair or her father's weathered face and blue eyes.

But by the time she'd found both pieces of her luggage, neither her father nor son had shown up. "Wonderful," she muttered as she hoisted the shoulder strap of her garment bag closer to her neck and started threading her way through the crowds of people milling in the terminal building.

As she walked down the concourse, she looked around, hoping to see her father's familiar wiry frame or Korey's expectant face. Her eyes darted anxiously from one knot of people to the next.

When she didn't see anyone she recognized, she made her way to the area restricted to the use of private planes and asked about her father's Cessna.

"Not in yet," the man in charge of the flights of small aircraft replied as he checked his schedule and listened to a report from the tower. "No…wait a minute. He's just coming in now."

Ainsley paused, watching her father's small plane land and taxi to a stop. Picking up her bags, she started for the plane, smiling expectantly as the door over the wing opened.

Though the sun was in her eyes, she knew instantly that the pilot wasn't her father. Stopping short, she shaded her eyes with her hand and recognized Trent McCullough poised on the wing of her father's plane.

CHAPTER THREE

AINSLEY COULDN'T BELIEVE her eyes. "What in the world—"

Bare-headed, the bright rays of the sun catching in his thick, coffee-brown hair, Trent climbed down from the wing. Ainsley's throat constricted and her heart fluttered rapidly. She hadn't seen him for nearly a decade, yet her pulse still raced at the sight of him.

Sunglasses shaded his eyes and his jaw was tight. His dark hair ruffled in the wind over features more craggy and rough-hewn than she remembered. His broad shoulders were rigid as he approached and his gaze, behind the dark glasses, was trained on her. "Ready?" he asked, without so much as a greeting.

"What're you doing here?"

"I came to pick you up." He glanced around the field.

"I see that. In Dad's plane. Where's he?"

"At the ranch."

"At the ranch?" she repeated and started to question him, but he cut her off by ignoring her and walking into the building. "Wait a minute—" She followed him inside and found him talking to the supervisor, going over his flight plan. Steamed, she gripped her suitcase more tightly but didn't interrupt as he made sure that his flight plan had been filed and that he was allowed to head back to the Circle S.

"We'd better go," he said, taking her bags and hoisting them over one shoulder as he crossed the hot tarmac to the plane. His free hand was planted firmly in the small of her back as he propelled her to the gleaming white Cessna.

"Just hold on a minute," she demanded.

His thin lips tightened.

"Where's Dad—and Korey? They were supposed to meet me."

"I told you—they're both at the ranch."

"But why didn't they come?"

Trent shrugged and his jacket stretched taut over his shoulders as he placed her bags inside the hold. "Beats me. Come on, climb in."

"Dad said he'd be here, with Korey," she said again, once she was in her seat and Trent was behind the controls.

He checked the gauges and the levers, not even once glancing in her direction. "I know. Maybe he had better things to do."

She'd forgotten how frustrating he could be. "Such as?"

"I don't know. Maybe he wanted to stay home and go fishing with Spike."

"You're trying to tell me that my father, whom I haven't seen in over six months, didn't come pick me up because he had to go fishing with a friend he sees every week?"

"Yep." He glanced at her, then looked straight ahead, his concentration entirely on the commands from the air tower and the runway ahead.

Knowing that he was teasing her, but goaded just the same, she clamped her mouth shut, waiting until they were airborne and she had his complete attention before trying to talk with him again.

She crossed her arms over her chest and pretended interest in a 747 as it took off, but from the corner of her eye, Ainsley watched him. His skin was dark and weathered, his features angular. His nose was long and straight, his eyes, when not covered with dark aviator glasses, deep set and a piercing shade of gray that she remembered as vividly as she did the feel of that one kiss. Thick brows, even darker than his hair, bunched together thoughtfully and his thin lips curved cynically. He looked tough and lean with a hard edge that was almost chilling. And still her heartbeat quickened at the sight of him.

The little plane lurched forward. Ainsley held her breath.

Within seconds they were in the air, and with a thud, the landing gear snapped back into the body of the plane. To the west, the craggy Rocky Mountains jutted upward through the wispy clouds that clung tenaciously to the uppermost peaks. High in the eastern sky, the morning sun sent bright rays of light that reflected off the white-painted nose of the plane.

Being so close to Trent made her uneasy. She watched the length of his leg resting so near hers, the way the soft corduroy fabric stretched and slackened over the tense muscles of his thighs as he guided the plane.

"Okay," she said, once Denver was far behind them and the air traffic had thinned, "why don't you tell me about Dad?"

"Nothing to tell."

"There had to be a reason he didn't come—and don't give me some malarkey about a fishing trip with Spike."

"Just telling you what he told me." But deep grooves lined his forehead and his thick brows drew downward below the metal rim of his glasses.

Ainsley's hands twisted in her lap. "Is he okay?" she asked softly and saw his mouth compress.

"As far as I know, but he's getting older. We all are."

"But he loves to fly."

He pulled off his headset and sighed. "Look, Ainsley, I'm not gonna lie to you. Your dad's been around a while, had a few hard knocks. A lot of things have happened at the ranch in the past few years. Some of them you probably won't like—or maybe you still don't give a damn."

"What's that supposed to mean?"

"Take it any way you like."

"The least you could do is try to be civil," she said, her eyes flashing.

"I am."

"Barely."

He didn't respond, but his fingers tightened around the controls.

Ainsley tried a different tack. "So why are you at the ranch?"

"I work with your dad now."

She was surprised. Her father hadn't mentioned Trent. The same cold unease she'd felt when she'd first seen him in the plane settled in the small of her back. "Doing what?"

The plane hit a bank of clouds and jarred a little. Ainsley's stomach jumped to her throat and she started to sweat, but Trent held the controls steady and kept the small craft on course.

"I didn't know you could fly," she said, breathing again.

"I can't."

She saw the twitch at the corner of his mouth. So he did still have a sense of humor. That, at least, was encouraging. "Very funny," she said, grinning and tossing her head back. Thick chestnut curls fell away from her face.

Trent glanced her way, then ground his teeth together as he noticed the thin dusting of freckles over the bridge of her nose and the way her sea-blue eyes peeked from beneath curling dark lashes. After all these years, he still couldn't tamp down the desire that fired his blood whenever he looked at her. "You're a fool," he muttered under his breath.

"What?"

"Nothing. Just a little off course," he lied—then changed the subject. "I met Korey."

Her eyes lit up and she looked straight at him. "And what did you think?"

"That he's a lot like you."

"Oh?"

"Strong-willed kid."

"I know." Sighing, she slid back into the plastic cushions of the seat and wondered how she'd ever control her son.

"Bullheaded like his ma."

And irresponsible like his pa, she thought, but held her tongue. Lifting a brow, she glanced in his direction and saw the quirk in his lips. "I suppose."

"Jefferson claims Korey got into a little trouble at school."

"A lot of trouble," she corrected, combing her hair with her fingers.

"Bad?"

"Well, not really. I mean, he's too young for girls… and he's not into drugs or anything. At least, not yet."

"But you're worried."

"Yes," she admitted, her brow puckering as she squinted against the sun. "Very."

"So you think a slower-paced life on the ranch will

help him," he guessed as he banked the plane and headed northwest.

"I don't know. I hope so."

"What about a little hard work?"

"That would help," she said, her thoughts turning dark as she considered Korey and the fact that he had never really adjusted to his father's death.

"You didn't seem to think that way when you left," he said coldly. "You wanted to get away from the Circle S— no matter what the cost."

"I was eighteen. I thought I wanted to see the world."

"And?"

She rubbed the tired muscles of her neck. "And I'm glad to be coming home."

"'Bout time," Trent muttered. He noticed her thoughtful expression, saw the sadness in her eyes and decided she was thinking about Robert. His jaw tight, he stared through the scattered, filmy clouds. "Want to talk about it?" he asked.

Shaking her head, she wrapped her arms around her waist. "There's really not much to say. Korey and his dad were very close…but, since Robert's death…" She lifted a shoulder and sighed. "It's been hard on him."

"And you?"

She glanced up sharply. He was still staring straight ahead. "It was hard at first."

"And now?"

"I'm okay," she whispered.

The engine of the plane droned on, cutting through the clear air. Ainsley looked out the window and down to the earth far below. A swirling silver river cut through a dark forest to wind through a patchwork of golden fields.

"No commitments back in the city?" Trent asked,

trying not to smell the scent of her perfume or notice the way the hem of her skirt fell around her calves.

The corner of her lips lifted. "None that can't be ignored, or put on hold for a while."

"Won't the galleries in San Francisco shrivel up and die without your work?"

"I wish," she murmured. "But it doesn't really matter. If I decide to stay, I can work right on the ranch. I used to have a studio over the garage...." She thought about the old studio with its sloped ceiling, how she'd loved to go up there and work until all hours of the morning.

"I remember," he said softly, "but you have to realize that things are different now."

"Don't tell me Dad tore my studio down!"

"Nope. But it's filled with all sorts of junk."

"Nothing that can't be cleared away, I'll wager." She looked at him through narrowed eyes. "You keep talking about changes on the Circle S. What are they? Do they have anything to do with the reason *you* picked me up?"

"I told you—"

"I remember—'Dad wasn't up to flying.' I can't quite get it out of my mind that there's something else going on. As long as I can remember, Dad hasn't let anyone else fly this plane. Now you're at the controls," she pointed out, running her fingers along the side panels near her seat. "And when I asked you what you did on the ranch, you didn't answer. I wonder why."

Trent took off his dark glasses and looked at her. She was still as intelligent and beautiful as she had been all those years ago and every muscle in his body ached from the strain of lying to her. Well, not really lying, just avoiding the truth so that Jefferson could tell her about the financial condition of the ranch himself. "I'm the foreman of the Circle S."

"You're the *what?*" She gasped.

"You heard me."

"But why? How? Dad's never had a foreman in his life!" Ainsley said, worried all over again.

"He's getting older."

"He's not even seventy! Hardly old enough to give up or hire a man to run the place!"

"Maybe he's getting tired."

"And maybe it's more than that. Come on, Trent, we've known each other a long time. Why don't you tell me what's really going on at the Circle S?"

"Why don't you wait and talk to your dad?"

Ainsley felt cold inside. All of the little doubts that had been nagging her, the little fears that she'd resolutely pushed aside came back with a vengeance. She reached over and touched Trent's arm, her fingers encircling his elbow. "Just tell me," she whispered, "that my dad is okay—that he's not sick."

"I don't know, Ainsley," he said quietly. "He hasn't said anything."

"Then...why? Why you? Did you need a job?"

Trent laughed when he remembered just how old Jefferson had badgered and bargained him into taking the position. "No. I still run my family's ranch."

"What about the oil company?"

"Brother Jonah handles that," Trent said, eyes shifting to her and then back to the front of the plane as his voice grew cold. "Division of duties."

"Wait a minute. Dad mentioned something about investing in McCullough Oil a few years ago."

Trent nodded slightly. "He did."

"And?"

"And what?"

"How'd it go?"

"As well as any investment in oil has gone."

"Oh," she whispered, lapsing into silence again, her eyes following the course of the silver river as it wound, serpentlike, far below. *Just what the devil was going on at the Circle S? And why was Trent McCullough entrenched so heavily in the ranch?* She closed her eyes and rested her head against the door as she tried to think.

The drone of the plane's engine didn't falter, nor did the wheels spinning in her mind. In a few minutes, she was sound asleep.

"HERE WE ARE," Trent said quietly, rousing her by lightly touching her shoulder. He hated to wake her. She looked younger and softer as she lay with her head crooked against the window, her hair a wild cinnamon curtain covering the side of her face, her neck arched against the back of the seat.

Ainsley stretched as she opened her eyes. She hadn't realized that she'd dropped off. With a soft moan she rubbed the crick in her neck. "How long have I been asleep?"

"Long enough. I thought you'd like to take a look at the place from the air."

"You were right." Far below, the spreading acres of the Circle S looked just as she'd remembered them. Dark stands of blue-green pines covered the sloping hills to the northwest. Wolverine Creek, a rushing silver stream, zigzagged across the tapestry of green-gold fields. White-faced Hereford cattle dotted the landscape. A cluster of buildings—the farmhouse, barns and stables—stood in front of the stately pines and aspen that grew in the foothills of the mighty Tetons.

"Wait a minute," Ainsley said, staring at the black towers in the southeastern field. "What are those?"

"Oil rigs," he muttered as the landing gear snapped into place. His mouth a firm line of concentration, he guided the little plane downward, approaching the old landing strip.

"Oil rigs?" she repeated, confused. "As in McCullough Oil?"

"Yes—hold on."

Ainsley gripped the armrests of her seat. The wheels touched down on the old asphalt, bounced, then screeched as they held, and the plane raced to the end of the runway before stopping just short of the field.

Trent unbuckled his seat belt, took off his sunglasses and reached for the door.

Ainsley grabbed hold of his arm. "Why are there oil derricks on the Circle S?"

He looked at the small hand clamped firmly around his wrist. "Didn't your father tell you?"

"He told me that he'd invested in McCullough Oil. He didn't mention anything about drilling on the ranch."

Slate-gray eyes looked deep into hers. Ainsley's heartbeat quickened and she dropped her hand.

"Maybe you should have come home more often," Trent said. "Like I said, a lot of things have changed at the Circle S."

"Like you becoming foreman?"

The brackets around his mouth became deep creases. "For one."

"And the drilling?"

"That's another. But it's more than that."

"What do you mean?"

"The whole way of life has changed since we were kids. It's just not the same."

"Dad never mentioned—"

"Maybe he shouldn't have had to," Trent snapped, his patience wearing thin at being put in the middle between Jefferson and his daughter. "Maybe you should have shown more interest! The least you could have done was show your face around here once in a while."

The insult cut deep into Ainsley's guilt. Her visits had been few and far between, especially since her mother's death. "I suppose you're right," she said, wanting to defend herself but unable to.

"Just don't try and tell me you were too busy, okay?"

"I won't! Because it's really not any of your business, is it?" she said, her chin inching upward.

Trent raised his hand. "Hey—look, I'm sorry." He raked tense fingers through his hair. "I just think there are a lot of things you'd better discuss with Jefferson—that's all."

"I will."

"Good. Looks like you'll get your chance right away." He cocked his head in the direction of a battered old pickup lumbering slowly up the dusty road to the airstrip.

Ainsley climbed out of the plane. "Dad!" she called. "Korey!" The pickup ground to a halt and Korey jumped out of the passenger side, while her father slowly climbed out from behind the wheel. Dallas, her father's dog, barked from the truck.

"How've ya been, sport?" she asked, hugging her son fiercely and blinking back tears of relief at the sight of him. It had been barely a week since she'd put him on the plane in California, but she'd missed him horribly.

"I'm okay, Mom," he muttered, a red flush climbing up his neck when he glanced at Trent.

She brushed back his hair and noticed it was beginning to streak with gold and that his skin had already begun to tan.

"How about you?" she said with a grin as her father approached.

"Can't complain," he said, clapping her on the back and coughing. At Ainsley's worried gaze, he grinned. "Don't look at me that way. It's just too many years of these," he said, patting the pocket of his worn work shirt and the crumpled pack of cigarettes inside.

"*You* can't complain? That's not the Jefferson Davis Smith I remember," she teased.

"Really, kid," he said, his blue eyes twinkling, "I'm fit as a fiddle." He grabbed her hard and hugged her tight against his wiry frame.

Ainsley looked over his shoulder to Trent and saw the disbelieving slant of his mouth. "If you're so fit," she said, stepping back and staring at her father, "why didn't you come and get me today?"

Jefferson's bushy gray eyebrows lifted. "Have to keep Trent busy, y'know. Now that he's foreman."

"I heard you hired him on."

"Just part of a business deal," her father muttered.

"Along with the oil wells?"

"Yep. All tied together," he said. "Now, let's not talk about business, leastwise not yet. Sarah's baked a fresh strawberry pie and she'll want to set her eyes on you right away." He placed one arm around his daughter, the other around his grandson and guided them back to the pickup.

"Okay, Dad," she said with a small smile. "But I want to know what's been going on around here the last couple of years."

"And I aim to tell ya. Now, quit worryin'! Everything's fine now that you're back home!" Ainsley looked back at Trent. He was busy moving her bags from the plane to a Jeep that he'd evidently parked near the landing strip before taking off.

"You comin'?" Jefferson called over his shoulder.

"In a minute. I'll take care of the plane—put it in the hangar—and then I'll bring Ainsley's things up to the house."

"Fair 'nough," Jefferson replied.

Once Ainsley was situated between her father and son, Jefferson started the old truck, put it into gear and grinned as it lurched forward to bump down the long, dusty road leading back to the house.

"So, how've you liked your first few days at the ranch?" she asked Korey.

He shrugged. "Okay, I guess."

"Just okay?" Jefferson laughed. He pulled a cigarette from the crumpled pack in his shirt pocket. "Better'n okay I'd guess. He's quite a horseman, your son is."

"Is that right?"

"Oh, Grandpa—"

"'Course it's right. He takes after me, don't ya know?" He lit his cigarette and grinned, his old eyes twinkling with mischief.

Korey bit on his lower lip and stared out the window.

"Go on, son, tell your mom what we did."

Korey slid a glance at his mother but didn't say a word, and Ainsley got the distinct impression that trouble had already begun to brew. "What happened?"

"Oh, nothin'—not like you're thinkin' anyway," Jefferson said. "You remember your ma's favorite little chestnut filly?"

"Jezebel?" Ainsley swallowed back the familiar lump

that formed in her throat. Her mother had loved that fiery little foal.

But Emma Smith had taken ill shortly after the filly's birth and hadn't been able to see her grow. Ainsley and Korey had flown to Wyoming, staying on at the ranch for the last three months of Emma's life. Ainsley had watched her mother die, day by day, and had never felt so helpless in her life.

"Yep. Well, that little filly's a mare now, y'know, and I never did have the heart to sell her. The winter before last, she foaled and dropped one helluva colt. He's a yearling now and as full of the devil as his dam." He shifted down as he drove across the cattle guard and through the gate. The old truck shuddered and groaned before lurching forward. "I gave him to Korey here."

Ainsley didn't move. "You did *what?*" she said, hoping she hadn't heard correctly.

"I told Grandpa you wouldn't let me keep him," Korey grumbled.

"You gave Korey a *horse?*" Ainsley repeated.

"That's right. We named him Crazy Luke."

"Wait a minute," Ainsley said, bracing herself with one hand planted firmly on the warm dash so that she could look her father square in his weathered, conniving face. "Let me get this straight. You had the nerve to give my son, who lives in a very small townhouse in the middle of San Francisco, a yearling colt named *Crazy Luke?*"

Jefferson laughed and ground out his cigarette in the ashtray. "Sure I did. And don't go givin' me no lectures, not before you take a look at him—"

"But we live in the city, Dad!" she said incredulously as she flopped back on the worn plastic seats of the old truck.

"I don't expect you to take him back there, for God's sake. And don't stare at me like that!"

"Just level with me, okay? What've you got up your sleeve?"

"Nothin'. It's just that I think the boy needs to know how to handle a horse."

"Why?"

"You knew how to ride before you could walk. And Wilson, Trent's nephew, he's already been to rodeo."

"Wilson?"

"Yeah. You remember—Lila's boy. Korey and he are friends."

"I don't see what Wilson has to do with—"

"Korey needs a horse," her father said authoritatively, his gray-stubbled chin jutting forward. "You had one when you were his age."

"But this is different! You can't just ride a horse down to Fisherman's Wharf or around Nob Hill, for crying out loud!"

Jefferson ground the pickup to a halt. "Unless the laws are different in California, I don't know where it's written that you *have* to live there! You could always come back here, y'know."

"But—"

"But what?" her father demanded gruffly, his gnarled hands searching his pocket for another cigarette. "Robert's gone. There's nothing to tie you to that damned city."

"But my art!"

"Can't you do that here?"

"The galleries—"

"Don't they know how to ship things? Dammit, I may be nothin' more than a Wyoming rancher, but you can't make me believe that Picasso lived in Golden Gate Park!"

Ainsley had to laugh. "No," she admitted, shaking her head.

"Then you see my point, don't ya, Missy?"

"I still don't understand why you gave Korey a horse—"

"Wait till ya see him, Mom!" Korey exclaimed, his brown eyes sparkling with excitement. "He's the best lookin' horse on the spread!"

"He is, is he?"

"You bet!" He opened the door on his side of the pickup and jerked on her hand. "Come on, I'll show him to ya!"

"Hold on a minute," Jefferson said. "I promised Sarah that I'd bring your ma up to the house for a glass of iced tea and some pie. After Ainsley gets settled in, then she can look at the horse. Okay?"

"'Kay," Korey mumbled, looking longingly at the stables as they walked toward the house. "But can I go see him?"

"'Course you can," his grandfather said, chuckling. "Maybe I'll come too. We'll brush him for your ma, put on his saddle and bridle—show him off some, eh?"

"Dad—"

But they were off, Jefferson pushing back the brim of his Stetson and placing an arm firmly around the skinny shoulders of his only grandson, the old dog following behind.

Feeling manipulated, she sighed, then shook her head and stuffed her hands into the pockets of her skirt. Her gaze swept the countryside. Whether she wanted to admit it or not, it was good to be home and see the clear Wyoming sky stretching out for miles as it covered the green-gold acres of the ranch.

The hot sun beat steadily down, warm on her crown and causing sweat to drizzle down her back. But even the heat was a welcome relief from the long San Francisco winter.

She eyed the old garage where her studio had been; she couldn't wait to fix it up. Though she was hot and tired from the long flight, she felt the urge to hurry, to explore every familiar nook and cranny in the old farmhouse, to ride through the dry fields and check on the old haunts of her youth. Yes, she decided, she was home and it was the best place in the world to be!

Walking up the brick path to the main house, she noticed the weeds growing where the mortar had chipped away. The front porch was covered in a thick layer of dust, and beneath the grime, the once-white paint had peeled away.

"Ainsley!" she heard as she opened the screen door. Sarah Martin, housekeeper and cook for her father, ran through the parlor to hug her. "Don't you look great!" Sarah's bright hazel eyes looked Ainsley over from her mane of lustrous hair to the pointed toes of her high heels.

"Thanks," she whispered, holding the round housekeeper close and smelling the familiar fragrances of cinnamon and nutmeg that always seemed to cling to her. "So do you! It's been too long!"

"Whose fault is that?" The older woman laughed.

"All mine! Guilty as charged," Ainsley said.

"Now, listen, you go on upstairs—I got your old room all ready—and get cleaned up. Then you hurry back here and tell us all about life in the big city." The hazel eyes behind thick glasses studied Ainsley's thin face and hollowed cheeks. "This past year's been hard on you, hasn't it?"

"A little."

"Well, we'll change all that." She held Ainsley at arm's length and eyed her, as if looking through the wheat-colored suit and blue silk blouse. "We'll get some meat on those bones!"

Ainsley heard the screen door slam shut. Turning, she saw Trent, her garment bag slung over his shoulder, her suitcase swinging from his other hand, as he walked into the house. "Where do you want these?" he asked, his slate eyes probing deep into hers.

"Up in her room—top of the stairs, first door to the right," Sarah said.

"I remember." He started up the stairs but stopped when Ainsley took hold of his arm.

"No…wait! Look, I'll take them myself," Ainsley said, glancing back to Sarah and dropping her fingers from Trent's arm. "But, if it's all the same, I think I'll stay in the old apartment over the garage. I'll be working a lot of the time, sometimes late at night."

The cook shrugged. "Wherever you want. Just make yourself at home. I'll bring over some fresh linens and towels."

"I can take them myself," Ainsley said, waving her aside. "You don't have to wait on me hand and foot, for goodness' sake!"

"Nonsense! I want to."

Ainsley started up the stairs to the linen closet. "You may as well know that I intend to pull my own weight around here."

"I doubt if your dad would have it any other way," Sarah replied.

"Probably not." She found a fresh set of sheets, towels, blankets and pillows and started back down the stairs.

"Always was a stubborn thing," Sarah muttered to Trent.

"I heard that!" Ainsley grinned as she returned to the first floor, her arms loaded. She looked over the large stack of linens and met Trent's mocking gaze. "Really, you can leave those here."

"Wouldn't hear of it," he said, his eyes glinting as one side of his mouth lifted into a crooked grin. He followed her down a short hall and through the kitchen to the back porch.

"Thanks." She hurried down the path leading to the garage and mounted the steps to the studio.

"Hold on a minute," Trent said when she reached the top of the landing and tried the door. "It's locked." He fished into his front pocket and extracted a huge key ring.

"*You* have the key?"

"Yep."

"To everything around here?"

"Just about." The lock gave way and the door swung inward. Following her inside he glanced around the old studio, noting the cobwebs and the dust. "You sure you want to stay in here?"

"Positive." She pulled the dust cloth off a round maple table and set the clean linens on the scratched surface. "Believe me, in a couple of hours, after I give this place a once-over—" swiping at the cobwebs clinging to the window, she flipped open the blinds and the room was filled with light "—you won't recognize the place."

"If you say so," he muttered, opening the closet and placing her bags inside. Seeing the thick layer of dirt on the shelf, he grimaced. "Maybe you ought to wait to move in until it's clean."

"I'm fine. Really. I grew up in this dirt. Remember?" She walked through the bedroom, then into the connecting bath and sighed when she saw the grimy fixtures. Running her finger over the basin she left a streak of dirt. "But I think I'll shower in the main house today."

"Smart lady," he agreed.

"You didn't think so when I left," she said, biting her

lower lip. She'd thought about their last meeting, wondered about it, and couldn't help but bring up the subject.

A muscle worked near his jaw. "Maybe we'd better forget about that," he said.

"I'd still like to know why you were so furious."

"Robert never told you?"

"I don't think he knew."

Trent's eyes grew dark. "Oh, he knew, all right," he muttered, his body tensing. "But there's no point dredging it all up again, is there?" He leaned against the doorway to the bedroom and watched as she stripped the dust cloth from the bed. The old brass headboard had begun to tarnish, but the mattress looked clean, and the air freshener that had been put against it years before had kept the mattress and springs from smelling musty.

She snapped up the blinds and pushed open the window. Fresh air invaded the room. "I think that, if I'm going to be here on the ranch, we should clear things up between us. We left a lot of things unsaid."

"Why now? Because Robert's gone?" he asked, his eyes fixed on the pout of her lips.

"Maybe partially. And because you're here. The last times I came to visit, I never even saw you. Now, whether we like it or not, we're going to see each other every day."

And it was going to be hell, he thought, looking at her innocent upturned face. He should never have agreed to Jefferson's deal in the first place. He didn't move, but his eyes searched her face and he shoved his hands deep into his pockets. "Just tell me one thing, Ainsley. Was I right about Robert?"

The question caught her off guard. His pose was relaxed but his face muscles were taut. "That's a tough one," she admitted. "Robert and I... Things weren't perfect."

"I'll bet."

"But he was a wonderful father! Korey adored him."

"Is that so?" he mocked.

"Yes!"

"And you loved him?"

She saw the pain in his eyes. "I thought so," she said, her throat suddenly tight. "A long time ago, I thought I loved him very much." *Before you kissed me.*

Trent's back teeth ground together and his gaze, when it touched hers, sizzled. He looked as if he was about to advance upon her, then abruptly changed his mind. "I'll go turn on the water outside," he said, pushing away from the wall and walking quickly out of the loft and down the steps. Ainsley heard his boots echoing against the old wood, and the bedroom, though filled with her things, felt suddenly empty.

"You're just imagining things," she told herself before carrying some clean clothes back to the main house and hurrying upstairs to shower.

The hot water felt good against her skin. She closed her eyes and let the steam billow around her as she thought about spending the summer at the ranch and all the wonderful things she would share with Korey and her father...and Trent McCullough, she reminded herself, frowning at the way his image kept slipping through her mind.

CHAPTER FOUR

AFTER CHANGING INTO a clean, faded pair of jeans and a boat-necked T-shirt, Ainsley pulled her hair away from her face, snapped it into place with a rubber band and hurried downstairs.

Sarah was already serving thick slices of strawberry pie and whipped cream. "What'll it be?" she called over her shoulder when she heard Ainsley step into the kitchen. "Iced tea or lemonade?"

"Tea, please."

Slices of lemon danced in the pitcher as Sarah poured a tall glass of the amber liquid. "If you'll carry this tray out to the front porch, I'll bring the pie."

"You've got yourself a deal!"

Sarah's eyes twinkled. "You don't know how good it is to have you back."

"And you don't know how good it is to be back." Ainsley lifted the tray, backed through the swinging doors to the dining room, then walked carefully outside, where her father was already sitting on a beat-up old couch on the covered porch.

Trent leaned against the rail, his long legs stretched forward and crossed at the ankles.

"Who had what?" she asked.

"I wanted coffee," Jefferson said, lighting a cigarette.

"On a day like this?"

"Coming," Sarah said, slipping through the door and balancing a tray of the plates as well as the rest of the pie and whipped cream. "Don't you pay him no mind, Ainsley. If it's coffee he wants, it's coffee he'll get."

"But it must be ninety degrees out here."

"Don't matter," her father grumbled.

"Bullheaded, I declare," Sarah murmured, but her hazel eyes gleamed.

Ainsley looked up at Trent. "What about you?"

"Tea's fine."

"A woman's drink," Jefferson said, and Trent laughed out loud as he took a long swallow from the glass Ainsley had handed him.

"So be it," Trent said, wiping his lips. "Always did say women were smart."

"Humph!"

"Here ya go." Sarah hurried back to the porch and handed Jefferson a steaming cup of coffee.

"That's better," he mumbled.

"You spoil him rotten," Ainsley said.

"Someone has to," Sarah said. "Now, who'll have a piece of pie?" She handed out the small plates just as Korey ran around the side of the house.

"Aren't you done yet?" he demanded. Standing on the porch, shifting restlessly from one foot to the other, he could barely contain himself.

"In a few minutes," Ainsley said. "Why don't you wash up, have some pie and then we'll take a look at that horse that Grandpa gave you?"

"You will?"

"I can't wait!" She sent her father a look that spoke

volumes before stabbing a large red strawberry. "Umm. This is better than I remembered."

"Thanks," Sarah said as Korey headed inside.

In a few minutes he was freshly scrubbed, back on the porch and had cleaned his plate.

"You're still convinced you want to stay in the loft?" Trent asked, his eyes never leaving her face.

"I think so."

"You're doin' what?" Jefferson asked.

"I decided to sleep in the studio over the garage while I'm here. Korey can sleep on the couch up there."

Jefferson set his plate aside. "But he's already settled in here. We got a room for him with a bed and a closet and a bureau. No sense movin' him. And you've got your old room."

"I know. But it will just be easier for me to work there. I can set up an easel by the north window," Ainsley pointed out.

"Humph. There's plenty of work for you on the ranch." He waved distractedly in the air. "Real work! You don't need any of that artist nonsense—"

She chuckled despite his obvious aggravation. "Yes, I do. It's what I do for a living. What I love! And I've got commitments to galleries that are showing my work. I just can't give it up for the summer."

"And why the hell not?" He stood and began pacing the length of the porch.

She met his gaze with a defiant lift of her chin. "Because I don't *want* to."

"Come on, Jeff, sit down," Sarah suggested. "I'll get you another cup of coffee and some more pie and you can quit walking up and down this porch like a penned dog."

"Don't tell me you're on her side!"

"I'm not takin' sides. But it seems to me she's a grown woman," Sarah muttered, cutting a thick wedge of pie and topping it with a cloud of whipped cream. "The way I see it, we should just be glad that she's home." Handing him the plate, she waited until he began to eat, then smiled at Ainsley. "Now, come on, let's hear all about your art."

"Not much to tell," Ainsley said, sliding a secretive glance at her father. "Just when I needed it most, right after Robert's death, I sold a couple of pieces through a gallery in the city. The Worthington Gallery. My friend Charlie's folks own it."

"Charlie?" Jefferson repeated, his eyes narrowing. "When did you meet him?"

Trent didn't move a muscle, but Ainsley felt his eyes on her.

"Charlie's her nickname."

"Her?" Jefferson repeated.

"Yes. Charlotte Worthington. We were friends in college."

"Never heard you talk of no Charlie."

"You just weren't listening."

Trent's face relaxed a little.

Ainsley smothered a grin. "Since then I've sold quite a few paintings and three or four sculptures. I haven't gotten rich, but I haven't starved, either."

"I still say a city the size of San Francisco's no place to raise a boy," her father said.

Ainsley stabbed at another strawberry and ate it slowly, all the while counting to ten. She knew her father disapproved of her work, her city lifestyle and the man she'd married, but she'd hoped that he'd mellowed a bit over the past few years and learned that he couldn't run her life.

"Otherwise you wouldn't be havin' all this trouble now, would you?" he asked.

Ainsley swallowed the strawberry and her eyes grew dark. "I don't know, Dad. That's why I'm back—to try and work some things out. Okay?"

His frown disappeared and his craggy face softened. "Okay," he whispered, avoiding her gaze by staring past the barn. "I don't mean to sound like a stubborn old mule; I've just missed you, girl. I've missed you like hell!"

"And I've missed you."

"Then don't argue," Sarah said. "Just no point in it!"

"Let's go have a look at that horse. What do you say?" Jefferson said, a twinkle in his eyes as he winked at Korey.

"About time!" Korey took off like a shot. "Wait till ya see him, Mom," he called over his shoulder.

She followed him with her eyes. "I hope you know what you're doing," she admonished her father.

"'Course I do."

"Good. Then maybe you can explain what I'm going to do when we have to leave at the end of the summer."

"Maybe you won't have to."

"Dad—"

"Come on. Korey's been at the stables all morning. On one foot and then the other. He couldn't wait till you got in!" Jefferson's face crinkled into a smile. He tossed a teasing look at his daughter. "Best thing I ever did for the boy!"

"Remind me of that in September."

"I will. And if I don't, Korey will."

Ainsley stood and stretched and Trent pushed himself upright as well. "Just let me help Sarah clear the dishes, okay?"

Sarah shook her head. "Don't bother. Jeff's right—you'd better look at that horse before Korey goes out of his mind."

Jefferson was already down the two front steps. "You come to the paddock in a couple of minutes. There's no reason for him to wait any longer. And when you get out there, try not to rain on the boy's parade."

"I promise," Ainsley said, "if you promise to quit spoiling him."

"I'm not!"

She lifted a disbelieving brow and leaned one shoulder against the post supporting the roof. "What do you call it—*indulging* him?"

"Well," Jefferson said, chuckling and turning to squint at her, "maybe a mite. It won't hurt none. I spoiled you rotten and you turned out okay, didn't ya?"

Sarah picked up the dishes and waved away Ainsley's help. "I can get these." Then her gaze turned thoughtful as she stared at the retreating figure of her boss. "The best thing that happened to Jeff was when that boy came here," she said almost to herself as she wiped one hand on her apron and backed to the door.

"That's good," Ainsley decided. "For Dad. But what about Korey? By the end of the summer, he'll think he can have whatever he wants. All he has to do is ask Grandpa."

"Jefferson means well," Trent cut in, wondering if his words rang true. Hadn't Jefferson tried to bribe him to marry Ainsley? The thought of that part of their bargain still stuck in his craw. Fortunately, he'd never agreed to it. Now, he glanced at Ainsley and wondered if he'd made a mistake.

"Just go on. I'll handle this," Sarah ordered.

"Okay, but I'll help with dinner."

"Get out of here."

Trent took hold of her arm and guided her down the steps and out of the shade of the roof. The afternoon heat still simmered, rising in waves from the parched land. Sweat began to dampen her brow.

"Jefferson's trying to help," Trent said.

"I know, but what's going to happen when I have to take Korey back to San Francisco and we have to leave the horse here?" she asked, pausing in the shade of a gnarled old apple tree.

"Jefferson thinks maybe you'll stay."

"He's wrong."

"Is he?" Trent's eyes studied the concern in the knit of her brow, the worry in her blue gaze.

"I can't live here," she whispered. "I made that decision a long time ago."

"I see," he said, his voice clipped, his eyes narrowed against the intense sun. "So you can't change your mind."

"I didn't say that."

"Then don't make rash statements. Things have changed. You've changed. We all have. Maybe this would be the best place for your boy."

"What is this?" Ainsley asked, her temper flaring a little. "Don't tell me you're in cahoots with Dad."

Trent's face slackened and a smile lifted one side of his mouth. "Nope. I'm just pointing out that staying here might not be the worst decision of your life."

"Probably not."

"So just relax about the horse."

"Would you? If it were your kid and the colt was named *Crazy Luke?*"

Trent laughed. The rich sound filled the air and touched a part of Ainsley's heart. "Maybe you've got a point."

"Of course I have! This is my son we're talking about!"

His fingers surrounded her arm and he tugged gently, prodding her forward. "You can't very well tell Korey to give him back, can you?"

"I suppose not."

"The way I see it," Trent drawled, "the damage is already done—so you may as well make the best of it. As for leaving the horse here when you go back to California, you'll have to cross that bridge when you come to it."

"Pearls of wisdom," Ainsley mocked, but she felt better and looked up at him with shining blue eyes. "You always did know what to say, didn't you?"

"Most of the time," he replied, frowning slightly. "Except for once."

Remembering the night she'd told him about her marriage to Robert, she swallowed hard and started for the paddock. "Let's just leave the past out of this," she suggested. *Until we're alone!*

"Do you think that's possible?"

"Who knows? But it's what you wanted a little while ago."

"I still do. I just don't know if we can leave it alone."

"I hope so," she said fervently, waving as she spotted her son in the middle of the dusty paddock, leading a shining, coal-black colt.

By the time Ainsley reached the stables, Korey had tied Crazy Luke to the top rail of the fence and was patting the silken nose of the rangy colt. "Isn't he great?"

"He sure is." Ainsley watched the horse toss his head and nicker.

"And Korey, here, rides him as good as any bareback rider in the rodeo," Jefferson added proudly.

"Is that right?" Ainsley asked.

"Grandpa says that maybe I can ride in the bareback race at the Pine Corners Roundup."

"You didn't!" Ainsley said, her blue eyes accusing her father.

"Why not?"

"Because it's dangerous! That's why not!"

"Aw, Mom."

"Tell him, Trent!" she demanded. "Tell him what happened to you! When you were fifteen!"

"Fourteen," Trent corrected, his lips turning downward at the unwelcome memory.

"Well?" Korey asked.

"I fell off."

"More than that," Ainsley said. "You fell off and you were trampled by Jonah's horse."

"Your brother's horse ran over you?" Korey asked, wide-eyed and filled with new respect for his grandfather's foreman.

"Not on purpose. At least I don't think so," Trent said.

"Nonetheless, you ended up in the hospital with two or three cracked ribs and a broken arm. And you were lucky to be alive!"

"Wow," Korey said, obviously in awe.

"He was in the hospital for over a week!"

"That won't happen to me."

"You're right. Because you're not riding."

"I have to! Besides it'll be safe."

"You don't know that!" Ainsley said, turning furious eyes to her father. "How could you get him all excited about the rodeo when you know how I feel about it?"

Jefferson shrugged. "Show your ma how you can ride," he told his grandson.

Korey didn't need any more encouragement. He slid

onto the nervous colt's back. Crazy Luke sidestepped and tossed his head, then shot off, racing from one end of the paddock to the other, twirling on his hind legs and running again, the boy clinging to his back like a burr.

"Dad—" Ainsley warned, but Jefferson didn't respond. Ainsley glanced at Trent. He was leaning over the top rail of the fence and studying Korey. "I suppose you were in on this, too," she accused.

"No way. This was all Jefferson's doing."

"Can't argue with that," the old man admitted. "And I'm proud of it."

"Proud?"

"That's right. It was high time Korey got out of the city—"

"—and onto the back of Crazy Luke. Right?" Ainsley said.

"Right," her father agreed.

"Well, Mom, what do you think?" Korey asked breathlessly, once he'd dismounted. His eyes were bright, his forehead streaked with sweat and dirt, his smile as wide as his face.

"I think he's beautiful," she said.

"Then I can keep him?" Korey asked, hardly believing his good luck.

"For the summer. Just until we go home."

"But Grandpa gave him to me."

"I know what Grandpa did," Ainsley said, shooting her father a rueful look. "I just don't know what to do about it."

Korey wanted to pout, but Jefferson climbed into the paddock and promised to work with him and the horse. With a sigh, Ainsley turned back to the house. "How could you let him get all caught up in this rodeo thing?" she asked Trent as he fell into step with her.

"Wasn't any of my business."

"I thought you were the foreman here."

"I am. But I can't tell your son or your father what to do."

"Unfortunately, neither can I," she said wryly as they approached the back porch.

"I need to talk to you," he said slowly as she started up the steps.

"Now?"

He shook his head. "Later. Right now I've got to check on things at home. But I'll be back."

"When?"

"Tonight."

She stared straight into his eyes. "Is anything wrong?"

"No. Don't worry." His smile slid from one side of his face to the other. "I'll be back after dinner. We can talk then."

"Fine."

She watched as he climbed into his Jeep and started the engine. The vehicle took off with a lurch, spraying dust and gravel in its wake.

Ainsley walked into the kitchen but her thoughts still lingered on Trent. In the past few hours, nearly ten years of her life had seemed to melt away.

"Where's he goin' in such a hurry?" Sarah asked. She was looking out the window and watching Trent's Jeep disappear down the lane.

"Back to the Rocking M, I suppose."

Sarah pursed her lips and continued dusting pieces of chicken with seasoned flour. "Don't know why he'd want to do that. His brother's back from Denver, you know."

"Jonah?"

"Yep. But just for a little while. Anyway that's what I heard and I hope I heard right."

"You don't like Jonah, do you?"

"Trent's the only one of those three McCulloughs with any sense," Sarah said thoughtfully as she took fruit from the refrigerator and began cutting wedges of cantaloupe and honeydew melon. "Jonah was always stirrin' up trouble. He used to be known as the meanest kid in the valley."

Ainsley shook her head and sighed. "Oh, come on. That was years ago. Jonah's not a teenager anymore."

Sarah's eyes narrowed. "Don't matter. A leopard doesn't change his spots overnight!"

"You're saying that Jonah is trouble."

"Yes."

"For who? Dad?"

"Anyone involved with him."

"Including Trent."

"I hope not," Sarah said, placing the chicken into a heavy skillet and watching the pieces brown in the bubbling oil.

"I think Trent can handle himself," Ainsley thought aloud, looking out the window. Trent's Jeep had disappeared over the softly rolling hills.

"I hope so."

Ainsley turned her attention to a nearby field where her father was sitting tall on a long-legged buckskin with Korey riding along beside him. The two horses ambled down a dusty trail in the back paddock, and Jefferson had his head cocked down, obviously listening to his grandson. "What about Dad?" Ainsley asked the cook. "How did he get involved with McCullough Oil?"

"I don't know. You'll have to ask him that yourself. But I sure wish he'd never had anything to do with the likes of Jonah McCullough."

"So it wasn't Trent?"

"Not to my knowledge. Trent, he spends most of his time ranchin'."

Ainsley didn't press the issue. Instead she scrounged around in the pantry and found a bucket, mop, rags and several bottles of disinfectant. "I'll be up in the loft if anyone needs me," she called over her shoulder as she walked through the back porch.

The studio was just as she'd left it. She started cleaning by scrubbing the bathroom fixtures and all of the floors. Then she dusted everything she could reach, polished the blinds and the light fixtures and put clean linens on the bed.

"Good as new," she told herself, surveying her work with a critical eye. The small interior gleamed.

"Hey, Mom! Time for dinner!" Korey called as he climbed the stairs and poked his head into the room. "Wow! This looks great! What did you do?"

"Just applied a little elbow grease."

"What?"

She laughed and rumpled his hair. "Never mind. Now, guess what? You've got the couch." She pointed to a foldaway bed but Korey shook his head.

"I'm not sleeping on that!"

"Why not?"

"'Cause Grandpa said I could stay in the house."

"Seems as if Grandpa's taking over," she observed dryly.

"Isn't it okay?"

"I suppose." Maybe he needed a room of his own. She looked into his eager young eyes and felt a sense of pride.

"You were the one who wanted to come here," he reminded her.

"And aren't you glad I forced the issue?"

"I guess," he admitted, glancing at the floor. "It's not as bad as I thought it would be." He started out the door and Ainsley caught up with him at the bottom of the stairs.

"Let's not keep Grandpa waiting." She draped her arm over Korey's shoulders as they walked into the house through the back porch. Inside the kitchen, the smells of fried chicken and cinnamon rolls greeted them. "If Sarah has her way, I'll gain fifty pounds this summer," Ainsley whispered to her son.

"Yeah. She told me you were too skinny," Korey said as he dashed into the dining room.

"I heard that!" Chuckling, Sarah scooped mashed potatoes into a bowl and drizzled butter over them. "And by the way, it's true."

Ainsley laughed and washed her hands, then grabbed the bowl and carried the steaming potatoes into the dining room. Her father and Korey were already seated at the table, engrossed in talk about the rodeo.

Jefferson glanced at her and frowned. "Where in tarnation have you been?"

"Cleaning the loft." Ainsley sat in a vacant chair and waited for Sarah.

"You're really gonna stay up there?" Jefferson said, helping himself to a roll and buttering the gooey cinnamon-flavored bread as Sarah seated herself next to him.

"I told you I was."

"Seems strange, if you ask me. You come all this way to stay in the garage."

"Because of my work."

Scowling, Jefferson lapsed into silence and conversation lagged as everyone began to eat.

"So tell me," Ainsley said, once she'd pushed her plate aside. "Why did you hire Trent as foreman?"

Jefferson avoided his daughter's eyes as he reached for a cigarette. "Simple. I needed a little help around here."

"You've got help."

"But I wanted someone to oversee the hands. I'm gettin' older, if you hadn't noticed." He laughed as he lit up.

"So it doesn't have anything to do with McCullough Oil?"

"Not really."

"What about the oil rigs in the south pasture? Why aren't they drilling?"

"Glut on the market." Jefferson blew a stream of smoke to the ceiling. "Jonah thinks it's best if we cap 'em until the price goes up."

"And he thinks it will?"

"Eventually."

She leaned back in her chair. "How is Trent involved with the oil company?" she asked.

"He's kind of a silent partner, I guess," Jefferson said thoughtfully. "He spends most of his time ranching, either here or over at the McCullough place."

"But he is part of the oil company, isn't he?"

"Yep."

"So why was he flying your plane?"

Jefferson took a last long drag from his cigarette and threw the butt into the empty fireplace that separated the living room from the dining room. Wrangling with private thoughts, he pushed his chair back from the table. "I just wasn't up to flying today," he admitted. "Sad as it is, Missy, your old man isn't getting any younger."

Korey glanced warily in her direction. "I don't like him," he said flatly as he pinched off a corner of his roll.

"Trent?"

"Right."

"Why not?" Ainsley asked.

"'Cause he bosses everybody around."

"Including you?"

"Especially me! I just don't think it's fair."

Jefferson chuckled. "I think Korey came up against the first person he can't hoodwink."

"I wasn't trying to hoodwink anybody!" the boy protested.

"Sure you weren't." Jefferson stood and stretched. "And a fox don't like chicken eggs."

"Grandpa—" Korey protested.

Jefferson's leathery face stretched into a grin. "Trent doesn't put up with any shenanigans or goofing off. The first day Korey was here, Trent gave him a list of chores he had to do."

"A lot of chores! Can you believe that?" Korey asked, his eyes wide.

Ainsley had to grin. "'Fraid I can," she admitted. "I grew up with Trent. He always was a workhorse. That's why I can't figure out why he's not running the oil company."

"Maybe he got sidetracked," Jefferson said.

"Yeah and maybe he just likes pushing other people around," Korey added. "Can I be excused?"

"Sure—just help Sarah clear the table."

"Okay," he grumbled taking his plate into the kitchen.

Ainsley helped clean the kitchen, then found her father on the back porch. Jefferson was staring out across the fields, his eyes trained on the distant smoky-gray hills. The first few stars had begun to glitter in the sky as he sat on the top step and smoked, his cigarette glowing in the gathering darkness.

"What's up?" Ainsley asked, plopping down beside him.

"Not much. Thought I'd go upstairs and read before the news comes on."

"How about a game of chess?" she asked.

He groaned as he stood. "Already got one planned with Korey. Then I'm gonna turn in. It's been a long day and I'm tired. Keeping up with that boy of yours isn't easy."

"Don't I know," she muttered, listening to the sounds of insects humming and an owl hooting in the nearby hills.

He placed a gnarled hand on her shoulder. "But I'm glad you're back."

"I'm glad to be here."

Jefferson grinned as he patted her shoulder.

Watching him walk into the kitchen, his wiry silhouette dark against the interior lights, she realized just how much he'd aged in the past few years.

A cool evening breeze picked up and blew across her face. Shadows lengthened across the land; the sky had darkened to a dusky shade of lavender.

Tugging the band from her hair, Ainsley shook her head so that loose curls danced around her face. She stood and stretched then followed the worn path through the dry grass to the series of paddocks surrounding the stables.

Leaning over the top rail of the fence, she watched several horses pick at the dry stubble. Spindly-legged foals scampered next to their dams, alternately kicking their heels to the heavens and tossing their heads.

She recognized Jezebel and called to the chestnut mare. "It's been a long time, girl," she whispered as the horse approached and nickered. Ainsley rubbed the soft nose of her mother's favorite horse. "Too long. Is Dad taking care of you?"

A shy little filly peeked from behind her mother. The young horse stared at Ainsley with wide, curious eyes.

"And who're you?" Ainsley asked.

"That's Emma's Girl." Trent's voice cut through the evening solitude.

Startled, Ainsley looked over her shoulder. "I didn't hear you drive in."

He took a spot next to her and placed one booted foot on the lowest rail of the fence as he stared across the fields. The sleeves of his work shirt were rolled over his forearms and the soft cotton fabric stretched tight across his broad shoulders. "I came in the back way," he said, his eyes moving over the small herd. "And you looked a million miles away."

"Not really. I just wanted to see the horses. You said this one," she began, hooking her thumb in the direction of the skittish foal, "was named 'Emma's Girl'?"

"That's right. This is Jezebel's first filly. Every other foal she had was a colt. So, Jefferson named this one after your mother."

"I guess he misses Mom."

"A lot." He rubbed the back of his neck, massaging his tired muscles. "He missed you, too."

Ainsley felt a sharp stab of guilt. "Maybe I should have come back more often."

"Maybe."

She looked at him. His profile was set, his angular features hard as he watched the horses. Lips slanting pensively, he narrowed his eyes against the encroaching night.

Ainsley felt the same wave of emotion that had enveloped her eleven years ago. Just standing next to him, catching furtive glimpses of him through her lashes, she felt her heart begin to pound. "What about you?" she asked, her voice breathless. "Have you missed me?"

"What kind of a question is that?"

"Just curious."

Turning, he looked down at her, his eyes hard in their appraisal. "A little, I suppose," he lied. "I guess I haven't really thought about it."

"I always wondered," she whispered.

"What?"

"What would have happened if I hadn't already married Robert eleven years ago?"

Tiny points of light glittered in his eyes. "Hard to say, isn't it?" Reaching forward, he pushed her hair away from her face and then let his hand fall. "Doesn't matter anyway. It happened. You married him, moved to California, had a son and lived happily ever after."

"It wasn't quite that simple."

"I warned you about him, Ainsley," he said slowly.

"Too little, too late."

"If I'd told you earlier, would you have believed me?"

"Probably not," she admitted. Looking up, she was lost in the silvery depths of Trent's eyes. "But as you said, it doesn't matter anyway, does it? The past is the past, over and gone."

His lips curved downward and his jaw was so tight it ached. "That's right. It's better to just forget it. Besides, I have work to do. May as well get to it."

"I…er, thought you wanted to talk to me."

"I do. But first I want to check on the cattle. Are you going to be up in your loft or at the house?"

"The studio."

"Okay. I'll stop by."

"So what is it you want to talk about?"

"Korey," he said softly. "I think there are a few things you should know about your boy."

"What do you mean?"

Trent's eyes softened. "There's been trouble, Ainsley. And I think Korey's involved." He glanced over his shoulder. "But I want to talk to you when we're completely alone. I don't want anyone else to hear."

"You're scaring me," she whispered.

"Don't be scared. It's nothing serious. Yet. I'll see you in forty minutes." And then he was off, striding across the gravel road to the barn. Ainsley had taken two steps to follow him and demand to know what he was talking about when she heard Korey behind her.

"Hey, Mom!"

Turning, she forced the furrow from her brow.

"Guess what?" he asked.

"What?"

"I beat Grandpa at chess!" he said, beaming.

"No fooling?"

"Scout's honor!"

"Good for you."

"Oh, and here!" He handed her a thermos and a basket. "Sarah said you might need something to munch on later. It's some of her rolls, I think."

"She really does want to fatten me up, doesn't she?"

He shrugged and kicked at a piece of gravel. "Remember that Grandpa said I could stay in my room in the main house."

"Yeah."

"Is it okay with you?"

"I suppose."

"Then you don't mind?"

"No, not really."

He started to walk away but thought better of it. Stuffing his hands into the front pockets of his jeans, he faced her again. "What did you think of Crazy Luke?" he asked.

"I think he was appropriately named."

"He's the greatest!" Korey said fervently. "And you'll be proud of me. Because I'm gonna win that rodeo race!"

"I'm already proud of you and it doesn't have anything to do with a horse race." Bending down, she placed her arms around his shoulders and pressed her forehead against his. "I'm proud of you because of who you are— not because of what you can do."

"Aw, Mom—" He stepped away from her. "Are you trying to tell me I can't ride?"

"Aren't you too young?" she asked, hopefully.

"Nope. There's a division for my age."

"Wonderful."

"And Grandpa already has me entered."

"Good old Gramps. He's taken care of everything, hasn't he?" she said sarcastically.

"Uh-huh."

She straightened up, sighing. "Why don't you go back to the house? It's almost time for bed. And if you see Grandpa tonight, tell him I'm gonna corner him in the morning."

"Okay." Korey sprinted for the house, and Ainsley, taking a deep breath, watched him run easily down the path. Then, tucking the thermos under her arm and carrying the basket of rolls, she headed back to her room over the garage to wait for Trent and whatever it was he wanted to discuss about Korey.

Trouble, he'd said. *Good Lord, what did that mean?*

CHAPTER FIVE

AINSLEY WAS JUST pouring a cup of coffee when she heard Trent's footsteps on the stairs. "Here we go," she whispered, bracing herself, her hands trembling.

He knocked and her heart began to pound.

"It's unlocked," she called, then remembered it didn't matter. He had the key.

Entering, Trent closed the door behind him. His gaze skated around the clean rooms before landing on Ainsley. "You've been busy," he observed, eyeing the shining fixtures and clean floors.

"A little."

"A lot." When he smiled, the hard lines of his face relaxed. "I never would have thought you'd get this far," he admitted. "But then you've always done what you set out to do."

"So you've said." She poured him a cup of coffee and set it on the table. "Now, what do you want to tell me about Korey?"

Trent crossed the room, picked up his coffee and took a sip of the hot liquid. "There've been a few things missing," he said slowly.

"Missing? What things?" Her pulse jumped again.

"Tools, for one thing."

She met his direct stare. "And you think Korey may have taken them?"

"It's possible."

"I don't think so," she said hurriedly. "What would a nine-year-old boy want with tools?"

"Beats me. Maybe he's selling them. The other things that were taken—fishing tackle, chewing tobacco, a hunting knife—"

"Whoa!" she cut in, her eyes blazing. "Just hold on a minute. I think you're trying to blame Korey for taking things you've misplaced."

He shook his head and calmly sipped his coffee. "Not me. Some of the hands."

"And you believe them?"

"I have to."

"So why do you blame Korey?" she asked. "Is it because he's been in trouble before? Is that why he's such a handy target?"

"Of course not. But nothing had been missing, or at least no one had reported any thefts, until Korey got here last week. Since then—"

"Korey doesn't chew tobacco!" she cried, slapping the table.

"Slow down, Ainsley."

But she was furious and her cheeks burned with the accusations. "No way! You tell me what's going on, Trent. I come back to the ranch to visit my father and all hell breaks loose! First, I find out that you're his foreman. Then I discover that there are oil wells—capped wells not producing a penny, mind you—on his land. McCullough Oil wells that *you* got him into. The next thing I'm told is that Dad has given Korey a horse and entered him into the rodeo without my permission, and now you come up here and accuse my son of stealing! What's going on here?" She leaned against the counter and pinned him with her eyes, her heart hammering furiously.

"I'm not accusing him. Not yet."

"Sounded like it to me," she snapped.

"It's just something I've got to figure out. I thought maybe you could help me."

"How? By confronting him? Going through his things?"

"Whatever it is you have to do."

She blew a strand of hair out of her eyes and sat in one of the hard maple chairs surrounding the table. "And I thought Korey and I were coming here to relax," she muttered, shaking her head. "To get away from all of this…this whatever-it-is! Looks like we've jumped from the frying pan into the fire, doesn't it?" she mocked. *Korey wasn't a thief! He couldn't be!*

"Ainsley—" He reached forward to touch her hand, but she drew away. Frowning, he leaned back in his chair and finished his coffee. "Just keep your eyes open."

"Is this why you've been riding Korey?" she accused.

"Riding him?"

"You know, giving him a bad time. Lots of chores and extra work!" Shaking, she had to fight her temper.

"Is that what he told you?" Trent's gray eyes sparkled with amusement.

"In so many words."

He chuckled and shook his head. "Well, the answer is no." Raking his fingers through his hair, he glanced at the ceiling. "I just expect him to pull his weight. I haven't asked him to do anything you didn't do when you were his age."

"He's not used to—"

"Hard work? Maybe that's his problem. He's too soft."

Her jaw clenched furiously, but Trent held up his hand to ward off the blast of anger he saw coming. "Jefferson told me about the trouble you were having with him. And so did you."

"And you took it upon yourself to straighten him out!"

"Nope. That's your job."

"Glad you see it that way."

"All I have to do is run the Circle S. That includes seeing that Korey does his part. Especially with his horse." He forced a smile and his craggy features softened. "Simmer down, will you? I want to help Korey, too. Believe it or not, I like him. Even if his mother is a hot-head! However, I think he should look after his own horse."

Ainsley slowly counted to ten and some of her anger dissipated. "Oh, yes. The horse. The wild horse that he plans to ride in the bareback race on the Fourth of July."

"That was Jefferson's idea."

"I know." She looked out the window, through the clean panes to the house where lights still glowed within. "I just don't understand it—why Dad is indulging Korey with the horse and that stupid rodeo!"

"He's been lonely a long time," Trent said, sipping his coffee.

"Then why would he want to risk his grandson's life?"

"He doesn't see it that way."

"That race is dangerous, Trent. I can't let Korey ride in it."

"You'll get no arguments from me." His face softened into a smile. "I'm still carrying a few old scars from that one myself."

Ainsley wrapped her arms around her waist and walked to the window. "I wonder if I made a big mistake in coming here," she murmured. "Maybe I was just running from my problems."

"Seems to me they followed you here." He scraped his chair back and watched the lines of worry etching her brow, wishing there was some way to ease her pain. "Maybe I shouldn't have said anything about the missing tools."

"No. I'm glad you did." She looked back at him. "Really. It's just hard handling a son sometimes."

"It'll probably get worse before it gets better."

"Thanks for the vote of confidence."

"Let's just say I've got a long memory."

"Dad says that you're helping raise your sister's boy, Wilson."

Trent's expression darkened. He set his empty cup on the table. "Wilson's a handful."

"Like Korey."

"Two peas in a pod," he muttered to himself. "They've struck up a friendship, if you could call it that. The problem is they compete."

"Just like brothers. Like you and Jonah—right?"

Trent measured his words, watching her carefully. "I guess so."

"I think it's only natural. Because they're so close in age. I'm just glad there's someone around here that Korey can play with. It's hard growing up without a friend."

He shifted. "Sounds like you're talking from experience."

Smiling sadly, she shook her head. "I didn't have a sister or brother, but I had Mom and Dad and..." Her throat felt rough. "And I had you," she whispered. "We were good friends once."

His eyes grew dark. "And Robert."

"Yes, and Robert," she said. "God, that seems like a long time ago."

"It was. A lifetime." After setting his cup in the sink, he walked to the door. "I'll see you tomorrow," he said, the brackets deepening beside his mouth. "You know, Ainsley, I didn't come here to upset you. I just thought there were some things you might want to know."

"And you were right." Smiling, she showed off a dimple. "Thanks."

"Any time." He reached for the doorknob but hesitated. "Just for the record, I missed you, too." And then he was out the door and gone, his footsteps growing faint as he climbed down the stairs.

Trying to quiet the hammering of her heart, she wondered how her life would have changed if she hadn't married Robert. "And then you wouldn't have had Korey," she told herself as she poured the final dregs of coffee down the sink and began undressing for bed. Snapping off the lights, she crawled between the cool sheets. No matter what, Korey had been worth the unhappy years with Robert.

AINSLEY SPENT THE next few days putting the final touches on her studio. She moved extra furniture and junk she didn't need downstairs to the garage. With the extra space, she made room for her potter's wheel in one corner of the loft and found the perfect spot for her easel near the window.

"Not bad," she told herself after spending nearly three full days getting the two rooms in order. She threw her dust rag into the garbage and congratulated herself on a job well done. The old studio was beginning to feel like home again.

Humming as she arranged her tools and paints carefully in the drawers of an old buffet, she felt better than she had in a long time. Yes, sir, it was good to be back!

Glancing out the window, she could see Korey putting the black colt through his paces. Tucked high on the shoulders of Crazy Luke, Korey clung like a burr as he gave the colt his head and the horse sprinted from one end of the pasture to the other.

The stairs creaked and her father poked his head into the loft. "Hey, this place doesn't look half bad," Jefferson admitted, eyeing the studio. His old Border collie, Dallas, followed him inside.

"Are you surprised?"

"A little, I guess. Never did understand why all this painting and messing with clay was important to you. But if it's what you want to do—"

"It is."

"Okay, okay." He walked to the window and saw Korey through the panes. Poking at the glass, he said, "The boy's a natural rider, you know."

"You wouldn't be prejudiced because you're his grandfather," she teased, chuckling.

"Humph. Nope. He just inherited my instincts."

Ainsley laughed. "Is that it?"

"'Course it is!" Jefferson's thick gray brows raised. "I heard that Korey told you I entered him into the rodeo."

"He mentioned it."

Jefferson wiped a hand over his stubbled chin. "Maybe I should have asked you first."

"No 'maybe' about it."

He stretched out his stiff leg and sat in the old rocker. His hand dropped down to scratch Dallas behind the ears, and the black and white dog panted and wagged his tail. "Well, you weren't here. It was the last day to register and—"

"And you wanted to see him ride in the race. I know. And I also know that you always wanted a son to fill your shoes and take over the ranch," she said. "Unfortunately, I didn't fit the bill," she said, her lips twitching into a wry smile.

"Hey, now—it wasn't 'cause you were a girl."

"No, it was because I wanted to get out and see the world. I was more interested in art than in branding cattle."

"Nothing wrong with branding."

"Nothing wrong with art."

Jefferson's weathered face cracked into a fond grin. "Guess you're right," he muttered. "You're so much like your ma sometimes…" Clearing his throat, he squinted through the afternoon sun, past the pines and cotton-wood surrounding Wolverine Creek to the house on the next piece of property. "Doesn't matter anyway. Trent works this place as if it were his own. Does a good job, too."

Nervously licking her lips, she asked, "So how does he get along with Korey?"

"Not too bad, considerin' that Korey don't like no one telling him what to do."

"Then you don't think Trent has it in for Korey?"

"Hell, no!" Jefferson's old eyes flashed. He fished in his breast pocket for his cigarettes. "Did he tell you that Trent was givin' him a bad time?"

"A little. Nothing serious." Ainsley put the rest of her brushes in the drawer.

"Well, you know Trent. Not a fairer man in the county."

Ainsley studied her father and the thrust of his chin. "So when did you become such a Trent McCullough fan?"

"Always have been. And if you'd had any sense when you were younger, you would've married him instead of Robert Hughes," Jefferson stated with a curt nod of his head.

"Dad—"

"Well, it's true. Hughes wasn't half the man McCullough is." He cupped his hands around his cigarette and took a long drag. Smoke curled up to the ceiling.

"Robert's gone," she reminded him. "And he was Korey's father."

"That makes it okay that he ran around on you, does it?"

"Dad!" She could feel her cheeks begin to burn.

"Oh, I see. So now Robert's a saint and…and… Don't look at me that way," he said, when he saw the surprise on Ainsley's face. "I knew what was goin' on. You don't have to be a genius to see when a man is strayin'."

"But you were here—"

"I saw you enough to know." He waved in the air as if to dismiss a bothersome insect. "No use bringin' it all up now. Just this time, Missy, don't be so foolish. This time you recognize a good man when you see him."

"Like Trent McCullough, right?"

"Right!" Jefferson squared his hat on his head, winced when he stood on his bad knee and walked through the door, pausing at the landing to take a final puff before squashing his cigarette with the heel of his boot. "Come on, Dallas." The old dog stretched and lumbered outside. Jefferson met his daughter's gaze. "Just remember that I won't always be around to take care of you, y'know."

"Take care of me? Dad, I'm nearly thirty years old—"

But Jefferson wasn't listening. He was already making his way down the stairs and heading across the parking lot to the field where Korey was exercising his horse.

"So why is Trent a god all of a sudden?" Ainsley whispered just as Trent's Jeep rumbled down the lane. She watched as he climbed out of the vehicle and pushed his dark hair out of his eyes. Tall and lean with a flat abdomen, broad shoulders, and carved facial features, he was as handsome as he was a part of the rugged land surrounding him. She wondered how her life would have changed had she married him instead of Robert. "It would never have worked," she decided shaking her head. "He's a rancher and you're an artist. He loves the open range and you love the lights of San Francisco. He eats steak and potatoes, and you'd rather have white wine and chicken Kiev."

Opening the window, she sat on the ledge and felt the soft rays of the afternoon sun warm the back of her neck as she watched him.

Trent stood beneath a solitary pine tree and studied Korey for a few minutes, exchanged words with Jefferson, then glanced her way before walking into the machine shed. Her heart tugged a little at the sight of him and she forced herself to get off the ledge. "You're an idiotic fool," she chastised as she dusted her hands together. "You can't live in the past, especially in a past that really didn't exist."

After changing into a sundress, she started down the stairs but stopped on the landing when she heard hoofbeats. Shading her eyes against the sun, she saw a dark-haired boy riding a buckskin gelding across the long field separating the Circle S from the McCulloughs' land. The horse was sweating as he ran and the rider was tucked high on his horse's shoulders as the rangy gelding raced over the cracked fields.

"Who's that?" she asked as she hurried down the stairs and walked up to her father.

"Wilson McCullough," the older man said with a grimace.

"Trent's nephew?"

"In the flesh." He watched the youth jerk hard on the reins and pull the gelding to a stop in front of them. The horse reared and shied, sidestepping away from the fence. "A wild one, too," Jefferson whispered to Ainsley.

"Is Trent here?" Wilson asked, eyeing Ainsley suspiciously.

"This is my daughter, Ainsley," Jefferson said.

"Hi," Ainsley offered.

Wilson's dark eyes narrowed. "You're Korey's ma."

"That's right."

"As for Trent," Jefferson said, waiting until the boy slid off the sweating horse, "he's either in the machine shed or the barn, I expect."

"Uncle Jonah wants him back at the ranch. He needs his signature on something."

"He could've called," Jefferson observed.

"Yeah, well, I said I'd come over. I wanted to see if Korey could go fishin'."

"Korey's got work to do," Jefferson said. "When he's done with his chores, he'll give ya a call."

Wilson didn't move.

"Anything else?" Jefferson prodded.

"Just tell Trent that Jonah wants him. Pronto!"

Jefferson's face hardened. "I'll give him the word."

Wilson climbed into the saddle and, hearing hoofbeats, waited as Korey came into view astride Crazy Luke.

"Hi!" Korey called to the other boy as he dismounted. "What're ya doin'?"

"Lookin' for you. I wanted you to go fishing with me but your grandpa says you can't."

Korey looked from Jefferson to his mother. "Why not?"

"Grandpa says you have some chores to finish," Ainsley said.

"I'll do 'em later."

"I don't think so. Besides you've got some homework to finish."

"But, Mom, I'll do it later, too."

Trent sauntered out of the barn, took one look at Wilson and frowned when he heard the tail end of the conversation. "I thought you had some chores of your own," he said slowly to his nephew.

Wilson avoided Trent's eyes. "I did. But Jonah wanted me to come and get you. Some guy is there and he needs your signature on some important paper."

The skin over Trent's features stretched tight. "I'll be over in a little while."

"But—"

"Tell him I'll be back around three. Like I said I would. And then finish your chores, okay?"

Wilson's face worked, but seeing that arguing wouldn't get him anywhere, he jerked on the reins, kicked his mount and took off in a whirlwind of dust.

"And you've got some work to do, too, haven't you?" Trent reminded Korey.

"I'm almost done," the boy complained.

"Almost isn't quite enough. When you're done, you can go fishing with Wilson. If it's okay with your mother."

"After the homework," Ainsley added.

His chin thrust forward defiantly, Korey climbed back on his horse and rode the sweating colt to the stables.

"You make Simon Legree look soft," she muttered to Trent, her teeth flashing in a smile.

"You disapprove?" he asked, dark brows quirking up as he took off his hat and wiped the sweat from his brow.

"I didn't say that."

"Well, I don't!" Jefferson said emphatically. "That boy needs all the direction he can get."

"I think I give it to him," Ainsley said, bristling.

"Sure, but you're a woman."

"What's that got to do with it?"

"Korey's nine, now. About the time a boy needs a father, a man to help him face all the, er, problems of growing up."

"I can do that!"

"You don't know what it's like to be an adolescent boy," Jefferson said. "What Korey needs is someone who can show him wrong from right."

"Meaning a man."

"Of course!"

Ainsley was incensed. "That's the most sexist thing I've ever heard!" Ainsley said. She glanced at Trent and saw the mocking glint in his gray eyes. "I can handle Korey, thank you very much, and I don't need some man to play daddy to my son!"

"Sure, sure," Jefferson said, rubbing his chin as he turned to the house. "That's why things were going so well for you back in San Francisco."

"Low blow, Dad," she said, but he was already out of earshot, walking up the path to the back porch. Letting out a long breath, she slowly unclenched her fists, and glimpsed Trent trying to hide the amusement in his eyes and the twitch at the corners of his mouth.

"I suppose you agree with him!" she charged.

"I didn't say that."

"Then what's so funny?" she demanded.

"Nothing," he said, but laughed just the same.

"Oh, you're all alike!" She started to stomp away, but he reached out and caught her arm, spinning her to face him.

"Don't let him get to you," he advised. "He means well."

"But he's so—"

"Mule-headed? Stubborn? Set in his ways?"

"All of the above!" she said, her teeth clenched as tightly as her fists had been.

"Hey, whoa. Calm down. It's just that he cares."

"Then he could give me some credit for having a brain."

"He's your father and you'll always be his little girl."

Some of her anger slipped away. "I suppose you're right," she said, still glaring angrily at the house. "And I asked for it, coming here."

"He just wants what's best for you."

"So you *do* agree with him?" She glanced at her wrist, where his fingers were wrapped so possessively, and then looked up into his eyes. They were as warm as she remembered. "You think I should go out and find myself a husband to help me raise my son?"

"No."

"But—"

A muscle worked in the side of his jaw. He dropped her hand and stared across the fields to the McCullough house on the hill. "But I just know how hard it is to raise a boy alone."

"You're talking about Lila, right?"

Trent nodded, his brow furrowing. "It hasn't been easy for her."

"What happened to Wilson's father?" she asked.

Trent's eyes flashed angrily. "He left. Before the baby was born."

"Did he know about it?"

Trent's expression grew dark and dangerous. "Oh, yeah, he knew about it. Claimed it wasn't his. Wouldn't be responsible. Didn't even bother to meet Wilson."

"And she never hears from him?" Ainsley whispered.

"Never."

"What happened to him?"

Trent looked down at her again and his eyes had grown distant. "It really doesn't matter, does it?"

"I guess not."

"Lila's done the best she could."

"According to Dad, you've helped."

His lips twitched. "She's busy a lot of the time. I try to help out. That's all. No big deal." He shoved his hands into his pockets and leaned one elbow on the fence. When he looked straight into her eyes, her pulse leaped erratically. "I'm sorry about Robert," he whispered, rubbing the splinter rail with one callused hand. "I know it's hard to lose someone you love."

"I'm over it. Really."

"And Korey?"

"He's learned to deal with Robert's death—and he doesn't need a replacement father. No matter what Dad thinks." She saw Trent's gaze move downward, to her lips...to the hollow of her throat. Then, stiffening, he pushed himself upright.

"Guess I'd better go see what Brother Jonah thinks is so all-fired important," he said, squaring his hat back onto his head and striding to his Jeep.

She watched him walk away, noted that his jeans hung low on his slim hips and the cotton fabric of his shirt stretched taut over his shoulders. She closed her eyes for a moment and remembered how he'd looked that long-ago summer, his tanned muscles glistening with sweat, his face still slightly boyish.

When the engine of his Jeep roared into life, she looked up to see him drive away. "You can't feel this way," she muttered, ignoring the warmth beginning to spread through her.

Disgusted, she walked into the barn. Cobwebs hung from rough beams. Dirt covered the wood floor and collected in the corners of small windows. The smell of dry hay and dust filled her nostrils. She ran her fingers through the hard kernels of wheat and corn as she passed the grain bins on her way down the two steps to the machine shed.

Shouldering open the door, she stood at one end of the building and looked at the equipment parked inside. She noticed the two old tractors in rusty disrepair. The flatbed trailer looked okay, but the rake and harrow had broken spikes and the combine's engine was torn apart and lying in pieces on a tarp on the cement floor.

"Oh, Dad," Ainsley whispered, biting into her lower lip. "What's happening to this place?"

AT THE MCCULLOUGH ranch, Trent parked the Jeep in the garage and walked across the asphalt path to the main house, a refurbished colonial structure painted white and surrounded by huge maple trees. Climbing the stone steps, he opened the door and walked straight into the den where his brother Jonah was seated behind the same old desk his father had used. The room was neat—everything in its place—a far cry from the mess that Jefferson Smith called a study.

"'Bout time you showed up," Jonah said, tawny eyes lifting as Trent strode into the room. A handsome man with angular features and light brown hair, Jonah was used to being obeyed. Trent knew that the fact that his younger brother constantly ignored his commands irritated him.

"I said I'd be back around three," Trent said.

"Three was too late. Parker's already left."

"Parker?"

"Jed Parker. Remember?" Jonah's nostrils flared. He finished looking over the deed in front of him and ran his fingers through his neat hair in frustration.

"Oh, yeah. He's a real estate agent. Right?"

"Not just any agent. The best in Idaho Falls."

"So what'd he want?"

"He wants to sell us the land on the other side of the Circle S. The Hammond place. He's heard that the bank's about to foreclose on it. We could get it for a song."

Trent walked to the bar and poured himself a stiff shot of Scotch. The Hammond place had been owned by four different generations of Hammond sons, the current being Nick Hammond. Nick was a friend, a good man with a wife and three kids who had made the mistake of investing in oil at the wrong time. Just like Jefferson Smith. "Not interested," he said, taking a swallow of his drink.

"You'd better be. This is a good deal—something you don't really care about, I know, but it's important to the company. After that fiasco you pulled with Jefferson Smith, we don't have much of a choice but to acquire land around here as cheaply as possible."

"Smith'll pay us back."

"When?" Jonah demanded. "You and I both know that the Circle S is only this short of going down the tubes." He held up his fingers in a small pinch and shook his hand in front of his brother's face.

"We got the plane, didn't we?"

"Big deal. Who needs it?"

"If you have to, you can sell it."

Jonah pushed away from the desk and sighed. "We're going to buy the land on the other side of the Circle S."

"I won't sign."

"Then Lila will. I'll stay here until she arrives. She's flying in from New York sometime soon, thank God. At least she's got some common sense."

"What's that supposed to mean?"

"That she doesn't care about sentimental value. Hard cash is good enough for her."

"And you think that's a virtue?" Trent didn't bother hiding his smirk.

Jonah squinted up at his brother. "No. A necessity. We have to make a few smart decisions or we'll be out of business. Not only the oil company, but the ranch as well. Is that what you want?"

Trent finished his drink. "I just want things to be simpler."

"Don't we all? But it's too late. And you may as well face the fact that we're all in this together. You, me, Lila *and* Jefferson Smith."

"And Nick Hammond?"

Jonah snorted. "Just quit feeling guilty about his investment, and for God's sake, don't let the fact that Ainsley's back at the Circle S sway your opinion."

"You think it would?"

"You never have thought straight when it comes to her," Jonah muttered.

Trent forced a cold smile. "Ainsley's always been a friend of mine—a good friend. I'm not going to be part of anything that ruins her or her father. Got that?"

"You don't have any choice."

Trent crossed the room and leaned over his brother's desk. "I still own a third of this ranch and the oil company."

"Not enough. Lila and I can override you."

"Try." Trent's eyes grew deadly. "See what happens."

Then he turned on his heel and strode outside. The sun was just beginning to set behind the mountains and Trent felt boxed in, caught between the proverbial rock and a hard place.

With a grimace, he jumped into his Jeep and headed into town. All he needed was a couple of beers to calm down. Maybe then he could quit thinking of Ainsley and the mess her father was in. He shifted down and the vehicle jumped forward onto the asphalt road leading to Pine Corners and a local bar named Diamond Jim's, where the booze was cheap and the women friendly.

He drove faster than he should have, parked on the street and sauntered into the smoky interior of Diamond Jim's. After ordering a beer, he sat in a corner booth, ignored the interested glances of a woman sitting at the bar and conjured up Ainsley's face. Her blue eyes and long chestnut hair were easy to visualize, and he imagined her smiling up at him and trusting him as she had once—before all of the pain and lies.

Frowning, he tried to shake her image, but she lingered. He just couldn't get her out of his mind. And maybe he really didn't want to.

CHAPTER SIX

AINSLEY HAD BEEN helping Sarah with the supper dishes when the sound of a diesel engine cut through the evening air. A large truck rumbled down the drive.

"What in thunder—" Sarah murmured.

Ainsley finished drying the last plate and walked outside to see the freight truck stop near the garage.

"What the devil's going on?" her father demanded.

"I'm looking for Ainsley Hughes," the driver of the truck said as he jumped to the ground and let the big rig idle in the drive.

"You found her," Ainsley said.

"Good. Sorry I'm late. I got a little behind schedule today," he said, mopping his brow. "But I've got several crates on the truck. If you'll just sign here—" He handed her a clipboard and pen just as Trent walked out of the stables.

Ainsley hadn't seen him for a couple of days and couldn't tear her eyes away from him. He squinted at the truck and the crowd of people gathered near the cab.

"Miss—" the driver repeated.

"Oh, yes!" She scribbled her signature in the space he'd marked, then waited as the driver went into the back of the truck to pull out three crates and a huge box filled with her art supplies.

"What's going on?" Trent asked as he approached.

"I'm back in business again," she replied brightly as the truck roared away. "Now, if I could get you to help me take these to the loft."

"You mean this is all for your work?" her father asked, eyeing the crates dubiously.

"Uh-huh. Except for that box. I shipped my extra clothes in there."

"More like it," the old man said.

Together, she and Trent and Jefferson managed to get everything into the studio. "Beats me where you'll put all this," Jefferson grumbled as he stood and stretched the pain from his lower back and knee. Trent pried open the crates. Paints, easels, palettes, drop cloths and canvases were tucked carefully into the wooden boxes.

"Don't worry about it, Dad," she assured him. "I'll find room."

"Humph. I reckon you will." He started toward the door.

"Oh, and Dad?"

"What?"

"If you don't mind, I'll need to add a couple of overhead lights in here," she decided, pointing to the ceiling.

Jefferson shrugged. "Why not? I'll see what I can do tomorrow—"

"I'll handle it," Trent cut in. "I know where some used fixtures are stored. I can rig those up for now. And Ainsley can pick out others when she's in town and has the time."

Jefferson glanced from Trent to Ainsley and decided not to argue. "Fair enough. Now, I'm gonna scare up my grandson and take him into town for an ice cream, if that's all right with you," he said, looking over his shoulder at Ainsley.

"As long as he's finished the homework I gave him this morning."

Jefferson left the room grumbling about slave-driving women.

"I think he resented your help," she thought aloud.

"Probably. Just like he resented *you* telling him how to raise his grandson."

Ainsley laughed. "I'm just Korey's mother."

The corner of Trent's mouth lifted into a crooked smile. "I'll be right back. I've got a couple of things to check on and then I'll bring a ladder and see what I can do about adding those fixtures." His grin widened and her heart leaped stupidly. Then he headed down the stairs.

"You're a fool," she told herself, feeling the flush in her cheeks. "Trent's just an old friend. Nothing more!" She started putting things away but kept glancing up, expecting Trent to walk through the door. She'd nearly finished by the time he returned with a ladder, a couple of saws, a small spool of electrical wire and two old fixtures.

"Nothing fancy, but they'll do the trick until you can run into town and pick out what you want."

Shadows had begun to darken the room, making it feel more intimate. Ainsley tried to ignore the feeling that she and Trent were completely alone.

After showing him where she wanted the extra light, she helped hold the ladder, trying not to stare when he stretched upward and his shirt slipped out of the waistband of his jeans to reveal the tanned skin of his flat abdomen.

She noticed the faded fabric of his jeans as it pulled across his thighs and hips; the way his belt hung just below his navel; his arms, veins bulging, as they stretched high overhead.

"Hand me those pliers, would ya?"

"Oh…sure." She picked them up from the table and placed them in his open palm, looking upward and seeing his eyes turn a smoky shade of gray. Swallowing hard, she glanced away.

"That should just about do it," he said, his voice a little rough. He climbed off the ladder but didn't move. Instead he reached forward and touched the side of her face. "You know, Ainsley, your dad isn't the only one who missed you," he whispered.

"So you said." Her fingers clenched around the wooden slats of the ladder. "It was hard to stay away sometimes," she admitted, closing her eyes as his fingers found the pulse near her neck.

"Why did you?"

"Lots of reasons," she said hoarsely. "Korey, for one."

"And Robert?"

"He was my husband."

"Even though he betrayed you?"

She felt the old pain again, but refused to cry, squeezing her eyes tight against the threat of tears. "There was nothing I could do."

"You could have come back to me," he said slowly, wrapping his arms around her waist and drawing her close. His breath fanned her hair and she could hear the beating of his heart, smell the familiar scent of him, feel his big hands splayed warmly against the small of her back.

"You would've wanted me?"

"Oh, Ainsley, if you only knew," he whispered, his forehead touching hers. "There were nights…" His fingers tangled in her hair and he pulled her head back to stare deep into her eyes.

She saw tenderness and pain, friendship and passion in his expression. "Knew what?" she asked.

"How much I loved you."

"You should have told me."

"I tried. But it was too late. You'd already married Robert." Disgusted with himself all over again, he dropped his arms and stepped away from her.

"I had no idea—"

"Because you were blind, dammit. A blind, spoiled little girl all caught up in her dreams of getting away from the ranch and seeing the world."

"Was that so horrible?" she asked.

Every muscle in his body strained, ached for her. His face twisted with the effort of his control. "No, I suppose not."

"Then why were you so angry with me?"

He hesitated, opened the door and then slammed it shut again. Leaning against the cool panels, he leveled his hard gaze at her. "It doesn't matter anymore. I thought you were making a big mistake and I wanted you to stay with me."

"But there's more to it! There has to be!" she said, re-membering his passion and anger at the creek all those years ago. "You thought that Robert had hurt me—"

"Leave it alone, Ainsley." He grabbed the knob and yanked the door open. "It doesn't matter anymore. Maybe it never did." Slamming the door, he stood on the landing and leaned over the rail. He took several deep breaths and tried to clear his head. He couldn't think about the past or the present, not when it concerned Ainsley. "Son of a bitch," he muttered clamoring down the steps. "Son of a goddamned bitch!"

Standing in the middle of the room, Ainsley heard him swear. In that moment she decided she was going to take control of her life: she was tired of people shutting doors in her face, making decisions about her son and running her life.

"Trent!" She threw open the door and saw him striding to the barn. There was tension in his shoulders, fury in the way his hands balled at his sides. He didn't look around. "You miserable son of a gun!" She raced after him, her cinnamon hair streaming behind her, her teeth clenched tight. "Trent, dammit, I want answers!"

The evening breeze was cool against her skin, but her anger was white hot as she marched through the open door of the barn, slammed it shut and waited as her eyes adjusted to the dim light. "Trent!"

"Go back to the studio, Ainsley," he ordered from somewhere high overhead. Though the interior was dark, she looked up and saw him in the hay loft, just before he pushed a bale over the side of the loft. The dry bale split open upon landing and another came crashing down to the dusty floor. "I have work to do."

"The cattle have already been fed," she said, eyes blazing, her hands firmly on her hips as she stared up at him. "Korey took care of it."

"Then I'm getting a head start on the morning."

She squinted through the dust swirling in the air. "You're avoiding the issue."

"Which is?"

"The past, dammit, and what it means."

"Believe me, you don't want to know." He stood high above her, balanced on the golden bales, staring down at her with silvery eyes that cut through her soul.

"I do and I will!" She started up the ladder to the loft. "If you won't tell me, I'll find out from someone else."

"There's nothing to find out."

She reached the top and climbed onto the mountain of stacked hay. "Then why're you so touchy about it?"

He leaned on a pitchfork and looked beyond her, as if

seeing the past through new eyes. "It was hard—watching you take off with Robert."

"He was your best friend."

Gray eyes flashed and he kicked another bale to the floor below. It crashed and split open below with the others. "I didn't really know Robert," he said slowly. "There was a side to him that I hadn't seen."

"Not until I married him?"

His jaw worked and his fingers clenched around the handle of the pitchfork. "Yes."

"But you hardly saw him since."

Tiny lines whitened around his nose. "Let's just say I learned about some of the things he'd done."

"Which were?"

His eyes held hers. "You don't want to know," he said quietly. "And what would be the point? I don't want to tarnish your memory of Robert." His gaze slid from her eyes, past the dusting of freckles on the bridge of her nose to the pout on her lips.

"It's already tarnished," she whispered, her throat becoming hot. "I should never have married him." She pushed her hair out of her eyes and sighed. "I knew it almost right away once we reached California, but I kept thinking that things would work out."

"You could've come back."

"I didn't want to give up," she said.

"You never do."

"Then, of course, I got pregnant and I decided that my marriage to Robert and bringing up the baby were the most important things in my life."

He dropped the pitchfork and massaged the aching muscles of his neck with his fingers and tried not to think about Ainsley and what he longed to do with her. She looked so small and vulnerable, her eyes wide and innocent; he had trouble keeping his hands off her.

"Besides, I felt guilty."

"Guilty?" He took a step closer to her and brushed a piece of hay from her hair. "What could you possibly feel guilty about?"

"The last time I saw you. By the creek."

A frown creased his forehead. "You shouldn't have thought about it. Nothing happened."

"Unfortunately, that's not entirely true," she said, wrapping her arms around herself. "I…I had trouble forgetting about it. Things changed between Robert and me." She sighed and felt Trent's arms slip around her waist. Leaning back against him, she closed her eyes.

"I didn't mean to cause any problems."

"I know," she whispered, feeling his hands, warm through her jeans as they held her against him. "You didn't. I should have been honest with Robert about my feelings for you."

Turning her around, he stared into the pain in her eyes. Lavender shadows filtered through the one window, shifting across the rough features of his face.

"If only I'd known you cared *before* I married him."

"Then what would you have done—stayed and married me? A rancher?" he mocked.

"Maybe—"

"Oh, no, lady, you were bound and determined to get away from here, no matter what it took. You had things to do." Studying her eyes, bright with tears, and the way her chin quivered when he touched it, he slowly lowered his head and brushed his lips over hers. Ainsley tried to draw away but couldn't. His hands tangled in the thick strands of her hair, cradling her head to his and his tongue slowly rimmed her mouth, tasting of her sweetness.

She pushed hard against his chest, feeling the rigid muscles under his work shirt, but he paid no attention. Instead, he groaned and the sound struck a primitive cord in Ainsley's heart. Her hands slipped upward, around his neck, and without thinking she was kissing him with all the passion she'd held at bay for eleven long years.

She didn't protest when his hands found the hem of her T-shirt and explored the soft muscles of her back, kneading them gently as the weight of his body forced her down to lie on the uneven hay.

"It's been so long," he whispered, kissing her eyes and lips, the flames of passion burning hot inside him.

She moaned softly against his neck, tasting his skin as his hand moved to capture the weight of one breast. "Oh God, Trent," she whispered, her nipple growing taut beneath his rough hand.

"Ainsley, sweet Ainsley," he murmured, his lips moving slowly downward, past the neckline of her T-shirt and lower still, his breath hot through the soft fabric. He lifted the shirt over her head and gazed down at her, seeing her dark nipples through the lacy fabric of her bra. "Dear God, you're beautiful."

Slowly he lowered his head and touched the pointed tips with whisper-soft kisses.

Ainsley curled her fingers through the thick, coarse strands of his hair and held him close, feeling liquid fire burn bright in her center, radiating outward as he teased and nipped at her breasts.

Shivers darted up her spine when his hands opened the snap of her jeans and his lips caressed the soft flesh of her abdomen. "Oh, Trent, please..." she moaned, writhing and straining upward, feeling the hard pressure of his desire pinning her against the hay.

"Please what?" he rasped.

"I...I can't think."

"Don't, Ainsley. Just *feel*." He slanted his mouth over hers, kissing her long and hard, his hands moving sensually over her rib cage as his tongue darted quickly in and out of her mouth, teasing her, promising so much, much more.

Head spinning, Ainsley kissed him back, ran her fingers over the corded strength of his muscles as she pushed his open shirt off his shoulders and then felt him stop and listen. Poised above her, he forced his passion aside and went rigid. "Shh..."

She didn't move, but heard the barn door creak open. Hardly daring to breathe, she saw pale light flicker and die in the interior of the barn, heard shuffling feet on the floor below.

"Okay! Okay! I'll do it. Just get off my back!" she heard a boy whisper. *Korey. It had to be Korey.* "But I'll need five dollars. For each one."

Glancing up, she saw Trent's face harden, his gray eyes grow cold.

Boots scraped on the wood floor and Ainsley couldn't hear anything but a gruff grunt in response to Korey's demand. Then the door squeaked open again and closed with a thud.

"What was that all about?" Trent asked, his passion ebbing as his curiosity was piqued. He reached for his shirt and stuffed his arms into the sleeves.

"I...I don't know."

"Well I aim to find out." He didn't bother tucking the tails of his shirt into his jeans, but started down the ladder.

"You don't think this has anything to do with the missing tools, do you?"

He stopped, eyes locking with hers. "I hope not," he muttered as he jumped down the remaining few rungs to the floor.

Quickly Ainsley pulled her T-shirt over her head, snapped her pants and followed him outside. Dusk had settled over the valley. Above, stars winked in the purple sky.

Trent stood near an old maple tree, his shirt still unbuttoned and flapping in the wind.

"Lost 'em," he said, his gray eyes scanning the dark countryside.

Ainsley stood still and listened for the sound of whispered conversation or the crunch of boots on gravel.

Far away an owl hooted, and in the nearby fields horses neighed softly to each other. But there was no other sound. Lights were blazing in the windows of the old farmhouse and her father's truck was sitting in the drive.

Her spirits plummeted. She'd hoped she'd been mistaken, that in the darkness she'd only imagined her son's whispered voice. "So Dad's back."

"With Korey," Trent muttered.

"Maybe I should have a talk with my son."

"Not a bad idea, considering," Trent said.

"He's not a thief, you know!" she insisted.

"I hope not, Ainsley. I hope to God not." Trent picked a few strands of hay from her hair and then buttoned his shirt. "It's late. I'd better be shoving off."

She wanted to beg him to stay and her thoughts strayed wantonly as she considered how good it felt to be in his arms, how right it had been to lie with him. Swallowing against the urge to ask him to spend the night, she watched as he walked to his Jeep, climbed behind the wheel and started the engine. In a few seconds he was gone and Ainsley was left with the uneasy feeling that her life was slowly falling apart.

With a sinking heart, Ainsley hurried into the house to find Korey. No time like the present to find out the truth, she reasoned.

The kitchen was dark, but she could hear the sound of the television drifting in from the living room. "It's now or never," she told herself as she rounded the corner and found her father asleep on the couch, the TV blaring loudly. Korey was nowhere in sight.

She snapped the TV off and Jefferson snorted, his eyes blinking open. At the sight of her, he smiled.

"Caught me catnapping, didn't you?" Sitting upright, he ran his fingers through his thinning hair, smoothing the silvery strands back into place.

"Maybe you should go upstairs to bed."

"It's early yet," he grumbled. "Besides, the nights are long enough as it is."

She sat on the arm of the couch and looked down at him. "How was your trip into town with Korey?"

"Fine. Just fine. We each had a double scoop. Chocolate marble and cookies with cream."

"Been back long?"

Jefferson shrugged. "An hour, maybe. Why?"

"Just wondering. Where's Korey now?"

"Upstairs. He didn't even want to watch TV with me. Claimed he had to get a headstart on tomorrow's homework. But don't let him know I said anything. He wants to surprise you."

"And he's been in the house ever since you got home?"

"That's right." Jefferson grinned sheepishly. "Unless he snuck by me while I was restin' my eyes. But that don't seem likely now, does it?"

"I don't know," she whispered.

Her father turned sober. "Somethin' botherin' you?"

"A lot of things," she admitted.

"Want to talk about 'em?"

Her lips still pursed, she shook her head. "I don't think so."

"I don't like to see you worried."

Clasping her hands around her knees, she glanced out the window to the night beyond. She didn't want to tell her father about Korey, not until she'd settled some things in her own mind. For all she knew, Trent could be jumping at shadows.

"Ainsley?" Jefferson asked quietly, placing his hand over hers. "Something's on your mind."

"It's the ranch," she said quickly. "Seems like a lot of equipment has broken down."

"It has."

"Why doesn't Trent have it fixed?"

"He does the best he can."

"But the combine—"

"I know. It's in pieces. One of the hands from McCullough's place is handy—mechanically inclined. He's gonna come over and take a look at it."

"It better be soon. You'll be needing it next month."

"I know. But if we can't fix it, Trent has promised to let me use his."

"Big of him," Ainsley muttered.

"Well, Missy, we can't very well afford a new piece of machinery like that, can we?"

"No, I suppose not." She stood and stretched, her mind

filling with thoughts of Trent. One minute she knew she was falling in love with him, the next she didn't trust him again. She started for the stairs. "I think I'll check on Korey."

His room was the first door to the right. She knocked softly and then entered, finding him huddled over some books at his desk. "Working?" she asked.

He grinned lopsidedly. "Yeah, I thought I'd get a jump on tomorrow so I could go fishin' with Wilson."

Feeling like a traitor, she sat on the corner of his bed. "So tell me, how're things going in Pine Corners?"

"Okay, I guess. The whole town's getting ready for the rodeo!"

"You had a good time, then?"

"Yeah."

"And you've been in here ever since?"

"Uh-huh. What's with all the questions?"

"Nothing, really. I just thought I saw you and another person over by the barn a while ago."

Korey shifted his gaze back to his homework. "Wasn't me. Must've been one of the hands."

"I don't think so," she said slowly. "You see, I heard him speak. I thought it was you."

"Are you crazy?"

She looked up sharply. "No." Then she lowered her voice. "Were you at the barn earlier?"

"I already told you I wasn't!" His face was red. "Don't you believe me?"

"Oh, Korey, I don't know what to believe." She looked at him steadily and her gaze softened. He'd been through so much in the past year. "Trent, he says some things are missing from the farm."

"Things?"

Lines of worry creased her forehead and she forced

herself to meet her son's gaze. "Like tools, fishing gear, tobacco. That sort of stuff."

"Don't tell me—he thinks I took 'em."

"He wanted me to check with you."

Korey's little face twisted. "Don't you know me better than that, Mom? I don't take things that aren't mine."

"I know that, but Trent doesn't. He started missing some of the things about the time you came to the ranch."

"Great! Just great! You know that guy has it in for me, don't you?"

"In for you?"

Korey's eyes darkened. "I know the story, Mom. Grandpa told me that Trent was in love with you and you married Dad instead of him!"

"That's not exactly how it went."

"Close enough. And now he's trying to horn in on you again."

"I don't think—"

"Come on, Mom. I can tell! He never takes his eyes off you! Wilson says the same thing."

"Wait a minute. Even if Trent were interested in me—"

"He is."

"Okay. Even if he is. What's that got to do with the missing tools?"

"I don't know. Maybe…maybe he doesn't like me," Korey said defiantly, tears building in the corners of his eyes. "Maybe he's making the whole thing up!"

"You don't think that!"

"Why not? He's always bossing me around! 'Korey, feed the cows. Korey, make sure there's water in the troughs. Korey, clean the barn. Korey, go round up the calves!'"

"All part of living on the ranch. Sometimes he even bosses me around."

"That's different."

"Why?"

Korey sniffed and wiped his nose with the back of his hand. "'Cause he's interested in you—you know, like a woman and a man. Like Dad was interested in you."

Ainsley had to bite her tongue. Robert had lost interest in her soon after they'd been married. "Look, Korey, I didn't come up here to accuse you."

"You could have fooled me," he said bitterly.

"I just want you to know what's going on."

"And you want me to keep my nose clean, right?"

"I always expect that." She sighed as she walked to the door. "I know that living here is a big adjustment, but let's make the most of it, okay? How about you and me taking a ride and having a picnic tomorrow?"

His eyes widened. "You mean it?"

"'Course I do."

"Can Wilson come, too?"

Ainsley hid her disappointment. She needed time alone with her son. "Maybe. If you want."

"Then I'll finish this homework right away!" he exclaimed.

"Good. See ya in the morning." She walked down the stairs and outside. "He's a good boy," she told herself as she leaned against the fence. "Trent's wrong about him."

Gazing across the dark fields, listening to summer insects buzz through the air, Ainsley tried to push her doubts about her son aside. After all, those doubts had been planted by Trent and she still didn't understand his role at the Circle S.

Her chin stuck out in determination. She decided she'd find out exactly how Trent was connected—really connected—with the ranch. She wrapped her fingers tightly around the rough wood of the top rail. She'd leave no stone unturned in her quest.

CHAPTER SEVEN

AINSLEY SPREAD THE blanket on the shaded ground and looked across the valley. From her vantage point on the ridge, she could see the spreading acres of the Circle S. Cattle dotted the landscape and the golden fields shimmered from the heat.

"What did Sarah pack?" Korey asked as he dismounted and helped his mother unload the saddlebags.

"Your guess is as good as mine," she said. "Probably liverwurst sandwiches."

"Yuck!" Korey made a face, then grinned. "Hey, look at this!" He opened one of the foil packages and found several turkey sandwiches.

"It's too bad Wilson couldn't come," Ainsley said as she sat on the edge of the blanket and tossed Korey a half-frozen can of cola.

Korey's eyes clouded over. "Maybe we can do it again. Another time."

"We've got all summer." Leaning back on her elbows, she felt the sun warm her shoulders.

"I thought I'd go see him when we're done here." At her quizzical expression he let out an exasperated breath. "I did my homework last night, remember? And I finished my chores this morning."

"Okay, okay," she said, laughing. "I'm convinced."

"Good." Korey took a bite of his sandwich and then swallowed some Coke. "You like it here, don't you?"

"Yes," she admitted.

"So why did you leave?"

She chuckled and closed her eyes. "Some foolish notion that I had to see the world. You know, surf in California, climb mountains in Oregon, ski in Heavenly Valley and sail in Puget Sound. I thought I had to see it all."

"And did you?"

"Nope. Instead, I got horribly homesick," she whispered, recalling the lonely nights when Robert didn't come home and she was in a college town where she didn't know a soul.

"Why didn't you come back here?"

"Good question. I had lots of reasons at the time, one of which was my pride. I couldn't admit that I'd made a mistake."

"Grandpa would have understood."

"Yeah. I know that now."

"What about Dad?"

Ainsley's brows puckered. She took a long drink. "He never wanted to come back."

"Why? Was he afraid you'd leave him for Trent McCullough?"

"What?" She sat bolt upright and gazed at her son. "What kind of a question is that?"

"Don't get bent," he said, grinning when he saw the blush climb up her neck. "I just thought there was a reason he wanted to stay away."

"He was a construction engineer and loved his job in San Francisco. Before that, we were in college. He, uh, never felt comfortable on the ranch."

"But I thought *you* liked the city."

"I do," she admitted, squinting against the sun. "Hard to believe, isn't it? I love this land with all of my heart, but I really like my life in the city."

"So what're you gonna do?"

"You mean at the end of summer?"

"Uh-huh."

She winked at him and grabbed a sandwich. "I guess I'll cross that bridge when I come to it. But believe me, I won't make a decision like moving back here without asking you."

"Good."

"Relieved?"

"A little. You seem to get off on this ranch so much I was worried."

A hot breeze moved through the branches overhead, rustling through the leaves. "Would it be so bad—to stay here?"

"I don't know," Korey admitted. "I guess I'll have to cross *that* bridge when I come to it!" He reached for another sandwich and Ainsley leaned back again. She'd been back in Wyoming for less than a week and already she was wondering what it would be like to stay.

After they'd finished lunch and packed the saddle-bags, Korey took off for the McCullough place to find Wilson. Ainsley sat with her legs tucked up, her head resting on her knees and watched Korey ride Crazy Luke down the hillside. When he reached the lower fields, he gave the black colt his head and the horse raced off, galloping over the dry crusted fields to the fence at the southern border of the Circle S. "He's growing up," she told herself with a sigh. "And you've got to help him."

Dusting herself off, she stretched and climbed back on

Jezebel, following the winding, overgrown path that cut through the trees, and watching the sunlight flicker and dance through the branches overhead.

The mare picked her way carefully down the hillside and Ainsley, when she reached the bottom, didn't turn back toward the house. Instead, she cut through the pasture, leaning forward and urging Jezebel on, feeling the exhilaration of the horse as it galloped easily over the acres toward Wolverine Creek, where Ainsley and Trent had parted so long ago.

TRENT WAS STANDING knee-deep in the creek when he heard the sound of approaching hoofbeats. The horse and rider were as one: a galloping chestnut mare, ears flat, legs stretching forward, and Ainsley, face flushed, her long red-brown hair streaming behind, her eyes bright, pressed low over the mare's neck as she rode.

Trent squinted and felt the now-familiar tightening in his gut as he watched her. In the past few days, he'd found to be true what he'd suspected for a long time: he'd never really gotten over Ainsley Hughes.

All the women he'd met in the past eleven years faded when he looked at Ainsley with her intelligent blue eyes and dimpled smile. Maybe she was the reason he'd never married. Probably.

"Once a fool, always a fool," he decided, wiping the sweat from his brow with his shirt as she pulled Jezebel up short on the bank near him.

"Howdy," she said, casting him an impish grin.

"Aren't you supposed to be working?"

"Yeah." She nodded and tried to comb her long, tangled hair with her fingers. "I guess I'm playing hooky. I wasn't in the mood to paint."

He cocked a dark brow. "Oh, I get it. You're one of those free-spirited artists who only works when the subject moves her," he mocked.

Blue eyes flashing coyly, she pursed her lips. "Close enough."

"Bull!"

"What's that supposed to mean?"

"Just that I've never met a woman whose feet were more solidly planted on the ground than yours are."

"Is that right?" She leaned over the saddle horn and brought her face close to his.

"That's right. And if you're not careful, I'll drag you out of that saddle and throw you into the creek."

"Promises, promises," she quipped, then ducked when he reached for her. Jezebel neighed and reared, and Ainsley laughed as she controlled the anxious mare. "So what're you doing?" she asked.

"Checking the flow of the creek. The neighbor down the way claims he's not getting the water he should be. He seemed to think that there might be a beaver dam or something blocking the flow."

"Here?"

"Somewhere between here and his place."

"Never heard of beaver down here."

"Neither have I. But there's always a first time," he said, climbing out of the ice-cold stream. He was bare-chested, his tanned skin nearly bronze, dark hair swirling over firm muscles. The legs of his worn jeans were wet, but he didn't seem to notice.

"So did you find anything?"

"Not yet."

She slid off Jezebel and opened up one of the saddle-bags. "How about some lunch?"

"I thought you and Korey were going on a picnic."

"We already had it. As soon as he was finished eating, he made tracks to find Wilson. But I've got some leftovers…if you're interested." She spread the blanket in the shade of the trees near the creek.

"Leftovers. The story of my life."

Ainsley took in a swift breath and her fingers fumbled with the foil wrap on the sandwich.

"I wasn't talking about you," he said gently.

Embarrassed, Ainsley sat cross-legged on the blanket, and tried not to notice the way his muscles rippled as he sat next to her. Still lean and hard, they moved easily beneath his tanned skin, flexing and relaxing as he shifted. "I know you weren't," she said, her voice low.

Trent eyed her suspiciously. "Why're you here?" he asked, his eyes dark.

"Like I said, I'm goofing off today."

"I already heard that. But there's more."

She avoided his eyes and handed him a sandwich as he leaned close to her. "It's Korey. I talked with him last night. He claims that he doesn't know anything about the stolen things."

"'Course that's what he says." He took the cola she offered, glancing at her from beneath spiky dark lashes. "The question is whether you believe him."

"He's never lied to me before."

"What about all that trouble he had in school?"

Ainsley's jaw clenched. "He always told me the truth."

"*After* he was caught red-handed."

"He said he wasn't in the barn last night."

"We both heard him."

"We heard *someone*," she said. "Maybe it wasn't Korey."

"Maybe," Trent allowed, finishing his sandwich and settling back on his elbows. "But I thought you recognized his voice."

"The voice was hushed."

"And you haven't heard him whisper before?"

Ainsley looked up to the blue, blue sky. Her emotions were all jumbled and confused. "Of course I have. But I'm not sure that he was in the barn. I...I want to believe him."

"So do I," Trent admitted.

"But you can't."

"What I can't do is ignore the fact that since he's been on the ranch, things have been missing. Just watch him, Ainsley."

"I can't spy on my own son!"

"Don't spy on him—just keep your eyes open."

"Same difference."

"No reason to get belligerent on me," he said. "You don't have to condemn the boy, just because you're not turning a blind eye. Okay?"

"Okay," she said hotly, then tried to control her temper. "So what do you think the people in the barn were talking about?"

"Beats me, but it didn't sound good, now, did it?" His gray gaze seemed to pierce right through her.

Shuddering, she looked away. "No," she admitted. "It didn't."

"I'll keep a watch on the hands. Especially the new men."

"Good." Relieved, she allowed herself a glance in his direction. "Korey's had a lot of problems," she said. "But he's not a thief."

Trent's lips twisted into a wry smile. He lifted his can and held it in mock salute. "To Korey," he said. "The perfect child."

"Cut it out." But she laughed anyway, her cares seeming to melt away as she watched the rushing water of the creek slide over smooth stones to bubble in small eddies and pools near the banks.

Trent's eyes grew slumberous as he lay back, staring up at her. Sunlight glinted in the fiery waves of her hair and the trees overhead swayed in the hot afternoon breeze. "It's been a long time since I've heard you laugh," he thought aloud.

"I've been gone a long time."

"And maybe you haven't felt like laughing."

"Maybe." She tossed a stone into the creek and felt him shift closer to her, until his head was resting near her thigh.

His breath fanned hotly through the worn fabric of her jeans and despite her thoughts to the contrary, she began to ache deep inside. When he reached up to touch her shoulder, she nearly jumped out of her skin.

"I didn't sleep much last night," he admitted. His voice was rough, but the fingers stroking the slope of her cheek were gentle.

"Neither did I."

"I thought about you."

"Oh?" She tried to sound casual, but couldn't hide the hoarse tone in her voice.

"And the barn. And what almost happened."

"Nothing happened."

"Yet." His fingers touched her chin, forcing her to look into the gray depths of his eyes. "But it's going to. We both know it." He searched her face.

"I'm…not sure I can handle a love affair," she said, swallowing hard and noticing the rippling power of his shoulders as he shifted onto one elbow, lifting his head to stare straight into her eyes.

"Maybe I can't either," he admitted. "But what happens between us, it's not something we can ignore." He placed both of his hands around her face, tilting her head and meeting her lips with his.

It was a soft kiss that gently explored, questioning and commanding as he groaned and let his fingers move to her hair, to tangle in her wild chestnut curls.

Ainsley knew she should push him away, deny the heat spiraling deep inside her, wait until she was sure of just what she felt…but she couldn't. The length of his body, molded next to hers, made her dizzy, and the feel of his lips, pliant over her mouth, made her crave more.

Her fingers caressed his shoulders and back, feeling the hard muscles flex. Sweat beaded across his brow and glistened on his chest as he rolled and pinned her beneath him, his legs tangling with hers, his breath as ragged as her own.

"Oh, Ainsley—" his voice was a harsh whisper "—what you do to me should be illegal." And then he kissed her again, harder this time, stealing the breath from her lungs.

His fingers trembled as he found the buttons of her blouse and parted the soft fabric to expose her breasts, ripe and waiting, the white skin dappled by the shifting branches overhead.

Groaning, he massaged one rose-crested peak, feeling it turn button-hard in his hand as he lowered his lips to pluck at it, teasing the firm nipple between his teeth.

Ainsley moaned in pleasure. All thoughts of denying Trent had fled, and she could think of nothing save the sweet torment of his lips at her breast.

"Do you want me?" he asked, his hot breath tickling her skin, searing her deep inside.

"Y—yes," she whispered, her heart pounding unevenly, echoing in her mind.

"Now?"

"Oh, yes, please!" Gasping for breath, she closed her eyes and heard a soft click as the snap of her jeans gave way. His fingers dipped deliciously below the waistband and touched her abdomen as he lowered her jeans over her hips, down her legs, his fingers seductively brushing her calves.

Still straddling her, he watched the play of emotions on her face. Her lips were still swollen from his kisses and her hair was a wild cinnamon cloud, surrounding her face in tangled curls that crept past her neck to rest just above the heavy white globes of her breasts.

Her blue eyes, glazed in passion, stared straight up at him, through to his soul as his fingers slowly inched up her rib cage. "You know that I loved you?" he asked.

"Yes."

His brows pulled together and he tried to think straight. "And you know that I would never have done anything to hurt you."

"And...and now? What about now?" she whispered.

His hands stopped their gentle torture. Jaw working, he suddenly rolled off her and raked his fingers through his hair. His back was to her, his head lower than his shoulders.

"Trent?"

"Get dressed, Ainsley."

"But—"

"Get dressed before I do something we'll both regret!" he rasped, grabbing his shirt from the ground and stuffing his arms through the sleeves.

Cheeks burning she yanked on her jeans and buttoned her blouse with quivering fingers. "I don't understand—"

"Neither do I!" Walking over to a pine tree, he leaned

against it and clenched his teeth against the passion that was still throbbing mercilessly. "Oh, Lord, neither do I!" He clenched and relaxed his fists and stubbornly pushed his lust aside. When he finally turned to face her, she was staring at him with wide, confused eyes. "Don't look at me like that!"

"How am I supposed to look at you?"

"Maybe you shouldn't!" he said, and when he saw her swift intake of breath, hated himself. "Hey, look—"

But she was already striding toward her horse, wrenching on her boots as she walked.

"Hey, Ainsley, just listen—"

She didn't turn around and he had to run to catch up with her. Grabbing hold of her wrist, he spun her around.

Her face was flushed, her eyes filled with tears. "You don't have to explain anything, Trent," she hissed. "You wanted to mortify me and you did. Satisfied?"

"Not by a long shot, lady."

One glance at the white lines near his mouth confirmed that he was telling the truth. She jerked her arm away and grabbed Jezebel's reins. She couldn't stay another second; she was too confused.

"I just don't want to rush into anything we might regret."

"Then why let it go so far, Trent?" she asked, climbing into the saddle. "Then why the hell let it go so far?"

"Because I couldn't stop myself."

"Seems to me you did a damned good job."

"I just want things to be right."

"Right?" She dashed away her tears with the back of her hand. "And when will that be?"

"When I can get over the guilt of ruining things between you and Robert."

"Don't flatter yourself," she said, kicking Jezebel and

leaning forward as the mare reared and took off. Tears still collected in her eyes and she tried to blame them on the wind from her wild ride, but she knew, deep in her heart, that Trent was right. He had ruined any chance she had with Robert—and *she'd* let him. "Never again," she vowed, pulling up on the reins as Jezebel approached the barn. *She'd never let Trent get close enough to hurt her again!*

"Let's hope it isn't too late," she said to the mare as she slid to the ground and went about taking off the saddle and bridle before brushing Jezebel's gleaming chestnut coat. Once the mare had cooled down, Ainsley led her into the paddock where the little filly neighed eagerly for her mother.

DINNER WAS A disaster. Trent stayed and throughout the meal, Ainsley felt his eyes on her. She tried her best to be lighthearted and avoided speaking directly to him, but she could feel the tension in the room.

"A great meal again," she said to Sarah as she pushed her plate aside.

"Couldn't tell it by you," the older woman commented, eyeing the plate of food Ainsley had barely touched.

"I…I, er, just wasn't too hungry. That big lunch you packed, you know."

"Sure." Sarah began to clear the table and Ainsley helped her, glad for the excuse to leave the dining room.

"Something happen between you and Trent today?" Sarah asked when she and Ainsley were alone in the kitchen.

"Nothing, really," Ainsley lied, biting at her lower lip.

"Then why were you two at each other's throats?"

"We weren't."

"I don't know about that," Sarah said, slicing large pieces of apple cake. "I wasn't born yesterday, y'know. I recognize a lover's quarrel when I see it. Pour the coffee, will ya?"

Ainsley nearly choked. "What do you mean 'lover's quarrel'? Trent and I aren't—"

Sarah shook her head. "It's plain as the nose on my face that Trent's crazy about you. Don't tell me you haven't noticed, because I won't believe you."

"Trent and I are…"

"What? Just friends?" Sarah's old face crinkled with a smile. "Don't be giving me any of that malarkey."

"Our relationship is hard to define," Ainsley admitted slowly as she poured the coffee.

"I'll bet." Sarah carried a tray back into the dining room and Ainsley followed, trying her best to be as casual and unconcerned as possible. When Korey challenged her to a game of chess, she accepted, only to be trounced by her son.

"Check and mate!" Korey exclaimed.

"I can't believe you did that!" she said, staring down at the chessboard.

"Grandpa gave me a couple of books to read and I've been practicing."

"Obviously."

"What's the matter, Missy?" Jefferson asked, his eyes twinkling brightly. "Need a lesson from the old master?"

"No thanks. I think I just had one."

Jefferson laughed and Ainsley glimpsed Trent from the corner of her eye. His gaze was dark and unreadable, but he stared at her, his face bland.

As if nothing in the world were wrong.

"I think I'll go upstairs now," Korey said, leaving his plate on the coffee table. "Read a little more in that book."

"Just don't expect me to be such a sucker next time," Ainsley called after him.

Jefferson finished his dessert and took a final swallow of coffee. "Good cake," he said, winking at Sarah. "Almost as good as Emma's was."

"Her recipe." The cook beamed.

"Well, if you ladies will excuse us, Trent and I have business in the den," Jefferson said, pausing to pat old Dallas as he straightened.

"Let me help," Ainsley suggested. Maybe this was her chance to see exactly how the ranch was doing under Trent's care.

"With the books?" Jefferson rubbed his chin and tried to hide a smile.

"Why not?" Trent asked, looking directly at her. "Seems she's got a good head on her shoulders."

Jefferson chuckled and shook his head. "If I remember right, math wasn't exactly your best subject."

"That was years ago," Ainsley protested. "Believe it or not, I can balance a checkbook."

"Nonetheless, you'd better leave the accounting to me and Trent."

Burning with anger, Ainsley watched as Trent followed Jefferson into the den and shut the door behind them. "Dad has a lot to learn about women's lib!"

"If he hasn't learned yet, I don't think he will," Sarah commented, her hazel eyes gleaming.

Ainsley glared at the closed door. "What I wouldn't give to be a fly on the wall in there." With a sigh, she carried the dirty cups into the kitchen.

"Not me. I have enough problems of my own." Sarah

pursed her lips as she put the dishes into the dishwasher. "I don't want to know what goes on in there." She cocked her head toward the den.

"Then things aren't good around here?"

"Things haven't been good since your mother died." Sarah sighed loudly. "Your father loved your mother very much—he never really got over her death." Swallowing a lump in her throat, Sarah shut the dishwasher.

"I know."

"So, learn from his mistakes. You're young. I don't think you should lock yourself away just because Robert's gone."

"I don't think I have."

"Lord, I hope not!" Sarah snapped a tattered dish towel and folded it over the oven door before looking at Ainsley. "You're a beautiful woman. With your whole future ahead of you. No reason to be lonely. There are lots of good men out there."

"So I've been told. Over and over again," Ainsley complained.

"Well, one of them is right here on this ranch, if you'd only open your eyes."

"Meaning Trent."

"Of course, meaning Trent."

"What is this? Everyone around here thinks Trent should run for president or something."

"He's a good man, that's all. And he's crazy about you!"

Ainsley wasn't so sure. "And what about Korey?" Ainsley asked. "He doesn't much like Trent."

"Why would he? Trent's interested in his ma and that's threatening for a child. Korey lost one parent already, he's afraid of losing you."

"But that's ridiculous." Ainsley propped one hip against the counter and eyed the older woman.

"Maybe to you; but you're not a nine-year-old boy." Sarah took off her apron and headed for her room off the back porch. "I'm gonna turn in early. I'll see you tomorrow," she called over her shoulder. And then she was out the back door.

Alone, Ainsley was restless. She walked back to the den, knocked on the door and poked her head inside. "Just wanted to know if I could get you anything," she said.

Jefferson was seated behind his desk. His reading glasses had slipped to the end of his nose and he was silently smoking as he stared at the checkbook and a tall stack of invoices. He glanced up quickly. "We're fine. Really."

"You sure I couldn't help?"

"Positive."

Rebuffed, Ainsley closed the door and walked outside. The sounds of the night filled the air. Frogs called out their song and insects buzzed close to the windows. In the distance a freight train clacked on ancient tracks. She looked up, saw the light in Korey's room and decided to tell him good night.

Quietly she walked back into the house and up the stairs. Through the door, she could hear his radio playing softly. She knocked. When he didn't answer, she called through the heavy oak panels "Korey? You still awake?"

No answer.

Thinking he'd fallen asleep, she cracked the door open.

His homework was lying open on the desk, the radio was on, but he wasn't anywhere in sight and his bed was untouched. Frowning, she called down the hallway, but the bathroom door was open and no one was inside.

"Funny," she muttered to herself, looking at his bedroom again. And then she noticed the open window, curtains rustling in the breeze. "Oh, no," she whispered crossing the room and seeing that for an athletic young boy, it would be easy to walk along the ledge to the kitchen, where the roof was lower, and across that roof to the back porch, slide down the sloping metal and jump the remaining five feet to the ground.

But why?

The scene in the barn came back to mind and her heart fluttered with fear. *I'll need five apiece,* the young voice had said. "Oh, Korey, I hope you're not in trouble," she whispered, running from the room.

Hurrying downstairs, she ran out the front door and into the dark summer night.

CHAPTER EIGHT

HER HEART HAMMERING, Ainsley stood in the backyard and looked around the night-shaded buildings. Only a few security lamps were lit. Shadows shifted against the barn and stables as branches moved in the wind.

"Korey!" she yelled, waiting for a response and getting none. "Korey, where are you?"

"Mom?" She turned quickly toward the stables. Korey was just closing the door behind him.

"What're you doing out here?" she demanded, relieved as her son loped toward her.

"Just checkin' on Luke," he said, a half smile on his boyish face. "Why?"

"I thought you were in your room—studying."

"I was. I got bored and decided to take a break."

"I didn't hear you come down the stairs."

"Why not?"

"You tell me," she suggested, glad to see that he was safe.

He shrugged. "You were in the kitchen talkin' to Sarah. I didn't want to bother you. So I just went to the stables without saying anything."

"And that's all?" she asked, holding him by the shoulders and wanting desperately to believe him.

"'Course it is. What did you think?"

"You wouldn't want to know."

His young face fell. "You thought I was out stealing?" he said, reading the doubts in her eyes. "All because of Trent and what he said?"

"No," she said, shaking her head. "I was worried, that's all."

"Aw, Mom, I'm not a little kid anymore," he pointed out, stuffing his hands deep into his pockets and kicking a stone with the toe of his shoe.

"I know. That's what worries me."

"Nothin' you can do about it," he said, shrugging.

"Yeah, but it comes with the territory of being a mother."

"Don't worry, Mom. I'm all right. Really." He gave her his most charming grin. It touched that special place in her heart that was all his. "I'll see ya tomorrow."

"Sure." She watched as he hurried to the back door and jumped over the two steps leading to the porch. "How could you ever doubt him?" she asked herself, heading for her loft over the garage.

Once inside the studio, she kicked off her shoes, made a cup of tea on the hot plate and looked at the empty easel standing near the window. "You'd better get with it," she muttered, thinking back to the afternoon on the ridge and the gorgeous view of the ranch. But painting hadn't come easily since she'd been back in Wyoming. Her mind had been distracted with worries over Korey and thoughts of Trent.

She heard footsteps on the steps and then a sharp rap on the door. Her heart fluttered stupidly when she heard Trent's voice through the heavy panels. "Ainsley?"

"It's open."

He strode through the door and his face was set—a hard mask without emotion. "Were you outside earlier? I thought I heard you."

"I was, but there was nothing wrong," she assured him. "Korey had been checking on his horse and I thought he should go upstairs and get ready for bed."

"Oh." He eyed her suspiciously, but let the subject drop. There were too many lies between them as it was.

"Want a cup of tea?" she asked.

"If it's no trouble."

"No trouble at all. Besides, I think maybe we should call a truce." She poured a cup and handed it to him.

"A truce?" he repeated.

"Yes. We both got a little…upset this afternoon."

"Seems that it's always that way between us."

"Water and oil?"

"Exactly."

She took a chair at the old table and cradled her cup in her hands. "I've had a lot on my mind."

"Me, too." His eyes stared deep into hers. "I've been doing some thinking—I thought maybe we should clear up a few things."

"About what's happening here—on the ranch?"

His dark brows lifted. "That, too."

"What else?"

"Us."

She looked into her tea. "I didn't really think there was an 'us.'"

"Oh, there is. Very definitely," he said. "I just don't know what we should do about it."

"Maybe leave it alone," she suggested.

"Maybe." But his gray eyes bored into hers. "If that's possible."

Uncomfortable, she tried to change the subject. "Hard to tell—there's so much involved. Including the secret you've been keeping from me for these eleven years."

His eyes narrowed. "What secret?"

"You tell me," she said. "I haven't been able to figure it out. I just know that you haven't been straight with me. And you thought about it again this afternoon. So, until we can clear up the past, I don't think we can deal with the present."

He rolled the cup in his hands and his throat worked. "Just leave it alone, Ainsley. In time—"

"In time, what? You'll get it off your chest?"

His fingers tightened over the cup. "If I think it'll help."

"Okay," she said, seeing that she couldn't push him any harder. She leaned back her chair and blew across her cup. "Then tell me about the ranch. I've seen the equipment and know that we have less livestock—and fewer hands than we used to. And I can tell that lots of things around here are in sad need of repair. What I don't understand is why Dad hired *you*. Or was that all part of the deal when he agreed to have the oil wells put on his land?"

Trent's mouth turned into a cynical line. "Believe it or not, I'm only trying to help your father."

"Sure—then why the capped wells? How does that help Dad?"

"That," he admitted, tugging on his lower lip, "was a mistake."

"A big mistake," she countered, her eyes flashing angrily. "The last time I was here, about four years ago, everything was fine. The equipment was kept up, the livestock looked after, the buildings painted and fixed. So what happened?"

"Maybe your dad lost interest," he thought aloud. "It wasn't easy on him when he lost your mother."

"I was here, remember?"

"But you went back to San Francisco. To Robert."

She winced. "So Dad just gave up? Is that what you're trying to tell me?" she asked incredulously, not believing him for a minute. "My dad's always been a scrapper. He would've fought anything to save this ranch, and he did. Several times."

"When Emma was still alive."

"If things were so bad, then why did he invest in the oil company?"

Trent grimaced. "You'll have to ask him that yourself. He worked it out with Jonah."

"Don't try to pass the buck to your brother!" she said hotly.

"I'm not. That's just the way it was."

"Then why are *you* here? Is it all part of the deal?"

"Not exactly." Seeing the disbelief in her eyes, he continued. "It's true that investment in the oil was a last-ditch effort to save this place, and it worked for a little while— until the market went belly-up."

"And now that investment in the wells is killing the ranch, right?"

"It's been a drain," he admitted.

"Great. Just great. And now you're working here! Look, I don't even know why I'm discussing this with you!" She finished her cold tea and then set the empty cup in the sink. "Maybe you should just leave."

"Not yet."

"Why not?"

He stood and walked up to her. "We have unfinished business."

She stared up at him and held her ground. Her chin thrust defiantly outward, she stared straight into his erotic gray eyes. "If you're talking about this afternoon at the creek, you can forget it! I'm not interested in taking up where we left off!" she lied, her chest rising and falling rapidly. *Dear Lord, he was too close.* She couldn't think straight. Old emotions she'd tried to keep hidden kept boiling to the surface.

"I didn't think so. But you know it's going to be damned hard to ignore what we feel for each other when we have to see each other every day."

"Are you suggesting I go back to San Francisco?"

"No." He touched her cheek, but she drew away.

"Good! Because I'm staying! Now, if you want to bag out, that's just fine with me!" She planted her fists on her hips and glared up at him.

"I can't."

"Then try to keep out of my way, okay?"

His expression softened and one corner of his mouth lifted. "I just don't know if that's possible," he whispered, his hands coming up to capture her waist.

"Don't, Trent," she said, feeling his fingers pull her close.

"I can't help myself."

"Sure you can."

He bent down and placed his mouth over hers, cutting off her protest and feeling her lips yielding to his.

Ainsley knew she should try to fight him, break away while she could still think straight, but the feel of his muscles pressed hard against hers, the warmth of his hands as they slid around to her back and the heady scent of him, took control of her senses and caused her head to spin. Rational thought ceased, and emotions, whirling and dancing, took control of her mind.

"Don't, please," she whispered, when he began to kiss her neck, but she let her head fall back, allowing him to get closer, letting his lips sear her skin, permitting his breath to seep beneath her blouse and cause shivers of anticipation to dart down her spine.

"Tell me you don't want me," he groaned.

"I…I don't."

"Tell me you won't make love to me."

"I can't!" *Dear God, why couldn't she think straight? Why was her concentration controlled by the movement of his fingertips against her skin?*

"Tell me to stop," he commanded, his voice hoarse, his emotions running ragged.

"Please…please, Trent, stop…oh, God!"

He cradled one firm breast in his hand, and she was lost in a pool of swirling emotions, hot and breathless and drowning with the want of him. Closing her eyes, her head lolling back, she felt the buttons of her blouse give way, then the soft cloth was pushed over her shoulders to fall to the floor in a useless heap. Her fingers dug into his shoulders, hanging on as he leaned over and touched the tip of one nipple with his tongue.

Ainsley squeezed her eyes shut tighter, trying to fight the shard of desire that cut through her core, turning her insides molten.

Falling to his knees, he brazenly plundered the rose-crested mound, suckling and nipping, driving all thoughts of denial from Ainsley's mind. "Let me love you," he whispered. "Tonight, let me love you."

And what about tomorrow? But he toyed with the snap of her jeans, slid the rough fabric down her legs and followed with his eyes and lips. She swayed against him and he caught her, deftly picked her up and carried her to the bed.

The bedroom was dark except for the light from the

other room and the moonlight, splintered by pine needles, reaching through the window.

His lips never left hers as he laid her on the handmade quilt that covered the old brass bed. As her back touched the cool patchwork, she sucked in her breath, her abdomen curving inward.

Knowing he was probably making the worst mistake of his life, Trent unbuckled his belt, kicked off his jeans and covered her body with his, capturing her lips and feeling her soft, pliant muscles press against his hard counterparts.

"Just love me," he whispered, settling over her and cradling her face in his hands.

"I always have," she admitted, her voice cracking as she clung to him, wrapping her arms around his back. "I...I never stopped." Hating herself for never forgetting him, she felt tears gather in her eyes. Her throat clogged with all the years she'd lived a lie.

"Sweet Ainsley," he whispered, moving over her. She felt the hard length of his desire press against her and she gasped as he kissed her again. Her blood heated as he slowly massaged her breasts and his tongue slipped between her teeth, dancing and teasing hers until her fingers dug into the hard muscles of his back and her world was spinning crazily out of control. She couldn't think, could only feel as he parted her legs and entered her.

"Oh, God, Trent," she cried as he moved atop her. His rhythm was slow at first, questioning. But as he felt her sway with him, his strokes became more powerful and she felt hot and wild and wanton, as wave after wave of pleasure overcame her.

"Trent..." Her fingernails dug into his back, and she moaned lustily as a shaft of pleasure cut her to the core, convulsing her body around him.

"Ainsley," he cried, shuddering in a storm of emotions that ripped through him as they became one. "I'm sorry…"

Tell me you love me, she thought, still holding him close. *Please, Trent. Tell me you love me.*

But the words never came. Instead he cradled her next to him and sighed. "What am I going to do with you?" he whispered into the night.

Her heart twisted painfully as the seconds ticked by. "I think that's my line."

Gazing down at her, he grinned, his lips quirking in a crooked smile. "Just trust me."

"Sometimes that's difficult."

"Try." He outlined her eyebrow with his finger and kissed her forehead. "Maybe I'd better be going," he said slowly. "We wouldn't want anyone to get the right idea, now, would we?"

"I don't know. I think my dad would be thrilled," she said, staring up at the ceiling. "He's been singing your praises since I got here. If I didn't know better, I'd think that he was paying you to be with me."

Every muscle in his body flexed and his slumberous gray eyes hardened to cold silver. "Fortunately you know better, though. Right?" Without so much as looking over his shoulder, he swung his legs over the edge of the bed, grabbed his jeans and quickly dressed.

"I hope so," she said.

Scowling, he buttoned his shirt. "You still don't trust me, do you?"

"There are just some things I don't understand," she said quietly, seeing his jaw work and the way he glanced out the window. "Like the past."

"We talked about that."

"Not enough."

"Drop it, Ainsley," he warned, his voice sounding weary.

"I can't! And you shouldn't either!"

"Even if innocent people will be hurt?" he demanded, turning to face her, his gray eyes darkening dangerously.

"The truth never hurt anyone."

"Oh, God, Ainsley…"

"I have to know!"

"Dammit, just forget it!" he yelled, smashing his fist against the wall. Ainsley jumped. Then, he squeezed his eyes shut to control himself. "Believe me, it's over!" Sitting on the edge of the bed he felt the mattress sag. "Please. Just leave it alone."

"I can't, dammit!"

"Then that's your problem," he said coldly as he stood. "I've done what I can to clear things up." Striding out of the room, he slammed the door behind him and didn't stop until he reached the Jeep. Once inside the old rig, he turned the key. "You're an idiot, McCullough, a damned idiot!" he muttered as the old engine roared to life.

As he shifted into first, he saw the door of the loft open and Ainsley's silhouette against the light from the studio. Her hair was still wild and she was wearing some white, gauzy cotton wrapper that sent his fantasies spinning again. The wind blew the robe around her legs and arms, outlining in minute detail the slim, sensuous body he had so recently ravished.

His heart began to pound again and before his loins could respond, he snapped on the headlights and stomped on the accelerator. Gravel sprayed from under the tires as the old rig jumped forward.

"Don't even think about it," he warned himself,

glancing in the rearview mirror and seeing Ainsley on the landing. His body screamed to go back to her, take her again, tell her he loved her as much as he once had, but instead, he forced his sweating palms around the wheel and clamped his jaw shut.

Ainsley watched him speed away and she couldn't shake the feeling that the past would destroy them both. "Or maybe he's just using you," she thought aloud, but dismissed the unwelcome idea. She knew him too well, knew that he cared for her. The question was—just how much. Were they friends who had become lovers of convenience or did he feel something special for her as he had in the past?

Her stomach in knots, she walked back into her studio, turned off the lights and fell across the bed. It was still warm and scented with recent lovemaking. "Oh, Trent," she said with a sigh as she stared out the window to the ghostly white moon. "How can I ever stop loving you?"

FOR THE NEXT few days, she managed to avoid him. She spent most of her hours in the loft, sketching some projects on paper before trying to transfer her work to oil and canvas. Only stopping for meals, or an occasional chat with Korey, she lived like a hermit in her studio. Fortunately, Trent never bothered to knock on her door. "All for the best," she decided, but couldn't help feeling a little depressed that he hadn't bothered to find her.

"This is ridiculous," she told herself. "He's probably having the same doubts you are." Once her sketches were complete and she was ready to start painting, she got up from the table and looked out the window to see Korey riding his black colt, practicing for the race at the Pine Corners rodeo. Trent and Jefferson were standing in the shade of an old maple tree and watching the boy put Crazy Luke through his paces.

Deciding it was time to face Trent again, she hurried outside and down the steps. She was just crossing the yard when she saw her father turn to her, his face becoming ashen as he started to double over. Trent caught Jefferson's arm, and Ainsley began to run, her heart pounding in fear. By the time she reached him, he was leaning against the tree, some of his color returning.

"What was that all about?" she asked, breathless, her eyes clouded with worry. "Are you all right?"

"Fine. Fine. Just a little pain."

"Looked like more than a little to me."

"You worry too much, girl. Same as your ma did."

Trent eyed the older man. "You're sure you're okay?"

"Fit as a fiddle," Jefferson snapped, his spine stiffening. "Nothin' to get all flustered about."

"You've had these pains before?" Ainsley asked.

"Once in a while."

"Have you seen a doctor?"

Jefferson laughed and reached into his pocket for his pack of cigarettes. "What's a doctor gonna tell me? That I'm gettin' old? That I shouldn't be smokin' these? That I should be takin' it easy?"

"I don't know—"

"All the doctorin' in the world didn't save your ma," he said, striking a match to his cigarette and taking a long puff. "And I'm not about to be spendin' my last years takin' one pill for this and another for that and eating food without salt or any of that nonsense! I'm just fine the way I am."

"But—"

"Don't argue with me, Missy. I aim to live my life just

the way I see fit. Always have and always will!" He sauntered over to the fence and called to his grandson. "Now, slow him down, see if he'll ease up a bit. That's as important as going as fast as you can!"

Trent's lips twisted wryly. "At least now I know where you get your stubborn streak," he whispered to Ainsley.

"Didn't you already know it?"

Jefferson glanced their way. "Don't be talkin' about me when my back is turned," he said, grinning. "Some parts might be slowin' down but I hear just as good as I ever did!" He hooked his finger toward Korey. "What do you think of your son? Turned out to be quite a horseman."

Ainsley's eyes sparkled with pride. "Can't argue with that."

"Then you'll forget all this nonsense about not letting him ride in the rodeo."

She looked at Trent, but all of his concentration was focused on the galloping horse. "I guess I'm outvoted," she said wearily, "though I didn't really know that I was in a democracy."

"You won't be sorry," Jefferson predicted, slapping the top rail and hooting.

Ainsley watched her son maneuver Crazy Luke through the pine trees at the far end of the field. "I hope you're right, Dad," she said as clouds passed over the sun, shadowing the land. "I hope to God you're right."

CHAPTER NINE

AINSLEY SET HER brush on the counter, stepped away from the canvas, tilted her head to the side and surveyed her painting with critical eyes.

"Still needs work," she thought aloud, disgusted with her attempts at capturing life on the ranch. Several paintings in various stages of completion were propped against the walls, and the only one worth her effort was a portrait of her father, his eyes squinted against the late afternoon sun, his weathered features drawn as he stared across the fields.

Still muttering to herself, she decided to take the rest of the afternoon off. The past week had been difficult. Avoiding Trent had taken all of her energy. He was everywhere and she couldn't seem to get away from him. Each time she crossed his path, she could feel his eyes boring into her back.

He'd been cordial and reserved and had never once come back to her loft. And she hadn't invited him. Her feelings for him were too hard to define and she knew that if she thought about Trent too much, she'd discover that she was head-over-heels in love with him. She probably always had been.

"You'll never get over him," she said, feeling the warm summer air against her back as she crossed the yard and walked through the back porch to the kitchen. Pausing to pour herself a tall glass of lemonade, she listened and couldn't hear a sound in the house.

"Sarah?" she called, once she'd finished her drink. "Dad?"

No response.

"That's funny." She walked down the short hallway to the living room, but didn't hear the drop of a footstep or the muffle of quiet voices. Outside Dallas was barking loudly, as if he'd cornered a gray digger in the woodpile; inside the grandfather clock ticked quietly in the front hall.

Sarah was probably working in the garden, and her father resting.

"Dad?" Knocking softly on the door to his den, she waited impatiently, then turned the knob.

The study was dark and as cluttered as ever, but her father wasn't in his chair or napping on the couch. The room was quiet. She was about to close the door when she noticed the checkbook lying open on the desk.

Feeling a little like Benedict Arnold, she crossed the room and quickly scanned the figures, gasping when she saw the balance and the stack of unpaid invoices sitting on the desk. "Oh, Dad," she murmured, biting her lip.

Dreading what she was about to find, she looked in the file cabinet and found more unpaid bills and letters from attorneys for the creditors of the Circle S.

"So where is all the money going?" she asked, her brow knitting with worry. Nervously, she flipped back through the pages of the checkbook register. There were checks written for wages, feed, machinery repair and various other incidentals, but an astonishing amount of the checks had been written to McCullough Oil.

"Oh, God." She felt as if she'd been kicked in the

stomach. On instinct, she looked through the files again, praying she'd find nothing more incriminating. Trent wasn't trying to steal the farm from Jefferson. He couldn't be! Her fingers began to tremble.

In a small folder in the back of the file cabinet, she found the agreement between Trent and her father. Her eyes skimmed the document and she felt sick inside. Her father had given Trent McCullough twenty-five percent of the Circle S as well as his plane for a mere fifty thousand dollars. The plane alone was worth that much! Dying a little, she leaned against the desk just as the door opened and Trent walked into the room.

He didn't say a word but stared at her.

Startled and embarrassed, she dropped the document onto the desk and walked to the window, to sit on the ledge. Her throat was so tight, she could barely breathe.

"What are you doing?" he asked coldly.

"I was looking for Dad."

"He's not here."

"I know. But…" She pointed at the checkbook. "This was open."

"And so you decided to snoop."

Her temper flared. "I just wanted some straight answers, that's all."

"And now you have them?"

"Yes," she whispered, her voice shaking. "I think so."

"Then you know the ranch is in trouble."

"Big trouble. It's worse than I thought," she said, swallowing as she glanced at the incriminating agreement.

A pained expression darkened his gaze. "Maybe things will get better. We have cattle to sell and sheep and—" He stopped short, seeing the accusations in her eyes. "Oh, hell, Ainsley, if things don't turn around by the end of the summer, this place will be forced into foreclosure."

"But how—"

"Bad breaks."

"Like investing in the oil company?" she demanded.

"For one thing."

"What else, Trent?" she asked, walking to the desk and lifting the agreement into the air. She held it out to him. "You were one helluva foreman, weren't you? Somehow, you managed to get my father to invest in your floundering oil company and then you gave him part of *his* money back, for his plane and a percentage of this land!"

"It was your dad's idea," he said slowly.

"Sure, after you had him in such a financial squeeze, he couldn't do anything else!" She was shaking, but held her ground. "You know, I almost made a big mistake with you. I almost trusted you."

"You've never trusted me," he said, eyes flinty and dangerous. His features became hard and angular and it was all he could do to keep rein on his temper.

"Do you blame me? Eleven years ago you claimed that Robert had only married me in order to get his hands on this ranch. But it wasn't Robert who was interested in the money, now, was it? It was you! You!"

Trent pinched the bridge of his nose and hooked one leg over the desk. "That's not true and you know it."

"How? How do I know it, Trent? Because of what I feel for you? Because we made love? Because I wanted to believe that you cared for me as much as I cared for you?" she said, tears building in her eyes. "For all I know, that's a lie as well! You used me, Trent! With all of your concern about Korey and my father and me. And I believed you, dammit. I fell for you, hook, line and sinker!" She slapped the incriminating pages back onto the cluttered desk.

"And this changes it all?" he asked, thumping his fingers on the agreement.

"What do you think?"

"You're looking for excuses!"

"Then explain this, dammit!" she said, wadding the paper between her fingers and fighting tears of frustration.

"Just be careful before you go pointing fingers," he ground out, his skin dark with rage. "I think you'd better talk to your father about it," he decided.

"I will!" She turned to leave, but his hand snaked out and captured her wrist, spinning her around.

He pushed his face close to hers and she could see the bright spots of anger in his eyes. "Not yet. We have to get one thing straight."

"And what's that?"

"That I love you, Ainsley. I always have and always will. It's as simple as that. I might not like it, but I sure as hell can't deny it!"

"Oh, God," she whispered, her chest tight. "And that's why you're the foreman here?"

"I'm the foreman because your father asked me."

"Good old Trent," she mocked, tossing her hair away from her face. "And all your accusing Korey of God-only-knows-what. Is that because you *love* me?"

"I just wanted to help."

"Help?" she repeated sarcastically.

"He needs a man to help him grow up—"

"I'm sick to death of hearing that!" she said, her eyes blazing. "Korey's *my* son and I can handle him. Alone, thank you very much! Neither Korey nor I need a man pushing us around or telling him what to do!"

She looked at the pain in his eyes and melted a little.

"You've got it all figured out, don't you?" he asked.

"Not yet. But I promise you, I will soon."

His gaze dropped from her eyes to her lips and her rigid, angry stance. "I just want you to know that all of this—the oil wells, me working on the ranch, the plane, everything—was your father's idea."

"Sure it was. After you and Jonah backed him into a corner," she said.

"I would never have let Jonah railroad your father."

"Not when you could do the job. Right?"

His eyes narrowed. "I've got a deal with your dad and I intend to hold up my end," he bit out furiously.

"Of course you do. You wouldn't want to blow anything this sweet, would you?"

His lips flattened. "How did you get so hard, Ainsley?"

Her bravado slipped a bit and she felt tears stinging her eyes. "Maybe I've had good teachers," she whispered, her throat beginning to clog as she blinked back her tears. "You and Robert both knew how to play me, didn't you? I'm just surprised that I was stupid enough to fall for you twice."

It was all he could do to stay away. She slumped into her father's chair behind the desk and gazed out the window.

"Ainsley—"

"Just go away. Okay? I mean it, Trent. It's over. You go about your business and I'll go about mine." She forced her eyes to meet his. "It shouldn't be all that hard. In two months I'll be gone."

"Thank God for small favors!" He turned and left the room, slamming the door hard behind him. Tears began to slide down Ainsley's cheeks, but her fists balled over the scratched arms of the old desk chair. Never again would she be so stupid about a man—especially Trent McCullough!

She peeked through the blinds and saw him striding across the backyard toward the stables. His fists were clenched, the cords in his neck bulging. "If only I could stop loving you," she whispered as he disappeared through the door.

When she was sure he wouldn't be back, she reached for the phone and dialed operator assistance.

"What city please?"

"San Francisco," she whispered.

"And the party?"

"I'd like the number of Hillside Realty, please." Scratching the number on a piece of paper, she frowned and stuffed the note into her pocket. Somehow she'd have to raise the money to help save the farm from foreclosure. This ranch had been in her family for generations and she wasn't about to let it fall into the hands of the local bank or McCullough Oil.

The first step was to talk to the manager at First Federal Bank. If that failed, she'd put her townhouse in San Francisco on the market.

TWO DAYS LATER, she found Jefferson in the machine shed. He was talking with a man she didn't recognize, explaining exactly what had gone wrong on the old combine.

"What're you doing here?" Jefferson asked, glancing up. "And what's with the dress?" He looked at her white sundress with the rainbow of ribbons that wound around her waist.

"Looking for you. And I decided I needed a change from jeans with the knees about worn through."

Jefferson's eyebrows lifted. "Just as long as you don't

start in on me about seein' a doctor again, okay?" he said, coughing a little. "I've heard enough from you and Sarah both."

She lifted her hands in surrender. "Okay, okay," she muttered. "But it wouldn't be a bad idea."

"Not a good one, neither." He cocked his head toward the broken piece of equipment. "I just thought I'd help Jake, here, with the combine. Jake, this is my daughter, Ainsley."

The young man tipped his hat. "How'd'ya do?"

"Fine. I haven't seen you around here before," she said.

Jefferson rubbed his chin. "Jake works on the McCullough place. Trent asked him to come over and check the combine out."

Trent. Her heart tugged at the thought of him. She hadn't seen him since their fight in her father's den. She glanced at the broken-down combine and shook her head. "Do you think you can fix it?" Ainsley asked the dark-haired man.

Jake rubbed his chin thoughtfully. "Don't know yet. I just got here."

"Well, just give me a holler, if ya need anything," Jefferson said as he followed Ainsley outside.

"Will do." And Jake set about his task, his experienced hands fitting the old pieces of the machine back together again.

Jefferson touched Ainsley's arm. "Well, are you all ready for the Roundup?" he asked, stretching the crick in his knee and grimacing at the pain.

"I don't think I'll ever be."

"Starts a week from Friday, y'know."

"How could I forget?" She looked past the paddock to the large field where Korey and Wilson were riding their horses. The boys were huddled high on the shoulders of their mounts and the long-legged colts were running stride for stride across the dry grass. The sky was a brilliant shade of blue with just a few clouds floating high over the mountains.

"He's going to win, ya know," Jefferson predicted, pointing to his grandson.

"Spoken like a true grandfather."

"I mean it. That kid's got natural ability."

"Do you really think so?" Her brow puckered with concern as she watched the black colt, his long legs stretching forward as he ran. Crazy Luke was a head in front of Wilson's horse and though Wilson was kicking his buckskin for all he was worth, the race was over. The black horse surged forward, leaving Wilson and his mount in his dust.

"'Course I think so. Wilson, he won't like it much, I'll wager," he said, eyes twinkling. "He doesn't like to lose."

"Like his uncle," Ainsley muttered.

Jefferson's bushy eyebrows quirked. "Don't tell me you and Trent had a spat."

"More than a spat, I'm afraid," Ainsley admitted, glancing at her father. She'd talked to the loan officer who worked for the bank that held the mortgage on the ranch and gotten nowhere. "I found out that he owns a quarter of the ranch."

Jefferson blanched a little. "Ya did, did ya?" He reached into his pocket, found a cigarette and match and lit up. "Did he tell you?"

"No. I found out myself. I was looking for you, in your den," she said with a shrug. "The checkbook was there, lying open, and I read it."

He didn't say a word, just stared across the fields, smoke from his cigarette drifting toward the vibrant blue sky. "And the partnership agreement—you see that, too?"

"Yes."

"It wasn't on the desk."

"No. I looked through the files."

He frowned. "Always were a nosy thing, weren't ya?"

"A little, I guess," she admitted. "But what worries me is that it looks as if you might lose the ranch."

"It's looked that way before," he said, watching her from the corner of his eye. "But I've still got a few tricks up my sleeve."

"Maybe I could help," she said.

"You?"

"I've got some money saved, and my townhouse is worth—"

His tired eyes snapped angrily and he ground his cigarette out in the dust. "Now you just hold on, Missy. I've run this ranch all these years without your help and I don't need it now."

"But—"

"No 'buts' about it! I'm not taking one red cent from you, not even as a loan!" he said, anticipating her protests and turning back to the machine shed. "Darned fool woman! I think I'll go look in on Jake."

Furious, she fell into step with him. "I just want to help," she said. "Isn't that what families are all about?"

"Now you listen to me!" Jefferson replied, before his voice cracked and faded, his feet stumbled and he fell to his knees, clutching his chest.

"Dad!" she screamed, as he pitched forward. "Oh, dear God! Help! Korey!" she yelled over her shoulder. But Korey was too far away to hear her, and she yelled frantically toward the garden. "Sarah! Please, help me!"

Hearing the sound of footsteps in the drive she sent up a silent prayer and gently rolled Jefferson onto his back. "Dad—can you hear me? Are you okay?"

His face was gray, his eyes watery, his knuckles showing white where his fingers clenched his shirt. "It's nothing."

"Like hell!" Trent said, running to the fallen man and barking orders. "Call an ambulance. Now!" he yelled at Ainsley. "I'll take over." He was on his knees in an instant opening the front of Jefferson's shirt.

She didn't question him but ran across the yard, tears streaming down her face. Once in the kitchen, she picked up the telephone receiver and punched out the emergency number with trembling fingers.

"Police dispatch."

"I need an ambulance right away," Ainsley said, rattling off the address and looking through the window. Trent was crouched over her father, alternately forcing air into his lungs and pushing on his chest with the heel of his palm. "I think, I think my father's had a heart attack. We're giving him CPR."

"What's going on?" Sarah asked, brushing the garden soil from her hands and then stopping dead in her tracks when she saw the fear in Ainsley's eyes. She glanced out the window, then leaned against the wall. "Oh, my God! It's Jefferson!" Without another word, she was out the door.

The dispatcher took a little more information, then assured Ainsley that an ambulance was on its way.

She slammed the receiver down and flew out the back door. Trent, his brow covered with sweat, was still working steadily over the older man and Sarah was wringing her hands in her apron.

"Will he be all right?" Ainsley asked.

"'Course he will," Sarah said, crossing herself and whispering a prayer. "He has to be."

"Too soon to tell," Trent said grimly.

Thundering hoofbeats made the hard ground shudder. Korey, his face white, pulled up Crazy Luke, jumped off the black colt and bolted through the gate. "What happened?" he asked, stricken.

Ainsley held him close, wouldn't let him go to his grandfather. "I don't know. Grandpa had a heart attack, I think, or…maybe a stroke."

"Dear Lord," Sarah murmured.

Korey's eyes filled with tears. "He'll be okay, won't he?"

"I hope so. God, I hope so," Ainsley whispered just as she heard the distant wail of the siren. Then, as much to give Korey something to do as anything else, she gave him a pat on the rear. "Ride Luke to the end of the lane and make sure the ambulance sees you."

"You got it." He ran back to his horse and galloped off down the drive.

Several minutes later the ambulance arrived. Two paramedics jumped out of the car and rushed to the stricken man. They gave Jefferson oxygen and took his vital signs as they spoke with a doctor at the hospital on a portable phone.

Ainsley watched the entire procedure with dread settling cold in her stomach. The two men put Jefferson on a stretcher and carried him into the ambulance.

"We'll follow in our own car," Trent said, taking Ainsley's hand.

"I'm coming, too," Korey offered.

"It's best if you stay here," Trent said.

"No—"

"Please, Korey. Stay with Sarah," Trent said. "We'll call you as soon as we know anything."

"But I want to be with Grandpa."

The ambulance, its siren shrieking and lights flashing, roared down the drive. Ainsley's knees went weak and Trent helped her stand.

"Look, you have to take care of your horse," he said to the boy. Trent nodded in the direction of the black colt. Crazy Luke's coat glistened with sweat, his nostrils were still flared and he was blowing hard.

"Mom?"

"We'll call you from the hospital. Maybe Sarah can bring you by later," Ainsley said, glancing beseechingly at the cook.

"Of course I will! Now, go on, get out of here, all of you! And Korey, you mind that horse and then get yourself up to the house, quick as a cat."

Korey cast one last, longing look over his shoulder, then walked his horse toward the stables.

"Let's go," Trent said, gently pulling Ainsley to the Jeep.

She didn't protest. Couldn't. Her thoughts were with her father and all the years she'd been apart from him. "I can't lose him," she whispered, as Trent started the Jeep and took off down the lane. The old rig shuddered as the tires hit potholes. Dust clung to the windshield.

"You won't lose him," Trent said, his eyes dark.

"I wish I could believe that." She stared blankly at the gray ribbon of asphalt leading to Pine Corners.

The town was already getting ready for the rodeo. Red, white and blue banners had been strung across the main street and snapped in the wind, proudly announcing the dates of the Roundup. Vendors' booths were being constructed, and a traveling carnival was beginning to set up in a field on the outskirts of town.

But Ainsley couldn't pay any attention. Her eyes were riveted to the hospital. It was little more than a well-equipped clinic, and she felt a sinking sensation as Trent parked near the emergency room. Her father could already be dead!

She was out of the Jeep and into the single-story concrete building before Trent had even killed the engine.

"I'm Ainsley Hughes, Jefferson Smith's daughter. He was just brought in here by ambulance," she said breathlessly to the admitting nurse. She looked around the tiny waiting area, saw people with bandaged arms and pained expressions staring at her.

"If you'll just fill out the admitting forms," the nurse suggested, handing Ainsley a clipboard.

"But I want to find out how he is—"

"The doctor is with him now. We'll be sure to give you any information as soon as we have it."

At least he was still alive.

"But—"

"Please, Ms. Hughes, if you'd just fill out the admitting forms?"

Desperately worried, Ainsley dropped into the nearest chair and started filling out the papers as best she could. Name, age, date of birth, information that she knew by heart was easy. But then the questions got more difficult. "Insurance?" she whispered. "I have no idea—"

"Here, let me help." Trent reached into his pocket, took out his wallet and found an insurance card.

"You're covered by Dad's insurance?"

His mouth turned down. "Not exactly." He had Ainsley sign the forms and handed the completed information to the nurse behind the glass.

"Can I see him now?" Ainsley asked anxiously.

"Not yet. The doctor is still with him. I'll let you know." The nurse offered a reassuring smile and Ainsley's heart sank.

She sat in the nearest chair, nervously flipping through a tattered magazine about health and beauty, barely glancing at the articles or the worn pictures.

Trent took the chair next to hers and didn't say a word. Patients were called into the back rooms, and each time the door swung inward, Ainsley craned her neck, hoping for some glimpse of her father. How was he? Dear God, was he still alive?

"He'll be all right," Trent repeated, touching her hand. His voice was soft and reassuring.

"How do you know?"

"Jefferson's tough."

"Ms. Hughes?" the nurse called and Ainsley was on her feet. "Dr. Holmes will see you. Just go right through those doors—"

Ainsley and Trent pushed open the doors to the emergency room and a young doctor with reddish hair, a thick moustache and wire-rimmed glasses approached them. "You're Mr. Smith's daughter—Ainsley?"

"Yes." She shook the doctor's hand. "And this is Trent McCullough—he's the foreman of our ranch."

"McCullough? As in the oil company?"

Trent nodded stiffly. "One and the same."

Dr. Holmes's eyes returned to Ainsley. "Your father is resting comfortably."

"Thank God," she whispered, her throat catching.

"He had a heart attack and we're running more tests."

"Oh, God—"

"So, I want him to stay in the hospital a few days—just until we know what we're dealing with." The young doctor offered Ainsley a reassuring smile. "I don't think he'll like the idea much."

"You can count on it," Ainsley agreed, white-faced. "Can I see him now?"

"I don't see why not. But he's resting in intensive care." He pointed down the corridor. "Go straight down that hall and turn left at the corner."

"Thank you, Doctor."

"I'll see you later."

Ainsley and Trent walked down the tiled hallways and found ICU. Upon instructions from Dr. Holmes, the nurse at the station let them peek into Jefferson's darkened room. Poking her head inside, Ainsley saw her father, lying flat on his back, his eyes closed, his face a ghostly shade of white. Tubes ran into his arms and a heart monitor beeped overhead. He looked tired and old and beaten, and Ainsley had to fight a fresh battle with tears. "Dad?" she whispered, walking over to the bed and reaching over the rail to touch his hand.

Jefferson didn't move.

"Dad—can you hear me?" She felt Trent's hand on her shoulder.

"Come on. Let him rest." Trent gently tugged on her arm. "I'll buy you dinner."

"I don't think I could eat anything."

"Just try."

She sighed and followed him out of the room. "If my father wakes up, tell him I'll be back later," Ainsley said to the nurse, then headed for the nearest pay telephone to call Sarah.

The cook answered on the first ring and Ainsley told her everything that had happened.

"Bless the Lord that he's alive," Sarah said. "I don't know what I'd do if we lost him."

"That makes two of us," Ainsley agreed.

"I'll bring Korey down in a couple of hours. If it's okay."

"I don't think wild horses could keep him away," Ainsley said before talking to her son and finally ringing off.

"How's Korey?" Trent asked, once they were back in the Jeep.

"Okay, I guess. He wants to come visit, but I told him he'd have to wait until later this evening. Even then I don't know if the doctor will let him into intensive care."

"Then we'll have to change the doctor's mind, won't we?"

"How?"

"By letting him know that Korey is the best medicine Jefferson could possibly have."

Ainsley rested her head on the side window. "I warned Korey that he might not get to see Dad…just in case."

"How'd that go over?"

"Like the proverbial lead balloon." Ainsley closed her eyes as Trent drove to the edge of town and pulled into the parking lot of a quiet restaurant overlooking the river.

"I don't think I'm properly dressed," she muttered, eyeing the building. Originally a turn of the century hotel, the Country House was now the best restaurant in town. Creamy paint glistened in the late afternoon sun, and blue shutters adorned the windows.

"It's not exactly black-tie, you know. Believe me, you'll be the best lookin' woman in the place." A slightly off-center smile cut across his face as he glanced down at her white sundress and sandals. Her long hair fell down her back in tangled curls.

"You think so?" She laughed and it felt good.

"I know it."

Since he was still dressed in faded cords and a work shirt, she didn't protest when he tugged on her hand and led her inside.

Floral wallpaper and gleaming walnut wainscoting decorated the walls. A crystal chandelier bathed the stairs in golden light that gleamed on the hardwood floors and reflected in the windows.

"Trent!" the hostess called as the bell over the front door chimed. She was a slim woman with bright red hair and a friendly smile. "Long time, no see."

"I've been busy, Melissa."

"With what?"

Trent glanced uneasily at Ainsley. "Helping out on the Smith spread."

"Well, don't make yourself such a stranger," she admonished. "We see Jonah all the time! Well, at least whenever he's in town!"

"I imagine you do."

"Yes, sir, he's always bringing some big new client in here!" Melissa said, beaming.

Trent's smile hardened.

"In fact, he's got a reservation for later tonight. Would you like me to give you a table close by?"

"No, thanks."

"Okay," she replied, sliding an interested glance at Ainsley. "How about a private table upstairs?" she asked. "Maybe on the upper deck?"

"That would be great."

Within a few minutes they were seated on a private balcony overlooking the river. The jade-green water rushed by, moving swiftly along the outskirts of town.

Ainsley followed the river's winding course with her eyes. "Remember swimming in there?" she asked.

"How could I forget?" His gray eyes glinted. "I caught you skinny-dipping in the old swimming hole."

Ainsley blushed at the memory. "And you stole my clothes!"

"I brought 'em back, didn't I?"

"Half an hour later. I was frantic."

His thick brows lifted and he smiled, his eyes smoldering seductively. "It taught you a lesson."

"Not to trust you!"

"Come on, Ainsley." He touched her hand. "It happened years ago."

"I know, but it was a rotten thing to do." She chuckled and took a sip of wine. "I wanted to get back at you so badly it was all I could think about the rest of the summer."

His jaw slid to the side. "I guess you managed that, didn't you?"

She saw the pain in his eyes and shook her head. "I married Robert because I thought I loved him. I had no idea—"

The waiter came and took their order. Ainsley didn't bring up the past again. It brought back too many emotions that she'd rather forget. Right now all she could think about was her father and how to get him well.

"I didn't mean to bring up a sore subject," Trent finally said, when the silence between them became unbearable.

"It's all right."

"And it's water under the dam."

"So to speak."

He poured them each another glass of wine and touched his glass to hers. "Here's to…the future."

"And whatever it brings," she whispered, swallowing hard and thinking about her father. He had to be okay. Nervously, she rimmed the edge of her glass with her fingers. "You know I wasn't kidding about what I said in Dad's office the other day."

He grimaced and settled back in his chair as the waiter brought sizzling platters of steak and onions before disappearing again. "I thought you were just angry. Blowing steam. That you'd get over it."

"I don't think I can," she whispered.

"I love you, Ainsley," he said, slowly. "I always have and I probably always will. But it's a two-way street and you've got to learn to trust me."

"Why?" she asked, her throat suddenly dry.

"Because you want to love me, but you're afraid."

She wanted to laugh, but couldn't. "Afraid of what?"

"Afraid to trust a man, any man, again. Robert hurt you and now you've built a hard shell around yourself, so that no man can find out that you're a soft, vulnerable woman inside."

"That's got to be the most chauvinistic thing I've ever heard!"

"It's the truth."

She sighed and shook her head. Candlelight flickered and reflected off her hair, turning the curls a fiery red. "I'm not going to sit here and have the same argument I had with you the other day."

"Good. Then, just relax and enjoy your meal. When we're done here, we'll go check on your dad again."

She wanted to argue, but didn't. Instead she ate what she could, then leaned back to stare at the river. Dark shadows were beginning to color the water, and the wind had begun to pick up, catching in her hair and making the flame from the candle dance.

The dinner crowd had arrived and pieces of conversation drifted upward from patrons seated around the tables on the deck below. One voice was louder than the others, and Ainsley recognized it as belonging to Trent's brother, Jonah.

"Oh, don't worry about him," Jonah said. "He'll come around. We've already made an offer on the Hammond place and Lila's flying in tonight to sign the papers. She's probably already at the ranch right now!"

Ainsley didn't move. Her eyes locked with Trent's.

"So it's all wrapped up?" another voice asked, drifting upward.

"All we have to do is sign on the dotted line," Jonah agreed, laughing lustily.

Ainsley felt sick inside. Her eyes rounded as the wind carried the conversation away. "What's that all about?" she asked and saw the tight white lines surrounding Trent's mouth.

"Jonah's business," he spat out.

"Which is to run out all of the ranchers in the area?" she asked, horrified.

"I don't know."

"But Nick Hammond owns his place. Free and clear! It's…it's been in his family for generations!"

"It must be mortgaged," Trent said. He ran a hand through his hair. "According to Jonah, the bank's about to foreclose."

She felt a coldness deep in the pit of her stomach. "Don't tell me," she whispered. "Nick Hammond invested in McCullough Oil! Right?"

Trent's eyes grew as dark as the encroaching night. "Just a few years ago," he said.

"And now he's going to lose his ranch—just like my father! Oh God, Trent, how can you face yourself in the mirror?" she asked, furious. Throwing her napkin on the table she ran downstairs, not bothering to look back. She had to get away from Trent, from everything he represented.

She heard his boots pounding on the stairs behind her and she raced to the front door, yanked it open and ran outside, past his Jeep and across the street, oblivious to the traffic.

Headlights careened around her as a car swerved and honked its horn. Her heart was pounding, her eyes burning but she kept running.

"Ainsley!" he shouted, but she ran faster. Her sandals caught on the uneven pavement, but she kept on. "Ainsley, stop!"

Another horn blasted and she didn't look over her shoulder, didn't turn around but sprinted across the street to the park, where she could get lost in the large stand of pine trees. How could she ever have trusted him? she wondered, pressing her back against the rough bark of a tree and fighting the urge to break down and sob like a child.

She wanted to hate him so badly, but she couldn't. No matter what had happened, no matter how he and Jonah had maneuvered their friends and even her father, she loved Trent.

Sick at the thought of how he'd used her, she slid down to the ground and buried her face in her hands. How could she ever stop loving him?

"Ainsley!" he shouted, his voice closer.

She swallowed back her tears, hardly daring to breathe, her heart thudding painfully in her chest.

"Ainsley! Dammit, Ainsley, where are you?"

She tried to push herself upright. He sounded too close. But her feet slipped from under and she fell back on the ground. And then he was there, towering over her, looking down at her with furious silver eyes.

CHAPTER TEN

WHAT THE DEVIL do you think you're doing?" he demanded. "You could've been killed back there!"

"Just leave me alone."

"No way." He reached down and helped her to her feet, but she wrenched free, starting to run again. He caught up with her in an instant, his big hands surrounding her waist and pulling her tight against him. "Just where do you think you're going?"

"Anywhere! As long as it's away from you!"

"You can't run, Ainsley. I'll follow you and find you—no matter where you go," he vowed, his breath labored, his eyes dark as the shadows. Slowly lowering his head to hers, he kissed her, long and hard, and she couldn't find the strength to fight him. His lips were warm and tender, gently soothing the storm of emotions raging deep within.

"Don't," she whispered, but wound her arms around his neck.

"Trust me," he pleaded.

"But you heard Jonah," she said, pulling away and trying to ignore the pounding of her heart. "I just don't like what's going on."

"Neither do I."

"Then do something about it, for God's sake!" she

said, stepping away from him and brushing the dirt from her dress.

"I'm trying my best."

"Well, it isn't good enough, is it? Nick Hammond is going to be driven off his ranch—all because he invested in your damned oil company!"

"That might not be the only reason."

"Doesn't matter," she said, starting to walk back through the park toward the lights of the restaurant.

He was beside her in an instant, falling into step with her and jamming his hands deep into his pockets. "I think I owe you an explanation."

"You don't owe me anything. If you want to squeeze out your friends, that's your business."

"It's not mine."

She crossed the street, not even glancing at him. "Oh, don't tell me," she mocked. "Brother Jonah again."

"You heard him."

She stopped in front of the old hotel and lifted her chin defiantly. "You're the other man Jonah was talking about. You're the person he said would 'come around.'"

"But he was wrong." He reached forward and his fingers clamped around the smooth skin of her upper arms. Standing in the glow of the street lamp, her blue eyes dark with anger, her white dress mussed and her hair disheveled, she was as enchanting as the night. "Don't worry about Hammond," he said cryptically.

"Why not?"

"It's been taken care of."

"I don't understand—"

"Just trust me, okay?" He took hold of her hand, led her back to the Jeep and helped her climb inside.

"How can I?"

"Once in a while, Ainsley, you just have to take things on faith!" He slammed the Jeep into reverse and Ainsley stared through the window, watching as Jonah McCullough stepped out of the restaurant, smiling smugly to himself. His companion, a tall, raw-boned man with sandy hair and a surly grin, followed him. On the lanky man's arm was a beautiful woman with jet black hair and vibrant blue eyes.

Glancing at Trent, she saw his features harden and the white lines bracketing his mouth. "Who's the man with Jonah?" she asked.

"Jed Parker, a real estate man from Idaho."

"And the woman?" Ainsley whispered.

"I don't know."

Ainsley slid lower in the seat, resting her head on the hard cushion.

"And Lila's returning—tonight?"

"That's right. She and Jonah and Jed. It should be real cozy. And thick as thieves."

"Is that what they are?"

"Not really," he said, but his eyes squinted as the head-lights from a passing truck illuminated his face. "Let's not worry about them. We've got other things to think about. I'll take you back to the hospital to check on your dad."

They rode in silence for the rest of the short drive, and by the time they reached the hospital and ICU, Jefferson was sitting up in his bed. He was groggy but smiled when Ainsley rushed into the room.

"'Bout time you showed up," he chastised.

The sound of his voice made her heart turn over. "We were here earlier, but you were sleeping."

"Don't think I'm much good company."

"Neither am I. But I'll stay anyway." She looked up at Trent who was standing in the doorway. "You can go back to the ranch if you want. I can catch a ride with Sarah and Korey. They should be showing up any minute."

"Sarah's bringing the boy?" Jefferson asked.

"Korey wouldn't be left behind."

The old man chuckled.

Trent hesitated. He wanted to stay with Ainsley, make sure she was all right, but he had business back at the Rocking M—business with Jonah that wouldn't keep.

"Go on," she said.

"If you're sure," he said, looking at Ainsley.

"I'll be fine." She scooted a chair next to her father's bed. "Dad'll entertain me."

Jefferson laughed. "That'll be the day, especially when I'm all tied up to these infernal machines!"

"I'll be by the ranch early," Trent said. "Call me if you need a ride home." Then, turning to Jefferson, he said, "You take care of yourself. I'll see you tomorrow."

"And you take care of the ranch."

"Will do."

"And this daughter of mine!"

"Dad!" Ainsley protested and watched as Trent tried to smother a smile before turning on his heel and walking down the hallway, his boots echoing down the polished floors of the hospital. "You mind your own business," she said, still blushing.

"You are my business."

"Am I? I'm nearly thirty years old. I can take care of myself! And I don't need you or Trent telling me what to do."

"That's a bad attitude, you know," he said quietly, glancing toward the door. "And a lie."

"What!"

"I see the way you look at Trent—the way you watch him when you think no one's lookin'."

"I don't—"

"Sure you do!" He lifted his hand with difficulty and winced from the pain. "It's only natural. It's the way I looked at your ma."

"Maybe you should rest."

"Not until I have my say," he said, his eyes bright as they bored into hers, his fingers rough when they found her hand.

"And what's that?"

"I want you to marry Trent, Ainsley."

She was stunned and let the words settle in. "You're not serious—"

"And I want you to do it before I die."

The color drained from her face. "What're you talking about? You're not going to die, and I'm not marrying anyone, least of all Trent McCullough!"

"You always were a stubborn thing."

"This is my life we're talking about, you know."

"I know. But you're too proud to know what's good for you. Look, Missy, I know I don't have much time left in this world. All I want to do is see you married again, to a man who loves you and can take care of you."

"I don't want to be taken care of."

"Sure you do. Every woman wants the same thing."

She looked at her father's weathered face and felt tears burning behind her eyes. Touching his grizzled chin, she almost cried. "That's not the way it works any more."

"Then it don't work right!"

She laughed. "Maybe."

"Tell me you don't love Trent McCullough," he demanded.

"I don't."

"Look me in the eye when you say it!" His fingers curled around hers, his skin tight over his knuckles.

"Mr. Smith?" a young blond nurse said, poking her head into the room.

His gaze shifted.

"How're you feeling?"

"I've felt better," he admitted, wincing a little.

"Maybe I can take care of that. It's time for your pain pill."

"I don't want no pill!"

"Dad, come on. It won't kill you," Ainsley prodded, holding a cup of water while he took the medication. The young nurse took his temperature, blood pressure and pulse before walking to the door.

"Just a few more minutes," she suggested. "After that the medication will start to take effect, and he needs his rest."

"I understand," Ainsley said.

"Well, I don't!" Jefferson complained, frowning as the nurse left them alone. "Damned doctors and medicine!" He leaned back on the stiff white pillow and tried to focus, but his eyelids began to grow heavy. "Don't need no pills!"

"'Course you don't."

He forced his eyes open and frowned. "Hasn't he asked you to marry him yet?" he mumbled, the medication making him drowsy.

"Who?"

"McCullough," he said, his tongue thick.

"Why would he do that?"

"'Cause I told him to," Jefferson whispered, his voice fading.

Ainsley's fingers clamped tightly over the cold metal rail surrounding her father's bed. "You did what?"

"I told him to marry you—that way he'd give you a husband and Korey…give Korey a father…and…and he'd end up with all the land soon as I kick off…."

"You struck a deal with Trent?" Ainsley asked, horrified, her heart pounding heavily inside. Maybe her father was delirious—he certainly didn't know what he was saying. Or did he? A dull blade of doubt twisted in her heart.

"He called it…a bribe," Jefferson mumbled, drifting off to sleep.

"A bribe," Ainsley repeated, her eyes darting around the small room. She felt as if she'd been kicked in the stomach. All of her gut instincts about Trent had been right—and still she'd fallen for him. "How could he?" she whispered, her cheeks flaming, her eyes burning with shame.

"Ms. Hughes," the nurse said quietly.

"Y-yes?"

"Mr. Smith needs his rest."

"Oh, yes. Of course." Still reeling, she walked blindly into the hall.

"Mom!" Korey shouted, breaking into a run, while Sarah tried to hold him back.

Ainsley leaned against the wall. Her entire world was crumbling apart.

"Is Jeff all right?" Sarah asked, her face drained of color as she looked around the nurse's station.

"He—he's fine," Ainsley said. "But they gave him a pill."

"He's still awake, isn't he?" Sarah asked worriedly.

"Mr. Smith is resting," the nurse said, glancing worriedly at Ainsley. "Ms. Hughes, are you all right?"

"Fine," she whispered, trying to pull herself together. But she couldn't think of anything but Trent and his betrayal. He'd *used* her!

"You're sure?" Sarah asked.

"But I've got to see him," Korey insisted, his eyes wide. "There's something I've got to tell him."

"It'll have to be later, sport," Ainsley whispered.

"But—"

"Shh. You can peek through his door. That would be all right, wouldn't it?" she asked the nurse.

"For just a minute," the nurse replied.

Korey hung at the opening to the small, glassed-in room. "Is he all right?" the boy asked, his eyebrows pulling down when he saw his grandfather's hollow cheeks and ashen complexion.

"Yes. He just needs his sleep."

"So when will he get to come home?"

"That depends on the doctor and your grandfather."

"I tell him to slow down," Sarah said, shaking her head. "But he won't listen to me."

"He doesn't listen to anyone," Ainsley added. "Maybe we should go back to the ranch."

"May as well," Sarah agreed.

But Korey tugged on Ainsley's sleeve. "I really have to talk to Grandpa," he insisted.

"You heard the nurse—" But before she could catch him, Korey spun away and slipped through the open door of Jefferson's room. By the time that Ainsley caught up with him, he was standing over the bed, touching the old man's hands and fighting tears. "I'm sorry, Grandpa," he said. "Really, I am—"

"Ms. Hughes!" the nurse warned as she swept into the room.

"Come on, Korey," Ainsley said, then looked at the nurse. "I'm sorry about this. He and his grandfather are very close."

"I understand, but my first concern is Mr. Smith."

Ainsley put her arm over Korey's shoulders and noted his red-rimmed eyes. "You okay?" she asked.

He sniffed, but wouldn't meet her eyes. "Fine."

"What was that all about?"

"Nothin'." His lower lip protruded and then trembled.

"You sure?"

"Yeah." He shook off her arm and followed Sarah down the hallway and outside.

Once in the parking lot, Ainsley sat in the front seat of Sarah's old station wagon. Looking over her shoulder, she noticed Korey huddled in one corner of the back seat, his eyes glued to the windows and the dark night beyond.

"What's wrong, honey?" she asked, as the old wagon rumbled down the road to the ranch.

But Korey didn't answer.

Ainsley didn't really blame him. It had been a long day for all of them and she couldn't think about anything other than her father's condition and the fact that Trent had been bribed by her father to marry her.

"Over my dead body," she muttered, her teeth clenched in determination.

"What's that?" Sarah asked, her eyes never leaving the road.

"Nothing," Ainsley whispered. "Just something I've got to take care of myself."

TRENT STARED AT the house he'd called home for most of his life. Stark white against the black night, lights glowing in the windows, it should have been a welcome haven. Instead, he felt like an outsider. The little satisfaction he would get from his confrontation with his brother and sister wasn't worth the price he'd had to pay.

Jonah and Lila were both in the den. He could hear their voices before he opened the back door. The sound of their laughter and conversation irritated him.

"Well, if it isn't the prodigal son returning to the fold," Jonah said when he saw Trent standing in the door of the study. "Come in, come in, and pour yourself a drink." He held up a crystal decanter filled with Scotch.

One side of Trent's mouth lifted. "What's the occasion?" he asked, accepting the drink that Jonah poured.

Lila was lying on the couch, her long brown hair hanging over one of the arms, her eyes turned to the ceiling as she balanced her drink in her hands. "We're celebrating a new acquisition for McCullough Oil."

"Anything I should know about?"

She laughed. "You already do. The Hammond place. We made an offer on it today."

"Nick won't sell," Trent said slowly, sipping his drink.

"He won't have a choice," Lila replied.

"We made the offer to Valley National today."

"The bank?"

"They hold title to the land. Nick's mortgaged to the hilt and behind on his taxes."

"Is that so?" Trent swirled his drink and studied the amber liquor. "Has the bank accepted the offer?"

Jonah shrugged. "We don't know. Not yet. But we'll find out tomorrow."

"Well, if I were you, I wouldn't hold my breath," Trent said slowly and his tone of voice made Jonah's head snap up.

"What do you know?"

"Just that Nick Hammond is a fighter. He's not going to give up without a battle."

"He's got no recourse."

The corner of Trent's mouth lifted into a satisfied grin. "Haven't you learned that the fight isn't over until the referee counts to ten?"

Jonah's eyes narrowed. "What is it?" he asked suspiciously. "What have you done?"

"Not much," Trent allowed. "But don't count Nick Hammond out. He's not down for the count yet."

"What does that mean?"

"Just that I know Nick was looking for private funds."

"For what?"

"A second mortgage," Trent replied, sipping his drink.

"Or third?" Lila said, chuckling. "That place is so leveraged, it could topple right off the old seesaw."

"And you'd like that, wouldn't you?" Trent said slowly.

"What's that supposed to mean?" Lila's dark eyes flashed.

"Nothing."

Jonah crossed the room and stared straight into Trent's hard eyes. "What the hell have you done?" he whispered, his eyes gleaming angrily. "First there was that stupid stunt of investing in the Circle S and now, if you've blown this deal, so help me I'll—"

"What? Kill me?"

"Don't be so melodramatic."

"Or," Trent taunted, looking at his sister, "override my vote? Well, that's just fine with me."

"What's that supposed to mean?"

"I want out, Jonah. Out of the oil company."

"You're out of your mind," Jonah said. "It's Ainsley, isn't it? She's got you twisted all around."

"I've never been more sane in my life. I want the ranch and I'm willing to give up my share in the oil company for your two shares of this place."

"You've got it all worked out, don't you?" Lila said. "Don't tell me—this is all part of *Mrs. Hughes's* plan?"

"Ainsley has nothing to do with it. The corporate headquarters of the company are in Denver, the ranch is here in Wyoming. Jonah spends most of his time in the air."

"Maybe I like it like that."

"And what about your wife and your house in Colorado?"

Jonah shrugged. "Andrea and I go our separate ways. It works out."

"Does it?"

"What's gotten into you?" Lila asked, getting off the couch and eyeing her brother warily.

"I just don't like what's happened around here lately," he admitted. "I don't like what's going on with Jefferson Smith's wells, and I don't like this business with Nick Hammond."

"Smith's wells are no better or worse than any other," Jonah pointed out. "No one could have predicted the downturn in the market. As for Nick Hammond—he should have been more careful."

"We have plenty of land here."

"I know that."

"So you just want to get it cheap and sell it for a profit."

"The American way," Jonah said. "Capitalism."

Trent snorted and took a long swallow of his drink. "I'm all for that—just not at the expense of others."

"Get off it," Lila said. "I'm sick and tired of all your lofty ideals. They don't mean a damn."

"Spoken like a bitter woman."

"Wouldn't you be?" she asked, her lips drawn tight over her teeth. "And now you're taking up with Ainsley again. Sometimes I wonder about you, Trent. How can one man be such a glutton for punishment?"

Trent's shoulders stiffened and his lips thinned, but he wouldn't let himself rise to Lila's bait. "Let's get back to the business at hand. My share in McCullough Oil for the ranch and Jefferson's plane. Take it or leave it."

Jonah's eyes gleamed. "You're throwing away a fortune."

"Mine to throw," Trent said, starting for the hall before casting his sister a worried glance. "Where's Wilson?"

"Out."

"*Out? With whom?*"

"Does it matter?"

Trent could hardly believe her attitude. He'd always hoped that some latent maternalism would show up in his sister. "Of course, it does. It matters one helluva lot, in case you haven't noticed."

Lila shrugged and sipped her drink. "He's over at the Brandon place. Spending the night. He and that Brandon boy are planning their strategy for the big rodeo next week."

"I don't think he should hang out with Tom Brandon."

"Why not?"

"He's wild and he's a lot older than Wilson."

"You were wild once, too," she pointed out, raising her eyebrows and then turning her head coyly. "Wait a minute—don't tell me. You'd prefer Wilson to hang out with Ainsley's boy, wouldn't you? Well, forget it. As far as I'm concerned that kid is trouble and I don't want Wilson anywhere near him."

"Is that the only reason?" Trent asked.

"You know how I feel about Ainsley Smith."

"Hughes," Trent reminded her and wanted to kick himself when he saw the pain in her eyes. "Hey, look, I'm sorry—"

"Doesn't matter," Lila said crisply, tossing her hair away from her face. "Korey's too wild for Wilson. Everyone knows Ainsley can't handle that boy. That's why she's back here! So don't kid yourself that she cares for you, Brother dear. You'll only end up hurt. Again." Still fuming, she flounced out of the room and stomped up the stairs.

"Son of a—"

"Here, here, Brother," Jonah said, hoisting his glass into the air. "That was one of the best examples of rubbing salt into a wound I've seen in a long while. Fortunately Lila gives as good as she gets!"

"Stuff it, okay?" Trent said, glancing worriedly up the stairs as he heard Lila's door slam shut. "Just think about my offer. I want to sign the papers as soon as possible."

"So Lila's right," Jonah said, rubbing his chin and smiling to himself. "Ainsley's put the pressure on you."

"Just draw up the necessary papers."

"And get the hell out?" Jonah taunted.

"I didn't say that."

"You didn't have to." He downed his drink and set the empty glass on the edge of the desk. "But I'll think about it—and give you my answer tomorrow. As for Lila, you'll have to handle her yourself."

"Fine." Trent walked back outside and felt the warm summer air tickle the back of his neck. He stared down the hill, past the shadowed fields to the old farmhouse at the Circle S. A few lights still blazed in the night, including the light in Ainsley's apartment over the garage.

Not really understanding his own motives, he climbed the fence and started walking through the dark pastures, down the rolling hills to Ainsley.

CHAPTER ELEVEN

AINSLEY PINNED HER hair on her head and stepped into the shower. Tired and sweating from the heat, she felt used and dirty. All of Trent's attention had been because of her father! He'd been bribed to pretend to fall in love with her.

"It's your own fault," she told herself as she stepped under the cool spray and let the water soak her tired muscles. "You wanted to believe he would fall in love with you again." Squeezing her eyes shut, she tried to forget him and turned off the spigots angrily when his image kept coming to mind. "You're a damned fool, Ainsley Hughes!"

Pulling on a short cotton robe and a pair of old leather thongs, she walked outside and let the warm summer air evaporate the lingering drops of water from her skin. She glanced at the farmhouse. It was dark and quiet.

With a worried frown she rammed her fists into her pockets. She climbed down the stairs and headed down the worn path leading to the paddocks. Dry grass tickled her ankles.

She didn't really know where she was going but was content just to walk in the night, glancing up at the winking stars and pearl-like moon, high in the dark sky. The air was scented with the fragrance of new-mown hay and summer wild flowers. Crickets and frogs sang their summer songs and the wind whispered through the long-needled pines overhead.

Slipping through the gate, she heard mares snorting and little foals scampering to their sides. "It's all right," she whispered, smiling at the dark eyes peering curiously her way.

She walked a little farther, to a stand of pine behind the barn. Then, feeling as if she were being watched, she looked over her shoulder and saw Trent leaning against the fence, his eyes following her every move.

She stiffened and replayed the scene at her father's hospital bed in her mind.

Though Trent's face was shadowed, she could feel the amusement in his gaze.

"What're you doing here?" she demanded, furious all over again.

"Watching you," he drawled.

"For any particular reason?"

"Maybe I like it."

"And maybe you're paid to," she said, feeling her heart squeeze at his betrayal. How could she have trusted him?

"What's that supposed to mean?" He pushed himself upright and came closer.

She braced herself, but didn't move. When she could see his eyes, she read the anger in his silvery gaze, saw how his lips thinned. "It means I stayed with Dad and had a long talk with him," she said.

"And?"

"And he told me all about your little deal."

His brows pulled together. "But you knew about it already. You saw the contract in your father's den."

"I'm not talking about the written documents," she said, lifting her chin.

"What?"

"I'm talking about the verbal agreement you had with my dad."

"I don't get it. Everything's spelled out in black and white—"

"Not quite! What about the deal you had to marry me?" she asked, her voice cracking.

"What're you talking about?" But his face muscles grew taut.

"You can forget the dumb act, Trent," she said angrily. "It doesn't wash. Dad told me that he asked you to marry me and that in return you'd end up with the Circle S!"

She saw his jaw harden and his flinty eyes spark. "Do you believe that?"

"It all fits! I saw the contract. You *already* own a quarter of the ranch. And Nick Hammond's place—you and your family will have that by the end of the summer. All you need is the rest of this place, and you'll own the entire south end of the valley!"

"And you think that's what I want?"

"Of course it is! Between ranching and drilling for oil, this land could reap you McCulloughs a fortune!" She felt sick inside and just wanted him to leave.

"You're forgetting the current state of the oil market."

"But the downturn will change. In a few years, the prices will be up and you'll be rich."

He folded his arms over his chest. "And in the meantime?"

"You can run the ranch. Grow wheat, raise livestock. You might not be rich, but you'll be ready!"

"You've got it all figured out, haven't you?"

"Unfortunately, yes," she whispered, the pain inside her almost blinding.

"Do you really think I would prostitute myself like that?" he asked. "Give up my freedom and marry you, just for this ranch?"

"I—I don't know."

"I haven't ever been married, Ainsley. I'm thirty-three. Doesn't that tell you anything?"

She swallowed hard. "Maybe just the right 'deal' didn't come up."

He let out a long sigh. "God, you're jaded."

"I wonder why."

"I don't suppose your father said that I wouldn't have any part of his deal?"

"Don't try to put it back on Dad—"

"Well, I've never known Jefferson to be a liar. I don't know why he'd start now." He reached forward, touching Ainsley lightly on the chin and his eyes burned into hers. "It's true. Your father did offer me a deal—a bribe. I marry you and I end up with Circle S."

"You bastard!" she flung herself at him then, blind rage taking over her emotions. Her fists pummeled his chest and she began to sob violently. "How could you!"

"I didn't!" He caught her wrists and held them tight. His face was hard and dangerous, his voice low. "I can't believe you would believe that even for a minute I would—"

"Let go of me!" she hissed. "I don't want to hear any more lies! I…just…can't handle any more lies!" She sobbed violently now, betrayal burning bright in her breast.

"Oh, Ainsley—" He dropped her wrists to touch her chin.

She felt like dying inside and turned her head away.

Strong fingers held her chin and forced her to look into his eyes.

"But I didn't take the deal, Ainsley. I agreed to buy out part of the ranch and the plane—just until he got on his feet again."

"Oh, sure," she mocked, sniffing and holding her head up proudly. "And the reason he was behind? I saw for myself. It was because he was going broke on the oil investment."

He sighed into the night. "That was part of it, yes."

"And then you'd end up with it all—"

"No!" His lips tightened over his teeth. "You've just never understood, have you?"

"Understood what?"

"How much I love you."

"Save it, Trent," she whispered. "Save it for someone who'll believe it."

"That's the problem," he said slowly. "I saved it too long already. I should have insisted that you have your marriage to Robert annulled eleven years ago. It would have solved a helluva lot of problems." His voice was uneven. His breath unsteady.

"Why didn't you?"

"Because I wanted you to be happy," he said. "And you told me you loved Robert."

"I...I did," she said.

"I don't think so," he said quietly. "I don't think you ever loved Robert."

Not as much as I love you, she thought miserably, refusing to admit the damning words.

"I was too weak back then," he said, his eyes shifting to her lips and the V of her wrapper. "But I'm not any longer. I'm not about to make the same mistake twice."

His eyes were dark as midnight when they came back to hers.

"Neither am I. I fell for the wrong man once before; I won't ever let myself do it again."

"I don't expect you to, Ainsley. Because I'm not the wrong man. I'm the right one." His lips came crashing down on hers before she could move. Her mind screamed at her to back away and she tried, only to be stopped by the rough bark of a pine.

"Trent—I can't," she whispered, aware that the robe was being pushed off her shoulders. "Please—" But her protest sounded more like a plea as his lips plundered hers and his tongue pried open her teeth to explore her soft, moist mouth.

She felt dizzy and she closed her eyes, lolling her head back so that her throat was arched backward, the creamy white skin of her neck exposed.

"Oh, Ainsley," he whispered, breath hot against her throat. The robe slid off her body and he picked the pins from her hair, letting the thick chestnut waves fall downward past her shoulders and over the rounded swell of her breasts.

Holding her close, he slid to his knees, touching each proud dark point with his lips and hearing her moan in response. She shuddered when he pressed his nose and mouth against her abdomen. She couldn't move as his fingers softly grazed her buttocks, sending tingles of delight up her spine, making her warm and moist inside.

"I can't," she whispered as his fingers worked their magic on her skin. "Trent—please—"

But he was lost in the smell and taste of her. The fire in his loins burned hot and he gently pulled her to the bed of pine needles beneath the trees.

"Just love me, Ainsley," he whispered against her hair, moving over her and rubbing the length of his body against her smooth, fragrant skin as he shed his shirt. It fell in a crumpled heap on the ground.

"It—it isn't that simple."

"It's as simple as you want it to be." He turned his face back to hers, captured her lips with his, then stroked her, caressed her with his hands, made promises deep in his throat. "I've never loved anyone but you," he rasped, when her fingers gently touched his skin.

If only she could believe him. She felt him constrict, his powerful muscles tight as her fingertips brushed over his shoulders and down his back, tracing the length of his spine.

Her heart was pounding in her ears, thundering out any doubts that lingered in her mind. Aware only of his warm body and the silvery darkness, she listened to her heart instead of her head and helped him kick off his jeans.

His fingers wound in her hair, and there in the moonlight, his gray eyes warm with passion, he claimed her again, holding her close and putting his mark on her heart forever.

"I love you, Ainsley," he whispered, once his heart had stopped pounding. "And I always will. I would never do anything to hurt you or your family. You'll just have to believe that."

"Sometimes it's hard," she admitted thinking about all of the things that were wrong between them.

"I know. But trust works two ways."

She looked up through the branches of the pines to the clouds shifting restlessly over the moon. "I know. But there are so many things I haven't worked out yet."

"And then your dad said he bribed me to marry you and you came unglued."

"I wouldn't go that far."

"Admit it, you were as unglued as they come."

She laughed then, surprising herself. "Maybe I was. But what if the tables were turned? Wouldn't you be?"

"I don't know. Try me," he suggested, tracing her jaw with his finger. "Propose."

"Right now? Here?"

"Why not?" She laughed again, more quietly and felt his arms tighten around her. "Come on, Ainsley. Beg me to marry you. Tell me you want to live with me forever and won't take no for an answer."

"This is crazy," she whispered, as his lips pressed hard against her skin again, leaving a moist trail across her breasts, causing the hot ache deep inside to re-awaken. Her palms were flat against his chest and she could feel his heart begin to thud irregularly all over again.

"I love you, Ainsley," he promised and then went still. Snapping his head up, he listened. She started to move, but he shook his head, meeting her questioning gaze and pressing his finger to his lips.

She heard it then, muffled conversation and the snapping of twigs. Quietly, she reached for her robe and Trent slipped into his jeans. He followed the noise with his eyes and then whispered almost inaudibly, "Go back home. I'll meet you later."

"But—"

"I mean it, Ainsley." His hand was wrapped tightly around her wrist. "And follow the path through the trees so you won't be seen."

"But who—"

"Shh. Go."

She cinched the tie around her waist and then took off through the trees. Her pulse was running wild and she stumbled twice as she headed back to the blue glow of the security lights surrounding the ranch.

A horse nickered as she passed the stables and unlocked the gate. Then, hurrying down the dusty path, she wondered what was happening back in the fields. Certainly there was no danger....

Once up in her studio, she changed and waited, glancing out the window and wondering what Trent was doing.

TRENT SNAPPED THE waistband of his jeans together and slid his arms through his shirt. Then, he stealthily slipped along the stand of pine, walking quietly as he picked his way in the moonlight. The voices were growing louder and angrier.

"I said I don't want anything more to do with this!" Korey shouted.

"And you promised me five bottles!" Wilson taunted.

"I couldn't get 'em."

"You're chicken, that's it!"

"Am not!"

Trent stood in the shadows, watching the two boys square off. Korey, smaller and more wiry, Wilson a head taller and more filled out. He supposed he should let them fight it out. Maybe they could knock some sense into each other's thick skulls.

"You said that you could get the booze," Wilson taunted. "And I came up with my end. I've got twenty-five dollars."

"I'm out of this," Korey insisted.

"Why? I thought you didn't like your grandpa."

"That was when I first got here." Korey was on the balls of his feet, his fists clenched, his eyes bright in the night.

"And you've changed your mind."

"Yeah. He's okay."

"I heard he almost croaked today," Wilson said.

Korey lunged at Wilson, hitting the older boy and throwing him down. "You creep!"

"Get off me, you bastard!" Wilson screamed as Korey's fists pounded on him.

"That's enough!" Trent grabbed Korey and pulled him off Wilson. "Knock it off. Both of you!" His eyes were on fire as he glared at the boys. "What's going on here?"

"Nothing," Wilson said, rubbing the cut under his chin where Korey's fist had connected.

Breathing hard, Korey didn't say a word.

"So why are you out here? I thought you were supposed to be spending the night with Tom Brandon," Trent said to Wilson.

"I, er, I am. But that's later."

"That's not what Lila said."

"Maybe she's confused," Wilson said, backing away.

"Maybe. Maybe not." Trent turned to Korey and the boy paled. "Does your mother know you're out here?"

Korey avoided his eyes. "No."

"Then I don't suppose she knows you were planning to steal your grandpa's liquor, either."

Korey's head snapped up. "But I didn't. Honest!"

Trent's lips twisted downward. "What about you, Wilson?"

"What about me?"

"How're you involved?"

"I'm not involved in anything," Wilson said, swaggering a little.

"You expect me to believe that?"

"It's the truth."

Sighing, Trent raked his fingers through his hair. "What's going on here—no, let me guess," he added, when he saw the denial forming on his nephew's lips. "You're the middleman, eh, Wilson? You give Korey an order, then buy the things you instruct Korey to steal. After he's out of it, you turn around and sell 'em to Tom Brandon and his friends."

Wilson's jaw dropped. "No...I..."

"How did you know?" Korey asked, surprised, and Wilson shot him a glance that could kill.

"Because I was a teenager once myself. It doesn't make sense that a sixteen-year-old is hanging out with a ten-year-old. No offense, Wilson, but it just doesn't work that way."

"Tom's my friend!"

"Sure he is. As long as you're his supplier." Trent rubbed his jaw. "Now, what do you suppose I should do to the both of you?" They didn't say a word. He walked around them and sized them up. "I could cut a twig and whip you—or beat the tar out of you, I suppose."

Korey's eyes grew round.

"But I really don't like violence."

Wilson let out a long breath.

"So, two things are gonna happen," he said thoughtfully. "First, both of you are going home and tell your mothers what you've been up to. No, wait a minute. Wilson you tell Lila and you, Korey—"

"Y-yes?"

"You go back to the house to your room. I'll break the news to your mom. She's had a rough day."

"But—" Wilson protested.

"You heard me!" Trent snapped, his anger flaring. "What you're doing is illegal and dangerous. You just both better hope that when Jefferson gets out of the

hospital he doesn't want to press charges or you'll both
end up in juvenile detention centers! Now, the second
thing you're both going to do is muck out the stables
every other day for the next month."

Korey was about to complain but thought better of it
when he saw the fire in Trent's eyes. "Yes, sir," he mumbled.

"Now, both of you get out of here!" Wilson started
across the fields. "And you can tell Tom Brandon that I
want to talk to him!"

Wilson stopped dead in his tracks. "You wouldn't!" he
said and then swallowed hard. "He—he'll kill me."

"You'll live," Trent muttered, striding across the
fields, following Korey who'd taken off as fast as his feet
could carry him. "Damned fool kids," he muttered,
slipping through the series of paddocks and seeing Korey
run up the back steps of the porch before disappearing
into the kitchen.

Glancing at the garage, he noticed the lights in
Ainsley's studio and smiled. Tonight, at least, he'd
cleared up one mystery around the ranch. He climbed the
stairs, knocked softly on the door and let himself in.
Ainsley was seated at the table, her sketchbook before
her, a cold cup of coffee cradled in her hands.

"Well?"

"I found out who's taking the stuff around here," he said,
pouring himself a cup from the glass coffee pot on the stove.

"Korey?" she asked, her blue eyes glazed with worry.

"For one."

"Who else?"

"Wilson."

"Your nephew?"

"The middleman," he corrected, his mouth twisting
cynically as he turned a chair around and straddled it.

"The real culprit is Tom Brandon. Mr. Big. He puts out the orders and our boys hop."

"Who's Brandon?" she asked, not really wanting to know.

"A sixteen-year-old hotshot who's talked the kids into working for him."

"Great," Ainsley murmured, disappointed. "Just great." She leaned back in her chair and closed her eyes, fighting a headache.

"Don't worry about it. I handled it."

"I'm afraid I have to handle it. He's my son. Is he back?"

"In his room. I told him I wanted to break the news to you."

"He should have had to fess up."

"I know. But he was arguing with Wilson. He wanted out of the deal."

"The deal?" she repeated. "I swear there are more back-room deals around this place than in the Senate!"

Trent told her about the entire conversation with the boys and Ainsley didn't feel much better. "Well," she said, "it looks like it's time for a mother-son discussion." She started for the door.

"Ainsley?"

"Yes?"

"I could handle it for you."

"Not this time, I'm afraid."

He tossed the rest of his coffee down the sink. "Then I'll see you in the morning. If I remember right, you still owe me a proposal."

"Dreamer," she replied.

"I'll coax it out of you again."

"We'll see," she said, hurrying down the stairs and hearing him behind her. As she walked to the farmhouse, she thought about Trent and wished that things between them would be simple. "Now who's the dreamer?" she murmured. Their relationship had never been easy and probably never would be.

Looking over her shoulder, she saw him half running across the fields. Tall and rangy, he disappeared into the night. Ainsley felt an incredible loneliness settle over her before she walked up the back steps.

Sarah was just pinning her hair onto her head when Ainsley walked by the open door of her quarters. "Would you mind tellin' me what the devil is going on? I just saw Korey run up the stairs like his tail was on fire."

Ainsley shook her head. "It's a long story."

"Trouble?"

"Big trouble. Just let me talk to Korey and I'll come down and explain everything."

"I'll heat up some hot chocolate."

"Wonderful."

"Oh, and Ainsley. I called the hospital. Your dad's doing great."

"I know," she admitted. "I called, too. I'll be back down in a few minutes."

Upstairs, she knocked on Korey's door and heard him mumble a quick "Come in." He was lying on his bed, staring up at the ceiling.

Ainsley turned on the bedside lamp. "You want to explain yourself?" she asked, sitting on the edge of his bed.

"Don't you know?"

"I'd like to hear your side of it."

A muscle worked in the side of his jaw and he was fighting a battle with tears. "I guess I goofed up again."

"By stealing from Grandpa?"

"It wasn't like that!" he yelled, then lowered his voice.

"Not really—I mean, it wasn't supposed to be. Oh, I don't know what I mean." He rolled over, turning his back on her and closing his eyes.

"Come on, Korey. Just level with me," she said, tucking her knees under her chin. "Why did you take the things?"

"For the money. Why else?"

"You have plenty of money. Trent pays you for your chores." She tried to stay calm but her heart was pounding. There were reasons kids wanted money—none of them good.

"You don't know what it's like," Korey blurted out, his voice breaking.

"What what's like?"

"Coming here. Not knowing anybody. You weren't even here yet."

"When it started, you mean?"

"Yeah." He sighed and sniffed. "I met Wilson and I wanted him to like me."

"So you did whatever he asked."

"Not *everything*."

"But enough to get you into trouble. Oh, Korey, don't you know you can't buy friends or make people like you by doing things they want you to do? You have to be your own person."

"I know," he whispered. He rolled over again and looked at her with red-rimmed eyes. "Are you gonna tell Grandpa?" he asked.

She shook her head. "Nope. I think that's your responsibility. You got yourself into this mess, you can get yourself out of it. But not for a while. Wait until Grandpa's home and well."

"Wonderful," he groaned. "I already have to clean out the stables."

"I heard."

Korey pulled a face.

"That's not all," Ainsley said. "You're grounded, you know."

"I figured."

"For a month."

"But not the rodeo, Mom," he said, sitting up, his young face anxious. "I've been working so hard and Grandpa will be so disappointed—"

"I think he will be anyway," Ainsley said softly, and Korey studied the floor, big tears filling his eyes.

"I'm sorry, Mom. Really."

"I know, honey, but this isn't something that goes away with apologies. This is serious. You were *stealing*, Korey. And it doesn't matter if it was from Grandpa or the neighbor or a complete stranger. You can't do it. I won't have it!"

"So the rodeo's out, right?"

"Right." She got up from the bed and heard his sobs. "I'll see you in the morning."

"G'night," he whispered and her heart broke. She wanted to tell him that everything would be all right, that she believed that nothing like this would happen again, that Grandpa would forgive him and of course he could ride in the damned rodeo, but she didn't. This was one lesson he had to learn the hard way.

Sighing to herself, she hurried downstairs and smiled as the scent of chocolate wafted through the rooms. A cup of cocoa, some conversation with Sarah and then she'd go to bed. Tomorrow had to be a better day!

CHAPTER TWELVE

THREE DAYS LATER, Jefferson, cranky as ever, was released from the hospital and came home. "Don't know why they locked me up in that place," he muttered, once he was on the back porch and sipping lemonade. "Nothing more than a little spasm. Nothing to get excited about."

"Sure," Ainsley agreed, her blue eyes teasing. "And a seven-point-five earthquake on the Richter scale is just a tremor in the earth."

"Get outta here," he said, but grinned. Some of his color had come back and he was chomping at the bit to get to work. "So where is that foreman of mine?" he asked.

"Don't know," she admitted. "He said he'd stop by this morning and see you and then he had to take off for a few days."

Jefferson frowned and glanced slyly at his daughter. "So how're you two hittin' it off?"

"Funny you should ask," she said, arching a brow. "You said some pretty interesting things while you were all doped up—"

"I wasn't doped up."

"Good. Then you remember telling me about the bribe you offered Trent—the deal?" she asked.

Jefferson pretended interest in the horizon. "What deal?"

"You know, by telling him to marry me, you were dangling the carrot under his nose—letting him know that he could get the rest of the ranch."

Sighing, Jefferson began to rock in his chair. "Is it so bad to try and help your daughter?"

"It's called meddling, Dad."

"You need someone to look after you. And you've always liked Trent."

"That's not the point. My life is just that—*mine*. I'd appreciate it if you'd quit trying to run it."

He ran a tight-skinned hand over his brow. "No doubt you've already talked with Trent about this."

"No doubt."

"Never did know when to keep your mouth shut," he muttered. "Just like your ma, only with a shorter fuse!" He reached into his pocket for a cigarette and struck a match to it. "So what did Trent say?"

"That he couldn't be bought."

Jefferson's gray brows raised. "And you believe him?"

"Not really, but since he hasn't proposed, it's really not an issue is it?"

"He will."

"Then I don't have to accept, do I?" she quipped.

"I can't believe it. Most any girl in the valley would give her eyeteeth for a chance at him, exceptin' you, of course."

"Of course. And they can have him," she said, feeling her heart twinge. "Besides I'm not a girl. I'm a woman with a half-grown son and a job in San Francisco." She set her empty glass on the table, stood and stretched. Though she loved Trent, it didn't matter. She couldn't trust him and that was that. And she'd spent the better part of three days trying to convince herself of that painful fact. The trouble was, she couldn't forget that Trent had almost convinced her to propose to him.

She started for the door, but Jefferson called to her. "Korey talked to me this mornin'," he said slowly.

"Oh."

"He claimed he'd been stealin' tools and other things from me."

She sighed and faced her father. "Trent found out about it. Wilson and some older kid were involved."

"Tom Brandon," Jefferson said. "His father used to work for me. I had to fire him a couple of years ago for the same reason. He stole several head of cattle."

"Like father, like son."

"Except that this time my grandson's involved."

"Was involved," Ainsley corrected. "I don't think it'll happen again."

"Neither do I," he said, rubbing his chin and gazing into the distance. "You know I've enjoyed having him around, don't you?"

"And he's loved being here. Even though he thought it was going to be a fate worse than death at first."

"He claims you won't let him ride in the rodeo next week," Jefferson said.

"I can't. He's grounded and he'll pay you back the entrance fee *and* for all the things he's taken."

"I understand that. But he's got his heart set on that race."

"I know, Dad. But it can't happen. Please understand."

"I'm trying, Ainsley," he said, glancing at her. "You know you're a difficult woman?"

"Not really."

The back door opened and Sarah walked onto the porch. "How're we doin' out here?"

"Fine."

"Good. Good," the housekeeper said happily, grinning down at Jefferson. "Now, how about some lunch?"

"Just had breakfast three hours ago. Ever since I've been back you've tried to stuff me like a turkey for Thanksgiving dinner," Jefferson said, but his eyes sparkled when he looked at her. "The two of you've been spoilin' me rotten." He ground out his cigarette in a nearby tray.

"Oh, go on—" Sarah's broad face reddened.

Ainsley decided there was no time like the present to bring up a bad subject. "I've got to go back to the city," she said uneasily. She hated to lie, but saw no way around it. Her father's head snapped up. "There's a special showing at the Worthington Gallery."

"First I've heard of it."

"Me, too," Ainsley said nervously. "The director of the gallery called last night."

"Seems kind of a rush, don't it?"

"I know. But they had one artist cancel and since they had some of my work on hand…" She let her voice drift off so he could come up with his own conclusions.

"Humph." Jefferson folded his arms across his chest. "You're sure this don't have nothin' to do with Trent?"

"He doesn't even know about it. Besides it's just for a few days but—" she glanced at Sarah "—I was hoping that you could take care of Dad and Korey while I was gone."

"I'd expect to," Sarah replied.

"I could hire a nurse—"

"I don't need a damned nurse sticking her nose in my business!" Jefferson sputtered.

Sarah's eyes twinkled. "Don't bother. I worked in the medical corps in the war and I think I can take care of him."

"I don't need a keeper!"

"I know, Dad. But I just want some peace of mind, okay?"

"I don't see why you have to go," Jefferson grumbled. "What's back there?"

"My work! Remember?" Ainsley called over her shoulder.

It was early afternoon and the sun was warm against her back. Old Dallas lay in the shade of a juniper bush and wagged his tail as Ainsley walked by, but he didn't bother getting up. "Too hot for you?" Ainsley asked, scratching him behind the ears. The old dog rolled his eyes up at her and panted.

She heard Trent's Jeep coming up the lane and her nerves stretched tight. In the past few days she'd tried to avoid him because she was afraid of her feelings for him—afraid that she was already too involved in a relationship that would never work.

"I've got to keep a cool head around him," she said to the dog and Dallas thumped his tail in the dry grass.

"Afternoon." Trent hopped out of the Jeep and looked around the ranch. The air wavered with heat, and the tall, skeletonlike oil rigs stood idle in the fields. Frowning, he leaned against the trunk of an old apple tree. "How's your dad?"

"Grumpy," she said, looking up at him, her eyes bright despite the tension between them.

"So things are back to normal?"

"Pretty much, but he has to take it easy for a few days. He's not too crazy about that."

"I'll bet not."

She looked at his profile and her heart twisted. His hair glinted in the sun and he had to squint as he stared at the cattle grazing on the dry fields.

So many things had been left unsaid.

"I have to go to Denver tomorrow," he remarked, glancing sideways at her.

"Oil company business?"

His jaw tightened. "Yes."

She didn't want to tell him that she was going to San Francisco, but decided that there had been too many lies between them as it was. "When will you be back?"

"A couple of days. Jake will handle the ranch. Do you think you'll be able to hold this place together?"

"Dad'll scrape by. But I won't be here."

He turned to face her, his eyes drilling into hers. "Where will you be?"

"In San Francisco. If you'll give me a ride to Denver."

"What's in San Francisco?"

"An art show. One I can't miss. It, uh, came up on the spur of the moment," she added quickly. "One of the other artists backed out."

"Is that right?"

Her palms were sweating. She rubbed them on her jeans. "Of course it is."

"Will you need a ride back?"

"If you can manage it. I should be back in Denver the day after tomorrow."

"No need," he said, gray eyes flashing. "I'll come get you in San Francisco."

"Don't bother—"

"No bother at all."

"But you have business."

"It'll only take a couple of hours at the attorney's office. Then I'm free." One side of his mouth lifted into a cynical smile. "Besides, we could use a little time alone together," he said quietly. "To clear the air."

Her lips pressed together into a thin line. The last thing she needed in San Francisco was Trent nosing around. "Maybe the air doesn't need clearing," she said softly.

"You're satisfied with things the way they are?"

"I just don't think we should…get more involved right now."

"Too late," he said, pushing a strand of hair away from her face. "And whether you know it or not, I've been involved with you for years."

She felt his fingers trace the length of her neck and a shiver of anticipation shot down her spine.

"I just need time alone—to think things out," she said, staring at the oil derricks and frowning.

"So you're running away?"

"I didn't say that."

"You didn't have to." Hooking his thumbs on the back pockets of his jeans, he strode up the creaky back steps to the porch. She watched him leave and heard her father greet him heartily. "Maybe it's time Korey and I left this place," she thought aloud, her gaze sweeping the outbuildings and fields of the ranch. "For good. Before I start trusting that man!"

Dallas looked up at her and whined.

Laughing, Ainsley shook her head. "Don't worry, fella. I guarantee you, hell will freeze over first!" Then, planning what she would need to take back to San Francisco, she headed for her studio over the garage.

THE NEXT DAY she was a bundle of nerves as she climbed into the plane.

"Don't you worry about your dad or Korey," Sarah said, waving as Trent buckled himself into the pilot's seat. "I'll take care of them for you."

"Thanks!" Ainsley waved from her window and then braced herself as the little plane bounced down the runway and finally leaped into the air.

"You always were a white-knuckled flyer," Trent observed as the landing gear thumped back into place. "Now tell me. Why are you really going to San Francisco?"

"I told you—"

"You lied," he said bluntly. "I called the gallery."

"You did what!" She was incensed. "What business is it of yours—"

"I figure it might have a lot to do with me."

"How?"

He grinned and moved the controls. The plane banked to the south. "It seemed strange that you'd get a call to show your paintings on the spur of the moment, and the timing was pretty incredible."

"Because of my father's heart attack?"

"And the fact that you'd just seen the books of the ranch. The way I figure it, you're going to San Francisco to scrape together some money to try and save the ranch."

Cornered, she couldn't lie. "I'm not about to let what happened to Nick Hammond happen to my dad," she whispered.

His eyes grew dark. "Hammond hasn't lost his place yet."

"But it's only a matter of time, right?" she demanded, her eyes as cold as the northern sea. "Before McCullough Oil runs right over him." Looking out the window, she sighed and tossed back her head. Her cinnamon curls fell over her shoulders and her cheeks colored angrily. "But, as I said, what I do in San Francisco is really none of your business."

"We'll see about that," he muttered, as the nose of the plane slipped into a bank of clouds. "We'll see about that."

Ainsley didn't bother to say anything for the rest of the unsteady flight. Her stomach was already in her throat and she was furious that Trent had figured out as much as he had. The little plane landed at Stapleton, and she hurried toward the main terminal to catch her connecting flight to San Francisco.

Trent kept up with her, his dark aviator glasses in place against the bright glare of the afternoon sun. "You could stay in Denver, you know. Since there really isn't any reason for you to go to California."

"Why would I do that?" she asked, picking up her ticket at the gate and hoisting the strap of her bag higher on her shoulder.

He leaned an elbow against the counter and took off his glasses. His gray eyes pierced deep into hers. "We could have a good time here—all alone."

"I thought you had business with Jonah."

"I do. But it won't take long."

"I don't think so." She moved toward the ramp where other passengers were beginning to congregate. "I've got things to do."

"Nothing that won't wait, I'll bet." His cocky, self-assured smile was in place and she couldn't keep her stupid heart from fluttering at the thought of a couple of romantic days alone with him. She fought the urge to be impulsive and forget all the barriers between them.

The boarding call for her flight was announced. With a determined smile, she shook her head. "Some other time, maybe." Turning on her heel, she handed the flight attendant her boarding pass and headed for the plane.

A few minutes later, Trent watched the 727 roar down

the runway and take off. He didn't move until the plane was out of sight. Then he walked briskly back down the concourse and hailed a cab.

"Where to?" the cabby asked, punching his meter.

"Seventeenth and Stout," Trent replied, sitting back against the hard cushions of the cab.

"Oh, taking in Denver's own 'Wall Street,' huh?"

"Right," Trent said. The cab sped away from the airport, and melded into the traffic flowing toward the city's financial district and the offices of McCullough Oil.

HIS BROTHER WAS expecting him. Sitting behind his large cherrywood desk, the receiver of one phone against his ear, Jonah barely looked up when Trent entered the room.

"I don't care how hard-nosed he's being about it," Jonah was saying, "I want that lease signed—and I want it signed today!" He waved Trent toward a chair.

Ignoring him, Trent walked to the window and rested one shoulder on the cool glass. He stared past the skyscrapers to the craggy slopes of the Rocky Mountains to the west. Jonah's office had always made him uncomfortable, reminded him how far removed he was from the big city.

"Damned lawyers," Jonah said, slamming the receiver down. "Always making mountains out of mole hills."

"You'll straighten them out," Trent predicted.

"I wish. Now, how about a drink?" He stood and crossed the room, stopping at a mirrored bar.

"No, thanks."

"Too bad." Jonah arched a brow at his brother as Trent pushed upright and took a chair near the desk.

"I just want to sign the papers."

"And get the hell out?"

"Right."

Jonah couldn't help but smile. Trent had always worn his heart on his sleeve, especially when Ainsley Hughes was involved. "Don't tell me you've got Ainsley Hughes holed up in some hotel room nearby," he said, his eyes gleaming at the thought.

Trent went rigid, his eyes cold. "All right. I won't. And I'll forget you mentioned it."

Jonah's smile widened. "You never got over her, did you?"

"What's that got to do with anything?"

"Plenty. Getting Lila to agree to trade oil company stock for the ranch wasn't easy, you know."

"But you managed."

Jonah took a long swallow from his glass. "Yep. But I had one helluva fight on my hands. You know how she feels about Ainsley."

"Doesn't matter. If she agreed, that's all there is to it."

"Not quite."

Trent's eyebrows raised. "Meaning?"

"Meaning that she still wants Wilson to spend his summers at the ranch with you."

"Fine with me."

"As long as you're not married to Ainsley."

"Lila can't tell me what to do."

"But she insists that she doesn't want Ainsley anywhere near her son. I think you can understand why."

Trent grimaced and refused to be intimidated. "It's all water under the bridge. What happens between Ainsley and me, that's our business. If you won't tell Lila, I will!"

Jonah waved off the anger flashing in his eyes. "Slow down. And give our sister some credit."

"Why should I?"

"She handled that business with the Brandon boy pretty well."

"About time," Trent observed.

"So, she doesn't want Wilson hanging out with Korey."

Trent grinned wryly. "Ainsley would probably agree. For different reasons."

"Then there isn't a problem."

"Did you ever think of running for the diplomatic corps?" Trent suggested.

Jonah scowled. "I don't need your cynicism. Here you go." He leafed through a thick sheaf of documents before handing them to Trent. "One copy for you, one for me and one for Lila."

"You won't mind if I have my attorney look these over?"

"I expected as much."

"Good. I'll get back to you later."

Jonah's eyes narrowed. "Remember, this was your idea."

"Afraid I'll back out?" Trent asked.

"No. But Lila's feet are already damp. Don't stretch this out too long."

Trent looked over the pages. Everything seemed in order. "I have an appointment with my attorney in thirty minutes. If he has time to look these over, I'll bring them to your house this evening. If not, I'll see you tomorrow."

"Fair enough," Jonah said, his eyes still slightly suspicious as he clasped his brother's hand. "Though why you'd rather buck hay than work in the office down the hall is beyond me."

Trent surveyed the plush office and scowled. Thick carpet, fantastic view, comfortable furniture and no bars on the windows. So why did it feel like a prison? "To each his own, Jonah," he said, reaching for the door. "Just be grateful I don't want your job."

Jonah paled. "Oh, I am," he assured his brother, sweating at the thought of a power struggle between himself and Trent. "I am!"

Trent closed the door behind him and could hardly wait to get out of the building.

AINSLEY SHUT THE front door behind her and looked around the townhouse she'd shared with Robert and Korey. Selling the narrow house in Twin Peaks would be harder than she'd imagined. She walked around the rooms, gazed at the dusty hardwood floors and the furniture draped with sheets, and sighed. Oriental rugs were rolled and pushed against the walls and her heels clicked noisily on the cold floors.

Slowly climbing the stairs, she opened the door of her third-floor studio. The room was still airy and bright, but it seemed lonely. Walking out the French doors, she looked at the sparkling waters of the Bay, but felt none of the excitement she once had.

All because of Trent. She couldn't get him out of her mind. She wondered if she should have stayed in Denver with him.

"Well, you'll never know, will you?" she asked herself.

The doorbell chimed and she hurried downstairs. Charlie was on the front porch.

"I thought you were going to be in Wyoming all summer," Charlie said, laughing.

"I was—I mean, I am." She stepped away from the door. "Come in. I'll see if I can find some tea or coffee. How did you know I was here?"

"An educated guess. Actually, I just got lucky. Oh, here, I sold two of your paintings and I was going to mail the checks, but—" she followed Ainsley down the hall "—I took a chance you might be coming home."

"Thanks." Ainsley glanced at the checks and set them on the counter. The dollar amount wasn't much, but it would help.

"And I brought us a treat. There's this absolutely heavenly bakery by the gallery and I couldn't resist." She handed Ainsley a white bag and Ainsley peered inside.

"Looks great." She searched for cups, a plate and tea bags. "So why did you think I'd be here?"

Charlie sat in one of the kitchen chairs. "Because I got this cryptic telephone call from a sexy-sounding man."

"Who?"

"Some hotshot oil tycoon."

Ainsley groaned and put the maple bars and doughnuts on a clean plate.

"And I was a little surprised to hear you've got a private showing at the Worthington Gallery," Charlie said, reaching for a glazed doughnut and smiling smugly.

"So you talked to Trent." She took two cups of boiling water from the microwave and handed one to Charlie.

"I don't know who I talked to, but he sounded great! And you, look at you," she observed, looking Ainsley up and down. "Tanned, smiling, a spring in your step. Seems Wyoming has been good for you."

Ainsley doubted it. "Cinnamon spice or orange pekoe?"

"Orange, and don't change the subject. Tell me all about this guy!" Charlie cradled her cup and leaned back in her chair, her eyes shining.

"There's nothing much to tell. I've known Trent all my life. He grew up on the ranch next to ours."

"He didn't sound much like the 'boy next door' to me."

"Well, he was. Only next door was about a quarter of a mile away." She placed her heels on an empty chair and looked at her friend. "So, what did he say?"

"That he was interested in your work because you were a local girl and he wanted to buy a few paintings before 'the show' this weekend. I'm sorry, but I'm afraid I let the cat out of the bag," Charlie apologized, blowing across her tea. "I'm a worse liar than you are."

"I think he'd have figured it out anyway." Ainsley sighed and frowned into her cup.

"Are you in love with him?"

"W-what?" Ainsley's head snapped up. "In love with him?"

"If I remember, you went back home looking for a man as a father for Korey."

"I did not!"

Charlie laughed. "Okay. Maybe you weren't looking, but you obviously found someone. Don't tell me. He's the boy you left behind. He never got married and spent his days working the ranch waiting for you to find out what a mistake you'd made with Robert so you'd come back to him."

"It didn't go quite like that." Ainsley sipped her tea and told Charlie most of the story, starting with the night she'd married Robert and ending with the fact that her father had actually bribed Trent to propose to her.

"So what do you care?" Charlie said. "It sounds as if he really loves you."

Ainsley shook her head. Lines of worry etched across her forehead. "I know he cares about me," she admitted, "but I'm not sure about love."

"Were you sure with Robert?"

"I don't know," she admitted, thinking back. "That was a long time ago. I was so young then. Maybe I didn't know what love was."

"Maybe you still don't."

The doorbell rang and Charlie grinned. "That could be your rugged cowboy now—coming on his white horse to take you so that you can ride off into the sunset together."

"The sun sets in the west, Wyoming is east," Ainsley pointed out, checking her watch. "And, actually, I think it's the real estate salesman."

"You're not really going through with selling this place?" Charlie asked, looking around the cozy rooms.

"Don't have much of a choice." Ainsley scooted her chair away from the table and hurried down the hall.

Charlie was right on her heels. "So quit blaming Trent. There's a chance your dad got himself into his current financial pickle all by himself, you know."

"All I know is that Dad needs help. Whether he wants it or not!"

"I think that's what Trent's tried to do—help him."

The doorbell chimed again.

"If he has, he's gone about it all wrong." Ainsley yanked open the front door and met the interested gaze of a middle-aged woman in a gray suit and red blouse.

"Mrs. Hughes?"

"Yes."

"I'm Barbara Anderson with Hillside Realty."

"Come in, come in, Ms. Anderson. I'll show you around and then I'd like to sign the papers as quickly as possible."

"You're making a big mistake," Charlie whispered, taking hold of Ainsley's arm as the real estate woman strolled into the living room.

"I don't have a choice!"

Sighing, Charlie let go. "Okay. But call me before you leave. Okay? Let me know what's happening."

"I will," Ainsley promised, watching Charlie run down the front steps and climb into her convertible.

"This is a lovely home," the real estate woman said, glancing around the rooms with a calculated eye. "If priced right, you should be able to sell it by the end of the summer."

"Good!" Ainsley said, wondering what she would do if the house really did sell. Would she come back to San Francisco so that Korey could finish school with his classmates? Or would she stay in Wyoming on the ranch and have to face Trent every day? Squaring her shoulders, she forced a smile and met the older woman's gaze. "Let me show you the rest of the house and then we can get down to business!"

CHAPTER THIRTEEN

AINSLEY SMILED AND leaned against the wall, the telephone receiver against her ear. She was staring out the window to the night and saw moonlight reflecting on the rooftops of the townhouses lower on the hill. "Then you're taking care of Grandpa?" she asked Korey.

"Sure I am. But he doesn't like it much."

"I bet not." In the background she could hear Jefferson arguing good-naturedly with Sarah.

"Sarah's beat him at checkers and chess. He claims she cheats."

Ainsley laughed. "What do you think?"

Korey whispered, "I think she's better than he is."

"I heard that," Jefferson bellowed and then laughed, coughing.

Ainsley's brow furrowed with worry. "You make sure he takes it easy, okay? I'll be home in a couple of days, whenever I get things wrapped up here. I'll call beforehand, to let you know the exact time."

"If Trent comes to get you, can I come with him?"

"Sure," she said, her throat catching when she thought of Trent in Denver. "I'd like that. I miss you."

"Yeah, uh, I miss you, too."

"I'll see you in a couple of days." She hung up and sighed, glancing around the lonely townhouse. "Don't let it get to you." Putting a cup of water in the microwave, she decided to drink one last cup of tea while watching television.

The tea was steeping when the pounding began, loud and incessant, on her front door.

"I'm coming," she called, setting her cup on the table and thinking a passerby had seen the Realtor's sign in the front yard. "Hold on a minute!" Tying her robe more tightly around her waist, she hurried down the hall and looked out the tall window by the front door. Her heart fluttered crazily when she recognized Trent on the front porch. His face was contorted, his nostrils flared angrily. "Well I'll be," she murmured.

"Ainsley!"

Grinning, she slid the dead bolt to the side and yanked open the door. He stood glowering on the porch, the real estate sign in his fist. "What the hell is this?" he demanded, shaking the sign in her face before tossing it onto a corner of the porch.

"Hey, wait a minute—"

"No! *You* wait a minute!" he said. "I'm tired of being lied to and turned inside out—"

"You! *You're* being lied to?" she repeated, her eyes rounding at his audacity. "How about me? Huh?"

He strode into the entry hall and slammed the door shut behind him. "I thought you said you weren't coming here to raise cash for the farm." He leaned one hip against the window casing and jammed his fists into his pockets. He was furious.

"I told you it wasn't any of your business."

"I'm foreman of the ranch. It is my business."

She crossed her arms over her chest. "This," she said,

indicating the house with the sweep of one hand, "is my property, and I'll sell it when I damned well please."

"To help get your father out of the red?"

"Yes!"

He strode up to her, pushing his face next to hers, his eyes blazing. She felt like taking a step backward, but her back was already pressed against the banister leading upstairs. "I didn't think you had it in you," he said, his eyes glancing down her body, noting the thick terry robe that crossed over her breasts and the way her hair was pinned onto her head. Her cheeks were pink, her eyes defiantly bright. "I didn't really think you gave a damn about that ranch."

"Then you really didn't know me, did you?" she taunted, lifting her chin, her blue eyes filled with challenge. "And don't you ever talk to me about lies. Our entire relationship has been based on them. From the beginning. Eleven years ago!" She saw him pale, but forged ahead. "You didn't have the guts to be honest with me then, and you haven't been these past few weeks! You keep talking to me about trust, but *you* can't even trust me with the truth!"

"Don't push me, Ainsley," he warned.

"Oh, but I am. I should have pushed you eleven years ago, found out what you were hiding, what you thought you *knew!* Then maybe we wouldn't be here arguing right now!"

A muscle worked in his jaw, and his eyes, when they stared into hers, were clouded.

"You're the one that keeps talking about love," she whispered, pushing him just a little harder. "You're the one who suggested *I* propose. But I can't—I can't get any more involved with you. Not until you level with me!"

Breathing hard, she felt her chest rise and fall, saw his eyes glance down before his gaze locked with hers again.

"Believe me, you don't want to hear it," he whispered.

"So you keep saying. Why don't you try me? Why did you think Robert had hurt me? What did you know that I didn't? You were positively stunned when I told you I'd married him."

"I didn't think you'd do anything that rash."

"You knew I was impulsive."

"I know. But deep down, I thought you'd come to your senses and see that I was the one who loved you."

"You…you should have said something."

His lips twisted sardonically and he reached forward to twist a strand of her hair in his fingers. "Would you have believed me?"

"I don't know."

Sighing, he sat on the lowest step and stared through the tall window near the door. "I was going to, you know. I'd come back from Houston with a ring in my pocket. A ring for you."

"A ring?"

"An engagement ring," he said softly.

Her heart ached. "Oh, Trent."

"Matter of fact—" he reached into his pocket and pulled out a faded velvet box "—I still have it."

"Oh, no." Her eyes were bright with unshed tears as he snapped open the box and a diamond ring winked under the lights.

"It's small. But I didn't have a lot of money then."

"It's…beautiful," she breathed, her throat burning.

She sat next to him on the stairs, watching the play of emotions crossing his face as he slipped the ring onto her finger. "You never said anything."

"Because when I got home, all hell broke loose."

"Meaning?"

"I found out that you were very serious about Robert, even thinking about running off with him."

"Then why were you so surprised?"

"Because I didn't think Robert was that serious about you," he said, seeing the wounded look that crossed her face. "He'd been seeing Lila on the sly."

"W-what!"

"I didn't know about it until I got home. And then, I assumed that you'd figured it out." He glanced up at her white face. "Dad was fit to be tied," he admitted, "and I thank God that Mom wasn't alive."

"Why?" she whispered, her knees weak, her mind running ahead to the horrible truth.

"Because Lila was pregnant with Wilson."

Ainsley's throat went dry and she thought she might be sick. "You're not saying that…that…"

"Yes, dammit!" he admitted, running his fingers through his hair. "Wilson is Robert's son!"

"No!"

His face was stern, his gray eyes pained, and Ainsley knew instinctively he was telling the truth. And, if she were really honest with herself, she'd have to admit that the thought had crossed her mind. There were too many unexplained coincidences.

"Oh, God," she whispered, collapsing onto the stairs, leaning against him and fighting bitter tears. Robert had betrayed her long before they'd been married. She wanted to throw up. Her fingers curled into an impotent fist. "No!"

"It's true, Ainsley. But only Lila, Jonah and I know the truth. Wilson doesn't even suspect."

"Then Wilson and Korey are brothers," she whispered.

"Half brothers."

"But Lila—"

"She wanted to tell the world," he said. "But Dad talked her out of it—sent her to live with an aunt in Chicago. We all pretended that she'd been involved with a boy who intended to marry her, but had joined the army and been killed in a freak accident."

"She must hate me," Ainsley whispered, her insides shredding.

"Probably."

"And Korey?"

"That hurt," he admitted. "Even though she was over Robert, when she found out you were pregnant and married to the man who'd turned his back on her, she just about hit the roof. Wanted to tell you that he already had a son."

Ainsley's eyes were dry but burning. "Did...did Robert know?" she asked, bracing herself for the worst.

"He'd seen Lila the night before you got married."

"And he lied to her?" she said.

"Yep. Claimed he'd marry her and give the child a name. The next night, he took off with you."

"Oh, God," she whispered. "And that's why you thought he'd hurt me. You thought I knew and that he'd broken up with me," she said, forcing the pieces of the old, ill-fitting puzzle together.

"Ainsley, I'm sorry—"

"What about my dad?" she asked, her eyes piercing into his.

Trent shook his head. "If he knows, it's because he pieced it together himself. No one in my family has breathed a word, and I think the gossip would have drifted back."

"Somehow I feel responsible," she whispered.

"For what?"

"Lila's pain."

"I wouldn't worry about that," he said. "She's comfortable now. And she was the one who was seeing your fiancé behind your back."

"You should have told me a long time ago," she said quietly, feeling his arm stiffen around her.

He swallowed hard and kissed her forehead. "You were already married. You told me you loved Robert. I believed you."

She shook her head.

"Honestly, Ainsley, I did what I thought was best. For all of us. Including Lila."

Sighing, she stood and stared blankly at him. They'd shared so much together, weathered so many storms, and finally, she knew the truth. Though it hurt, at least she now understood what had happened between them. Feeling a sudden chill, she wrapped her arms around her waist. "Thanks for finally telling me," she said softly, her insides still quivering.

"You're sure you can handle it?"

"Positive." She nodded and forced a small smile. "I have to. Now, the least I can do is offer you a cup of coffee."

"Nothing stronger?"

"I'll see what I've got. Just give me a minute." She went into the bathroom, turned on the tap and splashed cold water over her face, as if she could scrub away the dirt of the past. When she looked into the mirror she saw her reflection and had to look away.

"It's not your fault," Trent said. He was standing behind her and she met his worried gaze in the mirror.

"I know."

When he left, she sat on the edge of the tub, waiting until some of the sickness passed. Finally, her legs still weak, she walked back to the kitchen. Trent was already seated at the kitchen table, his boots propped on a second chair.

"You okay?"

"I—I'll be fine. It's just a little hard to accept."

"If I can help—"

"Thanks." It felt good to have him in the house. Standing on a chair, she rummaged in the cupboard over the refrigerator and found an old bottle of whiskey. "Will this do?" she asked, holding up the bottle for his perusal.

He stared up at her, watching her stretch and balance on the chair. "Anything," he said.

"Okay. Straight up or on the rocks?"

His grin widened. "Whatever."

Pouring him a stiff shot, she set the bottle on the counter. "Aren't you joining me?"

"No, thanks. I don't think a drink would help." She reheated her tea and tried to ignore the fact that her hands were still shaking.

He sipped his drink and eyed her over the rim of the glass. "Have I convinced you to take this house off the market?"

"Too late. I signed the papers today," she said quietly.

He frowned into his glass.

"You know, if I didn't know better, I'd say you wanted me to keep this place so that you could get rid of me at the end of the summer."

"Guess again," he said, his voice husky.

"I can't."

"I just don't want you to throw your money away."

"On my father's ranch?"

"We'll find a way to pull it out of the red. Without your money."

"We?" she repeated. "Who's we?"

"Me and Jefferson."

"Oh, I see." Nodding her head, she looked at him skeptically. "How?"

"I've already started the ball rolling," he admitted. "Today I traded my shares of oil company stock for the ranch."

"I don't follow—"

"I own the Rocking M free and clear as well as Jeff's plane."

She brightened a bit. "And Dad's wells?"

"Will remain as they are. Until the market turns around. But, I have enough working capital to give him back his plane and his part of the ranch."

"He won't like it."

"He can pay me back, slowly." He grinned to himself. "Besides, I'd like to keep everything in the family."

"The family? The McCullough family?"

He nodded, sipping his drink, his eyes crinkling at the corners. "The Trent McCullough family."

"Oh." Her pulse jumped.

"Right." He grinned at her and set his empty glass on the table. "You see," he said, walking close to her and touching her skin just over the lapels of her robe, his gaze locking with hers, "what's happening here is that I expect you to propose to me before the night is over."

"Tonight?" she whispered.

"I'm sure of it."

"Dream on," she teased, but his finger inched downward, sliding seductively against her skin and causing her heart to skip a beat.

Lowering his head, he brushed his mouth seductively across hers and she tasted the hint of whiskey lingering on his warm lips. "Admit it, Ainsley. You want me to marry you." His fingers went lower, pushing the fabric apart and toying with the knot of her belt.

"No!" she nearly screamed, as the robe parted and fell to the floor leaving her dressed in only a cream-colored slip.

He groaned as he looked at her, then encircling her waist with one hand, he took the pins from her hair with the other. Her long tresses fell in lustrous waves down her back, and over his arm. "Tell me you want me," he said, his voice low, his gray eyes glinting silver.

"I don't," she said, but laughed.

"Tell me you expect me to make passionate love to you all night long."

"I don't—" He kissed the swell of her breasts and she sucked in her breath when his tongue rimmed the delicate lace. "Oh, please, Trent—"

"I'll take that as a yes," he said, lifting her off the floor and carrying her through the hall and up the stairs. He paused at the second floor and frowned in the doorway to her room. "You shared this with Robert?" he asked.

"Yes, but—"

"What's up there?"

"My studio, but we can't—"

He didn't listen, but carried her up the final flight. Moonlight spilled through the French doors and sky-lights. He laid her on the daybed, gently lowering her to the soft mattress and then slowly, sensuously, stripped. She watched as his clothes fell into a pile on the floor until he was naked, his skin shadowed, his eyes dark.

"Now," he said, his voice low as he lay beside her. "Beg me to marry you." His big hands touched the bend in her waist, before skimming the smooth skin of her inner thigh.

"Not on your life," she whispered, but knew that she'd already lost. There wasn't a doubt in her mind that before the grey light of dawn filled the room, she would plead with him to become her husband.

"This is going to be fun," he said.

"I don't know. You're in for the fight of your life."

"And it's going to be worth every second of it," he said, "when you propose."

"Never."

SUNLIGHT WAS STREAMING through the panes when Ainsley stretched and opened her eyes. She looked up and found Trent lying next to her, propped on one elbow, his eyes fixed on her face. "Say it again," he commanded, his crooked smile smugly in place.

"Say what?" she groaned.

"You know."

Sighing, she looked at the ceiling. "Please marry me," she repeated, wondering how many times she'd already asked him. She'd lost count.

"I just wanted to make sure you hadn't changed your mind."

"I haven't changed my mind, but I'm not sure getting married would be practical," she said, thinking of the ranch, her father's health, and her career here in San Francisco.

"Not practical?" He touched the tip of her nose. "Since when have you been practical?"

"I'm not eighteen anymore," she said, stretching and yawning, the sheets falling off the bed. "And not as impulsive. Where would we live?"

"In Wyoming."

"And Korey?"

"He'd live with us, too. I'd adopt him."

She rolled her eyes. "You don't exactly top his list of his favorite people, you know. Besides, I promised him I wouldn't make any decisions about where we would live without asking him."

He studied the perturbed knit of her brow. "Did you tell him that you were selling this place?"

"No, but—"

"And what were you going to do? Leave your dad with your money and take off? Just tell him, 'Here, Dad—here's the cash you need, now I'm off to San Francisco? Hope you don't have another heart attack and that you don't blow the bucks?'"

She laughed, despite her worries. "Of course not."

"Well? Admit it. In your mind you've already moved home."

"I've given it some thought."

"Good. Give it some more. Last night I tried to talk you out of selling this place because I don't want you to give up your life out of some sense of duty to your father. But if you're coming home because you *want* to, then I'm all for it."

"I want to be with you," she admitted.

A satisfied smile flashed across his jaw. "That's more like it."

"But there are still a few things I have to know."

He kissed her forehead, looked deep in her eyes and touched the tip of his finger to her chin. "Just ask."

"Nick Hammond. What's happening to him?"

"Nothing."

"Isn't the bank foreclosing?"

"No."

Her eyes narrowed. She propped herself on one elbow and met his gaze. "What did you do?"

"Nothin' much. Just bought his oil wells back."

"You didn't!"

"Brother Jonah's comments, exactly," he said, chuckling when he remembered the consternation and anger on Jonah's face when Trent had shown him the contract he'd signed with Nick. "One of the reasons he decided to give up ranching, I think."

"If you don't watch out, you'll be broke," she warned.

"The chance we all take."

Her throat was dry and she threw her arms around his neck. "I love you," she whispered, clinging to him. "I only wish I'd realized it eleven years ago."

"You and me both," he said. "It would have saved all of us a whole lot of grief." He kissed her and brushed the hair away from her face with his hand. "But don't worry about it, we have the rest of our lives. Now, come on!" He slapped her playfully on her behind and rolled out of bed. After putting on his jeans, he threw open the French doors and walked across the flagstone deck. "Let's take a look at this city of yours."

Snatching her robe from the floor and cinching it around her waist, she followed him outside. "It's beautiful, isn't it?"

He nodded, his eyes squinting against the brilliant morning sun as it shimmered on the dark water. "I thought it was supposed to be foggy here."

"It is. Sometimes." She took a deep breath of air and saw that the sunlight glinted in her diamond. "If you want, I'll show you some of the city before we go home. There's someone I want you to meet."

"Who?"

"Charlie! She's dying to meet you!"

He groaned.

"So don't talk to me about lies. You're a master," she teased.

"I'm not sure I want to meet this Charlie person."

"Sorry, you can't get out of it," she quipped.

"We're scheduled to fly out at three."

"Then we'd better get moving!"

"We could spend all day in bed," he suggested, taking her into his arms and holding her close. The wind ruffled her hair and caused her cheeks to color.

"What about Charlie?"

"She can meet me at the wedding."

Ainsley laughed and tossed her head back. "Whatever you say," she said, sighing as her arms wrapped around his waist. Hooking her thumbs in the belt loops of his jeans, she let her head fall to his chest and heard the rhythmic beating of his heart.

"I love you, Ainsley," he whispered across her crown. "And this time, nothing's going to keep us apart."

"Promise?"

"Promise," he vowed, his voice filled with emotion. "If you want, we could fly to Reno this afternoon and get married today."

She shook her head. Her soft cinnamon hair brushed against his abdomen. "No," she whispered. "This time I'm going to do it right. I want my whole family with me—and yours."

"Mine might not be too crazy about this," he said, thinking of the fire in Lila's eyes when they'd discussed his marrying Ainsley.

"Maybe not, but they're going to be invited to a wedding, whether they like it or not." She squeezed her eyes shut and kissed the firm muscles of his chest.

"Fair enough." He tilted her chin up and placed a

morning-soft kiss on her lips. "This is forever, Ainsley," he said, warning her. "I'll never let you go."

"And I won't want you to," she vowed, pulling his head down to hers and returning his kisses with renewed passion. Finally, at long last, she would marry the man she'd always loved.

CHAPTER FOURTEEN

AINSLEY'S STOMACH WAS in knots by the time Trent circled the ranch. "Take a look down there," he suggested.

She gazed out the window and saw the silvery waters of Wolverine Creek winding through the patchwork of land.

"You see the creek?"

"Of course."

"See where it goes under the fence, connecting the Circle S and the Rocking M?"

"Yes—"

"You remember that's where this all started—the day after you married Robert?"

"How could I ever forget?"

"Well, don't. Because someday, we're going to finish what we started right there, where the two ranches join."

She looked at him to see if he was teasing, but his face was set. "You're serious about this, aren't you?"

"I never thought what happened there turned out right." Banking the plane, he approached the longest field and landed the plane at the ranch's small landing strip.

Ainsley's throat was tight. The diamond ring on her left hand felt heavy and awkward and she knew that facing Korey would be one of the most difficult confrontations she'd ever had.

They drove back to the house in Trent's Jeep. "Second thoughts?" he asked, parking the rig by the barn and seeing the worry in her eyes.

"No—"

"But?"

"But Korey might not handle this very well."

"Maybe you're underestimating him. Give him a little credit, okay?" He winked at her. "You're going to tell your son that you're getting married again. It's not like you're going to the gallows."

"You're right!" she said, not really believing him, but kissing his cheek and climbing out of the battered vehicle. "And the sooner we get things straight, the better!"

After taking her bags to the loft, she and Trent walked into the kitchen through the back door. The screen creaked, and banged shut behind them.

Sarah had been rolling out pie dough but she looked up and grinned when they came into the kitchen. "Well, I'll be! I didn't expect you back for a couple more days!" She dusted the flour from her hands. "Jeff? You hear that? Ainsley's back!"

Jefferson walked stiffly into the kitchen. "What happened with the art show?" he asked, eyeing her suspiciously.

"First, tell me how you're feeling."

"Good as new and don't tell me I look good, 'cause I don't. I haven't for a long time, and I'm sick to death of people tellin' me how good I look. Gives me a complex, you know. I can't tell when people are lyin' or telling the truth."

"Well, you look good to me!" she exclaimed, kissing him on the cheek.

"You're prejudiced." But his gaunt face broke into a wide smile.

"Where's Korey?"

"Up in the shower. He spent the whole mornin' out in the stables, cleaning 'em out, just like Trent told him to," the old man said, grinning craftily. "Oh, he's been stompin' around here and carryin' on about all the work he has to do, but he's doin' just fine. I think the whole thing taught him a lesson!"

"Let's hope so," Ainsley said as Jefferson sat at the table.

"Well, sit down, sit down, and tell us all about your trip," Sarah said, pouring coffee into ceramic mugs. "Just let me get this pie into the oven and I'll join you."

"Always fussin'," Jefferson muttered, but his old eyes gleamed as he watched Sarah.

"And you wouldn't know what to do if I didn't fuss," she said. "Now, go on, tell us about the show."

"It, uh, didn't really exist," Ainsley said, cringing under her father's critical gaze.

"Then why in tarnation did you go to California?" Jefferson demanded.

"I put my house on the market," she said slowly.

Korey walked into the room and then stood stock still. "You did *what?*" he cried, disbelief written all over his young face.

"I'm going to sell the townhouse."

"But you promised that you'd talk to me first!" he said. "That's what you said when we came out here!"

"I know, but—"

"You lied!" He swallowed hard, his eyes bright with tears as he looked around the room to the sea of worried grown-up faces looking at him.

"I didn't lie, I just—"

"Fibbed! I get it. It's okay when grown-ups lie, but not kids, is that right?"

"No, but—"

"And I bet he was with you!" Korey exclaimed, pointing an accusing finger at Trent. "You sold the house because of him!"

"I haven't sold anything yet."

"But you will!" Furious, his small fists clenched at his sides, he ran out of the room, his boots thundering down the steps.

Ainsley started to get up, but Trent grabbed her arm. "Give him a few minutes to cool off," he said. "Let him think about it."

"But I have to explain—"

"You will. When he's not so angry."

Glancing nervously out the window, she saw Korey run into the stables. A few minutes later, he was leading Crazy Luke out of the building. Throwing a look over his shoulder at the house, he jumped into the saddle. Then he leaned forward, and the ebony colt took off through the fields, dust billowing behind.

"I need to talk to him," she said quietly.

"You will." Jefferson looked pointedly at his daughter. "Now, what's all this business about you sellin' your house?"

"It's true."

"Why? You unhappy in the city?"

"No—"

He clamped his teeth together and reached into his pocket for his cigarettes. The pack was empty and he swore.

"You should stop smoking those things anyway," Sarah said, sighing as she reached into a drawer and took a fresh pack from an open carton and handed the cigarettes to him.

Jefferson ignored her and slowly unwrapped the cellophane from the pack. "I ain't ready to be put out to pasture, you know," he said. "You ain't movin' back here because you think I need to be looked after now, are you?"

"'Course not," she whispered.

"Well?"

"Originally, I thought you might need a little cash here on the ranch."

His face muscles squeezed together. "I wouldn't take a dime of your money."

"I just wanted to help."

He frowned darkly, lighting his cigarette and staring out the window. "It'll be a cold day in hell before I'll take any of your money, Missy."

"I know, but there's another reason I put the house up for sale."

"And what's that?"

"Trent asked me...no, I asked Trent to marry me," she said, her eyes gleaming, "and he agreed."

"That's wonderful!" Sarah exclaimed, wrapping her floured arms around Ainsley. "Oh, honey!" She sniffed and dabbed at her eyes with the corner of her apron. "A wedding! And here I am blubbering like a baby!"

"Wait a minute," Jefferson said slowly. "You asked him?"

"That's right, Jeff," Trent said, placing his arm around Ainsley's shoulders. "Didn't want to give you or anyone else the wrong idea—that marrying Ainsley was part of any deal I had with you."

"Craziest thing I ever heard—a woman asking a man to marry her," Jefferson muttered.

"Maybe it's a good idea," Sarah said staunchly, lifting

her chin. "That way a woman don't have to wait around wastin' time, tryin' to figure out if a man wants her or not."

"What're you talkin' about?" he asked, his weathered face slacking as the words sunk in. "Sarah? Are you talking about me?"

Her hazel eyes sparked behind her glasses. "If the shoe fits, wear it," she mumbled, ramming her pie into the oven.

"Well, I'll be," Jefferson said, dumbfounded.

Tension sizzled in the kitchen and Ainsley couldn't help but smile. "I think maybe I'll go unpack and then catch up with Korey. Unless you need some help in here, Sarah."

"Seems to me she's got everything handled," Trent observed, taking Ainsley's hand and drawing her out of the kitchen.

"Can you believe that?" she asked, once they were outside.

"Been comin' for years," he drawled.

"I never knew—"

"Why do you think Sarah hangs around? Couldn't be the pay."

"I suppose not," Ainsley said, still looking over her shoulder. "What do you think we should do?"

"Bribe your dad to marry her?" he teased.

"Oooh! You can be such a miserable thing when you want to be," she said, tossing her head back and laughing.

"Just leave them alone. They'll handle it in their own way." At the bottom of the steps leading up to her loft, he wrapped his arms around her and kissed her firmly on the lips. "I've got to go home and square some things there. But I'll be back later."

"Promise?" she asked.

"Promise." He kissed her again and then ran to the

Jeep. She watched him leave and sighed. Maybe she was wrong in wanting to marry him, maybe she should have talked things over with her son first. She unpacked her things and then went to the stables, intending to track Korey down.

LILA WAS SITTING on the front porch swing when Trent parked the Jeep. Sipping from a frosty drink, she gazed across the stubbled fields as he got out and walked toward her. "I wonder if I made a big mistake," she whispered, glancing at her brother as he slid down onto the swing next to her.

"What do you mean?"

"I mean that maybe I shouldn't have sold my part of this ranch to you. It's my home and Wilson's."

"You haven't been here much."

"Mistake number two or three or four. I've made so many I've lost count," she said with a grimace. "How about a drink?"

"No, thanks."

"Have a good trip?"

"It was all right."

She swirled her drink and stared thoughtfully into her glass. "Did you ask Ainsley to marry you?" she asked suddenly.

His jaw tightened. "Didn't have to. She asked me."

She closed her eyes and shook her head. "You've always been an idiot about her."

"I don't think so."

Standing, she looked up at him and her eyes seemed lifeless. "Wilson's not going to like it, you know."

"Why not?"

"He thinks of you as his father—since he never

knew his. And he's been jealous of Korey ever since he came here."

"He told you this?"

"Part of it. The rest of it I figured out for myself." When she saw the skeptical lift of his brows, her lips clamped together angrily. "I am his mother, you know, and whether you approved of the way I raised him or not, I know him better than anyone. He adored you, Trent. And when you started showing interest in Korey and Ainsley, he got worried. Why do you think he started all this business with Tom Brandon?"

"I don't know, but I don't think we can blame Ainsley for that."

Lila's eyes flashed and she tossed her hair over her shoulder. "Think what you want. I really don't give a damn. But, I'm leaving at the end of the weekend, right after the rodeo."

"You don't have to go."

She smiled grimly. "Oh, I think I'd better. I'd like to say that I wish you all the happiness in the world, that I love the thought of having another sister-in-law. But it would be a lie. I never liked Ainsley and then she married Robert. Maybe you can forgive that, but I really can't!" Her chin trembled and she looked at her brother as if he were a traitor.

"She never meant to hurt you," he said softly.

"Probably not. But she did."

"Robert did," he corrected. "When he turned his back on you."

She shrugged. "Same difference." Taking a long swallow, she emptied her glass. "I'll be taking Wilson with me, you know."

"He could stay for the summer."

"Nope. I've expected too much from you already." She wrapped her arm around the post supporting the roof and looked to the stables where Wilson was still cleaning the stalls. "You've done a good job with him, Trent. Don't get me wrong. But he's my responsibility and it all came home to me—that I was shirking it—when you caught him stealing from Jefferson Smith. Despite my differences with Ainsley, I don't want my boy to grow up to be a thief."

"Whatever you say, Lila. He's your son. But if he wants to come back—"

"Oh, I know. You and your new little wifey will take care of him." She rolled her eyes to the vibrant sky. "I'll think about it, because I'm moving to Denver."

"I thought you loved New York."

"I do. But Wilson would hate it. Besides—" she glanced knowingly in his direction "—now that you're out of the family business, someone has to keep an eye on Brother Jonah, don't you think?"

"Wouldn't be a bad idea."

"I thought you'd agree. Well, good luck, Trent. You'll need it with Ainsley." Then she turned and went inside.

"I don't think so," he murmured, looking across the fields toward the Circle S.

SWEAT DRIZZLED BETWEEN her shoulder blades as Ainsley reined Jezebel to a stop and shaded her eyes against the lowering sun. Frowning, she squinted, staring into all the familiar haunts of her youth and wondering where Korey could have gone.

Jezebel pricked up her ears and whinnied. Ainsley followed the mare's gaze and saw Crazy Luke tied to the base of an old apple tree. "Finally," she whispered to the mare, nudging the horse's sides with her heels and heading for a shaded corner of the ranch.

Korey was tucked high in the leafy branches of the Gravenstein. He frowned when Ainsley rode beneath him and looked up. "What're you doin' here?" he asked.

"Looking for you." Tethering Jezebel to the tree, she climbed the rough lower branches, so that she was closer to her son. "I thought we needed to talk."

"Too late," he muttered. "You should have talked to me *before* you sold the house."

"It's not sold yet—just on the market."

"Same thing."

She leaned over one of the branches separating them and felt twigs and leaves catch in her hair. "Maybe you should try to listen to why I did it."

He didn't answer, but looked away.

"I didn't mean to hurt you, but you're right, I should have talked to you first. I had to put the house on the market to try and raise some money, for the ranch."

"Why?"

"Because it takes a lot of money to run a place this size and sometimes the cash just runs out. I don't know if you're old enough to understand all this, but I guess you should know that there's a chance Grandpa might lose this place."

"Because of the money?"

"Because of the *lack* of it."

"And so you were going to put the money from the house into the ranch?"

"Maybe—if Grandpa lets me. He's not real excited about the idea."

"Neither am I."

"There was nothing else I could do," Ainsley admitted. "He's my dad and he loves this place. So do I."

"Would it be enough—the money from the house, I mean?" he asked.

She lifted a shoulder. "I don't know. But I've got to get as much as I can and give it a shot. This land...it's important."

"You didn't think so once. You left a long time ago."

"I know," she said, smiling through the sun-dappled leaves. "But I'm back, and I want to be back for good." Leaning farther over the branch, she smiled and patted his knee. "I figure I can have the best of both worlds. I can still do the work I love, paint and sculpt right here, on the Circle S, and I don't have to leave—only when I want to."

He eyed her suspiciously. "This is all because of Trent, isn't it?"

"Partially."

"You gonna marry him?"

She bit her lower lip and glanced away before resolutely meeting her son's curious eyes. "Yes," she whispered. "I am."

"When?"

"I don't know. But soon."

Korey's face crumpled. "So all that talk about putting the money into the ranch was just an excuse, right? Because you never thought about going back to California! You planned to marry Trent all along!"

"Oh, no, Korey. I didn't plan it at all. In fact, I didn't really want to fall in love with him."

"Why not?"

"Lots of reasons, one of which was you." She felt her eyes burning, but didn't cry. "Believe it or not, I just want you to be happy."

"Sure." He looked as if he didn't believe a word she said.

"I mean it."

"Then let me ride in the race tomorrow."

Taking in a deep breath, she shook her head. "I can't do that," she said. "It would be going back on my word."

"Kind of like planning to stay here without asking me," he pointed out. "Wasn't that breaking a promise—or didn't it count?"

"It counted," she said. "More than you know." Letting out a long breath, she gazed at the distant mountains. "Look, I'll compromise with you."

"Compromise?"

"I can't let you ride in the rodeo race—we've been over that. But how about if we take Crazy Luke into town and you can ride him in the parade before the rodeo starts?"

He chewed on his lower lip. "Where would he be during the rodeo?"

"Under the stands, in the shade."

A smile tugged at the corner of his mouth. "Okay," he said slowly. "It's a deal."

"Thank God." Climbing down from the tree, she dusted the bark from her hands and looked up at him. "Come back to the house pretty soon, okay? Sarah will have supper on the table in less than an hour."

"Okay."

Feeling a little better, she hoisted herself onto Jezebel's back and urged the mare toward the house. The wind tore at Ainsley's hair and took her breath away as the horse galloped over the hard ground.

Her eyes stinging, Ainsley tried to ignore the feeling that she'd made a big mistake in agreeing to marry Trent and a bigger one in giving in to Korey.

SUPPER WENT WELL and there was a lot of conversation about the wedding. The tension between Sarah and Jefferson had dissolved, and though Korey was quieter than usual, he seemed to accept the fact that he would be moving to the ranch permanently. After cleaning the kitchen, Ainsley offered to play chess with Korey, but he mumbled something about homework and headed up the stairs.

A few minutes later, she went back to the loft and tried to paint, but couldn't. She kept listening for Trent, hoping he'd return.

It was nearly ten and she'd just about given up when her spirits suddenly soared at the familiar rumble of Trent's Jeep and the sound of his footsteps hurrying up the stairs. He swung open the door and she ran to him, holding him close. "Where were you?"

"I said I had business," he replied, grinning crookedly.

"Doing what?"

"Settling things with my family and especially talking to Wilson. He, uh, wasn't exactly jumping up and down at the prospect of us getting married."

"I don't imagine."

"I told him that he'd be welcome to come and live with us."

"And?"

"And he laughed." Trent's brows knit and he ran a hand wearily around his neck. "He said I didn't need him anymore. That now I had a real 'son.'"

"Meaning Korey."

"Right."

"Maybe someone should tell him the truth," she said, pouring a tall glass of orange juice from a thermos and handing it to him.

"I suppose Lila will. Someday."

"But not today?"

"No. The whole family has had enough shocks to last them a while. He and Lila are moving to Denver. Maybe they'll work things out. If not, he may end up with us."

"You can handle him," she predicted with a playful grin.

"And what about you?"

"He'll get used to me."

Taking her hand, he looked at the ring. The diamond winked in the dim light. "I want to get married right away, you know."

"How soon?"

"As soon as possible." His gray eyes met hers. "I think we've waited long enough, don't you?"

"Amen." She stood on tiptoe and wound her arms around his neck.

"How about next week?"

"Sounds perfect," she said with a sigh. "Sarah will be in seventh heaven. During supper, all she could talk about was the wedding and how we were going to have it right here, in the rose garden."

"Don't we get a choice?" He finished his juice and set the empty glass on the counter.

She laughed. "I don't think so."

"Then it sounds good to me," he said, kissing her lips. "Now, what about Korey?"

"He's coming around," she whispered. "We had our first compromise today. I told him he could ride in the parade before the rodeo tomorrow, but not in the race."

"Did he agree?"

"Begrudgingly."

"Sounds like he needs a stepfather and right away."

Ainsley cringed. "Don't start in on me, too," she

warned, her blue eyes dancing. "I'm marrying you because I want you for my husband, *not* because I think my son needs a father."

"Good. Now in the next few hours, I expect to show you just how good a husband I can be," he promised, lifting her off her feet and carrying her into the bedroom.

CHAPTER FIFTEEN

THE MORNING OF the rodeo dawned hot and sultry, and even with the windows rolled down, the inside of the Jeep was like an oven.

Ainsley felt restless. She blamed her worries on the weather as she glanced at Trent, seated beside her, but there was more to her unease than the heat. As Trent backed the trailer into a tight parking space on the rodeo grounds, he was sweating and dust filled the air.

Korey was seated in the back seat, fidgeting nervously.

"You okay?" Ainsley asked.

"Fine," he said quickly, but didn't meet her eyes.

"Good. Now, after the parade's over, you cool down Luke and then join us in the stands," Ainsley reminded him. "Grandpa's got a box right over the chutes."

"I'll be there," Korey mumbled, looking through the back window as the Jeep finally stopped.

"That's as good as it's gonna get," Trent decided, cutting the engine.

Korey was out of the Jeep and starting to unlock the back door of the horse trailer, his small fingers fumbling with the bolts.

Crazy Luke was kicking the sides of the trailer and had worked himself into a lather. "I don't think he likes traveling," Trent observed, grinning over at Ainsley as he helped Korey back the horse into the bright morning sunshine.

"I don't blame him."

Korey gave the horse some water and cooled him off, brushing his black coat until it gleamed midnight blue. "Doesn't he look great?"

"Radical," Ainsley replied with a grin. "How about a Coke?"

"Later maybe," Korey replied, still brushing Luke.

"I'll see you in the parade, then. Good luck," Ainsley said, paying for a Coke and carrying it up to the crowded stands. Trent was at her side, but kept glancing at Korey.

"Something bothering you?" she asked.

"Not really." But his eyes lingered on the boy.

"Don't worry about him. He's just had an awful lot to think about."

"Like a new stepfather?"

"And living in Wyoming, and riding in the parade and *not* being able to ride in the race—"

"Okay, okay. You've convinced me." But his eyes remained dark and Ainsley felt a cold chill in the small of her back.

Jefferson's seats were in the front row, directly over the chutes. He and Sarah were already sitting on the hard bench, shucking peanuts while waiting for the festivities to begin.

"You finally made it," Jefferson observed.

"Luke was a little touchy," Trent replied, sitting next to Ainsley and taking her hand.

"Um. Not used to the trailer."

"How about Korey? Is he all right?"

"Edgy," Trent replied.

"And none too happy about not getting to be in the race," Jefferson agreed.

"You did scratch him, didn't you?" Trent asked.

"No reason to. It was too late to get my money back."

Trent's hand tightened over Ainsley's and his shoulder muscles became taut.

"You're worried about something," Ainsley whispered.

"Just a feeling—"

The parade began and the crowd roared its approval as horses and riders, old and young, filed past the stands. Flags snapped in the wind, clowns did acrobatics, the high school band played and majorettes tossed batons high into the air.

Ainsley spotted Korey and waved frantically, but the boy didn't look up. Instead, he kept a tight rein on the black colt. Crazy Luke danced and sidestepped, frothing under the saddle and tossing his head nervously.

"Thank God he's not in the race," Ainsley said, once the parade had filed by and the first event began.

Trent didn't comment, his eyes glued to the red shirt Korey was wearing.

Ainsley watched the following events, only half paying attention through the calf roping and bull riding. Gray clouds gathered in the sky and the muggy heat was oppressive. Korey hadn't come up to the box and she began to worry.

"You're antsy about Korey, ain't ya?" her father said. "Well, don't worry. He's probably eating his way through two bags of popcorn and a spool of cotton candy."

But Ainsley couldn't help feeling nervous. Something wasn't right. "Maybe I'd better go check on him."

"Or I will," Trent said, his eyes moving over the crowd and around the stands.

"He'll be fine," Jefferson predicted.

"And now the bareback race," the announcer called over the loudspeaker. The microphone whistled as he began announcing the entrants:

"This is the nine- through twelve-year-old competition. That's the age of the riders, not the horses." A small wave of laughter rolled through the stands. "They'll take two turns around the track and end up at the finish line, right under the chutes. Here we go! Number one is Jacob Hammond riding his horse, White Thunder, number two is—"

Ainsley barely listened. Her eyes skimmed the stands, looking for Korey's red shirt and blond hair.

"Number eight is Wilson McCullough riding Blaze—"

She squeezed Trent's hand and watched as the entrants started filing through the gate at the far end of the arena. "And number twelve is Korey Hughes riding Crazy Luke."

"What?" she gasped.

Trent's eyes darkened.

"Did he say Korey?" Ainsley demanded.

"That's right."

"But—"

"I swear I had nothin' to do with this," her father said when she turned furious eyes on him.

"But he can't ride!"

"I don't think there's much choice now," Trent observed, his eyes narrowing. The gun went off and all twelve horses, their young riders clinging to their backs, hurled forward to race around the ring.

"Oh, God!" she whispered, her eyes wide, her hands clasped over her mouth and her heart hammering. The horses bunched together at the first turn.

Korey was bumped and Crazy Luke missed a stride,

but the game colt kept up, running around the inside of the stands as if there weren't another horse within miles.

Ainsley swallowed her fear as Korey guided the horse through one hole and then another. The sound of hoof-beats rocked the stands and people began jumping up and down, yelling to the horses and riders.

"Come on, Jason! Give him his head!"

"Hold him steady, Billy!"

The announcer's voice boomed through the stands. "White Thunder has the lead, but Moonshine is right on his heels and Blaze, ridden by Wilson McCullough, is making his move as they come into the final stretch."

The rangy buckskin caught the lead horse, but Korey and Crazy Luke were right with him, stride for stride. When Wilson broke free, Korey let out the reins, urging Crazy Luke forward. The black colt flattened his ears back and shot ahead, running neck and neck with the buckskin.

"Oh, God," Ainsley whispered, remembering the race where Trent had been all but trampled by his brother's horse.

Wilson took one look at Korey and began whipping Blaze. But it was too late. Crazy Luke's muscles bunched and he sprinted toward the finish line, right in front of the chutes.

Furious and desperate, Wilson slapped his mount and Blaze's shoulders rammed against Crazy Luke's flanks. The black colt stumbled and Korey was thrown over his head.

"No!" Ainsley screamed as her son hit the dirt and other horses rushed toward him.

Without thinking, Trent put his hands on the rail and vaulted over the fence, down the eight feet to the ground and threw himself forward, covering Korey's body with his own. Flailing legs and sharp hooves crunched all around him. The ground rocked and horses jumped over him.

People screamed, the announcer was yelling, but Trent heard nothing save the pounding on the hard earth. A hoof struck his shoulder and pain shot through his arm. Another rider fell and a horse reared, it's hooves narrowly missing Trent's head.

He huddled over the boy, trying to protect Korey. And then he felt an incredible stab of pain as a horse fell over them, crushing his chest and causing the world to spin crazily.

He heard Ainsley's voice screaming above the noise of the crowd before the world stopped spinning and went dark.

"LADIES AND GENTLEMEN, please—" But the announcer couldn't control the crowd. People raced into the arena and the ambulance screamed as it drove through the gate to the track.

Ainsley scrambled down the stairs and tried to run out to the track, but a huge, meaty hand took hold of her arm and restrained her. "I'm sorry, lady," a big cowboy said.

"But that's my son—and Trent, oh, God!" she screamed, fighting and clawing her way into the ring.

"You can't go in there."

"I have to. Please." She tried to jerk her arm free, but he held her back, his large face filled with compassion.

"Just let the paramedics handle it." She wouldn't listen to him and tried to rush into the arena where horses, running wild, were being caught, and paramedics were trying to evacuate the wounded.

"Missy!" Jefferson pushed his way through the crowd. "They've got Trent and Korey in the ambulance."

"Oh, no—"

The siren screamed again, and, lights flashing, the ambulance roared by.

"Come on," Sarah cried, breathing hard, her hair askew. She finally caught up with Jefferson. "We'll take my car."

Ainsley's heart was in her throat as she pushed her way through the crowd. She ran to Sarah's old wagon. She could hardly contain herself as the cook slid into the front seat and Jefferson sat in the back. Sarah put the car into gear and tried to drive through town to the hospital. The streets were clogged with pedestrians and traffic was at a standstill. The old wagon crawled and Ainsley felt as if she would go out of her mind. Each minute seemed like an eternity. Tears streamed down her face and she stared at a future without Trent or Korey.

It took nearly half an hour to reach the hospital. Sarah hadn't cut the engine when Ainsley was out of the wagon and racing to the doors of the hospital emergency room.

The nurse on duty recognized her. "Ms. Hughes."

"My son…and fiancé? They were in the rodeo race and accident."

"Oh, yes. The doctor is with them now—"

"Ms. Hughes?" Dr. Holmes stepped through the doors of the examining room. "Your son is going to be all right. Just a few scratches and a black eye. But no real damage."

"Thank God," Ainsley whispered. "And…and Trent?"

"He was unconscious when he got here, but I think he'll be okay, too. He's in X-ray right now. You can come back and see Korey if you like."

"Thank you." Ainsley didn't need any more encouragement. She hurried through the doors with Jefferson and Sarah on her heels. Korey was sitting on the side of an examining room table, swinging his feet and looking positively stricken. Aside from a cut across his chin a bruise over his eye and a deathly white pallor, he looked fine.

"It's all my fault," he whispered, tears in his huge eyes.

"Oh, no, sweetheart." She wrapped her arms around him and held him close.

"Yes, it is!" He swallowed hard.

"Look, I don't care. I'm just glad you're okay."

"But I shouldn't have—"

"Oh, baby." She kissed him and cried tears of relief. "It doesn't matter. It's over."

"What—what about Trent?"

"I think he'll be all right. I don't really know yet," she whispered, glancing around the sterile white rooms and silently praying that Trent wasn't hurt seriously.

"He must hate me."

"Of course he doesn't. Oh, honey!" She couldn't stop hugging him, telling herself that he was okay.

"I'm sorry I entered the race," he said, looking absolutely miserable. "And I'm sorry about all the things I said about Trent. He's really okay. I—I'm glad you're marrying him."

Ainsley's throat was so hoarse she could barely breathe. "I'm just glad you're okay. That's all that matters."

He looked up sheepishly. "Where's Crazy Luke?"

Jefferson's troubled eyes cleared. "I plumb forgot about the horse," he said and Korey began to cry. "Look, son, Sarah and I, we'll go take care of him. We'll hitch up the trailer to Sarah's wagon and he'll be home when you get there."

"Thanks, Grandpa."

"Don't thank me. Just don't go pulling one of these crazy kind of stunts again."

"I promise," Korey said.

"You, too, Dad. That's the *last* time you enter Korey in a race."

"I hear ya, I hear ya," Jefferson agreed, his mouth a thin line. "Next time—"

"There won't be a next time."

"He can go with you," the doctor interrupted, looking at Jefferson. "If his mother will sign the admitting form and the release forms."

"Gladly," Ainsley breathed.

Within half an hour, Sarah, Korey and Jefferson were gone, and Ainsley was left alone to pace the halls and wait for Trent.

When she finally saw him, her heart did a crazy little flutter. His head was bandaged and his skin had paled, but his eyes glinted at the sight of her.

"How do you feel?"

"Probably about as good as I look," he muttered, wincing.

"You look wonderful!"

"Then I feel lots worse." He forced a smile as Dr. Holmes read the X-rays.

"Well, Mr. McCullough, you were lucky. One cracked rib, a sprained ankle, a twisted shoulder and a slight concussion. Not too bad."

Ainsley's knees buckled.

"Then you're gonna let me out of here?" Trent asked.

The young doctor shook his head. "Not for a while. I want you to stay at least overnight. I'll look you over in the morning. *Maybe* you can go home then."

"I'll stay with you," Ainsley said.

"But Korey—"

"Is fine. More than anything I think his pride was

bruised, but he needed that. He even said he was glad I was marrying you."

"He must be delirious."

"No," she whispered, squeezing his hand. "That's me. Deliriously happy that you're going to be okay."

"GREAT DAY FOR a weddin' outside," Jefferson grumbled sarcastically, glancing out the window as he straightened his tie. Thunderclouds were turning the sky a pewter color, clashing overhead and promising rain.

"A perfect day, if you ask me. Now, you get onto the back porch and give that daughter of yours away," Sarah said, putting her hat onto her head. Ainsley smiled at the older woman's bossy tone.

"That, I'll gladly do."

The guests had all gathered in the side yard and the preacher, his collar stiff and tight, was in position under the rose arbor. Trent stood beside him. He'd been released from the hospital several days earlier. His head bandage had been removed, and he had trouble smothering a smile as Jefferson helped Ainsley to the arbor.

Ainsley's heart was in her throat as she joined hands with Trent and repeated her vows. She'd never felt happier in her whole life.

"I now pronounce you man and wife," the preacher said finally, and Ainsley's eyes glistened with tears.

Jefferson uncorked the champagne and friends and neighbors congratulated them.

As the afternoon slowly slid into evening, some of the guests began to leave. As the first few drops of rain started to fall, most of the remaining guests went into the house.

"We'd better go inside," Ainsley whispered, feeling the thick drops catching in her hair.

"Why?" Trent's gray eyes looked deep into hers.

"The guests—"

"The guests will keep," he said, his voice low. "We've got something more important to do."

"Oh?" She smiled impishly. "What's that?"

"I'll show you." Taking her hand in his, he led her to the stables where Trent's big bay gelding was already saddled.

"What's going on? Trent?"

He loosened his tie and swung into the saddle. "Come on. You can sit right here." He made a spot for her in front of him.

"You've got to be kidding. You're still recuperating."

"No better way," he said.

"I don't get it. And my dress—"

"Will be fine." Bending down and groaning a little from the effort, he helped her as she swung one leg over the saddle horn to ride sidesaddle.

"This is crazy—"

"Maybe."

He placed his arms around her, held her tight to him and slapped the reins. The bay took off at a soft lope, and Ainsley had to cling to his neck to stay in the saddle.

"Trent McCullough, you're out of your mind."

The rain had begun to pour from the heavens, but he didn't care.

"Where are we going?" she asked, blinking as heavy drops caught in her lashes and dampened her hair.

"You'll see."

The horse galloped through one field, then the next, and Ainsley finally understood. Trent stopped the gelding at the bend in Wolverine Creek, where the silvery waters washed under the fence, where, long ago, he'd pledged his love to her.

"I think we have some unfinished business here," he whispered, sliding to the ground and helping her out of the saddle. Her creamy gown was wet and clinging, but she didn't care. She wound her arms around his neck and felt the zipper slide down her back.

"Now, Mrs. McCullough, let's take up where we left off—" And then his lips claimed hers and he tasted the sweet summer rain on her skin.

"I can't wait."

"We have the rest of our lives," he said, deep in his throat, "and we're going to make every minute count."

"Promise?"

"Promise." Then he lowered her to the ground, sealing their love forever.

* * * * *

HURRICANE FORCE

PROLOGUE

A KEENING WIND whistled and shrieked across the roiling waters of Puget Sound, whipping Cord Donahue's dark hair in front of his eyes and sending sea spray across his face. Rain poured from the heavens, running down his neck as he worked to load the boat. Never once did he look up at the midnight sky.

The small craft rocked precariously against its moorings. Cord didn't care.

Deep inside he burned with betrayal—Alison's betrayal.

Eyes squinted against the darkness, he balanced on the slippery deck and packed the last crate tight into the small hold. His shoulders were tense, his jean jacket stretched taut as his mind spun in murky circles to a future that seemed empty and void. A future without Alison.

Yanking hard, he untied the rope and the boat was set free. His jaw thrust forward as vivid images of Alison and how she'd deceived him danced before his eyes. Jealousy coiled around his heart as he gripped the wheel. Glancing down at the tightly packed boxes, he swore. The damned crates represented his whole life. He hiked the collar of his jacket around his neck, then glanced to the menacing sky. A few clouds scudded across a full moon and the black waters of Puget Sound were punctuated by sharp-peaked whitecaps.

"Perfect," he muttered under his breath as he started the engine. The old Evinrude sputtered and caught with a roar.

"Hey, buddy!" a man on the dock yelled above the noise of the engine and the howl of the wind. "You, there! You can't go out. There's a storm brewing."

But Cord didn't pay any attention. He narrowed his gaze on the inky water, slammed the boat into gear and took off. From the corner of his eye he saw a woman in a white dress running along the dock and his gut wrenched. Her black hair was streaming behind her in lustrous, night-darkened waves, and her arms were waving frantically over her head.

Alison! Bitter betrayal sliced deep into his heart. What the hell was she doing out here? Jerking recklessly on the wheel, he turned the boat in the water, sending foamy spray over the docks as he headed out to sea.

"Cord!" he thought he heard her scream, but it could have been the shriek of the wind and he didn't bother turning around. He'd heard the last of her lies. "Cord! Wait—"

The small craft skimmed along the choppy surface of the water, the bottom of the boat hitting each swell with a thud as he left the winking lights of Seattle behind. Freedom— at last! Back teeth clamped together, his hair blowing away from his face, he could think of nothing but escape.

He steered crazily, ignoring the warning buoys, his mind screaming at him to turn around, face her, confront her with the truth! Then his thoughts turned dangerous and he imagined being with her again, her luminous hazel eyes, her pouting lips, the silky texture of her skin...

Crack! The boat jarred from bow to stern. Wood splintered with a sickening ripping sound.

Cord's fingers clenched around the wheel.

He hadn't seen the rock until it was too late. Now his eyes focused on the looming shadow to the starboard side of the craft and he wrenched on the wheel, nearly twisting his arm out of its socket.

The boat spun and the stern crashed against hard rock, scraping loudly. Shuddering, hull tearing apart, the vessel reeled out of control.

Searing pain shot through Cord's shoulder and he fell to his knees, striking his head on the wheel. It spun crazily as if the devil himself were at the helm.

Blackness surrounded him and frigid water spilled over the rail and through the deck, tearing the wood and dragging him down. He heard the engine sputter and die. Fumbling with one hand he searched in the darkness for the hold that contained the life jackets.

Numb fingers found nothing. His mouth, nose and eyes were filled with saltwater, and he tried frantically to stay afloat. A jagged piece of wood struck his head and pain seared through his brain. He groped for something, *anything,* to keep him above the surface. Choking and coughing, he couldn't get enough air. His lungs ached, threatening to explode. Everything was black and cold. He couldn't distinguish up from down.

Oh, God, help me!

His fingers scraped across rough planks as he scrabbled for a handhold, flaying in the water, swimming in circles, gulping saltwater. His hand bumped against the rough edge of a broken board and he held on until, nearly frozen, he could cling no longer.

"Alison!" he cried desperately as his fingers slipped. "Alison—" Gasping for a final breath, he called her name as one last black wave crested over him and he was dragged down.

CHAPTER ONE

"CORD DONAHUE'S ALIVE!" Celia Davis announced breathlessly as she shouldered her way into the office, the door banging against the wall behind her.

The words rang through the old building and tore at Alison's soul—a cruel joke. She looked up sharply, her eyes wide as Celia shook the rain from her golden blond hair, took off her coat and slung it over the curved arm of the brass hall tree near the door.

"Didn't you hear me?" she asked, serious.

"Y-yes," Alison managed to whisper, unable to move, her heart hammering wildly in her chest. *Cord alive? Impossible!* But a little part of her wanted desperately to believe it.

Celia walked across the room and slapped a copy of the afternoon edition of the *Seattle Chronicle* onto Alison's cluttered desk. "Right here—page one!" She pointed to a photograph and article. A grainy black-and-white picture of a bearded man stared upward and Alison recognized the familiar features. But it couldn't be true! Not after four years.

She studied the man in the picture. Though his dark hair was longer than Cord's had been and the firm line of his jaw was hidden by his beard, the man in the photo was either Cord Donahue or his double.

But Cord is dead, her mind protested, the horrid thought bringing tears to her eyes. Dashing them quickly away, she stared at the newspaper and the bearded man claiming Cord's identity. He was dressed in old jeans and a flannel shirt and his face was set in a hard scowl. Dark eyes glowered from beneath thick brows, and a hawkish nose was prominent above his silver-streaked beard.

Shivering, Alison skimmed the article and tried to calm down. But her face had drained of color, her heart was beating out of control and she had trouble breathing. Her throat burned against a new onslaught of tears, but she wouldn't let herself believe this wonderful but crazy tale.

"Hey," Celia whispered, eyeing her. "You okay?"

"I don't know," Alison admitted, still staring at the photograph. Though a part of her wanted to believe every printed word so that she could rush right out and find him, tell him she had never stopped loving him, force him to explain why he'd left her...she couldn't. This story was too fantastic and the more rational side of her mind took over. Whether this man was actually Cord or some impostor, he could tear her world apart.

Swallowing hard, she picked up the newspaper, her gaze fixed on the picture of the bearded man.

She tried vainly to get a grip on herself. Maybe there had been some mistake; maybe this man was just a dead ringer for Cord! If by some miracle Cord had escaped with his life, why, after four years of silence, would he return? Surely he knew he would be prosecuted by the insurance company, sent to jail for embezzling and running from justice.

Therefore, she reasoned, no man in his right mind would want to impersonate Cord Donahue.

The man's dark eyes seemed to mock her.

Her heart did a stupid little flip. "I thought you'd be doing handsprings," Celia said with a perplexed smile. Though she was the secretary for Donahue Investments, she was also Alison's best friend.

"Handsprings?"

"Yes, or at the very least be dancing in the streets! Cord Donahue is alive! He has been for the last four years, ever since he was supposed to have drowned in the sound!"

Alison trembled at the memory of that terrible night, but Celia didn't seem to notice.

"It's incredible that nobody knew about it! He's been in some small Alaskan fishing village doing God only knows what." Shaking her head, Celia rested her hip on a corner of Alison's desk and pointed an index finger at the story. "This might just be the greatest hoax ever pulled on the citizens of Seattle!"

"Maybe he's an impostor," Alison said, still afraid to let herself believe the article. For so long she'd prayed Cord would be found alive. But as the weeks had passed, she'd given up any hope that she'd ever see him again.

"Are you kidding? Look at him, for crying out loud!"

"But it could be a hoax—someone who looks just like him."

"But why?" Celia turned her palms to the ceiling. "For this place? No way. Everyone knows that the Donahue fortune is past history. No one would go to the trouble of impersonating Cord for this." She gestured to the bare walls and sparse furniture. A few leafy plants, two austere desks, several pastel watercolors and a couple of worn leather chairs were all that remained in the once-plush office. At one time, before the scandal, Donahue Investments had taken up the entire first and second floors of the building. "Besides, if this man were intent on stepping into Cord's shoes," Celia went on, "he'd have some serious explaining to do, especially to the police and the insurance company who bailed us out. *No one,* that is no one who isn't certifiably crazy, would want to be Cord Donahue."

"I can't argue with that," Alison admitted.

"Don't. Just read." Celia tapped on the newspaper. "It's all here in black and white."

Dear God, was it really possible? Was Cord alive?

Stomach churning nervously, Alison ran her fingers through her long black hair as she read the two-column article. She had hoped the scandal of the past was finally behind her. Now it was right smack in the middle of the *Seattle Chronicle!* But all the pain was worth it, if Cord were really returning to Seattle. Lifting her eyes to meet Celia's, she forced a weak smile and managed to hide the storm of emotions that was tearing her apart. "It's just so hard to believe."

"That's the understatement of the year. And I thought you'd be thrilled. Finally your mysterious brother-in-law, a man whom everyone thought had stolen the family fortune and subsequently drowned in a boating accident, shows up with hardly a scratch and—read this…uh, right here." She flipped through the pages and pointed to a paragraph on the fourth page, a related story dredging up all the old scandal again. "Here it is. This article says he's going to be in Seattle today."

Not today! There was too much to do! Panicked, Alison tried to hide the fact that her hands were shaking. She thought about her daughter, Mandy, and a new fear swept over her. What if he found out about Mandy—or already knew?

"I'm surprised he hasn't called you."

Alison's hazel eyes clouded. "We weren't very good friends," she lied, her throat dry as she remembered the last time she'd seen Cord—that very night when he'd roared away from the dock in the boat. She'd watched until he'd disappeared into the night, only to learn the next day about the accident that had taken his life.

Her fingers clenched around a pencil and the office seemed suddenly small and confining. "Do you think you could close up today?"

"No problem," Celia said. "Not much going on here anyway." She hopped off the desk and settled into her own chair. "I wonder why he didn't come back sooner? Or why he left in the first place," she mused, tossing back her short blond curls and looking through the window to the rain-drenched streets of Seattle below.

"Maybe he was hiding out," Alison suggested, straightening her desk.

"Doesn't seem the type."

"You knew him?" Alison asked, looking up.

"No, but I've heard the rumors. You know, the black sheep of the Donahue family. Wasn't he always in trouble as a kid?"

"I didn't know him then."

"What I heard is that he was always walking a thin line with the law."

"Is that so?" Alison said, biting back a hot defense of a man she'd sworn to hate. Why did she feel the need to protect his name when he'd let her think he'd been dead for four long years?

"They say he was the sole reason Donahue Invest-ments came apart at the seams."

Lifting a shoulder, Alison reached for her coat and

tried to appear as calm as possible. "I don't think it was *all* his fault," Alison said, though the evidence had been damning. Cord's initials had been on every falsified trade, and then he'd taken off with the money. But why? Why had he stolen from the company and thrown away their chance of happiness? She'd promised herself long ago that if she ever faced him again, she'd demand answers. Winding her hair into a rope and tucking it under a hat, she cocked her head toward the newspaper. "Do you mind if I take that with me?"

"Be my guest. I've already read it."

"Thanks." She folded the paper into her briefcase and snapped the case closed. Then slipping into her coat, she tried vainly to steady her nerves. One way or another she was going to face Cord, or a man who wanted to impersonate him very badly. She clutched her umbrella in one hand and opened the door with the other. "I'll be back in the office Monday," she called over her shoulder.

"You mean D-day, don't you? Remember, that's when the bank threatened to foreclose."

"How could I forget?" Alison murmured, her lips twisting at the irony. Ever since Celia had mentioned Cord's name, Alison hadn't been able to concentrate on anything but the fact that he might, miraculously, be alive. The door slammed shut behind her.

Walking briskly down the hall, Alison headed straight for the staircase. A rising sense of panic made her hurry down the stairs, her boot heels echoing on the old wooden steps. With her heart in her throat she pushed her way out of the brick building on Pioneer Square and turned north, ignoring the rain that fell from a cloud-darkened sky and splashed upon the steep sidewalk.

Ducking her head, she half ran, passing other pedes

trians in her dash to the parking lot across the street. Her fingers were shaking as she unlocked the car door and slid behind the wheel.

"Calm down, Ali," she told herself, glancing at her worried hazel eyes in the rearview mirror. "Just because he might be back doesn't mean he's going to bother you." *Right, and geese don't fly south for the winter,* she thought grimly.

The problem was that part of her—that stupid little feminine part that had never stopped loving him and had never really believed he was dead—wanted desperately to see him again. "Don't get any crazy ideas," she told herself as she started the old Mustang and maneuvered the car onto the hilly side street leading to the freeway.

Traffic seemed to crawl. Glancing again in the rearview mirror, she could see the steel-gray reflection of Puget Sound, the huge arm of the Pacific Ocean where she'd thought Cord had lost his life three years before.

Shivering, she threaded the old car through the rush-hour clog. Her hands were clenched around the wheel, her teeth sinking into her lower lip. The radio played pop tunes, the windshield wipers slapping time, but she could think of nothing but getting home to Mandy before Cord—if it were really he—arrived.

She drove as quickly as traffic allowed, her wipers fighting the rain as the Mustang climbed to the crest of a steep hill and passed through the wrought-iron gates of the Donahue estate.

After parking in front of the garage, Alison climbed out of her car and looked at the grand old house she'd called home for the past three years. The old Tudor manor stood dark and forlorn. Rising three full stories, with high-pitched gables and large windows, the house was far from the road, hidden in a thick cluster of fir and maple trees. Some of the attic windowpanes had been broken and had been boarded shut, and a few bricks in the foundation had chipped away, leaving unsightly gaps that Alison had tried to fill with stones just this past summer. Once proud and elegant, the immense house was now sorely neglected.

Alison refused to glance at the Realtor's sign in the front yard, and she didn't notice the untrimmed hedge or the weeds poking through the chipped mortar of the flagstone path. Her thoughts were far ahead to her inevitable meeting. She looked forward to the confrontation with a mixture of anticipation and dread. It was her most cherished fantasy—and her darkest nightmare. Maybe she could find a way of avoiding him....

"Impossible," she decided, her pulse racing at the thought.

Starting toward the front door, she startled a cat who had been hiding in the laurel hedge. Birds squawked and rustled through the branches of the trees overhead, sending down a fresh shower of thick drops. "Lazarus, you should be ashamed of yourself!" she scolded the old gray tabby, but smiled as she bent to stroke his head. He arched and purred, his prey forgotten for the moment. "If you come around back, I'll feed you," she promised, straightening again before walking up the uneven stone path to the front door. She dodged under the low-hanging fir boughs, not pausing to appreciate the pink-blossomed rhododendrons flanking the porch as she searched in her purse for her key.

"Norma?" she called, unlocking the dead bolt and swinging the door open. Her steps echoed on the tile of the foyer. "Mandy? Mommy's home!" As she stared up the curved wooden staircase, she listened for the sound of excited footsteps but heard nothing.

Taking off her hat and shaking her long hair loose, she hung her coat in the closet and walked to the kitchen, listening for any signs of life in the old house. She heard nothing but the ticking of the study clock and the soft purr of the furnace. Obviously Norma had taken Mandy out for the afternoon.

With a sigh, Alison snapped on the kitchen lights and found a piece of paper taped to the refrigerator door. The quickly scribbled note was filled with excitement and explained that Norma had taken Mandy shopping for groceries for a special dinner to celebrate Cord's return.

"Great," Alison murmured, her heart sinking, "just great." She wiped some raindrops from her forehead and glanced at the table. The afternoon paper was spread open on the maple surface. The article about Cord had been circled in red ink, and Cord's fierce eyes seemed to glare up at her from the picture. "Damn you," she muttered. *Four years. And not one word.*

Lazarus meowed loudly from the back porch. "I'm coming, I'm coming," Alison called, letting the wet animal inside and pouring a saucer of milk for him. "Looks like it's just you and me," she quipped. "How about if I build us a fire?"

Lazarus, his nose deep in the saucer, didn't even look up. "Yeah, a lot you care," Alison whispered, smiling as she petted him fondly. "Well, I don't know about you, but I intend to make a cup of tea, build a fire and curl up on the couch until Mandy gets home."

Shivering, she placed a cup of water in the microwave, left the cat contentedly lapping and walked back down the hall toward the den.

The heavy cherrywood doors were open, but the curtains were drawn and the room was dark except for a few smoldering coals still glowing red from a fire banked the night before. She started into the cozy room, but stopped dead in her tracks when she heard the sound of a boot scraping against the wood floor.

The hairs on the back of her neck prickled. Motionless, she stood in the archway, squinting into the darkened room.

Then she saw him. He sat in a leather wing chair in the corner, one jeans-clad leg draped over the arm, the other stretched out in front of him. The heel of one boot was propped insolently on a corner of an antique table, and his gaze, shadowed and dark, was trained on her face. Recognition and disdain flashed in his eyes.

Alison's heart stopped for a second. There could be no mistake—Cord Donahue was very much alive!

"Cord?" she whispered, her knees weak, a thousand emotions tearing at her soul. Her fingers searched blindly for the molding surrounding the doorway.

"Well," he drawled slowly, his voice as low and familiar as if she'd seen him just yesterday. "If it isn't the merry widow."

She had to lean against the smooth wood of the archway for support. "What are you doing here?" she demanded, her hands shaking as she crossed them under her breasts. Good Lord, it was still hard to believe he was alive! Her heart pounded at the sight of him, and she remembered all too clearly how much they'd shared and how their love had been based on lies. She met his gaze boldly, but inside she was melting as memory after painful memory washed over her. "How did you get in? And where the hell have you been?" she asked, hearing the tremor in her voice.

One side of his mouth lifted and his eyes glinted in amusement. "No 'Hi, Cord, how've you been'? No 'It's good to see you'? No 'I missed you—for a while. Until I married your brother'?" He reached into the front pocket of his jeans and extracted a key ring. Tossing it into the air, he watched in silent mockery as it clattered to the floor at her feet. "I still have the key. This was my house once. Remember?"

How could I forget? "That was a long time ago."

"Right," he said, nodding, his lips pulled firm over his teeth. "Before you married David."

Alison's jaw tightened but she refused to be baited. "For God's sake, Cord, we all thought you were dead! You let us think that for four years!" Anguish gave way to anger. How could he have left her—let her believe he'd died a horrible death in the icy waters of the sound? *How?*

He lifted a shoulder, then took a long swallow from his glass. "Your mistake."

"My—*what?*"

"One of many," he said, his boots falling to the floor as he stood and stretched before crossing the room to the bar. Lifting a bottle, he squinted to read the label. With an indifferent shrug he splashed some Scotch into his glass. "Can I get you anything?" he asked, his tone scathing.

Dumbfounded, she watched as he poured a second glass. "I don't want a drink," she replied. "I just want some answers."

He picked up both drinks. "Well, you probably need this whether you want it or not." Striding close enough to touch her, he handed her a glass. His fingers brushed hers and didn't linger, but his eyes, a near-black color, cut her to the quick. His mouth was drawn into a hard, cruel line. "You've had a helluva shock today."

"I...think I can handle it."

"I'll just bet you can."

He's enjoying this, she realized, sick at the thought.

He crossed to the fireplace, leaned his shoulders against the marble mantel and propped one boot heel against the red bricks as he glanced around the familiar room. "So, you're going to sell this place, huh?"

She didn't answer but instead took a drink of the Scotch. It burned her throat and almost came back up when it hit the bottom of her stomach. Swallowing hard, she watched him over the rim of her glass. What kind of a man had he become?

"The house too big for you? Or does it have too many memories?"

"I don't have a choice," she said slowly. "Back taxes."

"Oh, come on, Ali, you don't expect me to believe that you're in debt." He took a long draft and his eyes glittered. "You're wealthy now, and you don't have a husband telling you what to do. The perfect setup."

"Is that what you think?"

"That's the way it is," he said simply. "You played your cards right. Married a wealthy man who died young. You finally got what you wanted."

"If you only knew." Tired of the game-playing, she snapped on the nearest table lamp and sank into a leather chair. With an effort, she met his gaze squarely, though her insides were shredding. She took another slow sip of her drink and cocked her head to look up at him, feeling her hair tumble over one shoulder. "What do you want? Why did you come here?"

"Isn't it obvious?"

She didn't take her eyes off the rugged contours of his face. He'd aged in the past three years, the silver in his beard and hair evidence of a harder life than he'd ever known in Seattle. His skin was dark, almost swarthy, and his eyes, deep-set and bold, never left hers. Her heart pounded stupidly under his uncensored gaze. "Why did you let everyone think you were dead?"

"It solved a lot of problems," he said simply.

"Like facing the police?"

His teeth flashed in a hard smile. "That was one. I wasn't quite ready to admit to all of my crimes."

So it was true! He had stolen everything, just as David had guessed. Deep in her heart she'd never believed him capable of the crime. Until now. She ran a trembling hand over her brow. "It would have made it easier for all of us," she said quietly. "To know that you were alive. David died thinking you'd drowned."

"I don't think he really cared," Cord said, his muscles bunched tight under his shirt. "There wasn't a lot of love between us. You took care of that."

"For God's sake, Cord, you were brothers!"

"And obviously had the same interests," he remarked, his gaze slicing into hers. "But that's where it ended. He really didn't care if I was dead or alive. I'd always been a thorn in his side, and I'll wager he was glad to be rid of me!"

"No—"

"No?" He laughed hollowly. "Come on, Ali, you don't have to protect your dead husband. I know what he was like. He was my brother, remember? I grew up with him." His hands tightened around his old-fashioned glass, knuckles showing white. "It didn't take him long to stake out his claim on you, now, did it?"

"You left me," she said quietly. "You let me think you were dead. What was I supposed to do? Wait for a dead man to walk back into my life?" Setting her drink on a nearby table, Alison stood. "I don't know why you're here, Cord, or what you want, but I really don't care. I think you should go."

"Back to the grave? Or to hell?" he asked, his voice low as he picked up a Lucite cube with snapshots of Mandy, David and Alison. Then he tossed the plastic cube back onto the desk and advanced upon her, his quick strides closing the distance. "Because that's where I've been, Ali. To hell and back. But that's all behind me now. I'm not leaving. Not until I clear my name, get everything I should have gotten years ago and sit by to watch you lose it all!"

She didn't move but tilted her chin up proudly, her lips pursed, her eyes flashing defiantly. "So that's it. That's why you're here!"

His hands reached up to take hold of her shoulders, his fingers digging deep into her muscles. His brown eyes glinted with pinpoints of angry light. Every muscle in his body seemed rigid, tensed with some fierce hatred. "Do you understand me, Ali? I'm going to ruin you. And I'm going to enjoy every minute of it."

Alison was shaking inside, but she didn't show it. Instead she rose slowly, ignoring the pressure of his hands on her shoulders. "If you think you can come waltzing back into my life, right out of the grave, for God's sake, you've got another think coming! I don't know what you've got up your sleeve, Cord, but believe me, it won't work. You can threaten me all you want, but as far as I'm concerned, you gave up all your rights when you walked out of here!"

His eyes softened slightly. "You still have it all figured out, don't you?" As his fingers eased a bit, a hint of the old tenderness she remembered crept across his face.

"I try," she whispered, throat tight when his gaze dropped to her mouth. She half expected him to kiss her, and the tension in his face made her heart pound.

Then, groaning, he closed his eyes and suddenly released her, stepping back as if just the touch of her was repulsive. "Well, *Mrs.* Donahue, I'd say you've got a lot to learn. I'm back for everything I lost. *Everything!*" His eyes bored deep into hers and her pulse jumped crazily. "And I'm going to take my own sweet time...."

CHAPTER TWO

ALISON DIDN'T BUDGE. She met the menace in his eyes evenly. Though warring emotions raged deep in her breast, she wouldn't let him come into her home and make wild threats. Too much was at stake and she had Mandy to protect. "Get out," she whispered, pointing to the door.

"Can't do it."

"You don't have a choice. Either you leave on your own free will, or I'll call the police."

Cord had the audacity to laugh. The hollow sound bounced off the rafters and echoed in her heart, reminding her of a summer four years past, when, as a secretary for Donahue Investments, she'd been so hopelessly head over heels in love with him.

One side of his mouth lifted craftily. "You can cut the melodrama, Alison. You're no more going to call the police than fly to the moon!" Sipping his drink, he fell onto the couch and placed his booted feet on the coffee table. "No way."

"Don't push me."

Some of the hatred in his eyes disappeared. He gestured grandly to the phone. "Go ahead, call. But first let me tell you that I've already been grilled by the police, over and over again. And believe it or not, Detective Donnelly seems to believe my story. In fact, he let me out of the police station without even a warning to stick around. Guess he knows I won't leave—I've got too much to do."

She arched an inquisitive brow, stuffing her hands into the pockets of her wool skirt to hide the fact that they were shaking.

"Oh, don't worry, your secret is safe with me," he assured her. "At least for a while. Until I get the proof I need."

"Secret," she repeated. *What was he talking about? He couldn't possibly know....*

"Right."

"Proof of what?" Her heart was hammering, her entire world balancing precariously on a weighted scale.

"Proof that you lied, Alison. Proof that you lied to David just as you lied to me. Proof that all you ever wanted was the Donahue name to make you respectable. Proof that you would have done anything, *anything,* to get what you wanted."

"What I wanted," she echoed, her fingers curling into fists deep within her pockets. She frowned, genuine confusion mingling with anger at his insinuating tone. "And what was that?"

Snorting contemptuously, he dropped his feet and stood, then sauntered slowly across the hardwood floor. Once in front of her, he picked up her left hand so that her wedding band caught in the light. "A piece of paper, proving that you were a Donahue." His eyes became angry, glaring slits. "A marriage certificate, Alison. And you got one, didn't you? Even if you had to trap David into it!"

Her cheeks colored. "I didn't trap anyone!"

Waving off her excuses, he bit out, "Don't bother lying to me! Because it doesn't work anymore." He dropped her hand and strode to the bar, then splashed another drink into his glass. "David told me all about it, how you slept with him, knowing that you would get pregnant."

Alison dropped her glass. "He *what?*" Her skin turned white. What was he saying? Everything was wrong. He couldn't mean—couldn't think that she—"No!"

"No reason to lie about it now, is there?" he said, a scornful smirk twisting beneath his beard. "We have proof positive, now don't we?" Picking up the Lucite cube he tossed it to her and she caught it, the plastic cutting into her palm. Swallowing hard, she gazed down at the snapshot. Mandy was only six months old in the photo, laughing gaily, cheeks rosy, brown eyes bright as she rode high on David's broad shoulders. "The Donahue heir."

Oh God. "That's not the way it was," she rasped, shaking her head.

"No?" he said, his eyes glittering as if he didn't believe a word she said. "Then tell me, *Mrs.* Donahue, how was it?" He bent down, reached for a newspaper and saw his picture on the front page. Grimacing, he crumpled the pages and stuffed them into the fireplace before striking a match and tossing a couple of pieces of mossy oak onto the grate.

"David and I didn't—I wouldn't have—"

"You wouldn't have what?" he mocked, disbelieving. Looking over his shoulder, he said, "This, I gotta hear!"

Alison felt her temper snap. "Maybe if you'd stuck around you would understand."

"No doubt," he jeered, watching the flames catch and crackle. The firelight accentuated the grooves in his face. "But since I wasn't here—"

"Because you took off in the middle of a near hurricane!"

"Doesn't matter," he warned. "I'm here now. Go on,

Alison," he said, leaning against the fireplace. "Tell me how you managed to con my brother into marrying you when you found out you were pregnant with his child?"

"I didn't con David into anything," Alison said tensely. "He knew about the baby already."

"How?"

She swallowed with difficulty, her cheeks burning unexpectedly. "He found a report from the doctor."

"Found it?" Cord mocked.

"In my apartment."

"You just left it out in the open, on the table?" Cord's jaw clenched, a muscle jumping furiously, as if he already knew what she was about to say.

"Of course not. I didn't know he'd be there—"

"So where was it?"

She swallowed back the urge to scream at him. "On my nightstand."

His eyes filled with censure. "In your bedroom."

"Yes. But—"

"What was he doing there?"

"It wasn't like that," she said flatly.

"Okay, what was it like? Tell me. What was he doing there?" he repeated, his voice a little louder.

Alison had to think; her old memories of that wretched time were buried deep. "Looking for you, I suppose."

"In your bedroom? Come on, Alison, use your imagination. You can do better than that!"

"You don't believe me," she decided, her heart aching, her eyes snapping with defiance. How had they gotten so far from each other? Where they once had shared love and trust, now all that remained between them was hurt and lies and a child—a child he didn't know was his.

"Never mind," she whispered, suddenly feeling defeated. "It doesn't matter."

"Like hell it doesn't!"

The back door banged open and scurrying footsteps echoed along the hardwood hallways. "Mommy! Mom-my!" Mandy called, starting up the stairs.

Alison's eyes darted to Cord and his head snapped up, his gaze focused on the double doors that led to the foyer.

"In here, Mandy," Alison managed, her throat tight, tears hot behind her eyes.

The little girl, still wrapped in a gray wool coat and pink mittens, burst into the room. She was running pell-mell but stopped dead in her tracks when she saw Cord. Turning wide brown eyes up at him, she frowned, her face puckering.

Alison had trouble holding on to her poise as father and daughter sized each other up, neither recognizing the other. "Mandy," she said tautly, "this is your... Uncle... Cord." She scooped her daughter into her arms and kissed her flushed cheek. "Say 'hi.'"

Mandy shook her head. Dark curls poked from under her pink knit hat, framing her round face. "Don't got an uncle."

"Well, we didn't know," Alison said softly, "that, er, Cord was back. He's been gone a long time."

Mandy's face squinched and she looked up at the mantel over the fire. A picture of Cord and David taken ten years earlier hung on the bricks. "Cord's dead," she said, examining the portrait and then looking at the bearded man before her.

"I know but—"

"Dead's dead," the child stated matter-of-factly, eyeing her mother suspiciously. "That's what you said."

"Cord!" Norma walked into the room. She had been taking off her gloves but stopped, her smile faltering at the sight of him, her eyes bright with tears. "Dear God, it is you!" she choked out, running across the room to wrap her fleshy arms around him. "Praise the Lord," she whispered, hugging him fiercely, tears running from beneath her glasses. "Praise the Lord!"

Cord circled her thick waist with his arms. "You don't look a day older, Norma," he teased.

"Oh, go on with you." But she laughed a little, then wiped her tears from her eyes and became sober. "We all thought you were dead!"

"No such luck," he replied.

"Luck, my eye!" She squeezed him again. "Thank God you're alive," she said brokenly, sniffing back her tears. Alison knew Norma had raised Cord and his brother as if they'd been her own. "Here, now, let me take a look at you." Holding Cord at arm's length, Norma smiled and blinked. "What's this nonsense?" She touched his beard and frowned.

"Part of my new, rugged-man image."

"Well, I don't like it. Not one little bit!"

Cord laughed, and some of the tension drained from his face.

"You know," she said, once she'd managed to control her relief at seeing him again, "I should make you go out and cut a switch for this stunt you pulled on us. Why the devil didn't you let us know you were alive?"

His gaze darted to Alison. "I had my reasons."

"Sure you did. And all of them not worth a plugged nickel, unless I miss my bet," she admonished, though her eyes were still soft. "Whatever they are, they'd better be good, 'cause Alison and me, we spent the past four years grievin' and there you were up in Alaska havin' the time of your life! The least you could have done is written!"

"I suppose."

"You suppose right," she said indignantly, then smiled. "And don't you go tellin' me you had to run from the police, 'cause I don't believe it—not one little bit. You didn't steal any of that money from the company, and not you nor the insurance company nor the FBI nor God, His almighty self, will make me believe it!"

Cord chuckled deep in his throat. The sound was so warm that Alison nearly forgot how furious she was with him. "Am I forgiven?" he asked Norma, a boyish smile touching his lips.

"For lettin' me think you were dead? Not on your life!" But she laughed when he hugged her again. "I read that some fisherman found you, saved your life."

"George Clemens," Cord replied soberly. "I was just lucky he was out there. He saw my boat hit the rock, found me in the water and pulled me out just in time."

Alison felt as if her heart would drop to the floor, and Norma's lips moved in a silent prayer of gratitude.

"You could have come back then," Norma pointed out.

"I know."

"Well, go on with your story now," she prodded. "What happened then?"

"George lives in the San Juans on a very small island. He doesn't have electricity or a phone and he doesn't take a daily newspaper, so he didn't know who I was."

"And you didn't bother tellin' him."

"No. I also wouldn't go to a hospital."

"Oh, Lord." Norma sighed.

Alison watched, stricken. Cord had certainly tried to cover his tracks, and cover them he had.

"Anyway, I didn't want to go to the hospital for medical attention because I was afraid I'd be recognized and arrested because of the embezzlement."

"It would have been a whole lot better if you did. Lettin' us think you were dead—and a thief. If I wasn't so glad to see you, I'd—" Norma let out a long sigh "—I don't know what I'd do."

"And so why didn't you come home when you'd recovered?" Alison interjected, holding a confused Mandy tightly in her arms.

His gaze sliced into hers, accusing her of a thousand unknown crimes. "I decided I wanted to put my past behind me."

Norma shook her head. "Sounds like the talk of a guilty man, but go on with you."

"So, I paid George from some of the money he'd found on board the wreck, then asked him to boat me to Canada. In Vancouver I bought a beat-up old Chevy and drove to Alaska."

"Without a second thought," Alison murmured.

"With plenty," he said.

"I guess we should thank our lucky stars for that," Norma muttered.

"So, I started working, saving what I'd earned. With what I still had, I managed to put together enough cash to invest in a salmon cannery. It's done well and I bought out my partner. So, I've done all right."

"You're happy?" Norma asked, obviously skeptical.

"I was. Until I read about David."

Norma glanced at Alison and Mandy. "A pity, that," she whispered, crossing herself deftly, then forcing a smile. "Now, listen to me, you'd better get yourself cleaned up and shaved. We're gonna need all the help we can get with the bankers on Monday, and they'll want to see you clean-cut and businesslike."

Alison cringed and saw the storm gathering in Cord's eyes again.

"Bankers?" he repeated, his smile fading as he released the housekeeper. His gaze narrowed on Alison again. "What bankers?"

"Oh, I don't know their names," Norma prattled on. "The men from the Federal Commerce Bank."

"Rex Masterson," Alison supplied, meeting his gaze.

"Why?"

"They're considering foreclosing," she admitted.

He held up his hands, warding off any more information. "You're saying that the investment company is in debt?"

"Yes."

"But when I left—"

"Three years ago," Alison said swiftly. "A lot can happen in three years! A person could even die!"

Norma shook her head and glanced from Cord to Alison, then to Mandy. "Come on, let's not argue," she said. "What's done is done and we can sort it all out later. This is a night to celebrate! I'm goin' to whip up Cord's favorite meal and Mandy, here, is goin' to help me. Aren't you, darlin'?"

"Sure!" Mandy's eyes grew bright. "Can we bake cookies?"

"Better than that," Norma said, taking her small hand and guiding her through the door. "I'll teach you how to make a Dutch apple pie!" Before leaving, Norma looked over her shoulder. "You've probably guessed that the phone has been ringin' off the hook since the reports in the paper."

Cord sighed wearily. "I guess it would."

"Come on," Mandy urged.

"Just a minute, you run on ahead," Norma whispered to her, then turned to Cord again. "Mainly the calls have been from old friends and a few reporters."

"Great," Cord said with a sigh.

"And there were a few from some fella in Anchorage."

"Lamont?"

"That's it. I've got a list by the kitchen phone."

"I'll call them later."

Norma glanced at Alison and her lips pursed into a disapproving line. "And one call for you—Nate Benson."

Alison forced a tired smile. Nate was a personal friend, the hunting buddy who had been with David when he'd been killed. "Thanks."

Cord's jaw slid to the side. "Benson," he repeated, thinking back. "Why's he calling?"

"Probably because of you," she snapped, then heard the harsh sound of her tone. "Aren't they all?"

"Mostly," Norma agreed, eyeing them both before Mandy, impatient, dragged the housekeeper down the hall.

Norma's footsteps retreated, and Alison, feeling some of her hostility wear off, let out a weary sigh. "She's got a point, you know. We shouldn't fight. It doesn't accomplish anything."

"She should talk. Right now she'd like to tear me limb from limb."

"With good reason. She loves you, you know. And you let her think you were dead." Alison's lips quivered a little, but she held her ground.

"I didn't have much choice, did I?" Cord stalked to the bar, picked up the bottle of Scotch but hesitated, turning the bottle over in his hands. "Why the hell is Nate Benson calling you?"

"I told you I didn't know."

"He was David's friend."

"Yes, and he was there when the accident occurred. He rushed David to the hospital, but it was too late."

"I just don't understand it," Cord whispered. "David knew how to handle a rifle."

"Nate said that David was sure it wasn't loaded," Alison whispered, growing cold at the thought of the brutal accident that had taken David's life.

The color had drained from the tense features of Cord's face. "He saw what happened?"

Her stomach knotting painfully, she nodded.

Numb, Cord replaced the bottle and twisted on the cap. "And now he calls you."

"He's been a good friend, Cord, and I needed one," she admitted softly.

"Yeah, you probably did. Maybe Norma's right," he decided, his eyes growing distant and his shoulders relaxing as he gazed out the rain-spattered window. "Maybe we should try to get along, at least for now." He turned on his heel and faced her, his dark gaze centering on her mouth.

Alison's heart leaped unexpectedly.

"But I need answers, Alison, and I expect straight ones."

"So do I." Her gaze locked with his, and for a single moment she remembered what it was like to be with him, confide in him and hold him in her arms until dawn.

As if reading her thoughts, he snorted derisively, then strode purposefully out of the room, his footsteps ringing through the old house as he climbed the stairs. A few minutes later a door on the upper level banged shut.

"Wonderful," Alison muttered, frowning into her drink

and staring at the amber liquor. "Cord's back—with a vendetta!" Her fingers tightened around the glass as she heard Mandy's muted laughter coming from the kitchen. Alison's heart twisted with her deception. But she couldn't tell Cord about his daughter. Not yet. Not until some things were settled between them.

CORD STOOD NAKED to the waist and gazed at his reflection in the mirror. His eyes looked haggard and the lines around his mouth were deep. His beard was streaked with gray, though the hair on his head and swirling over his chest was still dark brown. His muscles were taut and firm, but he was tired. God, he was tired. He'd aged in the past few years, whereas time seemed to have stood still for Alison. Her skin was still unlined and creamy, her eyes a brilliant hazel shade, her smile easy and unjaded. She was as beautiful today as she had been when he'd last seen her on the pier, her black hair blowing wildly around her face, her dress white and clinging as she ran along the dock.

"Quit it!" he muttered, turning on the taps and letting steam fill the small bathroom, distorting his image. He'd thought he was over her. In Alaska he'd driven all thoughts of her from his mind. But now that he was back, all his old emotions stormed back to the surface. He wanted her—as much as he'd ever wanted her, if not more.

Disgusted with himself, he clipped off the longest part of his beard with scissors, then began scraping away the rest of the stubble on his chin. "You're a fool!" he chastised himself, swishing the razor through the hot water in the sink, then toweling off the remains of shaving cream and water from his face. "A goddamned fool."

Glancing at the lower corner of the mirror, he saw Mandy's impish face staring up at him. She was hanging on the doorjamb, peeking into the room.

"This is my daddy's room!" she announced.

Cord frowned. "Not anymore."

"Sure it is!"

"Well, now that I'm back, it's mine," Cord said, glancing around the private bath. "It was mine before I left and I'm reclaiming it. Besides, your daddy shared a room with your mom."

Mandy stuck out her lower lip and shook her head. "This was Daddy's room."

Cord's brows drew together. He'd grown up in the spacious bedroom with its private bath. David's room had been down the hall and his parents' on the other side of the landing. It bothered him a little to think that David had claimed this room along with everything else, including Alison, but he shook off his dreary thoughts. What could it possibly matter? David had been killed three months before, and the past was dead with him. He felt a stupid pang of remorse when he thought about his brother. There had been a time, years ago, when they had been close, their rivalry only the stupid cocksureness of teenagers. But later, after their father had died, when they'd both started working at the investment company, things had changed. The affable boyhood rivalry had turned dark and dangerous. Cord had been left with the bulk of the fortune and David had resented his older brother.

Cord had intended to make things right, to give David his fair share of the company as soon as David had proved himself capable of handling it. But, of course, that hadn't happened. There hadn't been enough time. And now

David was dead. Cord could still feel the loss of his brother, and a white-hot pain sliced through him.

He remembered his harsh words and wished he could call them back. A few hours before, he'd wanted to hurt Alison—to the point that he'd renounced his true feelings for his brother.

Hell, maybe it didn't matter what Alison thought.

All of the Donahue unhappiness could be blamed on Alison, a woman who had used both men for her own selfish whims.

So why was he still attracted to her? Why did he still yearn to trust her and tangle his fingers in her lustrous black hair?

"Because you're a fool, Donahue," he told his reflection. "A damned fool!"

"That's a bad word!" Mandy said, cutting into his cynical thoughts.

"What? Oh. Yeah, I guess it is."

"Mommy won't like it."

"Probably not," Cord said, not really caring what Mommy would or wouldn't like.

"What're you doing?" Mandy asked.

"Shaving." He slung the towel around his neck and tried to remind himself that this child was the sole reason he'd left Seattle three years before. This little girl was proof positive of Alison's infidelity.

She eyed his clean, square jaw and lifted her chin. "Looks better."

"You think so?"

Nodding fervently, she ducked out of the room only to poke her head back in again. With dancing brown eyes, rosy cheeks and black ringlets surrounding her face, Mandy Donahue was the most beguiling child he'd ever met. It was impossible not to be taken in by her impish smile and gleaming eyes.

"You're a scamp, you know that?"

She squinched her face up and squealed in delight when he bent down and pretended to reach for her.

"Mandy?" Alison called.

"You'd better skedaddle," Cord teased, but instead of running into the hall, Mandy did a nosedive under the bed, giggling to herself as the dust ruffle billowed and fell back into place.

"Mandy?" Alison repeated, her voice stronger. "Where are you?" She walked past the open door of Cord's room and glanced inside, her pulse jumping at the sight of him. Dressed only in a pair of blue jeans slung low on his hips, with a towel draped casually over his neck, he caught her eye, motioning silently for her to enter the room.

She hesitated, her heart thudding wildly when she noticed his clean-shaven jaw, the delighted twinkle in his eyes, the amused lift of one side of his mouth. Her gaze slid lower to the familiar, corded strength of his shoulder muscles, the swirling dark hair covering his chest and the lean, ribbed muscles of his abdomen. She didn't dare enter the room. Her fingers curled over the casing surrounding the door.

"I...I'm looking for Mandy," she said, mortified when she felt a blush creep up her neck.

"Haven't seen her," Cord replied, but his amused eyes darted to the skirt around the bed and Alison, following his gaze, noticed the toe of a sneaker being hastily withdrawn.

A smile curved her lips as she caught on to the game. "I guess I'll have to go look in my room then," she replied, warm inside at the first signs of tenderness she'd seen in Cord. Could this be the same man who had cut her to the bone just hours before?

"I guess so," he agreed, and a twitter of laughter came from under the bed.

"What was that?" Alison asked.

Coughing, Cord shook his head. "I didn't hear anything."

"No?"

"No."

This time the smothered giggle was too loud to pretend it didn't exist. "She is in here!" Alison said. "I wonder where?" Stretching out the game, she peered into the bathroom, opened the shower door and walked noisily to the closet. "She must be in here!"

"No, Mommy!" Mandy laughed and Alison bent down to lift the dust ruffle.

"So there you are! Come on out of there. Norma needs your help in the kitchen. It's almost time for dinner!"

Mandy reluctantly gave up her hiding space and crawled from beneath the four-poster. Her round face was smudged and dust had collected on her clothes.

"Oh, look at you!" Alison groaned, brushing the lint from Mandy's sweatshirt and corduroys. "You're a first-class mess!"

"It's okay," the little girl replied seriously, and Cord couldn't help but chuckle. Then Mandy pointed a finger at him. "He says this is *his* room, not Daddy's!"

Alison's good humor dissolved and her face went white. "Well, yes, he's right," she said quickly, nervously licking her lips. "Cord lived here, uh, before Mommy and Daddy were married." From the corner of her eye she saw Cord's muscles become rigid, felt his eyes boring into her.

"But then it was Daddy's room!" the child insisted.

"Yes, for a while," Alison admitted, scooping up the little girl and carrying her to the door. "Look, I think we'd better see what Norma wants, don't you?" She started down the hall, but heard Cord's footsteps behind her. She was halfway down the stairs, at the landing, when his voice arrested her.

"When you're done in the kitchen," he said slowly, leaning over the glossy wood rail, "I think we should talk."

"But there's dinner and then I have to give Mandy a bath and read to her and—" Hearing the babbling anxiety in her voice, she stopped short and glanced up, her gaze locking with his.

"Later," he insisted.

Alison could read the determination in his eyes, and seeing the way his fingers coiled tightly around the cherry-wood banister, she decided it wasn't worth the fight. "Later," she agreed, her voice soft. Then she dashed down the stairs, holding Mandy tightly to her chest as if afraid he might guess the dark-haired girl was really his child.

Soon she would have to tell him. But how? And maybe he'd given up all his rights when he'd run out on her without so much as an explanation three years before.

Her heart was pounding crazily. Sooner or later Cord would guess. And then all the gates of hell would surely open!

CHAPTER THREE

THE DINING ROOM hadn't been used for several years, but tonight it gleamed. Candles flickered, their small flames reflecting brightly on the recently polished mahogany table. Clear panes of a single bay window overlooked Lake Washington. The best crystal and china were on display and the silver, its patina glowing under the dim lights from the chandelier hanging high overhead, had been freshly polished.

"This looks like it was worth waiting for," Cord said as he assisted Norma with her chair. Dressed as Alison remembered him, in dark slacks, crisp white shirt and burgundy tie, his square jaw shaved clean, he was as handsome as ever. Alison's heart did a stupid little flip when his hand touched hers as he held out her chair.

"I helped!" Mandy declared. Balanced on a thick phone book, she giggled when Cord scooted her chair in to the table.

"*That's* why it smells so good," Cord decided, winking at Norma as he sat in the chair directly across from Alison.

"Next time I'll do it all by myself!"

Norma chuckled, but Alison wondered how she'd ever get through the meal with Cord, his eyes fixed on her lips, sitting across from her.

The mouthwatering scents of grilled salmon, herb-flavored rice and apple pie wafted enticingly through the rooms, but Alison couldn't eat a bite. Aware of Cord's eyes watching her every move, she pushed her food around her plate and had to concentrate to keep up with the conversation. She was positively unnerved and furious with herself for letting him get to her.

Only once in a while, when she reached for her water goblet, would she meet his insolent stare. At those times her pulse would leap expectantly—until she reminded herself that he'd left her, letting the world think he was dead.

Thankfully, Mandy was more animated than usual and kept up a steady stream of chatter. Alison's silence seemed to go unnoticed, and when Cord did catch her eye, she glanced away, afraid that all her emotions were painfully evident. She couldn't, wouldn't, let Cord know that a part of her still cared for him.

"Aren't you hungry, Mommy?" Mandy asked, eyeing her mother's plate.

"Not very," Alison admitted.

"Why not? Don't you like it?"

Alison forced a smile. "It's wonderful, you did a great job."

"Then finish it!" Mandy said impishly, her dark eyes dancing. "Or you won't get your pie."

Cord coughed loudly into his napkin, and Alison guessed he was hiding a smile. His brown eyes flickered with amusement.

"I'll remember that," Alison replied, wishing she could change the subject. "Now, you just worry about Mandy and I'll take care of myself."

Cord, lips still twitching, turned to Norma. "You really outdid yourself this time!"

Norma positively beamed. "And you, Cord Donahue, are still as full of it as you ever were."

"The best cook in King County," Cord pronounced as he took a sip of Chablis from his wineglass. "Maybe in the entire Pacific Northwest."

"Oh, go on," Norma said, waving aside his compliments but grinning just the same.

"I'm not kidding."

Laying it on a little thick, aren't you, Cord? Alison thought, wondering just what exactly was his game. Cord Donahue was a dilemma: hard-edged and breathing vengeance one minute, charming as ever the next. Would she ever understand him?

Pretending interest in her plate, she glimpsed him surreptitiously through a veil of dark lashes. His jaw was set and hard, the angular planes of his face chiseled and firm, but his mouth curved slightly upward and his eyes, dark and foreboding one second, sparkled with devilment the next.

"...Isn't that right, Alison?" he asked, grinning boyishly as he glanced back at her.

Startled from her thoughts, she looked up sharply. "What?"

"Haven't you heard a word I've said?" Mockery filled his gaze.

"I, er, was thinking."

"Obviously," he said dryly. "I was just saying that if the sun is out tomorrow, we should do something special."

"Special?" she echoed.

"A picnic at the carnival," Mandy decided, adding her own two cents' worth.

"There is no carnival."

"But we could go to the zoo or the aquarium, or just walk through the Pike Street Market and the piers," Cord suggested. "It's been a while for me, you know. I'd like to see the waterfront."

"Maybe we could go on a boat ride!" Mandy said eagerly.

Alison blanched. The thought of boating in the sound where she'd been convinced that Cord had lost his life was too much to bear. "I don't think—"

"Hell of an idea," Cord said, rubbing his jaw. "It's been a few years since I've been at the helm. I might be a little rusty, but—"

"That's enough!" Alison exclaimed, swallowing back the hot, angry words that had formed deep in her throat.

"I'll, er, get the coffee," Norma interjected, her worried eyes glancing from Cord to Alison and back again. "Come on, Mandy, you can help me with the pie." Hurriedly helping the child away from the table, Norma pushed through the swinging door to the kitchen.

"How dare you!" Alison hissed, standing and glaring at him as he casually sipped his wine. She was shaking so badly she had to brace herself by planting her palms on the edge of the table. "You might find that little stunt you pulled in the middle of the sound amusing, but I think it was despicable! Letting us think you were dead, for God's sake! If you only knew how much torment and anguish and fear we all felt—"

"Tell me about it," he suggested, his gaze searing into hers. "Just how long did it take you to march down the aisle with my brother? Three, maybe four weeks?"

She was suddenly speechless. What could she say? He'd already made up his mind about her. "I...I was nearly destroyed," she faltered.

"So destroyed that you married David the first chance you got," he finished.

"It wasn't like that."

Cord's patience snapped. His gaze narrowed onto her pouty lips, the flush on her cheeks, the pain in her eyes. "So tell me, *Mrs. Donahue,* what was it like? Didn't you have a big wedding? A honeymoon in Mexico? Didn't you live in this house, have David's child, inherit everything? Come on, Alison, don't hold back. Spit it out. Just what was so terrible?" he demanded, his voice rising.

"Losing you," she whispered, unable to stop the words.

The anger in his gaze wavered and his jaw, which had been thrust forward in righteous indignation, slackened. "You expect me to believe that?" he asked quietly.

"Yes."

"Here we are!" Norma announced, backing through the door and carrying a silver coffee service. "Coffee and pie."

"With cinnamon!" Mandy added brightly.

Alison was still staring at Cord, her shoulders square, her delicate chin lifted proudly. Without a word she sat down and tried to force a smile when she looked into Mandy's delighted face. "It looks positively yummy!" she said, winking at the little girl.

"It is!"

Norma passed the plates around and poured coffee, but Alison, though she tried, couldn't taste the cinnamon or apples for the life of her. She went through the chewing motions, managing pleasantries, feeling Cord's gaze boring into her, until dessert was finished. "Let me help you in the kitchen," she offered, picking up her plate, glad for the excuse to get away from Cord's excruciating stare.

"I wouldn't hear of it! Go on, take your coffee into the

den, have Cord stoke the fire and relax. I'll get this little girl to bed and handle the dishes. Then I've got to run."

"Really, I can manage—"

"Nonsense," Norma insisted, bustling around with the dishes. "I'll just stack these in the sink and then put Mandy into the tub. Now, go on. Scoot!" Norma made brushing motions with her hands, and Alison did as she was bid, listening to the sound of Cord's footsteps behind her and dreading the evening ahead.

She crossed the foyer, her heels clicking on the tile and felt Cord's arm brush against her shoulder as he reached for the door to the study and pushed it open. Without a word she entered, feeling the evening chill despite the fire still glowing in the grate. She heard the door click shut behind her and could see Cord from the corner of her eye. *How would she ever be able to tell him about Mandy?*

"I think I deserve a few straight answers," he said quietly, his voice low and rough.

Her patience finally snapped. "You deserve answers?" she repeated, facing him defiantly. "What about me?"

"What about you?"

"For crying in the night, Cord! You can't just waltz in here after pretending to be dead and expect no one to ask any questions!"

"The police have already made that point," he said, his voice bitter as he leaned one shoulder against the mantel. "By the way, they're going to want to reopen the files on the embezzling and that means they'll be down at the offices."

Just what she needed, she thought wearily, then turned back to the questions darting through her mind. "So where have you been? Why didn't you let anyone know you were alive?"

"It was better that way."

"For whom?"

"Everyone," he said tightly, his shoulders bunching uncomfortably. He tore off the tie he'd donned for dinner, letting it drape around his neck, and undid the top buttons of his shirt.

"Everyone," she repeated, shaking her head. Disbelief clouded her eyes. Silently she relived all those dark nights when she'd felt so alone and remembered the nightmares that had tormented her, the tears that had never seemed to go away. "Why?"

"Why do you think?"

"Because of the theft, right? You took off with all the investors' liquid assets and let us, David and me, deal with the consequences."

His eyes glittered dangerously. Did she really believe what she was saying? Had she told herself the same old lies for so many years that she really didn't know the truth any longer? Or was she, true to her nature, saving her own beautiful neck? Her lustrous black hair was twisted into a loose knot at the base of her skull. It glistened in the fire glow, shimmering from blue to ebony. Her dress, made of some dark green fabric, awakened the emerald sparkle in her hazel eyes. He glanced away from the proud lift of her chin and the creamy texture of her throat, vowing to himself that he would never let himself fall for her again. "What would you have done if I'd stayed?" he asked.

"I…I don't know," she admitted, watching him pour himself a drink. Was it her imagination or did his hands tremble a little? "I've thought about it often, how things would have been different." Wrapping her arms around her waist for warmth, she sat on the ledge of the bay window and watched the raindrops, shining gold in the fire's reflection, drizzle down the cool glass. Outside, the wind was blowing hard, forcing the branches of the nearby firs into a ghostly dance. The night was pitch-black; clouds covered the moon and stars. Thinking back to that other night, four years past, she shivered. She saw again, in her mind's poignant eye, the frigid black waves of Puget Sound and a small boat, Cord standing rigidly at her helm, rocking dangerously on the open sea.

"And?" he prodded, tossing a couple of chunks of pitchy fir into the fireplace. The fire crackled and hissed.

"And I've never come up with any answers."

"But you think things would have been better?"

"Oh, yes!" Conviction rang in her words. "We could have faced anything—together."

"So what about now?" Rubbing his jaw, he didn't move away from the fireplace.

"Now it's too late. You took off with the money, David is dead and the investment company is about to go broke."

"End of story," he said, his words clipped.

"Not quite. You're back. Why?"

Swirling his drink, he looked into the glass and scowled, his dark brows drawing together to form a single line of concentration. "I just found out about David's death two weeks ago. News doesn't travel too fast."

"Especially when you're supposed to have drowned."

Ignoring her remark, he said, "It took a couple of weeks to wind things up in Alaska."

"And that's done now?"

"Just about." Taking a long draft from his glass, he raised his eyes to hers. "But I couldn't wait."

She looked for something in his gaze, just the hint of tenderness and longing, but saw only scorn. His lips were white and pinched, his gaze condemning. "Why?"

"Because I wanted to see you, and your daughter. Find out what had happened to you while I took all the heat and left."

"Took all the heat?" she repeated. "What're you talking about?"

Cord squinted across the room, pinning her with his eyes. Alison, better than anyone, knew what had happened. *Who was she trying to kid?* "When I left here, I took some things—"

"The family fortune and some of the investors' capital."

"No."

Though she knew he was lying, she saw the sincerity etched in his expression, as if he really believed what he was telling her. "But the wreckage—things washed up."

He finished his drink and sighed, leaning back on the couch. *How long could she keep up this ridiculous charade?* "Only those things that were mine to begin with. The things I'd purchased or were given me. You remember, a Picasso, the coin collection, some of the bearer bonds."

She felt a cold prickle of doubt settle deep in her stomach. "But the rest—the cash in the general accounts? All of the bearer bonds?"

"Was already gone."

"I don't understand," she murmured, her voice the barest of whispers, her heart pounding a sharp double time. Sweat began to collect on her palms. *What was he insinuating?*

"Sure you do, Ali."

At the familiar sound of her name, so soft it was almost a caress, she felt her throat burn with tears for what might have been. If only he hadn't boarded that damned boat!

"Think," he commanded, leaning forward, pinning her with his eyes. "Think real hard."

"I don't know what you're suggesting."

"Sure you do. You know what happened to everything, don't you?"

"You took it."

"No!" His voice boomed, echoing off the rafters. His eyes glittered impatiently.

"Then I couldn't guess," she admitted, dazed as she realized what he was suggesting.

"You took it, Ali. I knew it back then, just as I knew about your affair with David."

She felt as if she'd been slapped. "But I didn't—"

"You're going to deny the affair as well as your scam of ripping off everything you could get your hands on? I should never have given you so much power."

Stunned, she heard the accusation in his voice and couldn't believe it. "Ripping off? What're you talking about? You don't honestly think that I—" The censure in his stance convinced her. "Oh, God, no! I was your assistant. I couldn't have possibly taken anything, even if I'd wanted to. You took the money!"

"I took only what was mine." He set his glass on the mantel, then he advanced across the room to stand so close she could feel the warmth of his breath fanning her face. He placed a hand on either side of her on the windowsill, locking her against the cold panes. He appeared more cruel and determined than she'd ever seen him. "Save your excuses and your lies for someone who believes them."

He thought she'd been the thief and had an affair with David? That was crazy! How could he have twisted everything around so? Her head was reeling, her heart was thudding so loudly he had to hear it. "But—"

"But, nothing." His gaze delved deep into hers and then moved lazily downward, past the flush of her cheeks to center on her lips, parted in protest. "I took the blame, Alison, because I didn't want you sent to prison and put behind bars while you were carrying David's child."

"I didn't take anything," she said hoarsely, her eyes round with honesty. "And I didn't—"

"Damn it, Alison, don't lie!"

Reaching up, she placed her hand over his chest, feeling his warm, hard muscles beneath the smooth texture of his shirt. Her fingers curled tight, wrinkling the fabric, and she met his gaze bravely. "You have to believe me, Cord. I've never been a thief and I never will be. I swear to God that I didn't take one dime of the fortune."

"Can you prove it?" he asked, his voice thick.

"I…I think the law reads, innocent until proven guilty."

"It didn't work that way for me, now, did it?"

"Because you ran." Swallowing hard, she glanced at the slant of his mouth, the thin line of his lips.

"I left to protect you, damn it!" he said, fighting an inner struggle between sanity and desire. Every nerve-ending in his body was reacting, screaming to touch her again.

"But you said—"

"I said that I took what was mine. That's all." Leaning closer still, he could feel the soft pressure of her breasts against his chest. The emerald silk of her dress rustled quietly as she moved her hand away.

"Cord, please," she whispered, "I don't think this is such a good idea—" But when his lips brushed against hers, she moaned softly, and when he pulled the pins from her hair, she didn't resist, feeling the long, heavy waves of her hair fall past her shoulders, as his lips captured hers, claiming her all over again.

"I've never stopped wanting you," he admitted, drugged by the nearness of her body. "I've hated you, sworn to get revenge and even wished that I had drowned on the boat so I wouldn't think of you with David. But I never stopped wanting you." His hands were splayed against her back, moving the fabric against her skin, rekindling old fires she had hoped were dead.

Parting her lips still farther, she kissed him back, though a tiny voice inside her head told her she was making another treacherous mistake. *He's using you,* it screamed, but she closed her ears. Torn between loving him and losing him all over again, she had no will. "Cord, please," she begged, hoping he would understand. But her words were more plea than protest.

Hating her weakness, she twined her fingers in his hair and wondered why she felt no satisfaction that, at long last, the only man she'd ever loved was back.

Because he'll hurt you and use you all over again, the nagging doubt shrieked. But she didn't listen.

Alison felt the power of Cord's body, sensed the urgency with which he held her and knew that if she didn't break off the wonder of this kiss she would be lost to him forever.

Her body quivered beneath the warmth of his hands, her heartbeat thudding erratically as his tongue rimmed her lips, gently tasting and exploring the inside of her mouth.

She groaned but tore her lips from his. If she surrendered to him now, he would never trust her again. All of his ill-fated suspicions—that she would give herself to any man to save her skin—would prove true.

"Cord, don't," she whispered, still clinging to him and drinking in his warm, special scent. How long had she dreamed of holding him just so? She saw the questions in his glazed eyes but disregarded them. Until she had time to think things through, she couldn't explain herself. "I…I have to check on Mandy," she said quickly, slipping away from his embrace and adjusting her clothes as she hurried out of the room.

"Ali," he called, his voice thick.

With every ounce of will she could muster, she threw open the study doors and started up the stairs, nearly colliding with Norma on the second step.

"I was just comin' down to tell you Mandy wants to say good-night," Norma said, her gray eyes sparkling.

Alison nodded, knowing that Norma had to see the high color of her cheeks, the wrinkles in her dress and the tangled mass of her hair. *Damn Cord Donahue and his seductive ways!* "I was just going up to see her," Alison said. "Thanks for everything."

"Don't mention it. You know, I helped raise Cord. The least I could do was cook for him." Her smile faded and she touched Alison's arm. "It's a miracle that he's back with us."

"I…I know."

"Things will be better, now that he's returned. Just you wait and see."

Alison wished she could share Norma's optimism. "I hope so."

"He'll give old Rex Masterson and that blasted bank what for!" She winked broadly. "Maybe, if he works it right, we won't have to sell this place."

Wishful thinking.

Smiling to herself, Norma continued down the stairs, found her coat in the front closet, then poked her head into the study to say good-night to Cord.

Alison didn't wait. She wasn't up to facing Cord

again—not just yet. Her heart was still drumming stupidly and her thoughts were a jumble of the past and present. Hurrying up the stairs, she heard Mandy's voice coming from her open door.

"And God bless Mommy and Uncle Cord, even if he is dead," Mandy said softly as Alison entered her room.

Alison couldn't help but smile. "I guess he's not dead," she said, tucking Mandy under her pink gingham coverlet.

"Why not?"

"Because he escaped, somehow," Alison whispered, bending over to kiss Mandy's dark ringlets. "Go to sleep now and we'll talk about it in the morning. In fact, you can have Cord tell you all about it."

Mandy snuggled under the covers and, holding tight to her favorite blanket, closed her eyes.

Cord has a lot of explaining to do, she thought, sighing to herself. *And so do I.* Snapping off the bedside lamp, Alison murmured, "Good night, sweetheart," then turned to find Cord lounging in the doorway. He stood, a dark figure watching her, one shoulder propped against the doorjamb, his head cocked to the side.

"You must have loved David very much," he finally said, pain shadowing his eyes, as she tried to step past him.

"I thought you said I just used him," she shot back, wanting to hurt him as much as he'd wounded her with his vicious accusations. "Remember? Like I used you— for this." She held up her hand and her wedding band gleamed traitorously in the light from the hall.

He reached forward quickly, grabbing hold of her wrist and dragging her down the corridor away from Mandy's open door. His eyes were dark slits and the skin of his face was stretched taut over sharp cheekbones and a jutted jaw. "I'm just trying to figure you out, Alison, and make some sense of this mess!" he finally conceded.

"Maybe you should have thought about that three years ago!"

"I tried."

"You *ran,*" she charged, shaking her head as he released her and she stumbled back against the wall. "That's what I couldn't understand—more than any-thing—is *why* you ran!" Her huge eyes drilled into his. "I had never seen you run from anything in your life, and you took off like a wounded rabbit."

"I had my reasons."

"Right," she said. "You were protecting me." Her teeth bit painfully into her lower lip. "If only I could believe you," she murmured, so softly he barely heard her.

"Believe." He was standing close to her again. His hands captured her upper arms, holding her against the wainscoting of the hallway, forcing her to stare into his clear brown eyes.

"Like you believe me?" she whispered, her throat swollen at the nearness of him.

"I'm trying."

"But it's hard, right? It's easier to think that, while I was having an affair with your brother behind your back, I was stealing from Donahue Investments and all our clients. But that wasn't enough for me—no, sir! When you took off, I just up and forgot all about you, turned right around and married David without once thinking about you giving up your life in Puget Sound."

He didn't move.

"Dear God, Cord, don't you see how ridiculous that sounds?"

He was still skeptical.

"Think about it, damn it! Remember everything we were to each other! Can't you trust me?"

He hesitated, balanced on the thin ledge between truth and lies, and then a quiet little cough from Mandy's room brought everything back into clear perspective. He glanced back to the open door, where David's daughter lay sleeping.

Alison felt him shrinking away from her, realized she'd lost. Again. She didn't have the heart to argue any longer because she knew in his mind she'd already been tried and convicted of a dozen crimes, including unfaithfulness. Swallowing against a thick lump in her throat, she stepped away from him and walked to her room. "This isn't getting us anywhere," she whispered. "I think maybe you should go now."

"Go?" he repeated, eyebrows cocked. "This is my house."

"But you can't stay here."

"Why not?"

"Because it wouldn't be right—" She stopped herself short. What did she or the rest of the world care, for that matter? This was a man who had turned his back on Seattle, let his clients and his lover think he'd stolen from his company and been killed, only to show up four years later. He obviously didn't give a damn what anyone else thought.

"Go on," he encouraged, mocking her again. Amusement touched the corners of his mouth.

"Never mind, you can stay in David's room."

"*David's* room," he repeated, shaking his head, light from the hall catching in his coffee-brown hair. "Why is it that you had separate bedrooms?"

Goaded, she reached her door and, throwing his own

words back at him, said, "Think about it, Cord. Think about it real hard."

"I will," he replied as she slammed the door behind her and leaned against the cool wooden panels. Why was it like this between them? she wondered, running a trembling hand over her forehead. Why couldn't they just start over again, ecstatic in the knowledge that they could be together at last?

She sank onto the edge of her bed, not knowing whether to laugh or cry. Cord was alive and back in Seattle, in this very house, only two doors down the hall. And yet she was as alone as she had been on that night when she'd last seen him on the docks of Elliott Bay in Puget Sound.

"Oh, Cord," she whispered, lying back on the pillows and kicking off her shoes. Though she stared up at the ceiling, her thoughts spun backward in time to that hot summer four years ago when she'd first met Cord Donahue....

CHAPTER FOUR

IT HAD ALL started so innocently the first day she'd met Cord. She'd spent the early morning dressing carefully and mentally preparing herself for a job interview at Donahue Investments. She'd been so anxious, she'd left her apartment much too early, then wasted time window-shopping and stopping for coffee and a muffin in a small coffee shop just off Pioneer Square.

Finally it had been time for the interview. Barely noticing the tall buildings of Seattle's skyline slicing into a vibrant blue sky, she'd made her way across a street heavy with traffic, then pushed open the door to the elegant old Victorian building.

She hadn't known her entire life was about to change as she'd walked across the cool tile floor.

Butterflies fluttered anxiously in her stomach. She wanted this job almost as desperately as she needed it, but she hoped her desperation didn't show.

Nervous as the proverbial cat, she twisted her fingers over the leather strap of her purse and saw her reflection in the glass of the elevator. Her black hair shone blue and was wound into a soft chignon at the back of her neck, her suit was claret-red, tailored and accented by a white silk blouse that tied at her throat. She was dressed conservatively, but she couldn't disguise the rosy flush of excitement on her cheeks or hide the sparkle in her eyes.

The elevator ground to a stop on the third floor. It was now or never. Her stomach was already in knots as she stepped into the executive offices of the investment firm. This was her second visit to Donahue Investment Company. Earlier this week she'd spoken with the personnel director. Now she was to be interviewed by the president himself.

Swallowing back any trace of her nervousness, she shouldered open a heavy door with a single brass plate engraved with Cord Donahue's name. Inside, the reception area was roomy, with floor-to-ceiling windows along one wall, several tufted-leather sofas surrounded by brass lamps, tall, broad-leafed plants, polished end tables and thick pearl-gray carpet.

Near the door to an inner office was a large wooden desk occupied by a receptionist with silver-blond hair, cool blue eyes and a confident grin. The girl, near twenty, whose nameplate read Louise Caldwell, glanced up from her word processor long enough to give Alison a smile.

"I'm Alison Banning," Alison said, forcing a smile to match the one offered her. "I'm here to see Mr. Donahue."

"Oh, Miss Banning, I've been trying to reach you all morning," Louise replied, obviously embarrassed. "Mr. Donahue's had a change of plans."

Alison's heart dropped.

"Then he's not in?"

"He's here, but—" she shrugged "—he's on his way out."

"We had an appointment," Alison reminded her, trying to control disappointment.

"I know, but—" Louise shrugged and sighed. "Maybe I can catch him."

"No, please wait—"

But Louise was already out of her chair and had knocked softly on a heavy wooden door. "Mr. Donahue?" she called, cracking the door.

"Please don't!" Alison pleaded, deciding she didn't want to give Cord Donahue the impression that she was brash and pushy. But Louise had already slipped into the room.

Alison had no alternative but to wait.

Louise appeared a few minutes later and held open the door. "He'll see you now," she said.

Thank God. Alison took in a bracing breath, expecting to meet a stiff, straitlaced, silver-haired executive with a bland face and a tailored three-piece suit.

Instead her gaze stopped on a young man, no more than thirty-two, slouched on a low-slung leather sofa. He was wearing faded jeans, an open-throated cotton work shirt and a suede jacket lined with sheepskin. His skin was tanned and his hair, coffee-colored and unruly, fell over his forehead in disarray. Deep furrows lined his brow as he studied some typewritten report, the pages of which were scattered over the couch. He was about as far from the executive type as anyone she'd ever met.

"Miss Banning to see you," the secretary said, rousing him from his dark reverie.

"What?" Glancing up sharply, he stared at Alison with deep-set brown eyes that sparked with intelligence and amusement.

"Miss Banning. About the administrative job?" Louise prodded, glancing nervously back to Alison. "I just spoke to you about her."

"Oh—right," he said, dark eyes flashing, a self-deprecating smile crossing his lips as the secretary left the room and closed the door behind her. "Sorry, I guess I got lost in this audit." He stood and offered his hand. "About the interview, you'll have to forgive me, Miss Banning. I had a change of plans and—oh, hell, the point is, I'm leaving here in—" he glanced at his watch "—twenty minutes for a meeting with an important client."

Alison was dumbfounded. Though she clasped his hand, feeling warm, firm fingers grip her palm, she couldn't help eyeing his unlikely jeans and work shirt.

"We're going fishing," he explained quickly, releasing her hand. "Don't ask me why—the client's idea." Then he chuckled to himself and shoved his hair out of his eyes as he hooked a leg over the corner of his desk. "No reason to pretend to be formal now, right?" Motioning to one of the side chairs, he said, "Have a seat. I'm sorry that I'm not ready for this. I tried to have Louise call you and reschedule but—" he shrugged, his big shoulders shifting beneath the soft rust-colored suede "—I guess she couldn't reach you."

"I was out." Fascinated by the mirth in his warm brown eyes, Alison asked, "Would you like me to come back later?" Though she wanted the administrative job so badly she could taste it, she was willing to wait another day or two. After four years of college, graduating at the top of her class with a degree in business administration, and three years' work experience in the management training program of First Puget Bank, she had the education and practical experience. If only she could have a chance to prove it to this man.

"No reason to," he decided, and she heard the dismissal in his voice.

He wasn't going to hire her. He'd already made up his

mind! "Look, Mr. Donahue, I want this job," she admitted, desperate for a chance to prove herself. His gaze sharpened and his thin lips tightened. "I…I'm willing to do whatever work you assign me, from getting your coffee to interpreting the quarterly reports, analyzing market trends to learning the business from the bottom to the top."

"Why?"

She lifted her chin defiantly. "Because I need a job and this is the best one I've found."

"I guess that's straightforward enough."

"I hope so."

His gaze never wavered but he thoughtfully rubbed his square jaw. Suddenly he rounded the desk, searched through a file drawer and withdrew a typed sheet, which she recognized as her résumé. He read the single sheet of paper with a concentration that made Alison feel as if her life had been laid bare.

She held her breath.

"Okay, Miss Banning, let's have this interview and make it quick." Changing before her very eyes, his face becoming stern and determined, he started firing questions at her.

"Why did you quit working at the bank?"

"I'd gone as far as I could go," she said, omitting the fact that the man in charge of her department, securities, had been pressuring her to go out with him. If it had been as simple as a date, she wouldn't have left, but Doug Feller had expected more and Alison had refused to compromise herself, even for the sake of a promotion. She was determined to make her way in the business world on her own qualifications, not by dating or sleeping with men in positions of authority.

"But you're willing to learn about this company from the ground up. Why?"

Forcing a wavering smile, she told him of her interest in investments, her need to grow, her desire to work in downtown Seattle for an investment company with a reputation such as Donahue Investments had.

"Any other reasons?"

She thought about telling him about Doug Feller's advances, but decided to hold her tongue. No reason to get off on the wrong foot. "Of course. The employee stock-option plan—it's the best available in the area."

He smiled then. "So you want to be part owner in Donahue Investments?"

"Yes." She didn't bat an eye, but instead held his gaze.

"You know, it takes ten years before you're fully vested and you're able to get your hands on the stock."

"I intend to be with the firm at least that long."

He let her résumé slide to the desk. "What about your family?"

"As I mentioned, both of my parents are dead."

"No, I'm talking about your husband."

"I don't have a husband."

"Yet," he finished for her, offering an understanding smile. "Look, Miss Banning, you're only twenty-five. Within the next ten years you'll likely marry and have children. Your interest in the company might wane."

"But maybe it won't," she said, her hazel eyes bright with conviction. "I promise you, Mr. Donahue—"

"Cord. Let's drop the formality." His entire face softened and she realized just how handsome and contradictory he was; hard-edged one minute, soft the next.

"All right…Cord. I promise you that I'll work twice as hard as any man you'd hire."

His eyebrows lifted skeptically. "The job as my assistant will be very demanding. Long, irregular hours and—" he grabbed the lapels of his jacket to emphasize his point "—days turned around because a client has a whim to go fishing or hunting or God only knows what else. This position might very well cut into your social life quite a bit."

What social life? For the past few years she'd spent most of her time studying and working. "I'll give it my best shot," she promised with a confident smile that only trembled at the corners. "If it doesn't work out, what have you got to lose? Just a few months."

"Just," he muttered, rubbing his jaw and staring at her with new interest. "I can be a real bear."

"So can I."

He laughed. "I'll just bet you can. All right, Alison, you're hired," he said, checking his watch again. "I'll see you tomorrow at eight."

She wanted to whoop out loud but she managed to contain herself as he shook her hand again. This time she felt the warmth of his touch, the power in his grip, and when her gaze touched his again, she saw more of him than before. Her heartbeat quickened unexpectedly as he escorted her out of his office.

She fairly flew down the hall and to the stairs, holding in her exuberance until she was down the two flights of stairs and on the sidewalk in front of the building.

Hallelujah! She'd done it! She'd actually landed the job she'd been wanting for nearly a month!

She felt as if she were walking on air and she wanted to savor the moment. So, instead of trudging uphill three blocks to her car, she hurried across the street and down the sharp hills to the docks to walk along the waterfront.

The sun was peeking through a few stalwart clouds and the wind, stiff against her face, was cool and scented faintly of salt. She thought about the next day, her new job and Cord Donahue. How lucky she was, she decided as she wended her way through the crowds of tourists, to be employed by the most devilishly handsome boss in the entire Pacific Northwest!

UNFORTUNATELY HER EXUBERANCE was short-lived.

The next morning, much to Alison's disappointment, Cord wasn't in his office or, it seemed, the building. He didn't show up while she filled out all the necessary paperwork in the personnel department.

Cord's secretary, Louise, showed Alison a small office with an enormous cherrywood bookcase and a tall window overlooking the street. "This is yours," Louise said, then pointed out the connecting corridors to the rest rooms, employee cafeteria and boardroom. "That door leads into Cord's office and that one—" she indicated a door on the opposite side of the room "—opens into David's domain."

"David?"

Louise's smile grew and her blue eyes shone a bit, though she tried to mask her emotions. "David Donahue, Cord's younger brother," Louise replied. "He's senior vice president. Cord's his boss, too."

So Louise was interested in David, Alison thought, warm inside. "And when will Mr. Donahue, er, Cord, be back?"

"I'm not sure. He phoned me last night and said he was called away for a few days," Louise explained. "It happens a lot. Be prepared, and catch him when you can. Now—" She gestured to a metal desk in the middle of the room. It was piled high with computer printouts and reports. "Cord seemed to think these would keep you busy."

"And then some," Alison murmured.

"Let me know if you need anything—coffee, paper clips, directions…maybe a tranquilizer."

"Will do."

Grinning, Louise left, and Alison spent the next three days and nights going over the information, never once seeing Cord. It was as if he'd vanished off the face of the earth, and she couldn't fight the idiotic sense of disappointment she felt each morning that he didn't show up at the office.

"You're being a fool," she told herself Friday morning in the ladies' room. Glancing at her reflection in the mirror, she touched up her lipstick and slung the strap of her purse across one shoulder, ready to tackle another day of eyestrain. So far her job had been less than exciting.

But when she walked into her office, her heart leaped. A man was seated in one of the chairs near her desk. *Cord!*

However, as he turned to face her, she realized her mistake. His features, though similar to Cord's, were softer, less angular. His eyes were a lighter shade of brown and his hair was a deep chestnut color. She didn't have to be told that this man was Cord Donahue's younger brother, a man who, though he worked for the company, wasn't in charge.

"You must be Alison," he said, standing, his navy suit slightly wrinkled, as he extended his hand. "I'm David, the 'other' brother."

"Other?" she repeated, at a loss for words as he gripped her hand. His shake was as firm as Cord's had been, his smile as bright, yet she didn't feel the same purely sensual magnetism she had with Cord. "Good morning." Quickly she skirted her desk, shoved her purse into a drawer and sat across from him.

"*Other,* as in the one who didn't inherit this place," he clarified, motioning grandly to the interior of the room as if to include the entire Donahue Building, carpet, walls, fixtures and anything else that happened to be within the premises. "Who'd want it, right?"

Maybe you, she mused silently. "Right. What can I do for you?"

David's grin widened, showing off perfect white teeth. "Let me buy you breakfast and we'll talk over ham and eggs. There's a little café across the street. We could grab a quick bite and I could tell you how you can help me...and Cord, of course."

"Of course." Alison felt a little uneasy with this brash, younger version of Cord, but she ignored her doubts. He was Cord's brother, for crying out loud, and senior vice president of the company. Technically, he, too, was her boss. But then there was Louise to think about. Cord's secretary had been wonderful to her, and Alison suspected that Louise was carrying a silent torch for David.

"Please?" he asked, his smile warm and sure.

She really didn't have a choice, and, after all, this was just breakfast, not a marriage proposal. "Sure," she said quickly, before she changed her mind. "Why not?"

David stopped at Louise's desk, explaining that he and Alison would be gone for an hour, then showed Alison the back stairs and door to an alley. Outside, he grabbed her elbow and helped her jaywalk across a four-lane street to a quiet café named Simply Sam's.

David pulled out a chair at a small table near the front window. Covered by an oilcloth and decorated with a single plastic carnation, the table had all the warmth and atmosphere of the inside of an empty refrigerator. "Best corned beef hash in the city," David insisted.

"If you like hash," she replied.

"Doesn't everybody?"

Laughing, she shook her head. "I don't think so."

A red-haired waitress in a tight white uniform sauntered up to the table. "The usual?" she asked, lifting penciled brows.

"Two," David replied. "And...coffee?" he asked, glancing at Alison.

"Black."

"You got it." The waitress disappeared through a swinging door behind a chipped Formica counter.

"Don't tell me," Alison said, grinning despite herself. "You lured me down here for ham and eggs and I'm ending up with corned beef. Right?"

David shrugged. "Couldn't help myself," he replied as two platters of hash and cups of steaming coffee were set on the dingy oilcloth. "Besides," he said, winking, "I wanted to impress you. Cord will probably take you to a boring, white-collar, upper-crust restaurant for lunch or dinner soon, but I wanted you to experience a place with more...atmosphere."

Alison glanced at the orange vinyl chairs, Formica-topped counter and yellowed overwaxed linoleum floors. "To atmosphere," she said with a chuckle, holding up her coffee cup and clinking it with David's.

"And good friends," he said, his eyes locking with hers over the rim of his cup.

"And good friends," she repeated, feeling slightly uneasy again, as if David wanted something from her. But that was crazy. She barely knew the man and he'd gone out of his way to be nice. She glanced at her plate and started to eat, surprised that David was right. The concoction of beef, potatoes and onions tasted delicious.

"It's the seasoning," he told her. "A special blend of herbs and spices."

"Sure." But she laughed despite her case of nerves, then seized the opportunity to change the subject. "You, uh, mentioned Cord. When will he be back?" she asked.

"Back?"

"Louise said he was out of town for a few days."

"Oh." He seemed surprised but hid his feelings. "I suppose he'll show up today. Probably already in the office."

Suddenly Alison felt guilty. Not that she was doing anything wrong, she reminded herself. But if Cord were back, she should be at her desk, ready if he needed her. Crazily, just at the thought of seeing him again, her pulse quickened. She took a final sip from her coffee. "I, uh, really should get back."

"Relax. We haven't had dessert."

"Dessert? For breakfast?"

"Why not?" he asked, amber eyes gleaming with humor.

"Because I'm stuffed and I really do have work waiting for me."

"It's not going anywhere," he said.

"But I have the feeling it might multiply if I ignore it too long," she quipped.

"Have it your way." With a sigh he crumpled his napkin and tossed it on the table, then paid the check.

They crossed the street again, and a few minutes later Alison walked into her office, only to find Cord sitting at her desk, reading her notes, barely glancing up as she closed the door behind her. Dressed in a crisp black business suit and white shirt, his hair neatly combed, he continued skimming a report on which she'd been working for three days.

"Enjoy yourself?" he asked.

Stupidly she felt her cheeks color. "It was fine. I was with David at Simply—"

"I know." He stood, his lips twisting wryly, anger flaring possessively in his dark eyes. "David feels it's his duty to show all the new female employees the back stairs and alley."

Alison drew in a swift breath. "It was just breakfast," she said, wondering why she was defending herself.

"Right." His eyes bored into hers and she thought he was going to say something more, something that was intended to wound. But he didn't. Instead, the tight angle of his jaw relaxed slightly and he cleared his throat. Alison couldn't help just staring at him, lost in his gaze. "I, uh, didn't mean to sound so…" he began.

"Much like a bear?"

He grinned then, a smile as crooked as it was endearing. "Right." He motioned to the computer printouts. "Did you have a chance to go over these?"

"Yes."

"And?" Leaning back in her chair, he folded his hands across his chest.

Alison knew she was being tested. She handed him one client statement. "And I think you could use an updated computer system, one that prints out monthly reports that are more easily understood, reports that show yield as well as potential growth, breakdown the assets by category and explain the diversification of a portfolio—something more readable for the layperson."

"Why?"

"Well, with reports like these—" she pointed to the old

statements "—I'd guess you get quite a few calls from confused customers."

"A few," he allowed, his interest sparking as she explained about the computer systems she'd worked with, the reports that had been generated by these systems and how she thought they might implement a more sophisticated system at the investment company. After searching through her file drawer, she withdrew a manila folder and handed it to him.

Cord sorted through the brochures and several reports she'd prepared on the cost of computer system installation as well as the proposed savings from cutting down on the time employees spent with dissatisfied or confused customers.

He seemed pleased, scanning her typewritten report as he asked, "Anything else?"

"Yes. Along with this system," she said, pointing to the software she considered best, "is a very simple but exact auditing system for the books. I talked with the local sales representative and he's willing to add the auditing program with no extra cost."

"You have been busy," he murmured, dark brows arching appreciatively. "I guess you earned your breakfast with David. I was out of line."

Grinning, she agreed. "Apology accepted."

"Now, how could I make it up to you? Dinner tonight?"

She almost leaped at the chance but stopped herself short. "I think I'd better tackle the rest of this," she said, touching the printouts with one finger and forcing a normal tone to her voice. She wasn't sure she was ready for an evening alone with her intriguing boss.

"But maybe later?"

Yes! "Maybe," she replied slowly, knowing she wanted to spend every minute with him and despising herself for being so tempted. She'd seen the kind of women who were promoted solely because they played up to their employers, and she'd sworn never to partake of that kind of dangerous game. However, this time, with Cord's warm eyes assessing her, she couldn't say no. "Okay. Later."

Later came the following Friday. After spending nearly a week working closely with Cord and trying to keep her stupid, schoolgirl fantasies about him at bay, she was finally alone with him in her office. They'd spent a frustrating morning and afternoon with computer salesmen, and both she and Cord needed a break.

His chin dark from the day's growth of beard, his tie loosened, his shirt sleeves rolled over tanned forearms and his hair tousled fetchingly, Cord slouched in a chair near her desk, shaking his head as the last of the salesmen left.

"Thank God," he muttered, once the door was closed behind the retreating figure of a short, rotund software analyst. "If I never see another hard disk, monitor or graphics color card, it'll be too soon."

"Amen," she whispered. Her shoulders ached, and she tossed down her pencil and glasses to rub her eyes.

Cord stood and stretched, the seams of his oxford-cloth shirt straining over his shoulders. "I think we owe ourselves that night out," he decided, glancing at her over his shoulder. "What do you say?"

This time she couldn't stop herself. "I'd love it," she admitted, pulse fluttering crazily. She thought about David's sarcastic prediction that Cord would take her to some stuffed-shirt hangout, but ignored it. Just being with Cord and away from the office would be heaven!

"Good. I'll pick you up at seven."

"What should I wear?"

Grinning crookedly, he said, "Anything but one of those damned suits. Surprise me."

And she did. For the next few hours she was jittery at the thought of being alone with him. Her mind warned her to be careful—he was the boss—but her heart told her to go and be with him every minute she could: take a chance. So she wore a simple black dress with a wide silver belt and let her long hair fall past her shoulders.

The night was perfect. Cord arrived at her apartment promptly at seven. He drove her to a small restaurant perched high in the hills overlooking the city, and as the sun settled behind the Olympic Mountains in the west, the calm waters of Puget Sound turned fiery, reflecting a deep magenta sky. Ferry boats churned across the sound, leaving huge frothy wakes. Sailboats, silhouetted against the blazing water, skimmed the horizon. Slowly, as darkness encroached, the lights of Seattle winked jewel-like below, mimicking the first twinkling stars in a dusky lavender sky.

"It's beautiful," she murmured, still gazing out the window, afraid to look at Cord, his features shadowed and unreadable in the glow of a single flickering candle on the table.

"I like it," he admitted.

They dined on lobster and crusty French bread, steamed asparagus and honeyed pears. Silent waiters whispered through the door to their private table to refill their glasses with white Burgundy, or offer dessert from a tiered silver cart covered with chocolate mousse, strawberry cheesecake, lemon tarts, raspberry crème and petit fours.

"I couldn't possibly," Alison said, when the waiter held a platter of sweets near her.

"For you, sir?"

But Cord just shook his head, his rich brown hair glinting with streaks of gold in the candlelight.

They lingered over coffee laced with brandy, staring through the window to the night-darkened waters of the sound. Alison felt warm under his gaze and when his fingers linked with hers to help her from the table, her heart went wild, pounding noisily.

He held her hand all the way through the restaurant and across the lamplighted parking lot to his car. A cool summer breeze lifted the hair from her face and pushed the black silk of her skirt against her knees. But she wasn't cold. It was as if being with Cord kept her warm, her temperature a few degrees hotter than normal.

Once they were both in the convertible, he drove quickly toward the glittering lights of Seattle. The wind tugged at her hair and rushed against her face as he turned north, away from her apartment.

"Wait a minute," she said, "I live on South—"

"I know. But I thought you might like a boat ride."

"At ten-thirty?" she asked.

"Why not?" And the smile he sent her, dazzling white in the dark night, caused her heart to trip.

"This is insane," she whispered, once he'd parked and opened the car door.

"Maybe." Grasping her hand, he ran along the docks, pulling her, laughing, behind. Their footsteps echoed on the wooden planks as he led her to a small white motor-boat and stepped inside.

"But we're not dressed for this," she protested.

"Do you care?"

Not when I'm with you. "I guess not."

He lifted her into the craft, his warm hands spanning her waist. The boat rocked slightly with her weight and his fingers clenched reflexively, holding her close enough that she could feel his warmth, smell the musky scent of his aftershave.

Entranced, she didn't move, tilting her head up to meet the questions in his eyes. For a breathless instant her gaze dropped to his sensual lips and she wondered how it would feel to touch them with her own.

"Let's go," he whispered, his voice husky and rough as he released her and turned to the helm. The engine sputtered once, then roared to life as Cord tossed the anchoring rope onto the dock, then maneuvered the craft through the moorings and to the ebony waters beyond.

Standing straight at the wheel, his hair rumpled by the wind, the white collar of his shirt stark against the ebony night, he squinted at the pitch-black waters. Cool air pressed against Alison's face, whipping her hair backward as the boat knifed across the sound.

You're out of your mind, a nagging thought taunted as she watched him. *What in the world are you doing out here, in the middle of nowhere, on a boat alone with your boss?*

But she couldn't stop the dizzy feeling of adventure that overwhelmed her and caused her cheek to crease with a small dimple. Irrationally she decided that if she were falling in love, nothing could stop her now. Shivering, more from exhilaration than a chill, she glanced up at Cord. He was staring at her and took time from the wheel to toss his jacket over her bare shoulders.

"I don't want you to have any excuses not to come in to work tomorrow," he said, white teeth glinting rakishly.

"Tomorrow?" she repeated. "Saturday?"

"There's a special meeting, remember."

She groaned.

"No excuses."

"I wouldn't dream of it," she replied, laughing as she tried to hold her hair in place with one hand. "You see, I have this boss, and he's got a reputation of being a regular *Ursus horribilis!*"

"A *what?*"

She laughed. "Make that a *non compos mentis Ursus horribilis.*"

"Which is?"

"A grizzly bear."

"Is that right?" With one hand at the helm he wrapped his free arm around Alison's waist and held her close to his side.

"Actually, a 'not of sound mind' grizzly bear."

"So, the truth comes out! You wanted a job at the firm just so you could insult me! Who put you up to this? David?" he asked, chuckling.

"You earned the insults by the way you acted the other morning."

"Guilty as charged," he agreed, glancing down at her. He almost said something else, something important. She could see the questions in his eyes, but he quickly looked away, his lips tightening though his hand still held her firm against him. "You have a way of making me crazy, you know," he muttered. "The *non compos mentis* part was true. At least since I met you."

She couldn't move, her heart pummeling her rib cage. Was it possible that he was experiencing this same wondrous feeling as she?

The warmth of his hand seeped through her dress, but

she tried to tell herself that she was imagining things. Though she was twenty-five, she'd never fallen deeply in love or really believed love existed. But now, under the silvery stars overhead, she began to doubt her own convictions.

"Cold?" he asked.

She shook her head, merriment dancing in her hazel eyes as she gazed up at him and felt the sweet pressure of his palm flat against her abdomen.

"There's something I want to show you. Hold on." With a secretive smile he opened the throttle and the prow of the boat knifed through the water. Alison nearly toppled into a chair, but Cord held her fast and she felt the sting of salt spray on her cheeks.

A half hour later he moored the boat on a private dock near a looming, dark island on the west end of the sound. Not one street lamp gleamed, though occasionally Alison could detect the flickering beams of headlights curving on a lonesome stretch of road through the trees.

"Where are we?" she asked.

"Bainbridge Island, a few miles north of Winslow."

"So what's here?"

"A secret place." After looping a rope around a mooring on the dock and checking to see that the boat was securely fastened, he found a flashlight in the hold and snapped on a beam of yellow light. Taking her hand, he helped her over the weathered planks and across a sandy strip of beach to an overgrown path.

"Who lives here?" she asked, eyes trained on the bobbing light as it lit up the path with its weak beam. Tufts of grass and weeds poked through the wet sand.

"I do—or I did when I was a kid," he said.

She stumbled over a rock and he steadied her. "You were right, we weren't dressed for this," he admitted.

"Next time I'll be prepared and wear my hiking boots."

Squeezing her hand, he shone the thin beam over a two-story log cabin that was surrounded on three sides by towering fir trees. As the light traveled the length of the house, Alison noticed that one of the steps to the front porch had rotted through and a few of the window-panes had been broken and boarded over.

"You haven't been here in a while," she observed.

"Five, maybe six years," he admitted, squinting as he surveyed the house. "Haven't wanted to."

"Why not?" She glanced across the ink-colored sound to the winking lights of Seattle. The soft noise of lapping water was countered by the sharp hoot of an owl. "All this place needs is a little elbow grease."

"A lot of it," he said, his smile fading as he stared at the deteriorating building. As if to add emphasis to his words a mouse scurried across the porch, and Alison jumped.

"You've got all summer," she pointed out.

"Too busy."

"Then why'd you bring me here?"

"I don't know," he admitted, perplexed as he stared down at her. Moonlight reflected in his dark eyes and Alison's heart nearly stopped as he studied her lips, then touched them gently with his thumb. "And I don't know if I should be out with you tonight, either," he said with a sigh.

That makes two of us.

She didn't move, couldn't breathe as he lowered his head, brushing his warm mouth over her chilled lips. Trying not to respond, she stood rooted to the ground until his arms slipped around her waist, holding her possessively, dragging her tight against him. "Oh, Alison," he murmured, his breath warm and scented with coffee, "what am I going to do with you?"

"Exactly what I'm wondering about you." She sighed into his mouth before his lips claimed hers in a kiss that was meant to be possessive.

She felt the gentle probe of his tongue, sensed the urgency with which he held her and she surrendered totally.

His hands tangled in her hair and his breathing was heavy, labored as he kissed her lips, eyes and cheeks. She wound her hands around his neck, feeling her blood rush hot in her veins, her heart thudding an irregular cadence.

"Alison," he whispered over and over again into the lustrous waves of her hair. His hands moved slowly downward, past her neck to slip beneath the jacket he'd tossed over her shoulders. The expensive suit coat slid noiselessly to the ground. "If you only knew how crazy you've been driving me!"

Closing her eyes, she ignored all the doubts in her mind and fell victim to the night. His lips were wet and demanding, his tongue searching.

The warmth radiating from his body, the feel of his hands firm against her back and the sweet pressure of his chest crushing her breasts sent her senses reeling. He was leaning heavily upon her, as if seeking support, but her knees were already weak and his weight pushed her steadily to the soft ground. Mesmerized by his touch, she couldn't move.

"Oh, God," he groaned, half lying across her. "Tell me to stop," he ground out.

"I...I can't."

"Tell me to stop," he said again, almost angry as he

stared down at her, his gaze caressing the contours of her face.

The wind rustled high overhead and she looked away from him, trying to find her common sense—her pride. But with Cord so close, all her pride seemed far away, lost in the pitch-black night. "St-stop," she finally breathed, then when his face fell, added, "No, please, don't stop. Don't ever stop."

Mouth drawn with restraint, he touched her hair. "I've wanted to be alone with you from the minute you walked into my office," he confided, bemused at his own weakness.

"Is that why you brought me here?"

He lifted one powerful shoulder but his muscles remained taut and the thin white lines of strain still bracketed his mouth. "I suppose. I haven't been here since my father died—haven't wanted to come back."

"Why?" Interested in this new side of him, she levered up on one elbow so she could meet his serious gaze.

He closed his eyes as if willing his desire away and hoping to regain some shreds of his composure. "It was symbolic, I suppose. The end of carefree youth, so to speak. My mother was already gone—she'd died years before and my father went into semiretirement here. He only spent a few days a week in the city, overseeing the business."

"But he died here?" she guessed.

"Yep." He let out a long, ragged breath. "The neighbors found him. Heart attack." As if the memory were still too painful, Cord swallowed hard. "He was only fifty-seven."

"I'm sorry," she whispered.

"We all were. Oh, God, Alison," he moaned, gazing at her mouth, then violently rolling over and forcing himself to his feet. Swearing loudly under his breath, he dusted off his hands. "I'm…I'm sorry."

"Don't be."

"I should never have brought you here."

"I'm glad you did." Touched, she pulled herself to her feet and leaned against him, feeling his warm arms circle her waist. Being alone with him on this remote stretch of beach, sharing his innermost secrets, she felt more alive than she had in years.

Cord glanced at the old house. "I had the place boarded up and never wanted to come back...until tonight. You made me change my mind."

"Me?"

An ironic smile twisted his lips. "That's right, Miss Banning. For the first time in six years I've wanted to share my past with someone and, believe me, I don't understand it. Now—" leaning over, he hooked a finger under the collar of his jacket and lifted it from the ground, shaking off the lingering grains of sand "—unless we leave soon, I might lose what little control I have left."

She wanted to say, *Would that be so bad?* but didn't. She was already flirting with danger, and she reminded herself to take one step at a time. After all, Cord Donahue was her boss.

Gently placing his jacket over her shoulders, he added, "After Dad died, I inherited the company, or most of it, and the house."

"Oh." Without thinking she asked, "What about the rest of your family?"

His jaw hardened. "There's only David," he said quickly, eyes shadowed with guilt.

"I...I didn't mean to pry."

"Didn't you?" Then the suspicion left his gaze. "Doesn't matter anyway. David will be only too glad to give you the details, so you may as well hear my side of the story."

"Really, you don't have to."

"You asked," he pointed out, helping her over the planks of the dock and into the gently swaying boat. "Dad took it upon himself to appoint me David's keeper and I can tell you, David doesn't much like it."

"I can imagine."

"So can I." He untied the mooring rope and coiled it over his arm. "He inherited a condominium in Snoqualmie, a small trust fund and a lifelong position with the company. Not a whole helluva lot," he added, as if reading her thoughts.

No wonder there was so much friction between the two brothers.

"He's been bitter ever since."

"Do you blame him?" she asked, as he flicked on the motor and the boat took off, skimming across the surface of the water.

"Nope. But he knows all he has to do is prove himself. I've already drawn up the papers. He'll get his half of the estate."

When you think he's ready, Alison thought, shivering with the cold. She wished she'd never asked about the inheritance; it was really none of her business.

Cord remained silent as he maneuvered the craft back to the city and Alison was too tired to bother with small talk. The evening had brought her closer to Cord—too close, perhaps—and she had trouble reminding herself that Cord Donahue was the one man in Seattle she couldn't fall for.

She watched his hard features, the firm thrust of his jaw, the dark determination in his eyes, the clench of his fingers over the helm, and she knew it was already too late. Despite the screaming objections of her sanity, she was falling in love with him.

When he finally dropped her off at her apartment, he stood just outside her door, took her chin between his palms and kissed her tenderly on her lips, with the unspoken promise of so much more.

"I don't want to leave," he whispered huskily, tracing the slope of her cheek with his thumb, his face so close to hers she could see small sparks of gold in his brown eyes.

She didn't think. The words just rushed out. "You don't have to."

"You don't understand," he said. "I don't want to go, *ever*." Then, abruptly, leaving his admission hanging on the air, he tore himself away, turning quickly and walking briskly down the hall to the stairwell. Without a glance back, he shoved open the door to the stairs and disappeared. Alison could hear the sound of his footsteps ringing on the steps, fading as he descended the four flights to the lobby.

"This is insane," she murmured, touching her lips. But her heart was soaring, her pulse throbbing, and she couldn't shake off the marvelous, breath-stopping feeling that she was in love.

She couldn't sleep. Even after taking a warm bath, sipping a cup of cocoa and trying to concentrate on a dull mystery, she was still wide awake, her mind working overtime with fantasies of Cord.

"Stop it," she told herself as she finally snapped off the bedside lamp at two-thirty and closed her eyes.

The phone jangled at three-fifteen.

She answered before the second ring, hardly daring to hope that the caller was Cord.

"Still awake?" he asked, and her stupid heart began to pound irregularly.

"Couldn't sleep."

"Me either."

She heard the hesitancy in his voice.

"I thought maybe you'd like breakfast."

"Now?" she asked.

"In a couple of hours, before the damned meeting that some idiot called."

"Meaning you?"

"Right."

She told herself all the sane, rational reasons why she should decline. He was the boss, for God's sake, the owner of the company. She didn't want to compromise him or herself by becoming involved in a sticky relationship that could only end badly. But her heart won over her head. "I'd love to," she admitted, sinking back against her pillows and listening as he told her about the morning and the weekend he'd planned for them.

NOW AS ALISON lay in bed some three years later, sick at heart as she recalled those painful memories, she sighed, remembering how the whole affair had started—innocently and wonderfully. The beginning of the summer romance had been so intense, so filled with fiery passion that Alison had been blinded to the pitfalls hiding beneath the calm surface of a love so deep she was sure it would never end. But end it had, bitterly and painfully, with Cord driving recklessly away from the marina on a black, storm-swept night.

Worse yet, she thought now, he'd let her believe for four agonizing years that he'd died in a horrific crash.

And now he was back—just two doors down the hall.

CHAPTER FIVE

CORD COULDN'T SLEEP. Just knowing Alison was a short walk down the hall made his heart pound and his blood race.

He was lying on the bed, hands under his head, eyes glued to the dark ceiling as he listened to sounds of the night: the steady drip of rain, the soft moan of wind and the creaking of ancient timbers in the old house. But his thoughts were with Alison.

Just two doors away, his mind taunted.

So what?

So here's your chance! Don't kid yourself any longer. You've been tearing yourself up over her. Go on, have it out with her. Find out why she betrayed you.

She claims she didn't.

And you believe her?

"God, I want to," he muttered, tortured all over again.

Then find out. A short walk down the hall—that's all it takes. She's lying there on your old bed, her black hair dark against the pillows, her white skin soft—

"Shut up!" Furious with the taunting voice in his head, he swung his legs over the edge of the bed and strode instinctively to the window. Outside, blue light from the street lamps cast an eerie glow over the rain-washed drive.

"Get hold of yourself, Donahue," he warned, gripping

the edge of the window—David's window. Why hadn't his brother and Alison shared a room? The question teased and tormented him. To make matters worse, Cord had never suspected his reaction to Alison would be so violent, an emotional storm he could barely control.

He'd convinced himself that he was over her, that he'd never really loved her and that she and David had deserved each other.

He'd been lying to himself, of course. He'd realized it the minute he'd set eyes on her again. It was as if all the emotions of that fevered summer had been waiting, simmering under the surface, to explode. And they had, just as they had on the Fourth of July at the company picnic four years past....

ALISON HAD BEEN dangling her feet over the end of the dock, her jeans rolled up over her calves, her toes splashing water as the last boat filled with Donahue company employees had slid from view. Cord had watched her, as he had for most of the day.

The Fourth of July celebrations were long over, and even David and Louise had left with her sister, a redhead named Francine. Unfortunately it had seemed as if David were more interested in Francine, a bank officer at Peninsula Bank, than in Louise.

Sighing, Cord told himself for the tenth time that day that he couldn't interfere in his brother's love life. If David didn't realize that Louise loved him, it was his problem.

Sitting on the rail surrounding the porch of the old cabin on Bainbridge Island, Cord studied Alison, watching as she tossed her head back, her hair shimmering in the last rays of sunlight. He'd known her two months, and he was as fascinated with her now as he'd been the day she'd strutted into his office, nearly begging for a job.

Since then they had worked together at the office, as well as at this old cabin, fixing it up, laughing together as they cleaned, repaired, varnished and added new furniture. Also, they had dated—and fallen in love. Cord, though it bothered him still, had honored her plea that they keep their romance a secret. But no longer. He couldn't wait to tell the world that he loved her and wanted to make her his wife.

Grinning to himself, he slid from the rail, poured two glasses from a last bottle of champagne and walked down the crooked path to the dock. "Enjoying yourself?"

She glanced up at him, hazel eyes twinkling. "Immensely! It was a great party, if I do say so myself."

"Can't argue with that," he agreed, sitting cross-legged on the weathered planks and handing her one long-stemmed glass. "To Alison Banning, administrative assistant and party-giver *extraordinaire*."

"Party-giver?" she repeated, laughing.

"Well, whatever you call it." Clinking his glass against hers, he winked, thinking himself the luckiest man in the entire Pacific Northwest.

Radiant, Alison glanced back at the cabin on the island, the log cabin that so recently had been boarded up and unused. "Then you finally agree that fixing this place up was a good idea?"

"Mmm. I suppose."

"You know it." She sipped from her glass, and Cord watched her throat work as she swallowed. "It was a perfect day for a picnic," she said.

"I guess you're right. Even David seemed to enjoy himself."

"And *you* didn't think that was possible, did you?"

Cord shrugged, trying not to think about his younger brother. Over the past few weeks David had become secretive, as if there were something bothering him, something he wanted to hide. Cord wondered if it had anything to do with his relationship with Louise, but dismissed the thought. Obviously, from the way David had dogged after Francine, he was still playing the field.

So, maybe David's problems were with the business. Twice in the past week Cord had attempted to talk to him and both times David had nervously tried to convince him that he was imagining things.

Cord wasn't so sure.

"You're still worried, aren't you?" Alison guessed.

"And you don't think I should be?"

"David's a grown man. He can make his own decisions."

"You couldn't tell it today."

"Oh. Well, Francine is good-looking." But she seemed unhappy at the thought and glanced out to sea, where the wake of the boat carrying David, Francine and Louise had recently disappeared. "She's…interesting."

And a flirt, Cord thought distastefully.

"Maybe David doesn't need an older brother looking over his shoulder," Alison suggested, her frown lifting.

"Maybe he does."

"Why don't you give him a chance?"

"I think I have." Cord leaned closer to her, watching her eyes darken as dusk streaked the sky with ribbons of lavender. "Don't you?"

"I'm not so sure," she admitted, wrapping one arm over her knees as she drew her legs out of the water.

"Sometimes I think that David's frustrated, that he needs to be his own person."

Something in her tone bothered him, touched a jealous part of his soul that he couldn't quite control. "Seems like you know a lot about David."

"We're friends," she stated, glancing at him. "That's all."

"Right." Finishing his drink, he stood and reached out his hand to help her to her feet. But she was quicker than he, and with a flashing smile and one swift movement she snaked a leg back into the icy water and splashed it upward, neatly sprinkling his jeans.

Cord gave a whoop as the cold water sprayed him. Alison jumped lithely to her feet and dashed along the length of the dock.

Grinning wickedly, he wondered how he could have doubted her as she started up the beach. She was fast, laughing as the cool sand pushed through her toes, her dark hair streaming bannerlike behind her. Fortunately he was quicker than she'd anticipated, and he caught her as she rounded a curve and was starting for a private cove where he and David had played years before.

"Not so fast," he taunted, grabbing her wrist and spinning her into his arms.

Still giggling, she struggled, but not for long.

He leaned forward and captured her lips in his. Already breathless, she responded instantly. He could hear her heart thudding rapidly, feel the warm promise of her mouth against his, smell the sand and salt spray clinging to her hair. "I love you," he whispered as they slid, as one, to the sheltered beach.

"And I love you."

He didn't think twice but slowly unbuttoned her blouse, letting the soft fabric fall from her shoulders to expose beautiful white breasts, bound only by a lacy camisole. "Marry me, Alison," he whispered against the soft mounds. "Marry me tomorrow."

"Not tomorrow, love," she said, her voice throaty and gentle as the first fireworks exploded high overhead. Screaming missiles and a vibrant burst of scarlet spider-webbed over a vast purple sky.

"Then the next day," he suggested, burrowing his face between her breasts, white beneath a layer of lacy fabric. His warm breath teased her soft skin.

She moaned, moving gently beneath him. "Next summer," she whispered against his ear.

Hot fire jetted through his blood, blinding him. He couldn't wait that long. Already his mind was throbbing with the want of her. His hands moved gently over her breasts, touching each peak, tracing the hard outline of her nipples with his thumbs. "I just have to convince you to change your mind."

"I…I won't." But her voice wavered as he lifted the camisole over her head, exposing soft, dark-tipped mounds. Without a word he rimmed each nipple with his tongue, toying with her, feeling her flesh heat beneath his touch. "Cord, please—"

"Please what?"

"Ooh…" Slowly he tugged at her jeans, lowering them insistently over her slim hips and legs.

"Next week?"

"Next *summer!*" But her voice cracked and she moved closer to him, writhing in the sand, fighting her natural response as he caressed every inch of her silken skin with his hands and tongue.

Another cloudburst of color rained across the sky, reflecting gold and silver in her eyes. Cord could restrain himself no longer. With a groan he stripped off his clothes, kicking them away. "You're the most frustrating woman I've ever met," he growled against her ear, poised over her.

She swallowed hard, gazing at him, her arms circling his neck as she drew his head to hers. His muscles ached beneath her touch, the feel of her fingers against his skin chased rational thought away. He felt the smooth cushion of her body as he lay over her and couldn't stop the desire scorching through his blood. He'd heard her damn excuses for not marrying him, for keeping their relationship a secret. She didn't want to compromise him, nor did she want to be accused of using him. She wanted to give their love time before they jumped into marriage.

Cord didn't buy a word of it. He loved her and that was that. To hell with the gossiping tongues at the company. Who cared what the rest of the world thought? Never before had he felt this incredible feeling of love and being loved.

"Sooner or later you're going to have to make an honest man of me," he growled against her hair, trying to control himself as her fingers slid slowly down his back, trailing down his backbone.

"Next year. I promise."

She was doing dangerous things to him; his body screamed for her, but sanity prevailed for a split second. "Then we'd better be careful," he whispered, though he thought that impregnating her might be the best course of action—forcing her into marriage now. He couldn't trick her, though, and forever doubt her love.

"It's all right," she said with a sigh, her fingers digging into the muscles in his back. "It's a safe time."

"You're sure?"

"Positive. I took biology in college," she teased.

He didn't need any further encouragement. He'd waited two agonizing months, begging her to marry him. He wanted this moment to last forever.

With the shriek of Independence Day rockets overhead and the brilliance of fireworks exploding in his mind, he made love to her for the first glorious time and was oblivious to anything but the feel of her skin, the glazed longing in her eyes and the wonder of the night.

Once he thought he heard a twig snap in the forest near the beach, and for a fraction of a second he felt as if he were being watched, but he shrugged off the unlikely thought. He and Alison were alone on the beach and nothing else mattered.

THAT HAD BEEN nearly four years ago, and now, as Cord stared out the window, his fingers curled around the casing, he wondered how he had been so stupid. He knew now why Alison hadn't wanted to rush into marriage, and it hadn't been to give their love affair time. She'd been secretly carrying on with his brother behind his back. She'd wanted to have her cake and eat it, too. The proof of her betrayal was the little cherub sleeping across the hall.

Unless Mandy's your child.

His gut wrenched. Ever since he'd met the little girl, he'd considered the possibility of his paternity. After all, she was just the right age. And maybe, had he been less careful, he would have held the faintest hope that the bright-eyed little girl was his. But that wishful thought was too much to hope for, the dream of a desperate man.

If only he hadn't been so damned careful! If only he had just let nature take its course.

Unclenching his fingers, he walked barefoot to the

door, hesitated at the threshold, then strode down the hallway, pausing at Mandy's open door. Bracing himself, he walked into the room and stared at the dark-haired child in the dim glow of the night lamp.

Thumb in her mouth, one arm flung around the neck of a scruffy teddy bear, she slept, tousled black hair falling over her face in unkempt curls.

So what if this child were David's? Mandy was the only link he had left to his family, the last generation of Donahue blood.

And she could be yours.

"Sure, and there really is a Santa Claus," he mumbled, pushing a wayward strand of hair from Mandy's face. She sighed and rolled over, small lips still working on her thumb. "Good night," he whispered gruffly, unaccustomed to the paternal feelings that touched him as he watched her. Turning to the door, he discovered Alison watching him, her black hair tangled around her face and falling past her shoulders.

"Couldn't sleep either?" she guessed. Dressed in a white terry robe cinched tight over her waist, her hair as rumpled as Mandy's, she was disturbingly beautiful.

"It's been a...difficult day."

"That's one way of putting it." Most of her animosity had worn off and she even ventured a smile. Seeing him with Mandy had softened her a little and it was much too late to start fighting. "I thought I'd make a cup of hot chocolate," she suggested. "Want some?"

Cord cracked a tired smile. "Will it do any good?"

"Probably not, but it beats tossing and turning for another hour."

He couldn't disagree. He followed her downstairs and studied her as she heated two cups of milk in the microwave oven before stirring two hefty teaspoons of cocoa into each warm mug.

"Let's declare a truce," she suggested, taking a chair opposite him at the table.

"I thought we already did."

She smiled into her cup. "Yes. And we already broke it."

"I guess you're right," he admitted, chuckling. "I never have been able to think straight when I'm around you. But tonight… Okay, we'll settle on a truce."

"Thank God." Gathering her courage, she met his dark gaze and ignored the traitorous leap of her heart as his eyes searched her face. "Look, Cord, I know we have a lot to iron out and I know you don't trust me. But for Mandy's sake we've got to try and maintain some kind of…"

"Facade?"

"If that's what you want to call it," she said, sighing before testing her hot drink. He'd never trust her again— she could see it in his eyes. "We're not kids anymore."

"I don't think we ever were."

"Maybe not, but whether either of us likes it or not, we're stuck with each other until we straighten out this mess between us."

"What're you getting at?"

"Just that…none of what happened between us has anything to do with Mandy." Alison's throat went dry with the lie. "I, uh, don't want her to get hurt and upset. I don't want to argue with you when she's around."

Jaw tight, Cord nodded. "Fair enough. I'll give it my best shot—when she's not around and you're not baiting me."

"I don't—" But she stopped herself and shoved her hair out of her eyes. "Well, maybe I do," she admitted.

"Thanks." Feeling suddenly awkward under his uncompromising stare, Alison drained her cup and set it in the sink. "Good night," she whispered as she left the room, sensing Cord's eyes on her back.

"Night."

Guiltily she wondered if she were escaping as she hurried up the stairs. After a quick peek into Mandy's bedroom, she crossed the hall to her own room, closing the door behind her. She waited for the sound of Cord's heavy tread climbing the stairs, but a full ten minutes passed and she didn't hear anything but the quiet hum of her alarm clock and the wind blowing angrily against the old house, rattling the windows.

Exhausted, she took off her robe and climbed into bed, hoping that sleep would overcome her quickly. Tomorrow she would have to square off with Cord again and she was going to need all her strength.

ALISON AWOKE TO the smell of frying bacon and fresh coffee. She stretched and remembered that Cord was back in Seattle, determined to throw her world into a tailspin. "Let him try," she muttered, surprisingly refreshed and ready to deal with anything he could dish out.

Yawning, she slipped her arms through the sleeves of her robe and poked her head into Mandy's room. The bed was empty, Mandy's favorite teddy lying facedown and forgotten on the carpet. "It happens to the best of us," Alison told the frumpy old bear as she set him on the top shelf of Mandy's bookcase.

Her feet were bare and didn't make a sound as she went downstairs, noting that there was already a fire in the grate in the den and noises of banging pots and childish giggles coming from the kitchen.

"Good morning," Alison said as she pushed open the swinging door, expecting to find Norma and Mandy huddled together and cutting out biscuits at the table.

"Mornin'," Cord drawled, glancing over his shoulder. He was at the stove and Mandy was standing on a chair at the counter nearby, watching in earnest as he flipped pancakes high in the air to catch them in a frying pan.

"Mommy, look!" Mandy insisted, awestruck.

"I see."

Cord deftly caught another flying flapjack. "You don't sound impressed," he chastised, chuckling, as if their argument the night before were completely forgotten. A little glimmer of tenderness sparked in his eyes and Alison smiled. Maybe there was still a chance for them, her wayward heart hoped.

"Oh, I am," she countered.

"There's coffee in the pot."

"Thanks." Pouring herself a cup, she watched, mesmerized, as Cord let Mandy pour batter into the pan. She wanted to shout, *Be careful,* but caught herself. All of Cord's attention was centered on the child, and Alison knew instinctively that he wouldn't let Mandy burn herself or fall off the sturdy chair. He was poised right beside the little girl, his eyes fastened upon her, his body blocking any possible fall.

He must have been up for over an hour. He was dressed, showered and shaved. Wearing a loose-fitting cotton sweater and gray cords, he was as damnably handsome as he had been before. His dark hair had been combed but now fell fetchingly over his brow and the amused twitch tugging at the corners of his mouth as he talked to Mandy caused her heart to flutter. With a sinking feeling she realized she'd never fallen out of love with him.

"You two ladies go upstairs and get dressed, then, after breakfast, we'll take off."

"Take off?" she repeated, frowning.

"For the waterfront. We promised Mandy a day at the piers."

"But—"

"Come on, Mommy!" Mandy insisted, hopping off her chair and tugging on Alison's hand.

"Whoa, hold on," Alison pleaded, coffee nearly spilling on her as Mandy, tornadolike, rushed out of the room. She heard the child clattering up the stairs. "What's this all about?" she asked, turning to Cord.

He cocked his wrist, flipping another pancake into the pan. "You said you wanted a truce and you pointed out that none of the problems between us are Mandy's fault."

"I know. But I didn't expect you to capitulate so quickly," she admitted.

"Neither did I."

"I just can't believe that now everything's settled."

"Oh, it's not," he said, his face turning grave. "Far from it. But this weekend you and I are going to do our damnedest to keep peace."

"And after that?" she asked.

All his tenderness fled; she could see the tightening of the cords in his neck. "Then we'll have to talk," he said cuttingly. "I think it's time we faced what happened four years ago."

Amen, she thought, shuddering a little at the fierceness in his glare. Still cradling her cup, she met his gaze and said, "Good. Because I can't wait to hear your explanation of why you took off in the middle of the night and let me and the rest of the world think you were dead!"

He started to say something, but she added, "And don't give me any more lies about protecting me, because I was innocent and you know it!"

"So innocent you married my brother within weeks. If you remember, you wouldn't marry me no matter how many times I begged."

Sadness lingered in his eyes. "And all that time you were seeing David."

"I wasn't!"

"Save it, Alison," he muttered, turning back to the pan. "Truce—remember?"

Damn him! Slamming her cup onto the counter, splashing the final dregs of coffee, she turned and marched out of the room. The man could be so horribly infuriating! Loving and tender one minute, devious and condemning the next!

Telling herself she would fight any further attraction she had to him, she dashed upstairs and tore off her robe and nightgown. Then, fuming, she turned on the spigots of the shower until the bathroom was filled with steam, pinned her hair onto her head and climbed into the shower stall.

Still muttering under her breath, she started to lather her body and gasped when the shower door opened abruptly. Cord, his eyes blazing through the steam, his gaze raking over her wet body, was standing squarely in the middle of the bathroom, acting as if he owned the place.

"What are you doing? You *can't* come in here!" she gasped, trying vainly to cover herself with her hands and a pitiful old washcloth.

"Next time lock the door."

"Next time knock! Now, get out! Mandy could—"

"Mandy's eating breakfast downstairs. Besides, *I* locked the door."

Thank God. "Why are you here?" she asked, trying not to notice that the hair on his nape was curling from the mist. His face was flushed; his eyes lingered on the pulse at the base of her throat before drifting lower to the water running down her breasts, abdomen and legs in steamy rivulets.

He took a swift breath as his gaze slid down her slick body; then, as if realizing he'd made a vast mistake by chasing her down, he said through clenched teeth, "Because you walked out on me, Ali, and I had one more thing to say."

"Say it and leave." But she was trembling under his smoldering gaze, feeling her breasts respond despite her anger.

He swallowed hard, forcing his gaze level to hers. "I didn't take the money. Not one bloody red cent that wasn't mine to begin with."

"Neither did I!" If she didn't have to cover up, she'd wring his neck right then and there.

"So who did?" he demanded.

"I don't know, but I really can't think about it right now!"

Then she saw an awareness dawn across his harsh features and the set of his jaw slackened. Without another word he slammed the glass door shut and Alison, letting out a long breath, collapsed against the wet tiles. The nerve of him! How dare he walk brazenly up the stairs and into the bathroom? And yet, her stupid heart was beating wildly and she couldn't forget the scorching feel of his gaze sliding down her body.

"You're a fool, Alison Donahue," she told herself, stepping once again under the hot spray. "A stupid, idiotic female fool." To cool the stain of embarrassment on her cheeks, she doused her head, hoping the water could wash away the feel of Cord's eyes on her, silently praying she would find some way to control her ragged emotions whenever he was near. "Pull yourself together," she warned herself. "Cord's back and you're in for the battle of your life!"

Forty-five minutes later she was dressed and had found most of the dignity he had so ungraciously stripped away in the shower. Squaring her shoulders, she pushed her way into the kitchen to find Mandy offering Lazarus a small piece of bacon.

"You're late," Cord observed. Standing in the alcove to the back porch, his arms crossed over his chest, he couldn't hide the amused twinkle in his eyes.

"Someone disturbed me," she said.

"Who?" Mandy asked, looking up and nearly kicking over Lazarus's milk dish.

"Careful, Mandy."

"Yes, who?" Cord taunted.

"Never mind." Alison found her jacket on a peg near the back door and shoved her arms through the sleeves. She wasn't about to be baited—not again.

"You missed breakfast," Mandy said. "Cord wouldn't wait."

Alison darted Cord a meaningful glance. "I know, honey," she said to Mandy, refraining from adding, *Cord just does what he damn well pleases.* "Come on, let me help you with your sweatshirt." She tugged the hooded pink shirt over Mandy's head and tucked Mandy's jacket along with a few cookies and a couple of bananas into an oversize shoulder bag.

"Looks like you're packing for the army."

"Just one little girl," Alison remarked, hoping to appear unruffled, though the thought of spending an entire day alone with Cord and Mandy was unsettling.

Seeing the two of them together and lying to them both would be rough. Sooner or later she would have to admit that Mandy was Cord's daughter, but she had to wait, make sure of his feelings. Hadn't he said just last night that he was going to mete out his revenge on her, take everything away from her? If he knew Mandy was his daughter, what would prevent him from trying to take her away, too? Cold to the bone, Alison finished packing. But her fingers trembled at the wretched thought that Cord, as Mandy's father, might find a way to come between mother and child.

"Alison?" Cord asked.

"Wh-what?"

"What's wrong? You look like you've seen a ghost." The gentleness in his voice surprised her.

"I have," she whispered, her hazel eyes wide with a new, paralyzing fear. "You."

CHAPTER SIX

A FEW BRAVE rays of sun pierced through the steel-gray clouds hanging heavily over Elliott Bay in Puget Sound. The wind was brisk and only a few sailboats sliced through the water between churning ferries and large international ships. Alison strolled along the waterfront, staring across the choppy water and smelling the scent of salt in the air.

"Let's go on the boats," Mandy said from her perch on Cord's shoulders. She pointed excitedly to a swooping sea gull and beyond to one of the large ferries.

"Another time," Cord replied, laughing.

"Now!" She began to kick but Cord pinned her heels with one large hand.

"Hey, slow down."

"You promised!"

"Stubborn thing, isn't she?" Cord remarked, sliding a glance at Alison. "Must take after her mother."

"Or her father," Alison muttered under her breath, and thankfully Cord didn't hear.

Together they walked along the converted piers, window-shopping with other tourists in the various gift shops, delicatessens, boutiques and craft shops located in the old warehouses.

Finally, near noon, Cord suggested they stop for lunch

at a chowder house, and Mandy protested vehemently. "Picnic," she said over and over again. "You said picnic and carnival!"

"Correction, sprite. That's what *you* said," Cord pointed out. "I said we'd do something special, and we are."

Mandy didn't seem convinced and pouted.

Alison glanced at the leaden skies, then touched Mandy's cheek. "Not today, sweetheart," she decided. "It's going to rain."

But Mandy wouldn't listen and wailed all the way to the chowder house Cord and Alison had frequented before he'd disappeared. They stopped in front of the wooden plank door.

"How about Murphy's?" he asked.

"I…don't think so."

"Too many memories?"

"That's part of it," she admitted, and Mandy, sensing they were about to put off lunch, squirmed out of Cord's arms and tugged at the door. "I'm hungry!" she proclaimed. Feeling caught between the proverbial rock and a hard place, Alison reluctantly followed him inside the dimly lighted restaurant and pushed aside all the familiar old emotions as Cord found a table near a window overlooking Elliott Bay.

Alison helped Mandy into a booster chair and barely glanced at the menu. "Let's get you some fish and chips," she suggested, refusing to meet Cord's eyes. The restaurant with its long tables and blue checkered cloths was too familiar—felt too right. Though it was only a little past noon, the table lamp was lighted, the flame casting intimate shadows over Cord's features.

Mandy began to play with a plastic spoon and Cord studied her as he would a rare bird.

What was he thinking? Could he possibly guess that Mandy was his? Probably not, Alison thought. He was much too sure that Alison had betrayed him by sleeping with his brother. Anger burned bright in her heart. How could he be so blind?

After the waiter had taken their orders and a steaming bowl of chowder was placed in front of her, Alison ignored Cord, helping Mandy with her fish and fries and sipping her hot soup silently.

As he ate, Cord concentrated on Mandy, his dark eyes penetrating hers, his gaze noting her dark curls, slightly cleft chin and deep dimples. Alison wanted to scream. Surely he could see the resemblance that was so blatant.

"Your daughter's adorable," an elderly woman whispered to Cord as she hobbled with her cane to the front desk and paid her bill.

Cord's back teeth clenched together. He darted an inquisitive glance in Alison's direction, and though she wanted to look away, she met his gaze boldly, with forced calm. "Donahue genes," she remarked, swallowing.

"Right." He tossed his napkin onto his plate.

"You're not my daddy," Mandy clarified, having understood at least part of the conversation. "Are you?"

"Of course not," he said gruffly, and Alison let out a silent sigh. She was beginning to feel close to him again, almost as if the past four years had been nothing more than an inconvenience, a period in which each of them had marked time until they could be together again. If she let herself, she could almost trust him. And that trust would be dangerous. Just last night he'd sworn to ruin her, and she knew he hadn't changed his mind in less than twenty-four hours.

Uneasy, Alison watched as Cord paid the check and

lifted Mandy into his arms. Her thumb was already in her mouth and her eyes were beginning to droop.

"I think it's time to get you home to bed," Alison said.

"No nap!" But Mandy's protests were cut short by a huge yawn.

"Sure, no nap." Alison's lips curved, her sense of humor returning.

By the time they'd walked to his Jeep, Mandy was asleep in Cord's arms. "Here, let me," Alison suggested as Cord opened the vehicle's door and fumbled with the buckles on Mandy's car seat. She deftly strapped the child into place without waking her.

"I guess I haven't had much practice," Cord drawled, and Alison forced a smile.

"No babies in Alaska?"

"Not mine—or David's," he replied as he put the Jeep in gear and drove rapidly uphill toward the freeway.

Alison bit her tongue. Was he toying with her? Drumming her fingers nervously on the armrest, she didn't say a word during the excruciating trip home. Nor did Cord. He drove, eyes fixed on the red glow of taillights from the traffic ahead, hands taut on the steering wheel as Mandy made little sucking noises from the back seat.

Once back at the Donahue estate, Alison unstrapped her child and carried Mandy upstairs to bed. Cord didn't follow. He shut himself into the den.

Alison didn't take a chance on disturbing him. She understood him well enough to know when to leave him alone. So, while Mandy napped, Alison decided to wash the remainder of the breakfast dishes. She hurried downstairs, past the locked double doors of the den and into the kitchen.

Lazarus was meowing at the back door.

"Don't like the rain, huh?" Alison asked the old gray tabby as she opened the screen. Lazarus trotted inside, checked his empty dishes and hopped onto the windowsill where he promptly began washing himself.

Some of her restlessness disappearing, Alison soaked the frying pan from breakfast, then began rummaging through the refrigerator, searching for something to cook for dinner. She wondered vaguely if Cord would deign to join Mandy and her, then decided it didn't matter. He could do what he damned well pleased—he always did anyway.

Right, like pretending to be dead, she reminded herself, doubting that she could ever forgive him for such a heinous lie.

The back door swung open and Norma, backing into the kitchen and shaking rain from her umbrella, appeared.

"What're you doing here?"

"I've come to fix dinner, that's what."

"But it's your day off," Alison reminded her.

"Oh, I know that," Norma said, waving off Alison's protests, "but it's not just any day that Cord walks back into this house, now, is it?"

"You can say that again," Alison breathed.

Norma cast her a searching look as she tied on a faded apron. "You don't sound too pleased that he's back."

Alison lifted a shoulder. "Thank God he's alive," she said softly, measuring her words. "I'm so glad that he… didn't die in that horrid storm."

"But…" Norma prodded. She was already seasoning pieces of chicken, but she stared pointedly at Alison.

"But I'm furious with him for letting us think he was dead."

"You and me both," Norma agreed. "Although I'm

tryin' not to hold it against him. He wouldn't have done it if he didn't have good reason."

"You're sure of that?"

"I raised that boy, even when his mama was alive. I know what kind of man he is." She tucked the seasoned poultry into a long baking dish and shoved it into the oven. "And I know that when he left here he loved you very much."

Alison didn't move. Her affair with Cord had been a secret. No one had known. Not even Norma.

"And don't bother denyin' it," Norma said, not even looking in Alison's direction. "I have eyes, y'know. Seems to me you two had a row and he took off, lettin' everyone think he stole the fortune."

"And you don't think he did?" Alison asked, surprised. Never once had Norma said a word about the scandal.

"'Course not. And neither do you, unless I miss my guess."

"But all the proof—"

"Pshaw! Proof! What's that? I say a man's integrity is his proof."

"But he *ran*."

"I know," Norma said, dusting her hands on the worn apron. "As I said before, he must have had one whale of a good reason."

Like thinking he was protecting me, Alison's mind taunted, but she pushed the distracting thought aside.

"What I don't understand," Norma confessed as she rummaged for potatoes in the pantry, "is how you got yourself involved with David so quick."

"He…he was always good to me. Even before Cord left…"

Norma sighed heavily. "David loved you, too. In his own way, I suppose."

"Meaning?" Alison asked, afraid of what she was about to hear.

"I don't like to speak unkindly of the dead, especially because David was your husband. But, I raised him, too, you know, from a toddler. He...he was difficult—not that Cord wasn't, mind you. Cord was rambunctious and had a couple of scrapes with the law when he was in his teens. Nothin' serious, though. David, he avoided that kind of trouble. But where Cord was always straightforward, David tended to bottle things up, hold them in. He was...different. Secretive. I'd never know what he was thinkin'...." As if sensing she'd spoken out of turn, she added quickly, "I'm sure that, in his own way, he was a good man. But he never loved you like Cord did." Norma began peeling potatoes, her back to Alison.

But Alison wasn't finished with the conversation. Intrigued, she asked, "How did you know?"

"Any fool could see it, honey," she said. "He loved you then and he hasn't changed."

If you only knew, Alison thought, remembering Cord's cruel words the night before.

"This time, don't you let him get away," Norma added.

As if it were up to me. "I'll remember that," Alison said, sitting on the window ledge and scratching Lazarus's back. The old cat purred and rubbed against her but she barely noticed, her mind filled with Cord. Was it possible? Could Cord still love her? Or was Norma's insight just the wishful thinking of a dear older woman?

At that moment the kitchen doors swung open and Cord walked through the room to the back door. He was wearing a jacket over his shirt and was clutching keys in his palm.

"And where do you think you're goin'?" Norma asked.

"Out."

"Out where?" she demanded, wiping her hands on her apron. "Dinner will be ready in about an hour. I didn't come all the way over here for nothin', you know."

He grinned crookedly and waved several phone messages Norma had left for him the day before. "I've got some business to attend to, but I'll try to wrap it up quickly." He glanced at Alison and she thought she saw a glimmer of—what? love?—in his eyes. But it faded quickly and she decided she'd been fantasizing.

"An hour," Norma reminded him, though her old eyes gleamed. "We've been talkin' about you, you know."

Alison wanted to melt right into the window casing.

"Only good things, I hope," Cord said, his gaze moving to the window where Alison was sitting with Lazarus curled in her lap.

"Only," Norma teased.

"I'll be back at five."

"I'm countin' on it."

Grumbling under his breath, Cord yanked open the door and Lazarus scrambled off Alison's lap to whisk outside just before Cord let the screen slam shut behind him.

"I don't think he likes to be mothered," Alison decided, smothering an amused smile. Through the window she watched him, his shoulders bowed against the rain, as he climbed into his Jeep and roared down the drive.

"Never did." Her smile faded a little. "But you take my advice, he needs a woman in his life to settle him down."

"And you think I'm the most likely candidate."

"The *only* candidate unless I miss my guess."

Stupidly Alison felt buoyed by Norma's words and let herself for just one second think what the future could bring if only he did love her.

CORD DID RETURN for dinner. Barely. Just as Norma, muttering under her breath, was setting the table for four and Alison was pouring gravy into a bowl, Cord burst through the back door. His hair was wet, his face stern as he pulled off his jacket and hung it near the door.

"Glad you could join us," Norma remarked dryly.

"I said I'd be back."

"Where'd you go?" Mandy asked, eyeing him from the floor where she was playing with plastic blocks.

"Out."

"Out where?" Rolling huge brown eyes up at him, she offered a shy smile.

Cord smiled back. "Popular question in this household. I was doing business with a man from Alaska," he replied, kneeling and scooping her into his arms. "He's buying my cannery."

"Your what?" Mandy asked, clearly confused.

Laughing, he said, "You know, you're just about as nosy as Norma!" He touched the tip of her nose and she giggled.

"I heard that," Norma said, "and if you hadn't just resurrected yourself, I wouldn't forgive you."

"Sure you would," he said, winking.

"Well, maybe. Now, come on, all of you, sit down before it gets cold." They ate quickly and the conversation was little more than small talk. But every once in a while Alison would glance up and find Cord staring at her, studying her as if she were an enigmatic puzzle he couldn't hope to solve.

When dinner was finished, he excused himself, then left again. "Must have a lot on his mind," Norma observed as she watched his Jeep disappear down the drive.

"Don't we all," Alison thought aloud.

As Alison cleared the table, Norma started loading the dishwasher. "Now, young lady," she said to Mandy. "Are you all packed and ready to go?"

"Packed?" Alison repeated, still thinking of Cord.

"You haven't forgotten that Mandy was goin' to spend a few days with me in Spokane, have you?" Norma asked. "Remember? With my sister. We're goin' to be gone for a week."

"Oh Lord, Norma," Alison said, suddenly remembering, "I hadn't even thought about it. Since Cord's been back—"

"This house is turned upside down. I know, I know," Norma said with a gay laugh.

"I haven't washed her clothes, or—"

"Don't you worry about that. The idea was to get Mandy out of the house and give you some time to yourself this week."

Alison hadn't thought about the days ahead. On Monday she'd have to deal with the bank. Rex Masterson had been threatening foreclosure and, as Celia had so aptly put it, Monday was D day for Donahue Investments. If Alison couldn't come up with the money for the mortgage payment, the bank would foreclose on the old Donahue Building. Though she'd fought long and hard to retain possession, leasing out most of the extra space, she hadn't been able to keep up with the payments on the loan David had taken out just after Cord had supposedly been killed.

"What a mess," Alison worried aloud, resting one shoulder against the pine-paneled kitchen wall.

"It will all work out, you'll see," Norma predicted as she tucked a silvery wisp of hair into a tortoiseshell comb. "Now that Cord's back, all your problems will be solved."

Or intensified, Alison thought grimly as she took

Mandy's hand and headed upstairs to pack her clothes and favorite toys into a small suitcase.

THE BIG HOUSE was surprisingly lonely and quiet without Mandy's chatter and footsteps running across the hardwood. *And without Cord,* Alison's mind taunted as she tucked an old quilt around her feet and curled into a corner of the couch in the study. The phone had rung twice, both calls from real estate agents whose clients were interested in buying the old house if Alison would only lower the price. Alison had put them off. She couldn't sell the place, not with Cord back.

Norma had taken Mandy and Alison had spent the evening cleaning the house and trying to come up with a last-minute plan to stop the bank from foreclosing on the Donahue Building. Though she'd racked her brain, she hadn't discovered a way out of her financial dilemma. Short of selling the house in the next twenty-four hours, which she couldn't do, she hadn't a prayer of making up the lapsed mortgage payments.

Unless Cord has money...Donahue money.

"Stop it," she told herself. Closing her eyes against the horrid thought, she tried to relax.

The doorbell rang, jangling into her thoughts. Yawning, she stood and stretched, then crossed through the foyer and twisted open the door. Standing on the front porch, tall and blond and as full of confidence as ever, was David's friend, Nate Benson.

"Hi," he said, teeth gleaming. "'Bout time you answered."

"I guess I dozed. Come in," she invited, glad for the company.

"You haven't returned my calls," he accused as they

walked into the living room, which was to the left of the stairs. More formal than the study, the room with its velvet furniture and glossy tables seemed somehow heavy and depressing.

"I've been busy," she admitted.

"Because of Cord."

"That's had a lot to do with it."

"Reporters hanging around?"

"Not too bad. I think Cord handles them alone."

"I've been keeping up with his return from the grave," Nate said. "Fascinating. I wonder why he let you think he was dead."

"I don't know." Uncomfortable discussing Cord, Alison suggested, "How about a cup of coffee or tea?"

"Nothing stronger?"

"Let's see." They walked to the kitchen and Alison felt better. With its pine walls, crisp curtains and hanging brass pots, the room seemed warm and casual, not uncomfortable and stiff as the living room did.

Standing on tiptoes, she searched through the uppermost cupboard and found a bottle of Irish Cream. "How about Irish Cream and coffee?" she asked.

"Perfect." Nate's blue eyes gleamed. "What can I do?"

"Stoke the fire in the den," she suggested. "I'll only be a minute."

He left the room and she let out a long breath. Though Nate had been David's best friend and a comfort after the hunting accident, he'd always managed to put Alison on edge. She'd told herself it was her imagination, that she was overly sensitive, but now that Cord was back she felt more uneasy than ever around David's best friend.

The coffee brewed and she added liqueur and cream, then carried both clear glass cups into the study. The fire was already crackling by the time she handed him his cup.

"Where's Cord?" Nate asked as he took an experimental sip. "Mmm. This is great."

"Thanks. I don't know where Cord is. He, uh, comes in late a lot," she said, pretending interest in the fire.

"A woman?" Nate asked.

"Oh, I don't know. Maybe." She attempted to sound casual as she dropped to the couch, but the thought of Cord with another woman turned her blood cold. "He's been busy."

"I'll bet. Police, insurance people, the press. He's Seattle's number one notorious citizen right now." Grinning, he sat next to her. "But he does live here?"

"Yes. Claims it's his."

"Hey, whoa! You're talking to a real estate man, remember? Seems to me he gave it all up when he took off and left his brother high and dry."

"He doesn't see it that way," Alison said, feeling instantly defensive of Cord but managing to hold back a hot retort by drinking from her cup.

"It's my guess he doesn't have a leg to stand on. Let him take you to court."

"Court?" Dear Lord, the last place she wanted to deal with Cord was in a courtroom. Her hands were suddenly unsteady, her voice faltering.

"Sure. He'll probably sue you for the remainder of the estate, but his reputation isn't the greatest, if you know what I mean."

"I don't want a court battle," she whispered, thinking about Mandy and the possibility that, when Cord eventually found out about his daughter, he might battle Alison for custody.

"Don't back down. You're David's widow, for God's sake, you inherited all of this legally. And Cord's circus stunt of reincarnation doesn't change a damned thing. Fight him for it. I know you've had some financial problems, but surely there's still quite a bit of money tied up in this house, the business and that place on Bainbridge Island. Don't give up without a fight, Alison. Think about Mandy."

I am, she wanted to scream. Then she heard it, the quiet rumble of Cord's Jeep climbing up the drive. Her heart began to hammer.

Nate poured himself another drink and loosened his collar.

"I think Cord's home," she said.

He glanced up through the window, his face turning grave. "Bastard," he mumbled, as if to himself.

She heard the engine die. A few minutes later a door slammed and Cord's footsteps rang through the kitchen.

Every muscle in her body tensed.

"Ali?" he called, poking his head into the den. His voice was warm and friendly, so much like before.

The warm sound brought a smile to her lips. "In here."

Hands pushed into the back pockets of his jeans, he sauntered into the den, then stopped dead in his tracks. His mouth curved downward. "Benson," he said flatly.

"Good to see you again, Cord." But Nate's words sounded hollow and as false as his smile. "So, you're famous now—got your name splashed all over the papers."

Alison's heart nearly stopped as Cord tensed.

"I almost didn't recognize you without your beard," Nate added, downing the remainder of his drink.

Cord stood near the fireplace, asking with quick menace, "Something I can help you with?"

"I was just visiting here with Alison."

"As David's friend, right?"

Nate seemed a little flustered. "You know we were close."

Cord nodded thoughtfully. "So you saw the accident?"

Alison's stomach twisted at the memory of the shock of David's death.

"I was there." His face taut, Nate set his cup on the table and shuddered visibly. "I'd, uh, rather not talk about it. It was—" he glanced at Alison and paled "—gruesome."

"Fair enough," Cord murmured, his own face whitening at the thought of David's death.

"As a matter of fact," Nate decided, glancing at his watch, "I'd better shove off. Good night, Alison. Thanks for the drink. I'll call you."

"You don't have to—"

But he was out the door in a hurry, the heels of his leather shoes clicking loudly across the foyer.

"I must have bothered him," Cord observed, watching through the window as the taillights of Nate's sports car disappeared down the drive.

Now they were alone, Alison realized, and nothing stood between them but the truth. Nervously she set her glass on the table.

"You could have been more civil," she said.

"I doubt it. He's a bastard."

"Exactly what he said about you."

Cord's lips curved sardonically. "Well, maybe he's smarter than I gave him credit for. I just don't like him hanging around." He glanced sharply at Alison then, as if he'd said too much. "Where's the sprite? In bed?"

"Norma took her for a few days, to visit her sister in Spokane."

Cord's mouth twitched. "Sister? Rose?"

"Right."

"Poor Mandy," he said, grinning despite himself. His teeth were white against his dark skin.

"Something wrong with Rose?" Alison wasn't worried. She'd met Norma's sister several times and the woman was warm and friendly. Mandy had taken to Rose immediately.

"Nothin' wrong if you like dogs. She takes in every stray in the country—dachshunds to elkhounds, puppies to arthritic mutts—it doesn't matter. They all end up at Rose's," he said thoughtfully, remembering the few visits he'd had with Norma's older sister. "Unless she's changed."

Alison smiled and stretched. "Mandy will be in seventh heaven."

"So," he drawled, walking to the couch and standing in front of her, "finally we're alone."

Her throat suddenly tight, she nodded. "Looks that way."

"Good." He dropped into a chair across from her and met her gaze levelly. "Now maybe we can clear up a few things."

Warned by the darkening of his eyes, she felt her stomach knot. "I suppose that would be a good idea," she whispered, feeling the need to put him on the defensive, "now that you're among the living again."

He ignored her remark, his gaze never wavering. "Let's start with one basic question."

Here it comes. She could read the determination glinting in his eyes. "I'm afraid I have more than one."

"So do I. But first things first." He reached forward, picking up the Lucite cube filled with snapshots.

Alison's heart stopped for a split second before pounding in rapid double time. "What?" she asked, her voice breathless, fearing what he was about to ask.

"Tell me about Mandy," he suggested, eyes severe as they drilled into hers. "Is she David's daughter? Or is she mine?"

Alison gulped.

"Did you hear me?" Cord repeated softly when she couldn't find her voice.

"Y-yes." *Dear Lord, why now?* she wondered frantically.

"And?"

There was no way out. She couldn't lie. Licking her lips, she admitted, "Of course Mandy's your daughter." He didn't seem the least bit surprised, and Alison, though she wanted to throw herself in his arms and beg him to love her and their child again, managed to lift her chin proudly. "Can't you see it?"

He was strung tight, every muscle coiled. "You're sure about it?"

"Positive," she said angrily. "Whether you believe it or not, Cord, I wasn't involved with anyone but you!" Desperate for him to believe her, she advanced on him, touching him gently on the shoulder. "I *never* slept with anyone but you that summer. There's no chance Mandy is any other man's child."

Some of the tension left his mouth, and she was moved to ask, "Don't you remember how it was with us?"

"I remember how it was for me."

"Me, too," she cried. "God, how I loved you."

He closed his eyes, as if in so doing, he could find the strength to repudiate everything she said, to feed the fires of hatred and revenge he'd nurtured for so long.

"I loved you, Cord," she repeated, knowing he was aching inside. "*Only* you."

"Don't," he said shakily, stepping away.

But she followed him. "And it hurts me that…that you could possibly think I was involved with anyone but you."

"David had the proof," Cord pointed out, his teeth clenched against her touch, her scent.

"What *proof?*" she demanded and dropped her hand. Talking with him was useless. "Not that it matters," she whispered. "What matters is that you trusted me so little." Shaking her head, she picked up the picture cube, glanced at the snapshot of Mandy and set the clear plastic box on the mantel. "You were my whole life," she said simply. "And you couldn't trust me to be faithful to you."

If only he could believe her!

"You were pregnant. Why didn't you tell me?"

Whirling, her eyes filled with tears of anguish, she challenged him. "I didn't get a chance, now, did I? The day after I found out, you took off and let everyone think you were dead! Do you know what that's like, to think the man you love, the father of your unborn child, left because he was an embezzler—because he couldn't face the police—and that he *died* out there in that cold, black water?" she demanded, reliving the terror of those first torturous nights without him.

"No. I only know what it's like to be told that the woman you love, the woman you had hoped to marry, is pregnant with your brother's child."

"Oh, Cord. How could you believe that? Didn't you once think that child might be yours?"

"I was careful," he replied. "You were careful. That's the way you wanted it, so you wouldn't have to marry me."

As if slapped in the face, she stepped back. How could he have twisted the truth so horridly? "I was careful because I didn't want to trap you into a marriage you weren't ready for," she insisted.

As desperately as Cord wanted to believe her, he knew she was lying. His brows drew down over dark, glowering eyes as he took hold of her arms and pushed his face so close to hers that she could see the pores of his skin, feel the heat of his breath. "But you were the one who wanted to hide the fact that we were seeing each other."

"I didn't want to compromise you."

"Or were you just hiding the fact from David?"

"If you'll think for one blasted moment," she threw back, "you'll realize I didn't have time for another man—David or anyone else. You and I, we were together constantly! Don't you remember? Or has bitterness twisted your memory?"

"I remember a lot," he replied, his jaw working.

"Then you remember how it was with us."

His eyes narrowed cruelly. "I remember being out of town. I remember finding you having breakfast or lunch with David. I remember David showing me the key to your apartment. I remember *David* telling me you were pregnant, showing me the pregnancy test results and admitting to fathering your child."

"But he never—I wouldn't—" Then she realized what she was saying and the color drained from her face. All that she had held sacred was suddenly stripped away. Stunned, she whispered hoarsely, "David. He...he must have lied."

"Do you really believe that?"

"I...I don't know what to believe," she admitted, feeling tossed adrift without an anchor. David had been good to her, cared for her and Mandy, loved them both after Cord had left. "Why would he—"

"He wouldn't," Cord said, releasing her.

Shaken, she dropped onto the couch, her thoughts a torn web of truth and lies. Nothing was making any sense. "I think— You'd better tell me what you remember. All of it," she said, incredulous at the depth of David's deception. *Or Cord's.*

He hesitated, rubbing a hand tiredly around his neck. "There's not much to tell," he admitted wearily, staring into the coals of the fire. "David told me he had something he wanted to discuss with me, something he couldn't talk about at the office. I thought it had to do with the company." Snorting derisively at his own ignorance, he closed his eyes. "He drove to your apartment and walked right in as if he owned the place." The lines around Cord's mouth tightened. "Used his own key and walked straight to the bedroom where he told me you were pregnant with his child."

"But how could he have known?"

"You tell me."

"I...I can't." Alison's mind was spinning. "Did he tell you he knew about us?"

Cord opened his eyes, staring at her. "He acted as if he didn't know you were seeing anyone but him. He went on and on about how much in love you were and how you'd insisted upon keeping your affair with him a secret so that his position at the company wouldn't be compromised."

"Oh, God," she whispered.

"Sound familiar?" Cord stood then, pushing his hands deep into his pockets.

"He couldn't have known...."

"He said that you were afraid of gossip and didn't

want me to know about the two of you, that you were afraid of other employees thinking you were trying to sleep your way to the top by getting involved with him."

She let out a small sound of protest. The words were her own, but she'd never mentioned them to David—only Cord.

"He even suggested that you, embarrassed over your 'condition,' might want to get rid of the baby to avoid any embarrassment to him or me or the company."

"And you believed him?" she asked, incredulous.

"He showed me the results of your pregnancy test and a bottle of some kind of vitamins in your nightstand."

"Prenatal vitamins," she whispered, swallowing. "But even with all that, didn't you think for one minute that the baby could have been yours?" she asked.

"Of course I did."

"Then?"

Doubts raced through him, doubts he wouldn't share with her. "I didn't understand why you would tell David that the baby was his."

"Didn't you think he might be lying?" She was incensed. "Even the most foolproof types of birth control aren't infallible! Why didn't you confront me?"

"David showed me a letter."

"A letter?"

"That you wrote to him, telling him about the baby and that you would marry him."

"*What?*" Shaken to the core, she just stared at him. "I never wrote any letter…."

"I saw it, damn it! In your own hand."

"Oh, Cord, no…" She fell onto the couch, letting her forehead drop to her hands. Wounded to the soul, she couldn't speak, didn't want to believe that David had lied.

"Then…" His jaw went slack as all those damned, unwelcome memories tore at his soul. "Why did he lie?"

Alison shook her head.

Cord paced between the fireplace and a window. "Why the hell did he lie?"

"I don't know."

His fingers flexed and straightened as he thought, trying to remember exactly what had happened. "He must have known we were seeing each other," he decided.

"But no one knew." *Except Norma.* Somehow the housekeeper had gleaned that she and Cord had been in love. Had they been so transparent?

"He had to!" Raking tense fingers through his hair, Cord squeezed his eyes shut, concentrating on a past he'd tried vainly to keep buried. "Someone had to know and either they told David or he guessed. Somehow he knew you and I were having a relationship."

Alison swallowed. "Norma knew."

"Norma?" he repeated, shocked. "How?"

"I don't know…but somehow she guessed. She wouldn't have told David, I'm sure of it," Alison decided, remembering her conversation with the older woman. "But if *she* guessed."

"He might have, too."

"Yes." She thought back to those first painful days when she'd not yet given up hope that Cord would be dragged from the water, miraculously alive. Slowly her hopes had faded and she'd confided in Cord's brother. "He…he knew afterward, of course."

"How? Did you tell him?"

"Y-yes. You were gone. I…we thought you were dead. At the memorial service," she whispered, the old pain returning, "I…I had trouble getting through it. Afterward,

David brought me home and I was sick to my stomach. He knew it was more than grief and he just put two and two together."

"So he *deduced* you were pregnant."

"I thought so."

"He already knew, Ali," Cord whispered, skin tightening over his rugged features, the evidence of David's betrayal scraping his soul raw. "Damn it all, and I believed him!" Sick with disgust, Cord walked to the bar and poured himself a drink. "I believed the bastard."

"I never wrote a letter."

"Then he must have forged it—or had someone else do it."

Alison thought back, remembering David's kind words, understanding touches, as she told him she was pregnant with his dead brother's child. He hadn't been shocked but he'd immediately offered to take care of her, help her through the pregnancy, give the child his name, the Donahue name.

At first she'd resisted, wanting to tell the world that she was carrying Cord's child, but David had convinced her to think about the baby, offer the fatherless child a home and chance at a normal childhood.

"David wouldn't lie," she said, curling her fists.

"He did, damn it! There's no other explanation."

"Unless you're making all this up."

"Me?" His face went slack. "Why?"

She was quivering inside, afraid to confront him with her doubts.

"I had no reason to lie."

"You had a million reasons," she whispered, thinking of the fortune that had disappeared with him.

Cord saw disappointment coloring her eyes and

realized just how deeply she had loved David. He didn't doubt that Mandy was his child. Alison wasn't lying. But what caused the white-hot jealousy to curdle in his veins was the devastating knowledge that Alison had loved his brother enough not to believe that David must have deceived them both.

Maybe she and David had been in it together, he thought savagely, anger ripping through his heart. Maybe they had been planning to defraud the company together. Maybe Alison had been distracting him, playing games with him while David had been siphoning money....

"You don't believe me," she said, witnessing the grim set of his jaw, the bitterness in his eyes.

"I trusted you with my life, Alison."

"And then you left."

"If only I'd known about the baby." His voice was low, barely audible.

"If only you'd stuck around so I could tell you." Suddenly weary, she stood on quavering legs and said, "This isn't getting us anywhere." She started for the door but Cord was on his feet and across the room, blocking her exit.

"We're not quite done."

"I think so."

"If Mandy's my daughter," he said, eyes dark with determination, "I want her to have my name, not David's. I want all the records changed, proving that *I'm* her father!"

"If?" she repeated. "Don't you believe me?"

"It's...difficult."

"Take a good long look at her."

"David was my brother, he could have passed on similar facial characteristics."

She forced a brittle smile. "I don't care if you believe me or not. She's your daughter. I never slept with David until we were married, not that it's any concern of yours. And if you want to do a paternity test, forget it. I'm not about to subject *my* daughter to anything so demeaning!" Her voice began to rise as her temper flared.

"It wouldn't work anyway," he pointed out. "David and I had the same blood type."

"Fine!" she shouted, reaching for the handle of the door and yanking it open. He slammed it shut with the flat of his hand. "Move, Cord."

"Not yet." His broad shoulders fell. "Okay, okay. I *do* believe she's my daughter," he admitted. "I've suspected it ever since I saw her."

"Thank God." Alison was relieved, but only for a minute.

His eyes met hers but no longer with anger, just raw determination. "I want partial custody of Mandy."

"Not on your life!" she spat.

His voice was low and serious. Not threatening, just flatly telling her what would happen. "It's up to you whether we work this out or not," he said with grim certainty. "I want my child. Surely you can understand."

"But—"

"Either you give me partial custody or I'll make the biggest stink this town has ever seen."

"You already have," she reminded him. "By doing your return-from-the-grave routine. *You* should have been named Lazarus!"

"Don't push me, Ali." He touched her cheek, almost tenderly, and Alison wanted to cry.

Refusing to break down, she said, "And don't push me. I've changed, Cord. I'm not putty in your hands anymore and you can threaten till you're blue in the face. I will never, *never* give up any custody rights!"

Her small fists were balled and she would have liked nothing better than to pound her clenched hands against his chest, hoping to knock some sense into him. How could he doubt her? How?

As if sensing the fury burning in her breast, he dropped his hand. "Oh, Ali," he whispered, his features softening as he stared at her, "how did we ever let ourselves get this far apart?"

Though touched, she couldn't, wouldn't let him see how much she still cared. "It happened when you ran away, Cord, when you sank into the black water and *decided* to conveniently disappear." Yanking open the door, she marched upstairs and slammed the door to her bedroom shut, hoping she could find some way to forget that she still loved him.

CHAPTER SEVEN

ON MONDAY MORNING Alison snapped her briefcase closed, glanced at herself in the mirror and decided she couldn't put off the inevitable any longer. At ten o'clock she was scheduled for a showdown with Rex Masterson of Federal Commerce Bank.

She hadn't really thought much about the foreclosure, at least not in the past few days. Before Cord's return from the dead she'd thought of little but saving the stately old Donahue Building in Pioneer Square, but since Cord had dropped so dramatically back into her life she hadn't had a chance to think of anything other than him.

But no longer. This morning the building would revert to the bank, unless she could come up with twenty thousand dollars.

"Fat chance," she mumbled to herself as she walked downstairs, pausing at the front closet for her coat. Although she knew Cord was awake—she could smell the scent of brewed coffee wafting from the kitchen— Alison decided not to confront him this morning. She needed all of her strength to face the fact that she'd lost the single most valuable asset of the entire corporation: the Donahue Building.

Alison had just tucked her umbrella under her arm

when the doors to the den cracked open and she felt rather than saw Cord lounging against the casing.

"Morning," he drawled.

"Hi." She glanced up, her gaze touching his for a moment. His chin was still dark with stubble and his jeans and plaid work shirt were nearly threadbare. He looked ready for a day on the docks of an Alaskan fishing village.

"Out so early?" he asked.

"I still have a job, you know." She heard the bite in her words and regretted it. She didn't have time for childish games or bitterness this morning.

"Right." He held up one finger. "As president of Donahue Investments."

She didn't bother to answer.

"And today is the day you meet with…Masters, right?"

"Rex Masterson."

"Don't you think you need a cup of coffee or maybe some breakfast before you battle with the lions?" He grinned lazily, his eyes sliding over her.

She felt her breath catch in her throat. "I'm fine," she lied, though her stomach was twisting nervously.

"I'll cook," he offered, slanting her his most engaging smile.

"No thanks."

"Maybe I can help, with the bank, that is."

She thought again about the money he'd supposedly made in Alaska. Maybe Cord could grant the company a small loan. But she discarded the wayward thought almost as soon as it crossed her mind. This was the same man who had threatened to mete out his vengeance against her. With a careful smile she decided she'd never take one thin dime from him. "No thanks," she repeated. "This is my problem."

"Correction—our problem," he pointed out. "Remember, what's left of the Donahue money should be mine."

"You should have thought of that before you 'died,'" she said.

"I just want to help." He seemed so sincere, she almost believed him.

"I appreciate it." Then, before she fell for his charade hook, line and sinker, she pulled the door open and walked outside.

Fog hung low over the land, wisping skyward in a gray, opaque mist shrouding the uppermost branches of the tall evergreens and softening the harsh roof lines of the old Tudor.

Alison's cheeks and forehead were damp by the time she reached her car and climbed inside. She knew Cord was still watching her, but she didn't even glance in the rearview mirror, afraid she would change her mind.

In the office Celia was already sitting behind her desk, diligently stuffing client computer statements into preaddressed envelopes.

She glanced up when Alison entered and her wide eyes sparkled. "About time you showed up," she chastised.

"I've had…company."

"You mean Cord Donahue, right? He's been staying at *your* house." Celia was clearly astonished.

"He seems to think it's his."

"Oh, I never thought of that."

"Who would have?" Alison said resignedly, hanging her coat on the hall tree. "We all thought he was dead."

"So tell me everything," Celia demanded as she poured them each a cup of coffee and set a cup on Alison's desk. "I've been on pins and needles all weekend."

"You and me both," Alison admitted. She told Celia Cord's story, leaving out nothing, while her friend sat, without a word, in one of the client chairs near Alison's desk.

"He thought *you* took the fortune?"

"That's his story."

"And you don't believe him. Right?"

Alison leaned back in her chair and rubbed her temples. "I don't know what to believe," she admitted. "I never wanted to believe that he took the funds, but the evidence seemed to point to him."

"So if he didn't and you didn't, who did?"

"I don't know," Alison said. "Cord insinuated that David and I might have been in on it together."

"Slow down! Now he's trying to blame your husband?"

"And me. Collusion or something just as dastardly." Alison managed a small laugh. "How about that?"

"Sounds phony to me. I remember your husband. He, uh, was a nice guy."

"Thanks," Alison agreed, finally sipping from her tepid coffee. David had been kind and understanding and he'd let her work as much as she'd wanted. He'd taught her much about the business, just as Cord had, and with his help and her background she'd learned to run the company. If he'd had a fault, it had been his bitterness at Cord's inheritance of their parents' estate. But even his jealousy had died when Cord had disappeared. Cord had managed to make her doubt David, and she resented Cord for those doubts.

"So what're you going to do now?" Celia asked.

"About what?" she asked. There were so many problems to face, the most important being custody of Mandy.

"About the company. Doesn't this Cord guy want to get back into it?"

"I think so."

"And?"

"Well, he still has to clear his name with the police and the insurance company."

"But you think he will?"

"*He* seems to think so," Alison granted. "I guess I can't worry about that now. Rex Masterson and heaven only knows who else will be here soon."

"Oh!" Celia shot up from her chair, nearly spilling her coffee. "I almost forgot." She reached over and picked up a pink note from her desk. "Masterson's secretary called and claimed he won't make today's meeting. He'll call later and reschedule."

"Did she say why?"

"No."

Relieved, Alison sighed. "It doesn't matter. Now we have more time to figure out an alternative source of capital." She drummed her fingers on the desk. "Did anyone else call?"

Celia handed a few pink messages to Alison. "Two reporters and an insurance adjuster. They'll call later."

"But Cord's not coming here."

Celia lifted a shoulder. "They didn't seem to believe me. Also, there was a Detective Donnelly from the police."

"For Cord?" Alison asked, apprehensive.

"You guessed it," Celia said with a sigh.

"How did he sound?"

"That's the funny part. He acted as if he just wanted to talk. Nothing demanding or pushy, not like I've seen on TV."

"Maybe you've been watching too much," Alison observed, silently grateful that the policeman hadn't been overtly antagonistic. Mentally crossing her fingers, she hoped Cord really had proved his innocence to the police.

"So, what about Mr. Donahue? Couldn't he invest some money into the business and pay something on the loan?"

Alison frowned, thinking what Cord's reaction would be when he realized that the mortgage on the building had been arranged by his brother. "I don't think that would be such a good idea."

"Why not? The newspaper said he'd made a small fortune in the fishing business in Alaska."

"I think it would be best if we left him out of this," Alison said just as the door to the office burst open and Cord, clean-shaven and dressed in a pale gray suit, crisp white shirt and wine-colored tie, strode into the room.

Celia sat glued to her chair, just staring at him. "You—you must be—"

"Cord Donahue," he supplied.

"Celia Davis," Alison cut in, standing, her stomach tightening as she stood and made hasty introductions. What the devil was he doing here?

"Good." He shook Celia's hand. "I assume you're Alison's right-hand man—er, woman."

"And left hand," Alison said.

His gaze swept the offices, hardening as he noted how bare the two small rooms appeared.

"I didn't expect to see you here," Alison admitted, wondering what game he was playing.

He dazzled her with his near-perfect smile, but Alison's heart froze. She knew as sure as he was standing there that he must already have set in motion his plan to take everything away from her. First the business and the house—next Mandy.

"When I left here four years ago, I was president of this company. I don't see that it's changed much."

"Not changed?" she repeated, glancing at Celia.

Sensing the tension simmering between Cord and Alison, Celia grabbed a stack of letters and reached for her coat. "I think I'll run to the post office and make the deposit at the bank." Anxiously glancing over her shoulder, she shrugged into her wool coat and ducked out the door as quickly as Cord had walked in.

"What do you think you're doing?" Alison asked.

"Saving your neck."

"What?"

"I don't have a lot of time," he said, crossing the room to one of the cabinets and opening the top drawer. "I want to see all the ledgers, reports and any printout and investor research material you've got." Grabbing a couple of file folders, he scanned them rapidly. "And when Ms. Davis gets back, let's get her in on this. We'll need all the help we can get."

"Just hold on a minute."

"I'm serious, Alison," he said with quiet authority.

"What you're asking is impossible. We have client reports to mail," she said, indicating the small stack of printouts still strewn over Celia's desk.

"Not until I see them."

"*You?* What have you got to do with this?" But she knew.

"Everything. As far as I can tell, I'm still president of this company and—" when she opened her mouth to protest, he held up his hand "—I've checked with the family attorney. If you don't believe me call Carl Zimmerman. Right now you and I are a team, *Mrs.* Donahue. So you can work with me or against me. What's it going to be?"

"I don't know," she said in total honesty. "You've already contacted Carl?"

He smiled that damned cocksure smile that made her heart squeeze stupidly. "Several times. Now, why don't you grab all the ledgers, reports, computer printouts and whatever else you've got and bring them to me. I'll just sit here—" he motioned to the single couch near the windows "—until my desk arrives."

"Your desk?"

"It'll be delivered tomorrow afternoon."

"You have been busy, haven't you?" she asked, annoyed at his high-handedness.

"More than you know," he said cryptically as he scooped up the reports from Celia's desk and plopped comfortably down on the sofa.

Alison stood dumbstruck for a full thirty seconds, wondering what to do with him. If there were any of the old tenderness in his gaze, she might have stayed, but instead she said, "I think I'll go out for a while." More than anything she needed to clear her head—away from Cord. "My appointment canceled and I have—"

"I know."

She was reaching for her coat, but her hand fell back to her side as his words sank in. "*How* do you know?"

"I talked to the bank and Rex Masterson, as well as the insurance company and several clients."

"All in one morning?" There was no doubt about it, Cord was back and he was in charge, and he didn't give a damn about the way she'd had to struggle these past months, didn't care one whit that she'd tried everything she could think of to save a company that he had helped ruin when he'd pretended to die in the sound. Anger fired her blood. "But how could you, without consulting me, for crying out loud?" she demanded. "I've been dealing with these people for nearly four years."

"And you need help," he said soberly.

"Help? From you?" She shoved her arms angrily through the sleeves of her coat and swung the strap of her purse over her shoulder. "You're the man who just last week promised to ruin me, remember?"

"That was before I knew I was Mandy's father."

"And that makes all the difference?" She couldn't believe his gall.

"Yes," he said simply, lines deepening near the corners of his mouth.

"So one minute you're against me, the next you're on my side," she accused, her cheeks flaming with color. "Well, excuse me if I don't buy it, Cord. I haven't spent the past four years of my life waiting for you to tear up everything I've worked for. Nor am I going to just let you bulldoze your way back into my life or Mandy's!" Without waiting for a response, she tied the belt of her raincoat and stormed out of the office, hearing the door slam behind her.

Just who did he think he was?

Cord Donahue, rightful heir to the company, house and fortune. Mandy's father.

Damn the man! Her boots echoed furiously against the stairs as she shoved her way outside. Stuffing her hands into her pockets, she ignored the threatening dark clouds overhead and started walking up one hilly street and down the next, wending her way along the steep slopes of the city as she attempted to cool off.

She was furious with him for barging into the office,

bitter that he'd let her think he was dead and disgusted with herself for still caring about him. "You are an idiot of the first order," she muttered under her breath as she noticed a Viennese bakery and decided to treat herself to a cup of gourmet coffee and the gooiest slice of apple strudel she could find.

The bakery was filled with the scents of cinnamon, mocha and vanilla. Patrons sat around small, round tables, sampling the coffee and pastries as they read the newspaper or gossiped among themselves, while waitresses scurried between the counter and the tables, refilling cups, taking orders and offering genuine smiles and twinkling eyes.

Alison ordered at the counter, then, after being served a plate of strudel and a cup of thick Austrian coffee with cream, she found an empty table and resolved not to think about Cord.

But as she sipped her coffee, her thoughts continued to stray to him. His image, changing as it had over the years, teased at her mind. She remembered running carefree along the beach with him, waking up in his arms, feeling the warm, steady beat of his heart as she lay with him. She remembered the more recent cruel, accusing bearded man who had sworn his revenge, then the gentle, amused way he'd watched Mandy and a few small glimpses of a more tender Cord.

So who was he today? Was the neatly dressed, all-business president of the company friend or foe?

"Freshen your cup?" a pert young waitress asked.

Alison glanced up to stare into bright blue eyes and a friendly smile. "No thanks," she decided, and the young girl, who seemed a reminder of how naive and trusting Alison had once been, moved on to the next table.

Gritting her teeth against unwelcome memories, Alison paid for her pastry, then marched back outside.

Rain had begun to fall in big, pelting drops that pooled on the sidewalk and ran down the street before puddling over clogged storm drains. Bareheaded, she threaded her way down the steep sidewalks to the waterfront, breathing in the familiar scents of the docks—fish, salt, cigarette smoke and diesel.

Just a few days before she'd been on these same wet piers with Cord and Mandy, pretending to be a normal family. Today she felt morbidly alone.

Leaning against the railing and staring across the frigid waters of Puget Sound, Alison wondered what she was going to do. Obviously Cord was back for good. As he'd pointed out, she could either work with him or against him. The problem was that he wasn't reliable. One minute she was convinced he was out for blood—her blood; the next she was certain he still cared for her. "Damned if you do, damned if you don't," she worried aloud, feeling the wind push her hair away from her face.

She was left with only one choice. She had to wait him out. She would tread carefully and watch his every move, holding her tongue while he acted as president of the company and talked with the business associates she'd been dealing with for years. Sooner or later his true colors would surface and she'd know whether he was for her or against her.

She couldn't help crossing her fingers deep in the pockets of her raincoat, because the sad truth of it was, she desperately wanted Cord on her side.

THE WEEK SLOWLY passed. Cord's new walnut desk had been delivered, along with a chocolate-colored leather

chair, a personal computer and carpeting, which he'd put
into the empty office across the hall on the very day that
his phone had been installed.

Alison managed the days well, ignoring Celia's wondering stare and complying with Cord's every demand.
She hadn't made a scene when Rex Masterson from the
bank had stopped by upon Cord's request and extended
the mortgage. Nor had she done more than grit her teeth
when Lila Prentiss, an elderly client, had insisted on
meeting with Cord, treating Alison as an underling.

She'd forced a smile when the police had stopped by
to ask her a few questions.

"What do *you* think, Mrs. Donahue?" Detective
Donnelly had asked. "You worked here."

He'd been crusty but had seemed fair. And there was
a kindness in his eyes she hadn't expected from a man
who'd been on the force for over ten years.

"I don't believe Cord Donahue would steal," she
had admitted.

"Then who would? What about your husband?"

"I find that hard to believe as well. What do *you* think,
detective?"

"It's a baffler," he'd admitted, pouring himself a cup
of coffee. "Before I met Cord Donahue, I would have said
he did it. His actions speak for themselves. But he did
come back, and now, well, call it gut instinct, but I don't
think he took the money. I think he was framed."
Donnelly had studied his fingernails. "He's been more
than willing to help us out, give us anything we need. No,
ma'am, he certainly isn't acting like a man guilty of embezzlement, leastwise not anymore."

She'd been relieved and put up with the officer's questions, probing eyes and insistence on looking through every single file in the entire office.

However, if the days had been rough, the past few nights had been torture. Not knowing what time Cord would return and wondering if he'd come back to the house at all had been difficult. Most evenings his Jeep roared up the drive long after midnight. She would lie in bed, listening to him walk through the house and up the stairs, tensing as he passed her door.

One night she thought he paused in the hallway just outside her room. She even imagined that the doorknob twisted, but then his footsteps had continued down the hallway to David's old room. And stupidly she'd been disappointed.

By Friday evening she was near the breaking point.

"Get hold of yourself," she whispered to herself, yanking off her suit jacket and hanging it in her bedroom closet. Determined not to let him get the better of her, she changed into her favorite pair of jeans and an oversize plum-colored sweater before clipping her hair away from her face.

When the phone rang she jumped, then scolded herself as she answered the extension in the kitchen.

"Mommy?"

Alison's heart constricted. "Hi, sweetheart. How are you?"

"I miss you."

"I miss you, too. Are you coming home tomorrow?"

"I don't know. But I want to ride the ponies."

"What ponies?"

"Aunt Rose got ponies."

"Aunt Rose lives in the heart of Spokane," Alison said, mystified. "How can she possibly have ponies?"

"She got dogs, too," Mandy said, ignoring the question.

"So I've heard."

After a few more minutes of conversation that didn't make too much sense, Alison heard Norma's voice. "Did you get all that?" Norma asked, chuckling.

"Not really."

"Here's the gist of it. Rose's daughter, Judy, has a farm just outside the city. Judy raises Welsh ponies and has offered to give Mandy a buggy ride on Sunday."

"Can I go?" Mandy called from the background.

"So we were wonderin' if we could come back next Monday. It's up to you."

Alison's heart sank. "I suppose," she said, "if it's not too much trouble and if Mandy's okay."

"Mandy's havin' a ball," Norma assured her. "Oh, she misses you at night, of course, but the rest of the time, between seein' the sights and playin' in the backyard, she doesn't have too much time to get lonely. Rose's cocker spaniel has a litter of pups—nine of 'em—and Mandy can't leave them alone."

"I'll bet not."

"Then it's okay?" Norma asked.

"If you can handle it."

"Good. No problem on this end." She took in a deep breath, then asked, "Now, tell me—the truth, mind you—how're things going at home?"

"Okay, I guess." Alison attempted to sound more sure of herself, but she couldn't lie to Norma. She leaned against the kitchen wall and twisted the phone cord in her fingers.

"And Cord?"

Alison tensed. "He...seems fine."

"I suppose he handled the bank."

"I guess," Alison admitted, still annoyed with him for keeping her in the dark. "Somehow he managed to pay a couple of payments and keep the building from being foreclosed."

"Saints be praised."

Alison wasn't so sure about praising saints. Not yet, anyway. She told Norma what had been happening at the office, blew a kiss over the wires to Mandy and hung up feeling entirely desolate.

"So do something about it," she muttered when she caught herself beginning to mope. "Take advantage of a weekend of freedom—no work for two days, no worries about the bank foreclosing on the investment company, no child to cater to…"

And probably no Cord. Strangely, that last thought was the most disheartening. Despite herself, she'd been hoping that Mandy would return and Cord would take them sight-seeing again.

Hating herself for being such a hopeless romantic, she grabbed the telephone directory and quickly punched out the number of a local travel agency. Maybe they had a weekend tour of the San Juan Islands.

An answering machine took her call and she hung up without leaving a message just as she heard Cord's Jeep come up the drive. She was surprised. He hadn't been home before midnight all week. Her pulse jumped as he walked through the back door.

His tie was dangling askew, his suit jacket was wrinkled and his jaw was dark with a day's growth of beard. "Mandy back?" he asked, eyes searching the kitchen and hallway.

"No. Norma called. They're staying over until Monday."

His lips tightened and disappointment clouded his gaze. "Why?"

Alison explained about Norma's call and Cord relaxed a little.

"So it's just you and me, huh?" His dark eyes met hers and she melted a little.

"Actually, I thought I'd try and catch a ferry to the San Juans tomorrow, maybe spend the night in Friday Harbor."

He frowned and ran a tired hand around the back of his neck. "You've already made plans?"

"Not yet."

His thick eyebrows lifted and some of the lines of strain disappeared from the corners of his mouth. "Good. I've got a better idea."

"Which is?"

"You'll see. Go pack for the weekend, just as if you were going to the San Juans."

"Wait a minute, Cord."

"Just do it."

"This isn't the office, you know," she reminded him, her temper sparking a little. "I've put up with you barking orders all week, but now—"

"Please," he interrupted softly. "Just this once, trust me, Ali. We need to talk. About Mandy. And…and I think we should take this chance to be alone, see if what we once had is still there."

She could hardly believe her ears. "Is that what you want?"

He closed his eyes. "I don't know what I want anymore," he admitted, his voice raw as he reached forward, pushing a strand of black hair off her cheek and grazing her skin with his fingers. "But I hope to find out."

"By being alone with me."

"Yes." His voice was low and throaty, and Alison's breath constricted. He didn't have to say what he was thinking; she could see the turn of his thoughts deep in his eyes. Was it possible? Did they have a chance together? Or was this another trick, one with Mandy as the prize?

"This is hard, you know," she admitted. "You've been running hot and cold with me."

"I can't help it," he admitted, throat working. "Just being around you is driving me crazy."

Alison felt tears sting her eyes at the memory those old, familiar words evoked. "I just don't know where I stand with you. One minute you're swearing to ruin me, the next…" Her voice trailed off as his lips lowered to brush over hers, warm and gentle, offering sweet relief from the stress of the week.

"Just this once," he said, wrapping strong arms around her, holding her close, "don't try to second-guess me." His breath fanned her face as he leaned his forehead against hers. "I know I came on strong when I got back."

"Came on strong?" she repeated, eyes rounding incredulously. "That's the understatement of the century. You wanted to rip me to pieces, Cord, and you didn't make any bones about it."

"I know. It was a mistake."

"Of monumental proportions!"

"Hey, give me a break," he whispered. "I'm trying to apologize and it's not easy."

"Just as it's not easy to accept. You…you change too quickly."

Sighing, he rolled his eyes to the ceiling. "Then don't trust me. That's fine. Just pack your bags."

"I'm not sure—"

"Alison, please." He straightened and his gaze grew dark. "I don't think either of us has time for games anymore."

"Meaning?" she asked, her heart nearly stopping.

"It's now or never. We've got to work this thing out.

We have a daughter to consider, a daughter I've grown to love. Either you're coming with me…or not."

Swallowing the huge lump of pride in her throat, Alison squared her shoulders. She didn't know if he was threatening her, warning her that he might try to take Mandy from her, but she had to find out. Besides, there might be just the slimmest chance that they could find each other again. "Okay, Cord," she agreed, pushing back her doubts. "I'll come with you, blindly trusting you to take me to God only knows where. But I'm not going to make any ridiculous promises about trust, okay? Too much has happened this week."

Jaw taut, Cord nodded as he pulled off his dangling tie. "Fair enough."

Silently praying she wasn't setting herself up for the worst fall of her life, Alison left the room and ran upstairs to pack.

CHAPTER EIGHT

CORD STARED THROUGH the windshield to the taillights glowing on the road ahead. What had gotten into him? he thought angrily. Why had he asked Alison to spend the weekend with him? Sure, the past week had been difficult and the nights alone in that drafty old house with Alison just down the hall had been murder.

He couldn't remember when he'd had a full night's sleep. To avoid being near her he'd spent long hours at the office, eaten late dinners in a nearby café and even spent some time in a local pub watching sports and drinking beer. Alternately hating her and loving her, he'd managed to make it through the grueling week.

Now he'd ruined everything by insisting she spend a weekend alone with him. Sliding a glance in her direction, he realized she was wedged up against the window, putting as much distance as possible between them.

He almost smiled. She looked about as happy as if she were going to her own funeral. Her skin was white, her eyes wide and staring straight ahead, and her hands were stuffed deep into the pockets of her down jacket. Her lips drawn into a thoughtful line, her arched brows puckered, she didn't say a word as he drove crazily through the streets of Seattle.

Just great! So what did he hope to accomplish this

weekend? Ever since returning to Seattle, he'd been drawn to her—more with each passing day. Though he knew she'd used him in the past, he was no longer certain of her betrayal. And he was convinced he'd been too hard on her.

At the painful twist of his thoughts, he winced. He believed that she hadn't slept with David, at least not until after she'd thought Cord had drowned. And he believed Mandy was his child. But what about the books, the god-damned accounting books that had proved she'd falsified company records? And what about that damned letter David had shown him? David, there was another matter. Why had he lied?

Because he wanted to get rid of you. Because he wanted Alison for himself. Because, no doubt, he was involved in the theft—the theft for which you were blamed.

"Son of a bitch," he muttered and Alison jumped.

"What?"

"Never mind. I was just thinking."

"Nothing good from the sound of it," she observed.

"No, nothing good," he agreed. The depth of David's betrayal still slashed through his soul and he felt a twinge of guilt. Should he have given David his due, dividing the estate equally and taking the chance that David would accept his responsibility? David had resented Cord, but had he hated him? The awful thought kept searing through his brain. Had he, in his self-important role as older brother, driven David to lying and theft and who knew what else?

ALISON STARED OUT the window, frowning. Stretching, she shifted involuntarily closer to Cord. "Where are we going?" she asked as Cord cranked hard on the wheel and rounded a sharp corner in the heart of the city.

"Can't you guess?"

She looked ahead, past the steep downgrade to the waterfront. Heart sinking, Alison leaned back against the seat. "The marina," she whispered, thinking about the sleeping bags and bags of groceries Cord had packed into the back of the Jeep. She'd known then this wasn't just a camping trip.

"Right."

She glanced toward the ominous sky. Dusk was giving way to night and the light rain had mixed with fog. Ahead, the lights of the marina winked eerily through the thick mist. "This isn't a night to take the boat out."

"You're probably right," he agreed.

"Won't the harbor patrol stop us?"

"Maybe."

"You don't care, do you?" she asked as he parked near a private slip and she recognized the boat—a boat replaced by insurance company money—rocking near the dock.

He offered her a crooked smile. "The police and I have become good friends," he said cynically. "Come on, let's go."

She didn't have much choice.

"Did David pick this out?" he asked, cocking his head toward the stark white boat. Bobbing on the water with its name, *Ali's Dream*, visible, the small craft was tied in the same slip where Cord's boat had once been moored.

"Yes. After your accident."

"After the appropriate mourning period, I hope."

She let out an exasperated sigh. "Of course. I've tried to sell it, but the one man who was interested defaulted and I've got it back."

"Why did you want to sell it?"

"Because I needed the money," she said with a sigh.

He frowned, staring at the helm as if gauging what the tiny white vessel was worth. "Is it still for sale?"

"Yes. But I haven't taken out another advertisement yet. The deal fell through the week you came back and…" She shrugged. "I've had other things on my mind."

Without another word she helped him load their gear into the gleaming craft. Once all the bags were packed tightly in the hold, Cord unleashed the mooring rope and stood at the helm.

As the engines roared to life Alison took a seat near the stern, then watched as Cord wended the boat through the marina and nosed its prow into the sound.

The cold April wind nipped at her face and tore at her hair, and Alison wrapped her arms around her waist. She had made a horrid mistake by agreeing to leave with him. Within a few minutes she realized where they were headed and she wondered why she hadn't figured out their destination before.

Cord was taking her back to Bainbridge Island, the remote stretch of beach where they'd first made love under showering skyrockets.

That piece of her life seemed so long ago, as if in another lifetime altogether.

The minutes ticked slowly by as the boat cut through the water. Eventually the island loomed, a foreboding mountain rising from the fog ahead. Shuddering inside, Alison braced herself.

Cord had been quiet throughout the ride. His eyes trained on the sea, his jaw thrust forward, he guided the craft through the inky water to the private beach near the Donahue family's log cabin.

When he cut the engine the ensuing silence seemed

tomblike. Only the sound of lapping water disturbed the still night.

"Did you and David ever come here?" he asked, tying the boat to the rotting posts supporting the dock.

"Never."

"Why not?" His eyes searched her face.

"Didn't seem right somehow," she whispered, her voice tight as she squinted against the darkness. She could barely discern the strip of sandy beach and, farther away, the cabin. "David wasn't interested in spending any time here, either. We had the place locked up. A couple of times a year a woman from Winslow checks up on it, cleans the interior, sprays berry vines, pulls weeds—that sort of thing."

"Mandy would love coming here," he observed, old emotions surfacing as he glanced quickly around the deserted dock.

"Probably."

He carried both suitcases and a flashlight, but when he heard a creaking noise he stopped. Sweeping the area with the thin beam, he picked out a faded real-estate signpost rocking in the wind. The words Price Reduced were nearly illegible, as was the telephone number of the listing agency.

"So much for nostalgia," Cord muttered, kicking the blasted sign and stalking up the weed-choked path to the cabin.

Guiltily Alison followed. "I didn't have much choice, you know," she said as he tried the lock and found his key no longer worked.

"Do you have a key?" he asked.

"Back at the house."

"In Seattle. That won't do us much good here."

Dropping her shoulder bag onto the porch, she let out a weary sigh. "You didn't tell me we needed it. I had no idea you intended to bring me back here."

His snort was derisive. "Then I'll just have to climb in like I did as a kid," he decided, letting the suitcases fall to the ground before springing onto the railing of the porch and shinning up the corner post to the roof.

"Are you crazy? What're you doing?" she called, just as she heard footsteps on the roof overhead, then a rusty hinge creak. A few seconds later he was at the front door, opening it from the inside.

"No electricity," he said as she walked into the cabin. "Turned off."

"And the water?"

"I…I don't know."

He turned the flashlight on the fireplace, the small beam moving slowly across the dusty mantel. "Here we go." The light settled on a box of wooden matches, and Cord struck one to the wick of a kerosene lantern. Slowly the room filled with a warm, yellow glow.

Alison's gaze skated around the small room. The furniture had been draped and a carpet was rolled against one wall. Every available surface, from the plank floors to the windowsills and mantel, was covered with a thin layer of dust.

"When was the last time your cleaning lady spent some time here?" Cord asked, swiping at a cobweb before checking the damper on the river-rock fireplace.

"Last fall."

"Hmph. Maybe we should have her come more often—like three times a year."

"Very funny," Alison said, but couldn't keep a straight face. There was something vital and romantic about camping in the old cabin with Cord. Slowly she began to relax. Maybe this weekend alone really was what they needed.

As Cord checked the back porch for firewood, Alison pulled the dustcovers off the furniture and managed to roll the carpet across the floor. She knew being alone with him was dangerous. If she wasn't careful, she'd let her emotions show and fall victim to him all over again.

But isn't that what you expected? her mind taunted as she glanced at the rolled sleeping bags. She couldn't pretend, not even to herself, that making love with Cord hadn't crossed her mind. She only hoped that, if and when the time came, she'd be able to think with her head and not her heart.

Despite her determined thoughts a flood of memories of that summer assuaged her. This very island was where they had first made love....

"It's looking better," Cord admitted, breaking into her thoughts as he carried two huge chunks of oak into the room and stacked them near the fireplace. "There's kindling on the porch and old newspapers in one of the kitchen cupboards, but not much else."

"You brought food," she reminded him, thinking of the two sacks of groceries still in the hold of the boat.

"Not all that much."

"I'm sure we'll survive for one night. Besides, I'm not very hungry," she replied, watching as he stooped before the dark grate and lit a match to old kindling. She couldn't help noticing the way he moved—so easily, as if his muscles were fluid. And his jeans hung low over his lean hips and slim waist, his denim jacket stretched tight across his shoulders. Working in Alaska had taken away any ounce of fat on him, she decided, wondering exactly how he'd spent those past four years, and with whom. Had there been a woman in Alaska? Or several? She couldn't expect him to have been celibate all that time—

"Something on your mind?" he asked.

Alison drew in a sharp breath. "I was just thinking."

"You looked a million miles away."

"Not that far," she admitted. "Only fifteen hundred or so."

In the firelight his dark eyebrows drew downward. "Fifteen hundred miles?"

"Alaska," she said simply. "I just wondered how you spent your time."

"Working."

"And when you weren't?"

"Sleeping."

Her mouth was suddenly dry and she licked her lips. "Alone?"

Then he understood and he sighed, his strong shoulders bowed. "I'd like to lie to you, Alison, and tell you I had women by the score," he said, "but quite frankly, I didn't have time. Not that I wouldn't have gladly traded a sixteen-hour day for one night with a beautiful woman," he added.

"That's hard to believe," she whispered. "Four years?"

His lips curved downward, his angular features suddenly hard. "Let's just say the opportunity never presented itself. I wasn't as lucky as you were. I didn't have another woman to fall back on."

Without thinking, she slapped him as hard as possible across his square jaw. "That's not the way it was," she hissed, quaking inside. "I've explained over and over again what happened, and I'm not about to spend this entire weekend being made to feel like some kind of cheap opportunist who just used whichever brother was around—whichever brother was *alive*—for her own purposes!" So furious she was shaking, Alison ranted, "I agreed to come on this trip with you to try to sort a few things out, but I will not—do you hear me, *will not*—be treated like some sort of…of…Jezebel!"

"I didn't mean to—"

"Then stop with the snide comments, Cord. Because I don't need them."

"You were the one who wanted to know about my love life in Alaska."

"Because I cared, damn it! Because I cared about you!" Swallowing hard, she started to turn away but he reached for her swiftly, twirling her into his arms and pressing his mouth to hers in an urgency born of four wasted years.

Alison tried to draw back, to ignore the sweet pressure of his hands splayed against her back, but she couldn't. And when his lips moved gently over hers, she couldn't resist. Her lips parted of their own accord, tasting him, feeling his tongue probe the soft recesses of her mouth, his fingertips hard pressure points on the small of her back.

A glowing fire spread through her, rivaled only by the heat and crackle of the flames in the grate.

"Oh God, Alison, what am I going to do with you?" he whispered raggedly, dragging his mouth from hers for a second.

Just love me, Cord. Pretend that all the pain of the past never existed. Pretend that we were always meant to be together, that nothing could ever come between us.

"I…I'm still wondering what to do with *you*," she

admitted. His hands twined in her hair, exposing her throat, and his lips touched her bare skin. Slowly, all rational thought spun away and she felt them both slide to the floor, with nothing but a tattered old carpet covering the hardwood.

Groaning, as if battling with himself, Cord hesitated, staring into her eyes. In his gaze she saw the reflection of the fire and a deep, hidden longing that was meant only for her.

"God, I've missed you," he admitted throatily, his lips seeking hers again as his hands worked wondrous magic over her jacket, zipping it open to gain access to her sweater. She felt his fingers against the soft wool as he gently kneaded the swell of her breasts.

Aching deep inside, she moaned his name, feeling the delicious power of his weight as he lay across her, pushing her jacket off her shoulders, gently tugging her sweater over her head, loosening the fastening of her jeans until at last she lay naked in front of the flames, her breasts firm with the need of his touch.

Her eyes locked with his, and she saw him swallow then lick his lips before leaning forward to capture one taut nipple in his mouth.

"Oh, Cord," she cried as bittersweet memories filled her mind and white-hot passion fired her blood. She could hear her heartbeat, echoed by his own as he caressed each breast before suckling hungrily.

She couldn't think about his promise of vengeance, wouldn't believe that he was using her. Though a small rational part of her mind screamed at her, warning her to be careful, to take things slowly, Alison paid it no heed: she was in the arms of the man she loved and nothing else mattered.

Alison's fingers sought and found the fastenings of his clothes. She pushed off his jacket and then quickly stripped him of his shirt, feeling the supple ripple of his muscular shoulders and abdomen, burying her face in the warm down covering his chest.

He groaned when she unbuckled his belt, his stomach muscles contracting as she slid his jeans over his hips and thighs. "I've wanted you so long," he murmured as he settled against her, his long body molding to the soft contours of hers.

"And I've wanted you," she whispered, her throat catching as he captured her lips with his and slowly, with the patience of one who had waited far too long, parted her legs with his knees and delved inside.

Heat, moist and pulsing, swept through Alison and she arched to meet him, pressing her body against his, falling willing victim to his rhythm.

"Alison…oh, love," he whispered against her hair, smoothing her brow, licking the soft drops moistening her skin as he moved silkily within her.

She felt a hundred different emotions tearing at her. Her breath was shallow and her eyes, locked with his, became glazed as she saw again that fragrant summer night when she was first his. "Cord," she cried, convulsing against him. Her fingers dug into his shoulders as reality shattered, a brilliant starburst not unlike that first skyrocket-filled night.

"Love me," he rasped, straining one glorious second, pausing over her, muscles taut, before, with a cry bursting from deep in his lungs, he fell over her, his welcome weight crushing her breasts, his body fitting perfectly against hers.

"I do," she murmured softly into the mat of hair on his

chest, the words muffled by the pounding of his heart and his shuddering breaths.

Lying with Cord, feeling vulnerable and lost, Alison blinked against tears forming in the corners of her eyes. She had waited for him so long, and now that she was with him she couldn't hold back tears of relief. As if to reassure herself, she clung to him, feeling his strident muscles beneath her hands, listening to his slowing heart-beat.

Lifting his head, Cord saw the shimmer of her tears. "Regrets?" he asked, kissing the salt-laden drops from her cheeks.

"Relief," she whispered. "I never thought I'd see you again. I'd given up hope."

A crooked grin slashed across his jaw, his teeth gleaming white in the semidark. "Oh, ye of little faith," he taunted, chuckling deep in his throat.

"How can you joke about it?"

Touching the tip of her nose with his finger, he said, "I think you and I need a little levity, don't you?"

Sniffing back her tears, she managed a wavering smile. "Aren't you the same man who promised to ruin me, and take his own sweet time about it?"

"Can't deny it," he groaned.

"Then you can see my dilemma."

He grinned again, more wickedly, and his eyes glinted mischievously. "You know," he whispered, moving his finger down her throat with painstaking leisure, "I could claim to have wrought my vengeance on you just now."

"Or mine on you," she whispered, sucking in her breath as he touched his finger to his tongue, then moistened the tip of her breast. It hardened to a taut little point. "T-two can play at this game."

"Oh?" he mocked, still teasing her breast.

She shuddered with delicious chills but managed to run her tongue down his neck and breastbone, breathing hot against his chest.

In response he groaned. "You never did like to lose," he ground out.

"Never." And she toyed with him as he had with her.

"God, woman, you're ruthless," he muttered at last and then, with all the strength he could muster, rolled onto his feet and, wrapping her in an old quilt from the couch, lifted her deftly into his arms.

"Hey, what're you doing?" she said, grinning, her black hair cascading over his arm.

"What I should have done the minute I got back from Alaska," he decided as he mounted the stairs, carrying her, laughing, to the darkened recess of the loft.

There, as rain drummed against the roof and fir boughs slapped the siding, Cord stripped away the dust cloth. "Now, Ali," he said huskily, laying her on the old mattress and keeping the quilt around them, "let me show you just how much I missed you." Slanting his lips over hers, he slowly moved against her. "This time," he promised darkly, "I won't be in such a rush...."

ALISON AWOKE FROM a deep sleep. The gray light of dawn had seeped through the windows into the room. Shivering and blowing a strand of black hair from her eyes, she rolled over to find Cord, one arm draped possessively over her waist, boldly staring at every naked inch of her.

Slightly embarrassed, she yanked at the quilt and was surprised to find herself tucked into a huge sleeping bag. "How—"

"You were sleeping," he said simply, still holding her.

"I decided we needed more than this—" plucking the quilt off the bed, he grinned "—to keep us warm. So I banked the fire, brought up our suitcases, unpacked the groceries, zipped two bags together and—voilà."

"And I didn't wake up?" she asked, yawning, as she propped herself on one elbow. His fingers tightened over her waist.

"Just made a few long-suffering sighs," he replied, nuzzling her neck.

"Oh, come on."

"You did." But his eyes crinkled at the corners and his mouth twitched into a boyish smile. His gaze locked with hers as he drew her close, burying his face in her long, tangled hair and breathing against her neck. "This is the way every morning should be," he whispered, pressing anxious lips to hers as they began to make love again, exploring each others' bodies, recapturing the feelings of a long-ago past.

Alison's nagging doubts reawakened with the morning, but she resolutely pushed them aside. This weekend she was going to spend every glorious minute with Cord; and she wouldn't allow herself to doubt him, wouldn't think about the future, couldn't face the past.

You're being a fool, a voice inside her head taunted, but she didn't care and gave herself to him time and time again.

When at last Cord had again fallen asleep, Alison slid out of the bed and found her clothes. There was no hot water, but she managed to wash in a basin of cold water, holding her hair away from her face with a tortoiseshell clip. Then she dressed quickly in plum-colored cords and a bulky cream sweater.

"Where do you think you're going?" Cord growled as she tried to sneak past him.

"Downstairs."

"Why?" His sable-colored hair was tousled, falling endearingly over his forehead, and his naked shoulders rippled as he moved.

"I think it's time to get up, don't you?"

"I have no idea."

"Well, look outside, for crying out loud." She pointed to the window and beyond where, high over the fir trees, blue sky peeked through wispy white clouds. "It's midmorning and I'm starved."

"So you decided to get up, rummage through the groceries we brought, light the fire and make me sizzling bacon, eggs—over easy—toast, coffee and home-baked cinnamon rolls."

"All over an open fire."

"Right."

"Guess again."

Stretching, Cord let out a rumbling laugh. "Okay. You want me to get up and get dressed so I can take you into town and buy you breakfast at one of the bed-and-breakfast houses."

"That's more like it."

Groaning, he rolled off the bed and tried to grab her, but she ducked and hurried down the stairs. She heard him whoop as he stepped into an icy cold shower, muttering obscenities about backwoods life and women who were so cheap they wouldn't keep the friggin' electricity turned on.

"You'll survive," she called up to him as he dressed.

He glared at her from over the railing above. "Barely," he growled, toweling off his dark, wet hair, then managing a brilliant smile.

"Then you'll love this—we don't have any coffee."

"Great, just great."

"Pretend we really are roughing it," she said with a laugh, seeing the consternation on his face. "Hurry up, I'd like to get into town."

"Why?" By this time he was buttoning his shirt as he walked barefoot down the stairs.

"I need to get to a phone and tell Norma where I am, just in case she wants to get in touch with me."

"What good will that do? The phone here isn't connected."

"In case there's an accident," she replied, her lips turning downward. "She could call the police and they would come here."

"There isn't going to be any accident. Not to my daughter," he predicted, touching her lightly under the chin, forcing her to meet his serious brown eyes.

"I hope not."

"Now, come on, let's get going." Cord found his boots and finished dressing while Alison zipped into her coat.

A few minutes later they were both in the boat, standing together as Cord steered. Sea gulls dipped over the gray water, crying noisily as Cord guided the craft toward shore several miles south of the cabin.

After docking at Winslow, Cord took Alison's hand and they walked along the piers crowded with fishing vessels and sailboats to the first telephone booth they found. She placed her call to Norma, satisfied herself that Mandy was fine, then returned to the docks.

"Everything okay?" Cord asked. He was leaning on the railing, watching several fishermen cast their lines into the water.

"Well, I guess."

He glanced up sharply. "She's not hurt?"

"No, nothing like that," Alison said. "But it seems she's grown rather attached to a certain half-cocker puppy and is insisting she bring him home."

"You object."

Alison glanced at him. "We already have Lazarus."

"A puppy won't hurt."

"Mandy is only three and a half. I don't think she's responsible enough for a—"

"Lighten up," Cord said, grinning and placing his arm over her shoulders. "Every kid needs a dog."

"I didn't have one."

"No?"

"We couldn't. The apartment wouldn't allow it, so Mom and Dad settled for a canary."

"But you don't live in an apartment."

Yet, she thought worriedly, wondering what would happen if the house sold. "I'm just not sure about the puppy."

"We'll think about it over breakfast," he said decisively, guiding her down a side street to a quaint restaurant with bright red shutters and a bell over the door.

"We?" she repeated.

"Have you forgotten?" he asked, holding open the door. "She's my daughter, too."

So it's already started, she thought. Cord was inserting himself into Mandy's life. Just how far would he go? If only she could trust him completely.

But she couldn't. Not yet. Not until she was certain he had no intention of taking Mandy from her.

"How about here?" he asked, indicating a table near a gas fire burning quietly in a tile fireplace.

"Perfect."

As Alison was about to sit down, a waitress ran up to

the table. "Cord Donahue?" she cried, her face filled with wonder. "Is it really you?"

"In the flesh," he admitted.

Tears filled her eyes. "I can't believe it! I read about it—in the papers, you know. But I really couldn't believe it." She called over her shoulder. "Len, Len! Come out here! It's true, Cord's back!"

A hefty man ambled from behind the counter. "Well, I'll be," he muttered, wiping his hands on a streaked apron. "I never thought I'd see your ugly mug again." But the cook's eyes crinkled merrily and he shook Cord's outstretched hand.

Cord laughed. "I guess your luck just ran out."

"And yours," Len said, his gaze sliding to Alison, "seems to have improved a mite."

"You could say that."

"Well, eat whatever you want, it's on the house," Len said, turning back to the kitchen. "And when you've got the time, come around and we'll celebrate. Then you can tell me all about what happened to you that night."

"I will," Cord promised as the waitress, Angela, handed them each a menu and poured coffee into their cups. "Old family friends," Cord explained, once they had ordered. "They've known me since I was a kid. Len straightened me out and saved my neck a couple of times when I was a teenager."

Alison took a sip from her coffee, feeling the hot liquid burn a little as it slid down her throat.

Angela returned with steaming platters of lemon muffins, scrambled eggs, crisp bacon, sausage and Belgian waffles filled with strawberry preserves and whipped cream.

"I didn't order all this," Alison protested.

"I know. Len did. He's showin' off," Angela explained, refilling their cups. "It's not every day of the week ol' Cord here strolls into this place. In fact it's been quite a while."

"Tell Len thanks," Cord said as Angela glided toward the next table. Then he speared his fork at Alison. "And you, eat! We don't want to offend Len, do we?"

"I suppose not," she agreed.

He shook his head and pronged a sausage. "Now, back to business. About Mandy's new dog—what're we going to name him?"

CHAPTER NINE

AFTER BREAKFAST ALISON and Cord stopped at a local store and bought a few groceries. Then they walked back to the marina and climbed into the boat. Clouds began to collect in the sky as Cord guided the small craft around the island. He pointed out all the private inlets and bays he'd discovered as a child.

By afternoon they had circumnavigated the entire island. Cord anchored the boat on a private, crescent stretch of beach north of the cabin. Graceful firs, gnarled with age, guarded the uninhabited stretch of white sand.

"You came here as a child?" Alison asked, dropping onto a faded blanket Cord had spread near the water.

"Every summer." His eyes swept the open sea.

"You miss this place," she guessed when he leaned his head against her. Together they watched a low-hanging sun peek through dark clouds. A few strong rays of sunlight sparkled and glittered gold on the water.

"Yeah, I miss it," he admitted, tossing a smooth rock into the quiet blue water. "Things were simpler then. Dad was alive." Frowning, he reached for another stone. "So was David."

Alison's heart squeezed. David, her husband. Had he really been a thief? Sighing, she leaned closer to Cord, placing her head in the crook of his neck. Half lying on the blanket, propped on elbows, touching him, she breathed the salt spray of the ocean and felt warm beside the man she loved.

"Things were easy then," he thought aloud. "No problems. No bankers, insurance agents, police. Everything seemed straightforward."

"And now?" she asked.

He squinted out to sea. "And now things are complicated—much more complicated." Picking up a handful of dry sand, he watched as it sifted slowly through his fingers until the last grain had fallen. In the distance the setting sun was covered by gray and roiling clouds. Cord eyed the ominous sky and dusted his hands together. "I think we'd better go," he said, helping Alison to her feet.

He shook out the blanket and tossed it over his shoulder. Fingers linked, they walked to the boat rocking just offshore. Cord started the engine as the first blast of wind blew in from the west. Thick drops of rain began to fall. Grimacing, Cord maneuvered the craft south as the sky turned dark.

A few minutes later the Donahue cabin was in sight. Cord cut the engine at the dock and Alison was grateful to be back.

"Just in time," Cord observed, as a gust of wind brought more rain. After securing the boat, he tucked the grocery sack under his arm, took Alison's hand and they dashed along the slippery planks of the dock.

Her hair was drenched by the time they reached the front porch, but she laughed and shook out the rain.

Inside, Cord started a fire and within seconds flames began to crackle against the dry wood. Smoke curled upward through the ancient chimney and soft light began to spread through the interior, leaving only the corners of the cozy room in shadow.

Alison watched him work, her gaze lingering on his back, strong shoulders and slim waist. All too easily, she thought, she could pretend that nothing had ever come between them.

As if he felt her gaze on him, he looked over one shoulder. "Just like that summer," he said, as if reading her thoughts.

"Almost." She gave him a quick smile. Before she said anything foolish, she retrieved the flashlight from the mantel and hurried upstairs.

Outside, the wind began to howl and rain splashed against the panes, but Alison, straightening the sleeping bags in the loft, cracked a couple of windows, allowing fresh sea-washed air into the cabin. The old curtains billowed and danced in the breeze. Glancing again at the bed, she frowned. Here she was, alone with Cord, falling in love with him all over again, giving herself to him in the face of her good sense. But she couldn't help herself. If there was just the smallest chance they could fall in love again, she had to take it.

"There we go!" Cord said.

Alison, from her vantage point in the loft, peeked over the rail. He was standing in front of the fire, wiping his hands on his jeans and watching as golden flames licked the dry wood.

"Looks good," she admitted.

"Glad you came?" he asked as she started down the stairs.

She couldn't lie. "Very."

"Maybe this was just what we needed—some time alone."

"Maybe," she admitted.

His gaze lingered in hers before he cleared his throat and looked away. "Maybe you should see if you can scrounge up a coffeepot in the kitchen. We'll heat water over the fire."

Fortunately, with the aid of the flashlight, she discovered another kerosene lantern and managed to light the wick. Then, while Cord stacked wood and worked on the water pipes, she rummaged through the cupboards and found an old cast-iron kettle.

In the flickering lamplight she diced onions, green pepper and garlic. Adding some ground meat, she poured the vegetables and spices into the old kettle and found a place for the blackened pot in the fire.

Once satisfied that the meat would indeed cook, she filled an old enamel coffeepot with water and balanced it on one smoldering log.

"I don't know about this," she murmured.

"What did you tell me this morning about roughing it?" he taunted, standing over her and appraising her work with an experienced eye.

She wiped her hands on her jeans as she stood. "Okay, okay. I just think we should have been better prepared."

"Next time," he suggested, arms surrounding her waist.

"Will there be a next time?"

"If you let it, Alison," he breathed into her hair. "And next time we'll bring our daughter."

Alison's pulse jumped. Mandy here—with Cord? Just like a real family? It was almost too much for her to hope for. "You tell her when we get home," she suggested, experiencing a pang of loneliness for her child.

Why did it feel so right to be in his arms? "There's

something I've been meaning to ask you," she admitted, throat suddenly thick.

"Shoot."

"What if I'd refused to come with you, or if I'd had other plans?"

"I would have convinced you." He looked down at her, his brown eyes glinting in the firelight.

"You were that sure of yourself?"

"Not sure, just determined. And we *did* need to talk, especially about Mandy."

That much was true. She sighed happily against him. As stupid as it was, she would have gone just about anywhere with him. Though he'd said he'd plotted revenge against her, she hadn't stopped loving him. "I...I'd better work on the chili."

The meat had begun to sizzle and eventually she added canned kidney beans and tomatoes to the concoction. As the chili simmered, Alison wrapped a loaf of French bread in foil and set it on the coals next to the coffeepot.

"Smells great," Cord told her, lifting the lid carefully so as not to burn his fingers.

"That's because you're hungry." But she laughed, light from the fire dancing in her eyes. "I just hope this works," she whispered, stirring the thick, steaming chili and studying it with a critical eye.

"Not much of a camper, are you?" he teased.

"Never was."

He sobered a little, his mouth thinning as he adjusted the logs with a blackened poker. "So how did that work with David? He was always the outdoorsman."

"It didn't," she said flatly.

Cord's brows quirked.

"When he wanted to go camping or hunting or fishing, he went. I stayed home with Mandy."

"*You* wanted it that way?"

Shrugging, she pretended to be interested in the fire. "I could have gone with him, I guess. He never *said* I couldn't. But David's trips were always planned with his friends."

"Like Nate Benson?"

She glanced up quickly, then looked back to the fire when she saw the possessive gleam in his eyes. "Yes. Like Nate. They usually went in Nate's camper and it was kind of an unwritten rule that no women were invited. Since I didn't think hunting trips would be the best place to take Mandy, I didn't argue. Some of David's friends were a little rough around the edges."

She could see a muscle jumping in Cord's jaw but decided to ignore it. "Let's see if this is done," she said, as much to change the subject as lighten the mood. Grabbing a dish towel as a makeshift pot holder, she lifted the kettle and set it onto the hearth.

Steam, scented with hot spices, escaped from the lid. "Here goes nothing," she muttered. As Alison served chili into two bowls, Cord cut the bread into thick slices and poured two cups of hot water into which he spooned instant coffee.

Then, together, they sat cross-legged in front of the fire and ate until they were full. "The best chili I've ever tasted," Cord proclaimed, patting his flat abdomen.

"Don't let Norma hear you," Alison said, giggling. "Remember just last week when you told her over and over again what a great cook she was? The best in King County or some such thing," Alison mocked.

"She still is."

"I agree, so don't try giving me the same line you used

on her." With a wink she picked up the dirty dishes and carried them into the kitchen.

She'd just finished drying the last dish and was staring out the back windows when she felt Cord's hands on her shoulders. Holding her close, he breathed into her hair. "I'm glad you decided to take a chance last night," he whispered, his voice low, his breath tickling her ear.

"I don't think I had much choice."

"Sure you did." Tugging her gently backward, forcing her shoulders against his chest, his arms circled her waist, hands clasped across her abdomen. "I know that when I came back to Seattle and first saw you again, I was an A-1 bastard," he admitted.

"Old habits die hard." She felt him stiffen and wished she could call back the biting words. "I'm...I'm sorry," she whispered. "I shouldn't have said that."

"Tit for tat, I suppose." He kissed the back of her neck and sharp little tingles crawled quickly down her spine. "Oh, Ali, why do we insist on hurting each other?"

"I wish I knew." She linked her fingers over his, feeling the warmth of his body permeate her sweater and flow into hers. It felt so right to be here with him, and she wanted desperately to forget all the pain of the past. "Maybe we should try to start over."

"Do you think that's possible?"

"I don't know."

His lips moved her hair. "Let's give it a try."

Closing her eyes, she thought of all the reasons she couldn't trust him; felt a storm of emotions ripping at her soul. "Why?" she whispered, hardly daring to breathe. The night seemed to wrap around her and she waited, hoping to hear that he still loved her, that he still cared.

"Because we lost so much," he admitted, his voice rough. "And now we have Mandy to think about."

So it wasn't love, just a sense of duty which had called him back to this deserted cabin. Of course. In her heart she'd known it all along. She felt her shoulders slump as she turned in his arms to stare into his eyes. "So Mandy makes the difference."

"Of course she does, just as you do," he said, kissing her upturned lips.

If only she could trust him again, she thought wildly, feeling desire awaken, stretching and uncurling lazily within her as his hands spanned the small of her back. *Love me,* she wanted to cry out but couldn't as his tongue rimmed her lips and darted deliciously into her mouth.

Her every nerve-ending strung tight, she kissed him back, moaning when she felt his fingers find the hem of her sweater and the warm flesh beneath. Her breasts felt heavy and ached for his touch. Hot and pulsing, her insides quivered as he slowly circled one straining nipple with the pad of his thumb.

"Cord," she whispered throatily, her knees melting, her lips seeking his.

"Slow down, love," he murmured against her hair, air from his lungs caressing the shell of her ear. "We've got all night...."

MORNING LIGHT, PALE and gray, was streaming through the windows when Alison stretched and opened one eye. "Cord?" she whispered and heard his hearty laugh from the room below. The smell of warm coffee and frying bacon filtered to the loft as his footsteps creaked on the steps.

"So, Sleeping Beauty, you've finally decided to wake up," he said, his dark eyes warm as they gazed at her.

"Mmm." She stretched and yawned again. "What smells so good?"

"Guess." Leaning one jeans-clad hip against the railing, he stretched his legs in front of him and crossed his ankles.

"Strawberry-filled crepes, a mushroom omelet and strips of barbecued ham," she said, laughing.

"Guess again."

"Okay. Chilled champagne, oranges from Florida, an apple-and-whipped-cream-filled German pancake and—"

"Sure," he growled, grinning as he lunged forward and pinned her, squealing, against the mattress. "You'll be lucky to get burned toast and day-old coffee." But he leaned over, his hair falling across his forehead, and kissed her soundly on the lips. Despite their passionate lovemaking of the night before, she wanted him again.

His fingers slid downward and he groaned as he touched one breast, feeling its warm weight against his palm.

"You're wicked," he murmured, shifting to lie next to her, his legs pressed intimately against hers.

"So are you." Kissing him, twining her arms around his neck, she molded herself against him, her blood igniting as one of his hands tangled in her hair, pulling gently to expose her throat. As his lips slid slowly down her neck to linger at the skyrocketing pulse at the base of her throat, liquid fire raced through her blood, throbbing with desire and forcing her to move wantonly against him. Without conscious thought she reached for the fastening of his jeans.

"Alison," he groaned, positioning himself over her as his pants slid downward.

A sharp pop from the fire startled them both.

"What in thunder...?" He glanced up, saw the cloud

of black smoke boiling from the fire. "Damn," he muttered, swearing violently as he yanked on his pants and ran down the stairs, clutching his waistband.

Alison snatched one of the dustcovers, which wasn't much more than a faded sheet, and wrapped it around her. Peering over the railing, she saw Cord bending over the hearth, muttering violent oaths under his breath, as he gingerly removed a blackened pan from the fire.

Charred bacon, still sizzling and crackling angrily, filled the house with smoke.

Alison giggled as Cord struggled, one hand on the hot pan, another holding his pants up, to take the spattering, hissing skillet outside.

She was still standing at the rail laughing when he stomped back into the cabin.

"A lot of help you were," he grumbled, staring up at her.

"Not my fault. You're the cook this morning."

"Like hell." But his eyes crinkled at the corners and the firm line of his mouth twitched upward. His brown eyes gleamed.

"Looks like you'll just have to start over," she quipped, knowing she was goading him.

"You know, Ali," he warned, "you better watch what you say."

"Or?"

His eyes slitted. "Someone might decide to teach you a lesson," he said, his teeth flashing white against his beard-darkened chin. He headed for the stairs, mounting them two at a time. "And I know just the guy."

"Cord—wait—" she protested.

But he was in the loft and grabbing for her before she could run away. "Now," he said, with mock severity, "I think I'm going to have my way with you."

"Have *what?* Cord, be serious." But she was laughing uncontrollably as he took her in his arms, imprisoning her against him.

"I am."

"Bull!"

Then he laughed, a hearty, rumbling sound that bounced off the rafters and echoed through the small cabin. "Why not? Breakfast is ruined anyway."

"You could try again," she teased.

"I intend to," he admitted, slowly pushing her backward so that the back of her legs met the edge of the bed, "right now." With a grin meant to be leering, he gave one gentle push and toppled with her onto the rumpled bed.

"You're the one who's wicked," she repeated, gazing into his eyes.

"Only with you, Ali. Only with you," he vowed, slowly opening her clenched fingers and pulling the sheet from her breasts. He sucked in a swift breath at the sight of her, his gaze sliding possessively over her. Swallowing hard, he calmly took his time stripping off his clothes, first unbuttoning his shirt and letting it fall to the floor, where his boots already lay.

Gazing up at him, feeling the electricity of his nearness, Alison was moved to honesty. "I…I've missed you," she admitted.

"And I you." He kicked off his jeans. "Oh, God, if you only knew." His lips slanted over hers and she felt the crush of his weight, the power of his shoulders, the corded strength of his chest as he claimed her again, slowly imprinting forever his special mark deep within. As the tides of passion swept over him, he pushed her into a tempest of emotions as wild as the stormy waters of the sound. She was lost, drowning in that heated sea, struggling for some sense of herself, but all she could see in a rush of breathless wind was the man she loved.

"Marry me, Alison," he cried, the sound torn from his throat as he strained and fell against her. "Please, marry me."

Rational thought crystallized in her mind. *If only I could.* "W-what?" she asked, her own breath rough and shallow. She hardly dared breathe for fear she'd misunderstood.

"I asked you to marry me," he admitted, burying his face in the tangled strands of her blue-black hair. "I want us to be a family. You and me and Mandy."

A cold certainty settled in her stomach. So that was it. He wanted to be a father to his child. Feeling tears sting her eyes, she bravely fought them back and tried vainly to keep her face emotionless.

"Alison?"

"I don't think that would be such a good idea. Not yet anyway," she said hurriedly as she rolled to the edge of the bed and quickly found her clothes.

"But why?"

"We need time, Cord," she said almost angrily. She knew her response was a flimsy excuse, but when David had died she'd vowed that if she ever married again it would be with love, for love. She couldn't ignore the lesson the reality of her less-than-perfect marriage had provided. David had never loved her as Cord once had. And now Cord hadn't said that he loved her. She didn't doubt that he cared for her and she was touched that he wanted Mandy, but David had cared for her in his own way, too, and her life had felt strangely hollow. Never again would she sacrifice love for security.

Cord grabbed her wrist, spinning her around. Surprised, Alison dropped her jeans. She had to lean over to retrieve them with her free hand when he wouldn't let go.

"That's the same excuse you peddled me four years ago and it still doesn't wash."

"Now hold on! I've barely gotten used to you being here."

"You were pretty 'used' to me a few minutes ago!"

She wanted to slap him but controlled her flare of rage. "And Mandy. Think of her."

"I have. She's mine. I want to claim her."

"So that's what you meant by telling me you wanted to talk to me. You want to stake your claim. Think about it, Cord. She's just a little girl."

"My little girl."

"But she doesn't know that."

"We'll tell her."

Frantic, Alison shook her head. "We have to give her time."

"It's Nate Benson, isn't it?" he challenged, every strident muscle suddenly flexed.

"Nate Benson?" she repeated blankly.

"You're in love with him," Cord charged, his brown eyes darkening.

"Me? And Nate Benson?" She had to laugh at his ridiculous accusation.

His fingers tightened. "That *is* it! Admit it!"

"You think I'm involved with Nate Benson, but I came here with you and…and… My God, you think I'm having an affair with Benson and now with you?" So incredulous and wounded that all the color drained from her face, Alison stood stock-still. "You don't really know me at all, do you, Cord?" Swallowing back hot tears of betrayal, she tried again to jerk her hand away but couldn't. "You never really did."

"I saw the way he looked at you."

"Hogwash!" she cried, wanting to scream that she'd always loved him, had never looked at another man. But it was no use. He wouldn't believe her because she'd married David. "This just proves my point. We need time."

Cord's broad shoulders slumped and he finally freed her wrist. "Don't you think we've already lost too much?" he asked softly. "Wasted too much time as it is?"

"And whose fault was that?"

"Yours, damn it."

"Mine?" she repeated, thunderstruck.

"For not marrying me the first time I asked you, way back when!" He stood, his anger returning. Every muscle in his body was stretched and rigid, the cords on his neck distended as he stepped furiously into his jeans.

"You've only been back a little over a week."

His dark eyes blazed as they bored into hers. "That doesn't hold water, Alison. You and I—we've known each other a lifetime." Then he stomped down the stairs, leaving Alison alone. *Damn him,* she thought, muttering under her breath as she pulled on her clothes. *He can't just charge back into my life, pick up where we left off and expect me to marry him just because he's Mandy's father!*

"Get ready. We're leaving!" he shouted from below.

"Believe me, I'm ready!"

She jerked her sweater over her head, tugged her hair from the collar and brushed it with quick, furious strokes until it crackled rebelliously. As she slammed her clothes into her suitcase, she heard Cord stomping and banging things below. Why had she agreed to come here with him? she asked herself over and over again. Why was she a glutton for punishment and heartache whenever she was with him?

The answer, like a cold blast of wind, knifed through her: *Because you love him and nothing will ever change that one agonizing fact.*

CHAPTER TEN

"MOMMY!" MANDY'S FOOTSTEPS echoed through the hallway as she raced into the study where Alison was trying to read a suspense novel.

Alison's heart twisted and she opened her arms wide to hug her daughter. "Oh, honey, hi!"

"I miss you," Mandy said, pressing her button of a nose into Alison's cheek.

"And I missed you."

"Where's Uncle Cord?" Mandy's dark eyes swept the room.

"He's, uh, gone for a little while," Alison said quickly. Ever since she and Cord had returned to Seattle, he'd been silent and brooding. It was as if their wonderful time on the island hadn't existed and he was back into his same mysterious pattern of behavior from the week before. "He'll be back soon."

"Good! I miss him, too."

"Do you?" Alison asked, her throat disturbingly dry. "And where did you leave Norma?"

"She's with Bangles."

"Who's Bangles?" Alison asked as she heard the back door slam shut.

"Mandy?" Norma called.

"We're in here," Alison replied just as Norma, her

face flushed, glasses unevenly balanced over her nose, her dress streaked with mud, bustled into the room. She was still attempting to catch her breath. "Good Lord, what happened to you?"

"Bangles!" Mandy said, giggling. "Wait till you see him."

"Him?"

Norma held up a soft hand. "Now before you go gettin' upset—"

"*Who* or *what* is Bangles? And please don't tell me we've got a Welsh pony stashed in our garage!"

"No, silly!" Mandy exclaimed, wriggling to the floor and tugging insistently on Alison's hand. "Bangles is a dog!"

"A *what?*"

Norma sighed and rolled her eyes. "A cocker spaniel pup. It was either that or the horse. I just couldn't tear Mandy away…."

Alison tried to smother a smile and failed. "You're just an old softie," she accused as she let herself be dragged down the hall, through the kitchen and into the garage, where in a corner, his tail wagging frantically, a blond puppy tugged on his leash. He yapped excitedly, straining on the rope that held him near the corner where Norma had placed a straw mat and bowls of food and water.

"He's adorable," Alison whispered, stepping closer.

"No! He's Bangles!" Mandy insisted.

"I mean—oh, never mind." Alison laughed, bending over and scratching the doe-eyed pup behind his drooping ears. "But look at the size of him." Alison didn't know much about dogs, but this was certainly the biggest cocker spaniel pup she'd ever seen in her life. "Well, now, fella, I wonder what's gonna happen when Lazarus gets a look at you?"

"Saints preserve us," Norma whispered fervently, standing in the doorway. "The chase will be on then, won't it? And the fur will surely fly!"

"You should have thought of that before you brought him home."

Chuckling, Norma gestured to Mandy. "You try to say no to Miss Stubborn. See how far you get."

"Okay, okay, but he can't stay out here. It's too cold." Alison tucked the old rug under her arm, instructed Mandy to carry in the food and water dishes and untied the leash. A quivering mass of unrestrained energy, Bangles leaped forward, sniffing the tires of the parked cars and all the lawn equipment as Alison tried to guide him into the house.

"He's not completely housebroken," Norma warned.

"We'll have to change that—in the house, where it's a little warmer."

"Now who's the old softie?"

"You don't have to rub it in. Let's keep him in the utility room on papers for the time being." She located an old toddler gate she'd used for Mandy and wedged it between the utility room and kitchen while Norma scattered old newspapers on the floor. "There, how does that look?" she asked, stepping back to survey her work.

"Like a booby trap," Cord said as he strode through the back door.

Alison had been so engrossed in her project she hadn't heard him arrive.

"Uncle Cord!" Mandy threw herself into his waiting arms and the look he sent Alison over Mandy's shoulder spoke volumes.

He wanted his child.

"Lookie at Bangles!" Mandy commanded.

"Bangles?"

The pup whined and begged, leaping against the mesh of the gate until Cord reached over and scratched his lopping ears. "So what kind of dog are you?"

"A cocker," Norma said. She had washed the dirt from her face and hands and was wiping her hands on her apron. Without meeting Cord's eyes, she reached into the refrigerator to retrieve an assortment of vegetables.

"Cocker?" Cord asked, lifting a disbelieving eyebrow as he glanced over his shoulder. "If that animal's a cocker spaniel I'm a—"

"Dead man?" Alison whispered to herself.

Cord scowled pointedly at her. "I was going to say Great Dane. That dog's no spaniel."

"Cocker mix," Norma corrected, looking decidedly guilty.

"How mixed?"

"Not much."

"With what?"

"Lab."

"Lab? As in Labrador retriever? As in big enough to eat us out of house and home?" he asked incredulously. "Norma—"

"Consider yourself fortunate," Alison interjected. "Mandy wanted a pony."

"I think she's got one. That dog is going to be—"

"A great watchdog," Norma cut in, giving Cord a swift glance, "so don't you go lecturin' me on the size of it, Cord Donahue. Just be grateful I didn't bring you back a barnful of Welsh ponies!"

"Believe me, I am," he said, chuckling, his spirits obviously lifting as he hoisted Mandy onto his shoulders. "Hang on," he whispered to her.

For nearly twenty-four hours he'd been short-tempered and pensive, refusing to take calls at the office and holing up in the study alone. Now, Alison noted, with Mandy jabbering excitedly about the ponies and a foreign dog whining expectantly, he was suddenly Mr. Wonderful.

"So where've you been?" Norma asked. "It's nearly seven."

"Working late."

At that moment Lazarus, who had been sleeping in the study, strolled into the kitchen to check his dish. The dog let out a yelp, slammed into the gate and the old gray tabby, spitting, hissing and stepping sideways, slunk swiftly toward the door.

"It's okay," Alison said, reaching for the cat, but Lazarus swiped a claw-extended foot at her, scratching her arm as he jumped on the counter, knocking over plants on the windowsill over the sink.

"You get down from there!" Norma commanded, and Cord quickly dropped Mandy, picked up the squirming cat and pushed him out the back door.

"World War III, right here in Seattle," Cord commented, glancing at Alison. "Are you okay?"

"I'll be fine." She washed her arm and cleared her throat, looking away from the tenderness in his gaze.

Staring at him only made the heartache worse. Remembering their wonderful weekend together, she longed to forget about their last fight. But, as if sensing her thoughts, he stiffened, and the censure of his rigid stance helped her control any wayward fantasies.

"Let me help you," she offered, grabbing an apron to stand near Norma.

"I can manage." Nonetheless, Norma pointed to a

bowl of flour shortening. "You can make the crust; I'm baking chicken pies."

"I don't wanna help," Mandy said. "I want to play with Bangles."

"Should we take him on a walk?" Cord asked.

Alison glanced outside. Rain was peppering the yard, sweeping against the windows. "It's raining."

"A little water never hurt anyone," Cord decided, reaching for Mandy's sweatshirt. "Come on, you, let's bundle up."

Alison was about to protest further but didn't see the point. She didn't want to risk another fight with Cord—not with Mandy around. Gritting her teeth, she turned back to her bowl of flour and shortening.

"You come, too?" Mandy asked, tugging on Alison's sweater.

"Not right now, sweetheart. I've got to help Norma."

"Oh, go on," the housekeeper insisted, but Alison continued to cut the shortening into the flour with a vengeance.

"Maybe I'll catch up to you."

"Promise?" Mandy asked, eyes upturned expectantly, pink hood surrounding her round face.

"Okay, promise."

"Yippee!" Then, having gotten her way, Mandy turned and grabbed hold of the leash. When Cord opened the door, Bangles bolted, dragging Mandy behind. "Catching up might be difficult," Cord muttered, letting the screen door slam shut behind him.

Still simmering from their argument the day before, Alison didn't respond.

"You two have a spat?" Norma asked. She was stirring sauce on the stove and didn't bother looking up.

"More than that, I'm afraid."

Sighing, Norma poured diced carrots and plump green peas into the sauce. "How much more?"

"Remember when Cord was talking about World War III?"

"If you two would ever quit fightin' long enough to find out you love each other, things would be a lot better for the rest of us," Norma pronounced. "And here I thought you two would be out at the island patchin' things up!"

"We were, but—"

"No buts, Alison. Lord knows Cord is mule-headed and his pride has always gotten in the way of his common sense, but I thought you were smarter than that."

Alison glanced out the window and saw Mandy running helter-skelter after the bounding pup. "Okay," she said softly, "I'll give it another chance."

"That's the spirit. Now, hand me that bowl and I'll roll out the dough. Dinner will be in an hour."

Mustering all her self-confidence, Alison jerked her sweatshirt off the hook near the back door and nearly tripped over Lazarus as she walked outside. The old cat scurried furtively into the house and Alison had to smile. "Better get used to him, Laz," she said. "I think he's here for good."

Then, keeping her smile in place, she dashed from under the overflowing gutters and past dripping rhododendrons to find Cord and Mandy laughing as the dog raced from bush to bush, sniffing and yapping each time he heard a robin in the trees or a squirrel chattering angrily from the overhanging branches of fir and oak.

"Mommy!" Mandy squealed, delighted at the sight of her mother. The rosy-cheeked child turned her attention away from Bangles and the hood of her sweatshirt slid off her head. Lunging, the pup tugged on the leash and the slippery leather slid through Mandy's plump little fingers. "Oh…oh."

Free at last, the pup galloped through the overgrown rose garden and down a mud-puddle-strewn path to the front yard. Swearing under his breath, Cord took chase, long, jean-clad strides sweeping him over the wet grass.

"Now you've done it," Alison said, but laughed as raindrops caught in her hair.

Mandy's dark eyes grew serious. "Will Cord be mad?"

"A little, but not at you." She rumpled Mandy's wet curls as the child blinked against the raindrops starring her lashes. "Here, let's put this back on." Adjusting the hood of the sweatshirt, Alison saw Cord, Bangles in tow, returning. Both dog and man were spattered with mud and Cord was breathing hard from the chase.

"I think that's enough exercise for me," he said, his face flushed.

Alison couldn't quite disguise her smile.

"Can I hold him?" Mandy asked, reaching for the leash.

"*If* you take him to the back porch and tie him there. He'll need a bath before he goes tracking mud through Norma's kitchen," Cord warned.

"I'll be real careful," Mandy promised soberly as she pulled a reluctant Bangles toward the back porch. Alison's gaze followed her child. Norma, chuckling and scolding at the same time, opened the back door, tied the puppy to a post on the porch and hustled a sneezing Mandy inside.

"He's going to be problems," Cord decided as Bangles whined pitifully.

"Then you tell her she can't keep him," Alison suggested.

"Me?"

"You were the one who wanted all your fatherly responsibility," she reminded him. "Take the bad with the good."

His thin lips twitched a little. "You're still angry with me, aren't you?"

"Very. In fact, I don't think angry quite covers it. I'm furious, enraged, annoyed and sick at the way you try to manipulate me. You've been toying with my emotions ever since you set foot back in Seattle, and you expect me to roll with the punches like some sort of mindless, simpering wimp!"

"Wimp? You?" He laughed, tossing his head back and letting rain drizzle down his hair and neck to disappear below his collar. His eyes were bright and warm as if he did, just a little, care for her. "You're a lot of things, Alison Donahue," he admitted, shaking his head, water glistening in the dark strands as he grabbed and pulled her, protesting, into a thicket of heavily bowed firs.

"What do you think you're—" she gasped, but her sentence went unfinished when she stared into the amusement in his eyes.

"As I was saying, you are decidedly the most stubborn, pigheaded woman I've ever met."

"Me?" she shrieked, hardly believing her ears. She tried to struggle away, but he pinned her with powerful arms, holding her tight against every inch of him.

The fresh scent of rain-drenched fir needles and wet earth invaded her nostrils. Nearby, heavy-blossomed rhododendrons added splashes of red and lavender to the greenery.

"But you are also the most intriguing and mystifying woman I've ever laid eyes on." He kissed her then, long and hard, bending his head to capture her rain-washed lips with his own. She thought she should try to struggle, but she knew it was useless; he wouldn't stop—nor did she want him to.

The same traitorous emotions that always took hold of her when she was in his arms captured her again. "You're a bastard," she whispered into his mouth as she circled his neck with her arms. "An arrogant, self-serving, pompous bastard." *And I love you, damn it!*

"Does that mean you still won't marry me?"

"Oooh." She felt angry all over again. Wasn't this the same man who had accused her of having an affair with Nate Benson, David and heaven only knew who else? Wasn't this the very same arrogant man who thought her capable of embezzling from and betraying him? She wanted to strangle him.

Yes, but wasn't this the man who was Mandy's rightful father? Shouldn't they be married, live as husband and wife, learn to love each other again—if not for each other, then for Mandy?

Emotions warring within, she jerked away from him. "I'll think about it," she said, running to the house, her boots slipping a little on the wet grass.

"Now who's running away, Alison?" he jeered, his voice ringing through the trees to mock her.

MANDY WAS EXHAUSTED. After dinner and a bath, she fell asleep curled in Cord's arms as he read a bedtime story to her in her room. "Must be my way with women," he murmured, kissing her forehead and smiling down at her small face.

"She's had a rather large day," Alison pointed out, turning down the lamp as Cord tucked Mandy beneath the covers. For the past hour she and Cord had been in quiet truce, and though the air had crackled with tension at the dinner table, they each had managed to get through the ordeal of sitting across from each other.

Fifteen minutes earlier Norma had left, shaking her graying head and muttering under her breath.

And now, as Cord gently lifted Mandy's arm and placed her teddy next to her, Alison's heart wrenched. He would have made such a wonderful father, if only he'd had the chance.

But he threw it away, her mind taunted, *by not trusting you to have been faithful to him.*

It was all such a horrid mess!

The doorbell chimed and Alison hurried downstairs, wondering who would drop by after nine. When she opened the door, she was face-to-face with a stranger, a man in a pressed wool suit, red hair, thick glasses and a bland expression. "May I help you?" she asked, frowning as she tried to place him. She heard Cord's footsteps on the stairs, knew that he was right behind her.

"I'm Carl Jenkins," the man said, handing her an ivory-colored business card. "I'm with Smith National."

"The insurance company," she said, her eyes skimming his card and her heart sinking. Smith National was the company that had bonded the employees of Donahue Investments; they had lost over a million dollars when Cord had taken off and had been presumed drowned in the sound.

"Right. I've phoned your office and here several times. Mr. Donahue never returns my calls." His small mouth compressed and Alison took an instant dislike to him.

By this time Cord was standing next to Alison. "Come in," he said, his voice edged as he stepped aside for Jenkins to enter. "I thought I squared everything with the insurance company."

"Not quite," Jenkins replied stiffly. He was unsmiling, his back ramrod stiff as Cord led him into the study. "We've consulted with our legal staff."

"About what?"

Jenkins's smile was faint. "About a lawsuit for the money we had to hand over to your clients four years ago."

"But I didn't take any of the clients' money. I've proved that to the police. Talk to Detective Donnelly. He seems satisfied and assures me that my name will be completely cleared."

Jenkins shook his head. "What you've proved is that you didn't cash in any of the stolen bonds or deposit money in any bank after your disappearance. It's the legal department's opinion that either you still have most of the money or it was lost with you when your boat broke apart in Puget Sound. Either way, Smith National is out a fortune."

"I never took the money," Cord said quietly, his eyes blazing.

"Well, if you didn't, who did?" Jenkins asked, and Alison's breath caught in her throat. The argument was a no-win situation.

"I don't know," Cord said through clenched teeth.

"And why did you run?"

Alison's pulse was leaping; she wiped her palms nervously on her slacks. Though she knew she had nothing to fear, had done nothing wrong, Cord was backed into a corner. Would he try to incriminate her or David? Would an entire new scandal sweep through Seattle, ravaging their lives all over again? Would Mandy learn the painful truth about David, the man she had considered her father all these years?

"I left for personal reasons," Cord said succinctly, his

eyes never wavering from the slight man in front of him. "Would you like a drink?"

"No thanks," Jenkins replied, adjusting his glasses, but undeterred. "What kind of personal reasons?"

Cord smiled coldly. "Too personal to discuss with strangers."

"Look, Mr. Donahue, I'm not interested in playing word games with you."

"Then what are you interested in?"

"A settlement."

"For?" Cord asked, his voice rising.

"Damages, of course. Damages to the tune of over a million dollars!"

"Oh, no," Alison whispered.

"And that would insure me that I wouldn't be sued?"

"Prosecuted," he replied.

Cord's dark eyes turned to slits. "As I said, I've already talked to the police. The D.A. won't press charges," Cord repeated, his voice rising.

Jenkins stuffed two fingers beneath his collar and began to sweat. "Unless our legal department convinces them you're to blame."

"You know what you can do with your legal department," Cord said with deceptive softness.

Alison wanted to die. The tension in the room was nearly visible. She wished there was something, *anything,* she could do.

"Mommy?"

No! Gasping, she turned and saw Mandy, her favorite worn blanket dragging on the floor, one fist rubbing her eyes. Dark hair surrounded her face in a tangled cloud and blue smudges circled her round eyes. "Who's he?" she said, pointing to Jenkins.

"A business associate of Daddy, er, Uncle Cord's." A flush of red swept up her neck. "Come on, I'll get you a drink of water and put you back in bed." *Before this show-down between Jenkins and Cord gets any more hostile.*

"I'm not tired," Mandy said, yawning.

"Sure, you aren't." Without a backward glance Alison hurried out of the room, away from the simmering argument. The last thing she wanted was for Mandy to hear this discussion and start asking questions about Cord.

As she climbed the stairs, she could still hear Jenkins droning on and crossed her fingers that Cord could handle him.

"SMITH NATIONAL ISN'T satisfied," Jenkins repeated.

Cord knew he was backed into a corner. Once he'd wanted revenge, now he felt the uncomfortable urge to protect Alison. Besides, he would like nothing better than to knock the smug smile off Jenkins's face. But he couldn't do that, unless he wanted to incriminate Alison or David, or both.

"I'll pay the company back," Cord said simply.

"Then you admit—"

"I admit nothing! And I'll expect a document to that effect!"

"But surely—"

"Look, Jenkins, I'll settle with the company. They'll get every last penny they paid in claims. Just bring all the invoices to the office next week."

Jenkins coughed. "It's a well-known fact that Donahue Investments doesn't have the resources to pay off that kind of debt. Most of your clients left after the scandal."

"I'm working on that," Cord replied tightly. "They'll be back."

"But we can't wait. We need to be paid immediately."

"It will take a little time," Cord said quietly, his patience with this self-righteous little jerk stretched thin. "I'm selling my cannery in Alaska and I have other assets."

Jenkins's thin brows shot up.

"Nothing to do with Smith National's loss," Cord clarified as Alison, her face chalk-white and eyes round with—what? guilt?—walked into the room and stood near the double doors. Cord advanced on the smaller man, and to Jenkins's credit he didn't back down. "Now, I suggest you leave us until you visit the office next week. By that time you'll have your money."

The neatly pressed insurance man seemed about to say something else but left the room quickly. The front door banged behind him, and Bangles barked wildly from the utility room. A few minutes later Jenkins's car roared down the drive.

"And good riddance," Cord muttered, stalking to the bar.

"Mandy would like you to say good-night again," Alison said.

Cord's black mood lifted a little. The sprite had a way of lining even the blackest clouds with silver. He set the unopened bottle back on the bar and strode quickly out of the room and up the stairs.

Mandy, lids half-lowered, was waiting for him.

"So why did you wake up?" Cord asked.

"You were yelling at Mommy."

"Not at Mommy," Cord clarified, touching her chin with the tip of his index finger.

"You do sometimes."

"Well, yes." *And sometimes she deserves it and a whole lot more!*

"She likes you," Mandy said innocently, fighting sleep.

"How can you tell?"

"Because—because she smiles when you're around."
Then, as if the discussion were closed, Mandy snuggled
into her pillow, her arm firmly clamped around the
loosely stitched neck of her tattered teddy bear.

"Does she?" Cord wondered, rubbing his chin
thoughtfully and finding the idea irresistible. If only for
a minute he could think, could hope... But then his
thoughts turned back to that worm Jenkins from Smith
National. Someone had been lying. Whether it was David
or Alison or both of them, he didn't know, but Cord had
to find out the truth before all hell broke loose and Mandy
was caught in the middle of the worst scandal in Seattle
since he had supposedly embezzled company funds and
drowned.

He glanced down at his sleeping child and his jaw
clenched tight. He half believed Alison, wanting desperately
to trust her, but first he had to dig up the past. All of it!

ALISON WAS ON pins and needles as she walked into the
office the next day. The night before, Cord had tucked
Mandy into bed and then left without a word. This
morning he'd taken off before dawn.

Celia wasn't at her desk, but a soft glow from the
lights in Cord's office filtered through the pebbled
glass of his door and she could hear him talking, probably on the phone. Deciding that she had to face him
and talk to him about the insurance company as well
as the police, she quickly heated water in the coffeepot, poured two cups and, with the *Investment Journal*
tucked under her arm, knocked softly on Cord's office
door.

"Come in," he said brusquely, barely glancing up

when she entered and placed a steaming mug on the corner of his desk. His jacket had been tossed onto the back of the couch, his shirt sleeves had been rolled over his forearms and the knot of his tie was loose. Huge circles under his eyes attested that he hadn't slept any better than she.

"You were gone early," she commented.

"Mmm."

"Up with the proverbial chickens."

He looked up then, lifting his dark head to stare at her through narrowed eyes. "You know what they say about the early bird."

Her stomach knotted. "So you're catching worms?"

"Someone has to—so we can get Jenkins and Smith National off our necks."

"But you said—"

"I lied," he said softly. "I can't come up with a million dollars in cash, even if I sell everything."

"But your cannery—"

"Can't possibly pay off the two mortgages on the house, the loan on this building *and* the insurance company." Leaning back in his chair, ignoring the aromatic coffee on his desk, he glared at her.

"Then why did you tell him everything would be taken care of next week?"

"To buy time," he said simply. "To stall."

"But you can't do that forever."

"Nope."

Weak inside, she sat on the arm of his couch and cradled her warm cup in her hands. "What do you hope to accomplish in a week?"

"I don't know," he admitted, some of the edge leaving his voice.

Then she noticed a stack of old ledgers and computer printouts on his desk. The papers had yellowed and smelled musty with age but were still very legible.

"Four years ago," he said, reading the question in her eyes.

Her fingers tightened around her cup. "And what have you found?"

"That *someone* covered his or her tracks well." He tossed her a ledger and she saw a withdrawal of cash from a client's account and noted the initials of approval in the appropriate column: C.D., written in Cord's distinctive hand.

"You did this?"

"That much of it—yes. Check the date."

Her heart stopped for a second. It was the day he'd supposedly drowned. All of her old pain resurfaced and she gazed at his strong, rough-hewn features, thankful that he was alive. How often had she wished for just such a second chance with him? How many times had she dreamed that he was alive and would return to her?

"Alison?" he asked, staring at her, his eyes dark as they delved into hers.

She blushed and tried to concentrate on what he was saying. "Now, look at this." He handed her a corresponding file. "There's even a letter from the client, signed for monies withdrawn."

"So?" But she'd already guessed the rest.

"No check issued. The letter's a fake. A forgery. And this is just one example of how money was shuffled out of the accounts."

"To where? There had to be a corresponding entry."

She tried to think; she'd gone through all of this with the police four years before.

"To the general account."

"And then?"

"Cashed in a personal advance to Cord Donahue." He handed her all of the paperwork. "The problem is, I never took it. I *never* cashed that check."

"But I don't understand. Someone did."

"This was done the day I left. It looks like I took this money, along with a lot more."

"And you didn't?"

"What do you think?"

She knew in her heart he'd never taken anything. "Then you think I did," she whispered, shoulders sinking, realizing he suspected her not only of embezzling but of forging his name.

"No. David showed me the ledgers. They had your initials on them in pencil. I changed them to mine."

"My initials? But I never—"

"I know. It had to have been David. He moved the money into the general account and slowly transferred it out, forging my name when he needed to, before I supposedly drowned, and then using his own name."

Alison had difficulty pulling all the pieces together. "But he would have had to have someone helping him in order to cash the checks."

"Yes. Someone in on it with him—an accomplice."

Alison didn't want to believe the depths of David's deception. "There has to be some other explanation," she insisted, remembering her husband. "You make it sound as if he was some kind of criminal. I just can't believe that—he was too good to Mandy and me."

"Was he?" Cord whispered, eyes sharp.

She could barely breathe under his accusing stare, but she had to defend David. "He...he tried."

Letting out an impatient breath, Cord scowled down at the ledgers, then shoved his chair away from his desk and stared outside to the foggy morning and the buildings across a back alley. "Do you think this is any easier for me?" he asked softly, his jaw tight. "Remember, David was my brother."

"And you never trusted him."

Cord's mouth thinned. "Not with money, no," he admitted.

"Or with me."

He cast her a glance and snorted. "Maybe that was my fault," he admitted wearily. "I never have thought straight when I'm around you." In frustration he raked stiff fingers through his dark hair.

"So why are you dredging all this up again?" she wondered aloud.

"Guess."

Suddenly she understood. "To prove to the insurance company that they weren't defrauded when they paid off the bonding policy of one of the employees of Donahue Investments. The dollar amount was right—they just had the wrong guy, is that it? Because even though you didn't steal the money, David did."

"That's part of it."

"Don't you think it's a little too convenient? Jenkins and the mucky-mucks at Smith National aren't going to buy it." But deep in her heart she wanted the trauma of all this pain over—the truth to be out.

"Not yet, I don't suppose. Not until I prove it."

"And how can you do that?"

Stretching, he turned to face her again. "I'm not sure.

I only know that it has to be done, and not just to satisfy the insurance company." His gaze held hers and he offered her a tentative smile. "I have to do this for Mandy," he said quietly, "and us."

Her heart somersaulted but she tried to hang on to some shred of common sense. "You're doing this no matter who gets hurt or whose reputation gets dragged through the mud," she said, suddenly defensive of the man who had taken her under his wing.

"I've had experience in that area," Cord pointed out. "My reputation's been about as blackened as anyone's in this town."

"But David can't defend himself."

Jaw working, Cord said, "Looks as if you're doing a damned good job."

"I'm just trying to be objective."

"Don't you even care about the truth?" Cord demanded.

"Yes! I care—"

"Good. That'll make things a whole lot easier on all of us. Now, tell me, do you know where Louise lives or works?"

Alison drew a blank. "Louise?" she repeated.

"My old secretary, Louise Caldwell."

Her throat went dry. "You want to see Louise?"

"Yes." Exasperated, he tugged on his tie.

"She used to work at Crestview Title Company at one of their east-side offices," Alison said, "but I don't know where she lives. Somewhere near Bellevue, I think."

"Thanks." He grabbed his coat and slid his arms into the sleeves.

"Where're you going?"

"Out," he replied mysteriously, and Alison felt suddenly cold inside.

She shouldn't have been jealous, not of Louise, but she couldn't help but feel a little nag of doubt. "What have you got planned?"

"I don't know yet." He reached for the door.

"But you have appointments."

"Handle them. You're still the president of the company, according to company records. Certainly you can deal with a few clients."

Then he was out the door.

Alison picked up his untouched coffee cup and, sighing, walked across the hall. She considered following him but quickly cast the thought aside. Whatever he was planning, she wanted no part of it. Frowning thoughtfully, she pushed open the door to her office.

"Where've you been?" Celia asked. All smiles, she was already at her desk and opening the mail.

"With Cord."

"I thought I just heard him leave."

"You did."

"But he has appointments," Celia whispered, glancing at her desk calendar.

"Phone them if you can. Explain that Cord was called away. I'll see everyone today or tomorrow, or they can reschedule for next week." Next week, when Smith National Insurance Company would be here, trying to squeeze whatever they could out of Donahue Investments, she thought with a grimace. She didn't blame the bonding company; they had every right to feel defrauded, and yet, she was just so tired of trying to keep the wolves from the door.

CORD DIDN'T STOP to think twice. He climbed into his Jeep, jammed it into gear and took off, heading east over the Mercer Island Bridge across Lake Washington. As if inspiration had struck, he pushed the speed limit, hoping Louise might give him the clue he needed to prove whether or not David had been the embezzler. *And what if she couldn't help?*

Then he'd start all over again, back at square one, checking with every other employee who had worked for the investment company four years before.

Half an hour later he wheeled into the parking lot of the Bellevue office of Crestview Realty. It was a small office with desks crammed into every available space. Despite the clack of typewriters, phones ringing and general buzz of confusion, he noticed Louise's pale blond hair and blue eyes the minute he walked through the door.

She glanced up and a huge smile lighted her pretty face. "Cord!" she cried, pushing back her chair and hurrying to the front counter. "My God, it *is* you!" She was grinning ear to ear. "I can't believe it!" She turned to a curly blond coworker and said, "Kathy, can you hold the fort? This is my old boss!"

"No problem," Kathy replied with an easy grin that was quickly replaced by her chin dropping several inches. "You're the man in the paper, aren't you?" she said, snapping her mouth shut. "The one that was supposed to have drowned."

"One and the same." Louise swung the strap of her purse over her shoulder as she rounded the counter. "Come on," she insisted, her long fingers folding over Cord's arm, "let's get out of here before the whole office gets wind of who you are and you have to hold a press conference." Looking up at him, her pale eyes sparkling, she whispered, "I just can't believe it's really you!"

She directed him to a small coffee shop three blocks down the street and they slid into a quiet booth near the back of the austere café. After ordering coffee and doughnuts and answering what seemed to be a million of Louise's questions about the boating accident and what he'd done since then, Cord was finally able to sip his coffee.

"Thank God you're alive," Louise whispered fervently when she'd finally calmed down and convinced herself that the man sitting across the table from her was indeed Cord Donahue. "I only wish we could say the same for David." Sadness darkened her eyes and she toyed with the crumbs on her plate.

Twisting his cup in his hands Cord said, "I suppose that was difficult for you—David's death."

Louise shuddered. "It was awful. I thought you'd both died."

Quietly Cord said, "I thought you always had a soft spot in your heart for him."

"For David?" she repeated, shaking her head. But her big eyes darkened. "He was Alison's husband."

"Not at first," Cord reminded her.

"Well, later." Louise glanced nervously at her watch. "Maybe I should get back. It's time for Kathy's break."

Cord's fingers grabbed hold of her wrist. "I know you dated David, and cared for him. It must have been quite a shock when he married Alison."

Sighing, Louise lifted one shoulder. "It hurt a little. But I knew he was seeing someone else." Her ice-blue eyes clouded.

Cord stiffened, his eyes fixed on her sad face. No doubt about it, Louise was telling the truth.

"I was just surprised when it turned out to be Alison," she continued, relaxing back against the hard wooden back of the booth and closing her eyes as if to ward off too painful a memory. "I knew that they'd gone to breakfast a couple of times, and lunch, too. But I never suspected..."

"That they were having an affair?"

She swallowed and avoided his eyes. "Right. I know this sounds crazy but I always thought Alison was interested in you."

"You did?" he asked, his muscles tightening. "Why?"

"She never said anything, of course."

Of course.

"But it was the way she looked at you and the way you were around her—I don't know—softer, somehow, that made me think the two of you might get together."

"So you were surprised when she married David?" he said, eyeing her over the rim of his cup.

"Yes! I...I knew he'd been seeing other women, too."

A faint memory darted across Cord's mind, something he'd forgotten that surfaced just for an instant. "Including your sister?" he asked slowly, watching as she turned ashen.

"My sister?"

"Francine."

Louise lifted one shoulder as she nervously fished in her purse, found a pack of cigarettes and lit up, inhaling the smoke as if to clear her mind. "They had dated," she admitted.

"About the time she worked at Peninsula Bank."

"That was a long time ago." She bit her lip and looked away.

Cord sensed she was holding back and he knew he was on the right track. "So you thought maybe David was involved with your sister."

"He was," she said firmly.

"During the time when money was being embezzled out of the company?"

She hesitated, then nodded, drawing in on her cigarette and blowing out a stream of blue smoke.

Realizing he was prying, possibly bringing back painful memories, Cord nearly stopped asking the questions screaming in his mind. But he couldn't. Because of Alison. Above all else, he wanted to protect her and, if possible, prove her innocence. "And then he married Alison. Is that why you quit?"

"I guess so," Louise admitted. "There was all that scandal when you left and then Alison and David. There just didn't seem like much left for me. All the clients were calling and the police kept hanging around, so I decided to leave."

"And now?"

Crushing out her cigarette, she brightened a bit. "I've worked my way up at Crestview," she said proudly. "I should be promoted to branch manager by the end of the year and then I'm going to get married."

"Anyone I know?"

She laughed a little. "I don't think so. He moved to Seattle about eighteen months ago, when you were still dead," she added with wry humor.

"Congratulations," he said sincerely.

"I'll send you an invitation to the wedding."

"You'd better."

Grinning, she talked at length about the man she was planning to marry, a longshoreman, and Cord sincerely hoped she was over David.

By the time he walked her back to the office, he didn't have much more information than before, but he had one more person to see: Francine Caldwell. Maybe after talking with Francine, he'd have some answers. If so, he could return to Alison and finally bury the pain of the past and claim Mandy as his daughter.

CHAPTER ELEVEN

BANGLES HAD CHEWED the corner of Cord's favorite leather chair.

Clucking her tongue, Norma wrung her hands in her apron and tried to apologize to Alison. "I guess Mandy opened the gate and he got loose while I was up changin' the beds," she said, surveying the damage and shaking her head. "Anyway, by the time I found him, he'd managed to rip a hole in it." Norma pointed to a ripped corner of the chair, where tufted white pieces of stuffing poked through the smooth, oxblood leather.

"Not too smart," Alison remarked to a totally unremorseful Bangles. He leaped high into the air, attempting to wash her face with his tongue.

"I feel just terrible," Norma said, eyeing the dog with a vengeful eye.

"It's not your fault." Alison tried to snap Bangles's leash onto his collar but he ducked out of her way and dashed around the room. "Come here!" Heedless of her calls, he raced through the door knocking against a brass lamp, which rocked crazily.

Alison tried to reach the lamp but grabbed only air. Glass shattered and the room went dark.

The dog clambered noisily up the stairs.

"Oh, merciful heavens!" Norma wailed while Mandy laughed and Alison ran up the stairs behind the frisky pup.

"Bangles! Come here!" She cornered him at the end of the hall. "You naughty dog," she chastised breathlessly, but couldn't keep a straight face when he tried to melt into the carpet. "You'd better be careful or I'll give Lazarus his chance with you!" Gently tugging, she led him, tail tucked between his legs, head lowered, down the stairs and back to the utility room. "We'll take a walk later, okay?" Alison said, scratching his ears. "But for now, you be good."

"Be good!" Mandy echoed, and Bangles immediately dropped his "poor me" act and started jumping up at the gate, hoping for another chance to escape.

"Maybe Cord was right," Norma admitted. "Maybe bringin' the pup back wasn't such a good idea."

"I love Bangles!" Mandy announced, perplexed. "He belongs with me."

"That he does, love, that he does," Norma admitted, chuckling, her good mood returning.

At the rumble of Cord's Jeep as it climbed up the drive, Norma glanced at the clock on the stove. "Oh, now, look. Dinner will be late. All because of you!" She cast the dog another scathing look but smiled when Bangles wagged his tail.

"I'll help," Alison offered, though she was on edge. Cord hadn't returned to the office all day. What had he done? Where had he been? And how could he possibly think he could straighten out the past when even the police hadn't been able to?

"No, I can handle the cookin'. And Mandy will set the table, won't you?"

"Can I really?" Mandy asked, already reaching in the silverware drawer.

"Hold on a minute, you've been playin' with that dog. First you wash your hands, then put out the place mats and forks and spoons—no knives," Norma said. "I'll bring the plates over."

Grumbling, Mandy stood on a chair and washed her hands at the sink just as the door swung open. Appearing tired and drawn, Cord strode in, forced a smile that stretched when his gaze landed on Mandy. "Uncle Cord!" she squealed, hopping off the chair and frantically running to him.

He grabbed her, tossed her over his head and listened to her laugh gaily. "How're ya, sprite?"

"Bangles eat your chair."

"What?"

"Come on, I'll show you." She wriggled to the floor and ran through the swinging kitchen door to the hallway.

Cord followed and Alison cringed when she heard him yell, "That blasted dog!" But by the time he returned to the kitchen, he was grinning again, amusement in his eyes, Mandy riding on his back.

"Cord says we should have gotten a pony! Can we, Mama? *Please?*" Her brown eyes were wide with excitement.

Alison wanted to strangle Cord and sent him a glance that conveyed her feelings.

"Just a little pony," Mandy enthused.

"Oh, honey, we can't. We don't have a place for a horse."

"He can sleep in there—" she pointed to the utility room "—with Bangles."

Cord laughed loudly then, some of the tension leaving his face. "We'll talk about it later, sprite. Oh, and Norma, we're having a guest for dinner."

"A guest?"

Alison's heart dropped. He'd invited Louise over, and foolishly she was disappointed. Though she'd always liked Louise, the thought of Cord with another woman, any woman, chilled her to the bone. Not that she had any hold on him, she reminded herself angrily. "It'll be good to see Louise again."

His thick brows drew together. "Louise? Oh, no. The guest tonight is Nate Benson."

"Benson?" Norma repeated as if she'd gone suddenly deaf. Her lips drew into a thin line, then she motioned to the child. "Well, I think we'll be eatin' in the other room. I've only got pork chops—"

"That'll be fine."

Still perplexed, Alison stared at him. The last time Cord had mentioned Nate's name, he'd had to spit it out. "Hold on a minute. Why is Nate coming here?"

"Business," Cord said succinctly, cutting her off. Then, as if seeing the worry in her eyes, he said, "Come into the den. I'll tell you about it."

Surprised by his change of attitude, she followed him down the hall to the study.

"I thought you couldn't stand Nate," she said, once Cord had closed the double doors and begun stoking the fire.

"I can't."

"This doesn't make any sense."

He glanced over his shoulder, offering her the barest of smiles. "No, I suppose it doesn't," he admitted, his eyes growing soft as he straightened. "I've been trying to figure out what happened. For us. All of us."

Alison's heart leaped.

Wearily he stretched, rubbing a hand between his shoulders and groaning. "You know that I love Mandy very much."

She nodded.

"I can't let her grow up thinking her father's some kind of criminal. It's important that I clear my name—for her. I wasn't kidding when I said I want her to know she's my child," he said.

"We will tell her," Alison promised.

"And I won't wait forever." He frowned a bit. "I can't." The clock in the hall struck six-thirty and Cord jumped. "Look, just bear with me tonight, all right? I think I've just about got everything figured out."

Astounded, she nearly gasped. "You do? But how?"

"It took a while, but Louise was a big help. Now, just give me time to shower and I'll tell you all about it."

"But I want to know."

He offered her a tender smile. "Just be patient." Striding quickly out of the room, he left.

And Alison, mystified, returned to the kitchen. Some of his words disturbed her. Obviously, once his name was cleared, he meant to have his daughter live with him—with or without Alison.

Shuddering, she shoved open the kitchen door.

Norma was busy peeling potatoes. She barely glanced up when Alison sat defeatedly at the table. "Why in tarnation would he invite the likes of Benson over here?" Norma wondered aloud.

"Something about the scandal," she said, tugging at her lower lip. Would Cord go so far as to try to take Mandy from her?

"He doesn't know anythin'."

"You don't like Nate, do you?" Alison remarked.

"No use for him. He never looks me in the eye. In my book, when a man can't meet your eyes, he's got somethin' to hide."

"But Nate was David's best friend."

"Believe me, *that* man is no one's friend but his own. I can't believe Cord would invite him. But then there's no accountin' for what Cord will do these days," Norma said with a snort. "Now you go on upstairs. Change if you want to. I certainly wouldn't, not for Nate. Mandy and I can handle dinner."

Alison's lips twisted wryly. "Just go light on the arsenic, okay?"

Norma scowled, but her faded eyes twinkled.

"I never knew you felt this way about Nate."

"You never asked, now, did you?" Then she glanced at Mandy, who was leaning over the gate to the utility room, playing tug-of-war with Bangles. "Come on, I'll show you where the good silver is."

"I already know," Mandy said, whisking through the doors leading to the dining room.

"But you have to wash your hands again…." Norma's voice faded. "It's no use."

Mandy poked her head back into the room.

Chuckling, Alison looked through the doors. "Mandy, when you're done setting the table, maybe you should come upstairs to change, too," she called, noting that the bands holding Mandy's pigtails in place had slipped and tendrils of black hair were curling around her smudged face.

"I'm okay," Mandy insisted, ducking back into the dining room.

"I'll send her up," Norma promised. "Now go on with you."

Knowing that Norma could handle the kitchen, Alison climbed the stairs and heard water running in Cord's bathroom. She thought about the time Cord had sneaked into her bath and, knowing he would probably be furious, decided to give him his due. Though the atmosphere between them had been tense lately, she couldn't resist paying him back, especially since he was being so mysterious. She pushed aside her worries about custody of Mandy and, smothering a smile, crept down the hall and into his room. The shower was still spraying noisily. Thinking of Mandy, she closed the door to the bedroom and locked it behind her. Then, hesitating a second, her teeth sinking into her lower lip, she reached for the knob of the bathroom door and twisted hard.

The door flew open and Cord, still dripping, a towel slung low over his waist, stood on the wet tile floor. "Looking for someone?" he taunted, his brown eyes bright.

"Oh!" she gasped, startled. "Uh, just you. I thought I'd pay you back." Then she glanced past his slick shoulders to the shower. "The water's still running."

His white teeth gleamed in a seductive smile. He was only inches from her, his rippling muscles taut as water drops glittered in his hair and ran slowly down the length of his throat. "I was expecting you."

"Y-you were? But how?" Confused, she met his eyes. They were dark and intent, dangerous as they focused on her lips.

He didn't bridge the small gap of the threshold between them, but she shivered under his provocative stare. "I've waited every time I've taken a shower."

"But it's been weeks."

"And, believe me, worth the wait." One hand reached up and his fingers curled around her nape, drawing her head to his as he pressed wet, warm lips against hers.

Alison's heart began to pound. After the past few days, when the tension in the house had been so thick it had been almost visible, she was relieved to fall against him and wrap her arms around his naked torso.

She could hear the beating of his heart, a cadence rapidly accelerating, could smell the scent of soap and water and feel the need firing his blood as his fingers massaged her neck.

She wanted to melt against him and didn't protest when he lifted her off her feet to lay her on the soft bed.

"Mommy?" A small fist knocked on the door. "Uncle Cord?"

Alarmed, Alison leaped off the bed and quickly straightened her hair.

"In here, sweetheart. I'll be out in a minute."

"The door's locked," Mandy protested.

"Thank God!" Alison whispered, then in a louder voice called through the door to her daughter, "I'll…I'll meet you in your room. Pick out what you want to wear."

Listening to Mandy's footsteps padding away from the door, Alison rubbed a trembling hand over her brow. What had gotten into her—into him?

"Dangerous game, isn't it?" Cord mocked, and any sign of amusement had vanished from his eyes.

"It wasn't a game."

"Sure it was, Alison. A charade," he accused, trying to get hold of his ragged emotions. "Here we are, her parents, for God's sake, hiding like teenagers caught in the back seat of a car! She's my daughter, *ours*, damn it! I just don't know what the hell we're doing in this room, feeling ashamed of ourselves!"

"But we—we're not married," she explained.

"Something you could quickly rectify." Then flinging himself back on the mattress and pulling her against him, he stared up at the ceiling, one hand draped possessively over the back of Alison's neck. Her head rested against his bare chest, and she could hear the beating of his heart. His fingers were gentle and soothing as they moved against her skin. "I won't give up, you know. Either you marry me, and soon, or I'll take you to court."

He didn't sound vindictive. Instead he seemed almost beaten. "Let's not fight about this."

"I'm not fighting with you, I'm just letting you know where I stand. The child is mine and I love her. Legally I have rights whether we're married or not."

Resting on one elbow, she gazed into his eyes, and if she'd seen one spark of tenderness, one chance that he loved her, she would have begged him to marry her at that very moment. Instead, she witnessed his features grow hard, his gaze become ice cold.

"You won't marry me, will you? Not even for Mandy's sake, which, if I remember right, was the reason you married David."

Just tell me you love me. "I think I should go," she said, sliding off the bed and moving to the door. "Mandy's waiting."

But he reached the door as she did, and though she managed to turn the lock and yank on the knob, he slammed the door back into its jamb and held it firmly in place.

"Cord—"

"There's one thing more I want to know."

"Not now—"

"Why did David sleep in here?" he demanded. "Without you?"

"He—he didn't, not at first."

Cord's skin whitened over his cheekbones and his eyes glinted. "Why, damn it?" he roared, and Alison was afraid Mandy might overhear.

"There's no point—"

"You're going to tell me," he said, pushing his face so close to hers she could see the pinpoints of frustrated light illuminating his near-black eyes. "And you're going to tell me before you leave this room."

She knew she didn't have a choice.

"Mommy! Come on!" Mandy called.

"I found out that David had a friend," she said quietly, her cheeks coloring.

"A girlfriend?"

"Yes." She tried to pull open the door but Cord's shoulder held it fast.

"Who?"

"I...I don't know."

"I thought he was so wonderful to you."

"Look, he was. Okay? He took me in, claimed Mandy as his own child, gave me a home and let me learn as much as I could from the company."

"But he cheated on you," Cord said bluntly. "Why?"

"How would I know?"

"You must have had a guess."

"Mommy?"

"Because of you, damn it," she said through clenched teeth. "Because of you!"

Cord's muscles slackened and Alison took advantage of his surprise by wrenching on the knob with all of her strength. The door opened and Alison slipped through, nearly knocking Mandy, half dressed and perturbed, off her stockinged feet.

"What were you doing?" Mandy asked.

"Arguing with Uncle Cord," Alison said, wondering if fighting with him was inevitable. "Come on, now, let's get you dressed." She knew Cord was still standing in the doorway watching her, irresistibly sexy in his low-slung towel, but she wouldn't give him the satisfaction of looking over her shoulder and seeing the smirk that was most probably squarely on his self-satisfied jaw.

NATE BENSON ARRIVED promptly at seven. Alison had just changed and was starting down the stairs when the doorbell chimed and Cord, striding stiffly from the study, answered the door.

"Benson," Cord said coldly. "Come in. Can I get you a drink?"

"Sure." Nate seemed decidedly uncomfortable in his soft blue sweater and slacks. He glanced at Alison as if hoping for some kind of explanation but she just shrugged her shoulders. She had no idea what Cord had planned. Stomach knotting nervously, she followed the two men into the study.

"So, what's this all about?" Nate asked, accepting a Scotch and water from Cord's outstretched hand. "You told my secretary you were thinking of listing the Donahue Building?"

What? Cord intended to sell the office building? But he couldn't! She had worked too hard to save it! Alison nearly dropped through the floor.

Cord didn't flinch. "That's part of it," he conceded. "But there's more."

"Oh?" Nate forced an even-toothed smile.

"I was hoping you could help me straighten a few things out. You were David's closest friend."

Alison's stomach knotted. She noticed the steel-hard edge of Cord's jaw and the cold determination in his gaze.

"I'd like to think so."

"Good. Then, after dinner, we'll talk a few things out."

"About David?" Nate asked uneasily.

"Right."

Nate took a quick swallow from his drink just as Norma, thankfully, called them to dinner. Alison shot Cord a questioning glance—what did he have in mind?—but he ignored it.

Dinner was delicious but nerve-racking. Though Cord talked of Seahawk football games and politics, his mind seemed only partially on the discussion, and Alison wished she were anywhere but sitting across from him and his damned omniscient gaze.

By the time Norma had cleared the dessert dishes from the table, Alison had put Mandy to bed.

Norma served coffee in the study, and Alison, knowing there was about to be a showdown, was as anxious as Nate.

Sitting on the couch, Nate could barely take his eyes off Alison. "Okay, Donahue," he finally said, glancing pointedly at his watch, once Norma had disappeared and was rattling dishes in the kitchen. "What about the building?"

Cord frowned and poured them each a drink. After handing a glass to Nate and another to Alison, he leaned one shoulder against the fireplace and said, "I'm considering selling it."

"Just considering," Nate repeated, obviously disappointed.

"It wouldn't be necessary except that it has quite a hefty mortgage against it. David took out a loan shortly after he became president of the company," Cord explained.

"I remember."

Cord seemed pleased. Alison sipped her drink and tried to understand just what Cord expected from Nate Benson.

"So then, as David's best friend, you probably knew what he did with the proceeds."

Nate shrugged and his lower lip protruded a bit. "Put them back into the company, I'd guess. There was quite a scandal when you left town. A lot of the clients pulled out."

"Most of the money didn't go back into the business—"

"Wait a minute," Alison interrupted.

"I checked," Cord insisted.

"But I saw the ledgers. I was working at the company…."

"For a few months. Then you took off for over a year to have Mandy and spend some time with her. Right?"

Alison nodded slowly as she started to understand.

"During those months you were off, David skimmed off most of the money."

"Cord, please," she begged, a part of her not wanting to hear this.

"You're sure about this?" Nate said, tugging at his collar.

"Yes. But there are a few things I don't understand; things that maybe you can clear up for me."

"I doubt it."

"Where did the money go?"

"I don't know."

Cord slowly advanced upon Nate. All pretense of friendliness faded as he stood, towering over the couch where Nate sat. "Think about it. And if you don't tell me, I know Detective Donnelly would love to talk to you."

"Hey, wait a minute, I didn't do anything," Nate protested.

"Except withhold evidence. Maybe you should get it off your chest," Cord suggested.

Swallowing nervously, Nate glanced at Alison, then swirled his drink and stared into the amber depths. "There's not much to say."

"David embezzled, didn't he?"

Nate squeezed his eyes shut tight. "Yes, but I didn't know about it at the time," he said. "He told me about it long after you were supposed to be dead. And then—" Nate shrugged "—he had a wife to think about. I couldn't see that turning him in would do any good. Especially since you were dead."

"But I wasn't."

"For Christ's sake, Donahue, no one knew!"

"So what else did David tell you?"

Nate pinched the bridge of his nose. "A lot," he admitted, as if suddenly relieved to unburden himself. "But most of it I didn't know until that last hunting trip, I swear."

Cord leaned over, eyeball to eyeball with the man. "Did David commit suicide?" he asked slowly and Alison gasped.

"Cord, no!"

"Of course not!" Nate replied, aghast, his eyes closing at the horrid memory. "The accident was just that."

Cord's face slacked slightly. "Thank God. Now, why don't you start at the beginning?" he advised.

Nate gave in. "I guess that's as good a place as any." Leaning forward on his elbows, avoiding Alison's confused stare, Nate said, "As you've probably guessed, David was in a lot of trouble financially. He'd gambled away a fortune—all the money in his trust fund, money he'd borrowed on his insurance policies and even the money he had received when he'd taken out a loan on the building."

"Gambling? What kind of gambling?" Alison asked.

"Any kind. His losses at the racetrack were only a small part of it. He got involved in betting on football games through Las Vegas and local high-stakes poker games. A lot of money was involved."

"Clients' money?" Alison whispered, stricken.

"You didn't know about this?" Cord asked her, seeing how pale she'd become.

"I…I never guessed. It was possible, I suppose. There were a lot of times when he'd come home late but he always said he'd been with clients."

"Nothing about gambling."

"Nothing *serious*. I knew he went to Long Acres for the horse races, of course." She shook her head. "This is all too farfetched."

"You think I'm making this up?" Nate asked, incredulous. "For God's sake, why?" He seemed so genuinely tortured, Alison believed he was telling the truth.

"I don't know what to think," she admitted. "Ever since Cord came back, this house has been upside down."

Cord drew in a long breath. "Did David tell you anything else?"

"Such as?"

"Who was his accomplice? Someone who worked for the bank had to be in on his scheme. A number of checks were made payable to me and cashed at Peninsula Bank."

Dear God, the bank where Francine Caldwell had worked. All at once, Alison understood and she felt sick inside. Cord's eyes met hers for an instant. *He knows. He knows all of this and yet he's grilling Nate.*

"I never saw the money," Cord said. "And David, in order to get money, had to cash some pretty sizable checks—made out to me. Either he had my identification, which is unlikely, or he forged the checks and a bank employee, probably an officer, okayed them for payment."

Nate licked suddenly dry lips. "It could have been anyone, I suppose."

"But it wasn't."

Alison felt cold inside with the extent of David's deception. She glanced at Cord, expecting to see some sort of satisfaction gleaming in his eyes. Instead she saw pain, and her heart went out to him. He, too, had loved David.

Nate's face fell and he avoided Alison's eyes. "Oh, hell! David—he, uh, had a girlfriend who worked at the bank. She was in on it. For a cut, of course. Look, Alison," he whispered hoarsely, "I'm sorry about all this."

Alison didn't move, just listened as this man, David's best friend, exposed him. She didn't doubt Nate for a minute; this confession was as excruciating to him as it was to her.

"It's all right. I suppose he told you this woman's name and a lot more, including the truth about Mandy."

Shoving his hands through his neatly clipped hair, Nate nodded. "David told me he'd guessed that you and Cord were seeing each other and he knew you'd gone to the doctor. He put two and two together and decided the best way to cover up what he'd done at the bank was to force Cord out of town. He figured Cord was the only person who might catch on to his scam."

"And me?" Alison demanded, color high, hands shaking so badly she shoved them into the pockets of her skirt.

"He thought if Cord left, you'd be devastated and turn to him."

"He was right," Cord pointed out, and Alison died a little inside. How had she been so blind, so manipulated by a man she trusted?

"So David made it appear as if Alison stole the money."

"Yes." Nate glanced at Cord. "And once he'd convinced you she was pregnant with his child and robbing the company to boot, he figured that you would try to protect her."

"And if I hadn't?"

Nate looked down at his hands. "I don't know. But I guess he would have let Alison take the fall."

"Oh!" Alison, wounded, placed her hand over her mouth. She didn't want to believe that David, a man who had given her so much, who had been so kind to Mandy, had actually been so callous and cruel. "But—"

"If it makes it any easier," Nate said, "he did care for you. He fell for you right from the start, but then he discovered you and Cord, saw you together at some Fourth of July party on the island."

Alison flushed to the roots of her hair, and tears gathered in her eyes. If only things were as simple as they had been all those years ago.

"And the girl's name?" Cord asked, glancing at Alison and noticing that she was trembling. He placed a steadying hand on her shoulder.

Nate swallowed. "I...I can't remember."

"Francine?" Cord prodded. "Francine Caldwell? Louise's sister?" His fingers tightened over her shoulder.

Letting out a tremendous sigh, Nate nodded. "I think so. She worked at some bank."

Mortified, Alison whispered, "She called here once." Staring at her hands, she felt as if every ounce of her pride had been shredded into tiny pieces. She was wounded, angry and embarrassed. "Dear God," Alison murmured, lifting her chin despite the fact that it quavered betrayingly. Would she always be such a fool where men were concerned?

"And Francine, did she write David a letter, a love letter, signing Alison's name?"

Nate nodded. "David didn't think you'd buy his story without some sort of proof."

Alison's stomach was roiling. She wanted to hit and scream and fight. How had she let herself become so manipulated? *How?*

Cord was still glaring pointedly at Nate. "Will you tell the police and insurance company what you just told us?"

Nate blanched. "I don't know. That could ruin my reputation here in town."

"You'll get over it." Cord's eyes glared furiously. "I did."

"But I'm a commercial real estate broker. If this gets into the papers…"

"That's a chance you'll have to take. After all, you heard all this after the fact, right? So you weren't a party to any crime. I'll back you up on that."

Nate's jaw clenched tight and his eyes showed signs of strain. "Okay," he finally agreed. "Why not? Now, look, if that's all there is to this, I'd, er, like to leave. We can meet again if you decide to sell the building," Nate added hastily.

"I'll call," Cord promised, walking him to the door. Nate was gone in a matter of seconds and Cord, grim-faced and tense, his hands stuffed into his pockets, returned.

"You lied," Alison said flatly. "You have no intention of selling the building."

"Or this house or anything, unless I have to. Benson has already figured that out."

Alison felt as if her insides had been shredded. It was one thing to suspect David of being unfaithful, but this… "But you think what Nate has to say will sway the insurance company."

"Time will tell." He found his drink, finished it and set his empty glass on the edge of the mantel.

"It's been a long day," Alison finally said, tired to the bone. "I think I'll go upstairs."

"Not just yet," Cord said, turning to face her again.

"What?"

"We have one more thing to settle between us."

"Tonight?"

"The sooner the better." He crossed the room and sat on the cushions next to her, taking her hands in his. "I know we've had our problems. Lord knows we'll probably have a whole lot more. But now that everything in the past is settled, we should wipe the slate clean."

His fingers were warm over hers. If she let herself, she could be fooled into thinking he still loved her—if only a little. "And how do we do that?"

"We tell Mandy I'm her father. Then we get married. It's time the child knew the truth."

"Just like that?" she said, hardly believing her ears.

"It'll take time, of course."

Relieved, she rested her head against his shoulder. "I'm glad you understand," she whispered. "We can't rush her. But in a few months, once all this mess has died down, yes, you're right, we'll have to tell her who you are." Alison's heart lifted. Finally things were going to work out!

But Cord's body became rigid. "Not in a few months, Alison," he insisted, his eyes fierce. "I want Mandy to know the truth by the end of the week. We'll work into it slowly, but then she has to know."

"That's not enough time," she said frantically, feeling her world start to collapse all over again.

"Why not?"

"She's thought David was her father for over three years. You can't just pull the rug out from under her and say, 'Oh, we made a mistake. Now that Daddy's dead and Uncle Cord's alive, he's your father.'"

"Why not?"

"Because she won't understand."

"She doesn't have to—not all at once."

"But a week?" Outraged, Alison drew away from him, ready to attack, but seeing the pain in his eyes all of the fight drained from her. "Please, Cord, let's think this through. For once we've got all the time in the world. Let's make the most of it."

Anger simmered in his veins as he remembered how she'd stalled the first time, and once again, though he could see the love shining in her eyes, he doubted her. "You want to wait, just like before," he accused. "Well, I can't do it, Alison. For too long I've lived a lie and I can't live it another instant. Either you marry me next week and we tell Mandy that I'm her father, or I'll fight you for her in court."

Alison's blood ran cold. "You're kidding," she whispered. "You wouldn't."

"Try me."

"Cord, just listen to reason."

"You don't understand, do you?" he said, advancing upon her, his voice low and threatening, his lips blade-thin. "This isn't a joke, Alison. I'm demanding right here and now to claim *my* daughter." He jerked his thumb at his chest.

"And that's all that matters," she said furiously, her highest hopes dashed to the cold, cruel ground. He didn't love her; he only wanted to marry her so that he could be near his child.

His hands flexed and opened, a vein throbbed angrily at his temple as he tried with all his might to make her understand. "We care about each other—you and I both know that. And for Mandy's sake we could make this work."

For Mandy's sake. "That's very noble of you, Cord."

"Nobility has nothing to do with it."

"Oh, no? What, then? Stubborn male pride? Ego?"

"She's my daughter, damn it!"

"She's mine, too," Alison said, standing shakily and jutting out her chin. "And I have to do what I think is best for her."

"Which is?"

"Give it a little time. Let her adjust. You've only been back a few weeks, Cord. You can't expect things to change overnight."

"Like they did for you and David?"

Fire leaped in her eyes and she raised her hand as if to slap him, but thought better of it. They'd wounded each other enough. "Good night, Cord," she whispered, knowing in her heart what she would have to do.

"I won't back down, not even if I have to sue you for custody."

"On what charges?" she asked, turning to face him. "That I'm an unfit mother? An embezzler? What?" But she didn't wait for an answer. Her thoughts were already spinning ahead. He'd left her no choice. He was bound and determined to fight for his daughter, and Alison wasn't about to lose Mandy. In the past few years she'd lost Cord, then David. And now, even though she loved Cord, she wouldn't sacrifice her daughter. He could damned well scream bloody murder. Alison and Mandy were leaving. Determinedly she mounted the stairs.

The closet was at the top of the landing, but she could still hear Cord stalking in the den, angrily muttering oaths under his breath. Then his footsteps clicked across the foyer and the front door slammed so hard the windows rattled and the timbers of the old house shook.

Swallowing back any second thoughts, she grabbed the suitcases and carried them quickly into Mandy's room. Glancing at the bed to make sure the child was still sleeping, she opened Mandy's closet and started packing her favorite toys and clothes.

Alison had no idea where she was going or how long she would be gone, but she knew she had to get away and give herself some time to put her life into perspective.

Could she marry Cord knowing he didn't love her? Was she willing to give up her ideals of a perfect marriage for the sake of her child? Maybe, but first she had to think things through. She wasn't about to be manipulated again—not by Cord or any man. But she loved him so much it hurt. Resting her forehead against the closet door, she felt tears burn in her throat.

"Mommy?" Mandy mumbled from beneath her comforter.

She straightened, forcing a brave smile. "Shh, honey. You just sleep a few more minutes. Then we'll go."

"Where?" Mandy asked, stretching, her brown eyes barely open.

Good question. "It's a surprise."

"Is Uncle Cord coming, too?" Mandy yawned and buried her face into the pillow.

"Not right away, sweetheart."

"I'll miss him," Mandy said.

"Me, too," Alison admitted, though Lord only knew why. Fighting back a fresh attack of doubt, she snapped Mandy's suitcase closed. She had to leave tonight before she changed her mind.

CHAPTER TWELVE

"WHAT DO YOU mean, gone?" Cord raged, stalking from one end of the kitchen to the other, glaring pointedly at Norma. His head was pounding from all the alcohol he'd consumed the night before, and he'd overslept in his wrinkled clothes. But though his temples throbbed, he had enough sense to know that Norma had to be wrong. Alison wouldn't have gone. Not now. She wouldn't have taken Mandy without a word.

"I...I don't know how to put it any other way," Norma said, her eyes red with tears. "But when I got here this mornin' Alison's car wasn't in the garage and Mandy wasn't in her bed. There was nothin'."

Cord glanced at the open utility-room door. No dog. No gate. No dishes.

Fear driving him, he ran from one room to the next, calling her name over and over again. "Alison!" he screamed, taking the stairs two at a time. "Alison, where the hell are you?" He threw open doors, banging them against wainscoting, tossing clothes out of closets, opening windows and yelling her name.

But no one answered.

He nearly ripped the phone out of the wall as he placed it on his lap and savagely punched out the number for the office.

"Donahue Investments," Celia answered.

"Is Alison there?"

"No, Mr. Donahue, she hasn't come in yet."

"Has she called?"

"No. Is there some kind of trouble?"

"Hell, I don't know! If she calls in, you make her tell you where she is. And if she shows up, don't let her leave!"

"But—"

"Just do it!" He slammed the receiver back into its cradle and left the telephone on the bed. Raw energy pumped through his blood and his mind was a kaleidoscope of pictures—Alison chasing after him in a white dress, Alison making love to him on the beach, Mandy being dragged by an overgrown pup, Alison's wet body in a steamy shower. *Where had she gone?*

He nearly ran into Norma as he stormed through the kitchen and grabbed his keys.

"Where are you goin'?" she asked.

"To look for them."

"Where?"

"I don't know, damn it!" His heart was thudding with the same fear that had overcome him years ago—the fear that he'd lost Alison forever.

"Just slow down," Norma advised, placing a comforting hand on his arm.

"I can't!" He jerked the door open so violently his arm ached.

"Saints preserve us," Norma prayed, fervently crossing herself.

Ignoring anything but the fear driving him on, Cord ran outside, sprinting through puddles and the sheeting spring rain to his Jeep. He threw the vehicle into gear, roaring out of the drive in a spray of water and gravel.

Somehow, though he couldn't recall the drive into the city, he was parking his car in the lot near the Donahue Building. Pocketing his keys, he jaywalked, heard the screech of tires and blast of horns, but dashed heedlessly into the building and up the backstairs.

On the second floor he flung open the door of the office and stood dripping and unkempt on the threshold.

"Good Lord," Celia gasped. "What happened to you?"

His shadowed eyes swept the office. "Has she come in yet?"

"No."

"Called?"

Celia shook her head, staring at him as if he were a creature from outer space. He ran a trembling hand over his rain-matted hair and down his jaw, feeling the rough stubble of a day's growth of beard.

"What happened?" Celia asked haltingly.

"I wish I knew," Cord said, sinking into the couch, all energy drained from him. He let his head loll back on the cushions, squeezed his eyes shut tight and tried to think past the dull ache of his hangover and the grim certainty that Alison had left him forever.

"I DON'T LIKE it here!" Mandy said staunchly, crossing her chubby arms over her chest and eyeing the furniture in the rented house with disdain.

"Sure you do," Alison cajoled, though she didn't sound convincing. Mandy had lived all of her few years in a roomy, though time-worn, mansion. This small cottage with its tiny yard, battle-scarred furniture and musty smell wasn't even close to the grandeur and spaciousness of the Donahue house in Seattle.

"When's Uncle Cord coming?"

"I don't know," Alison hedged, tired of the same question she'd heard for the past two weeks. *Maybe never.*

"Bangles misses him!" Mandy declared.

Hearing his name, the pup whined from the kitchen where he was confined.

"Bangles misses Cord's chair, his slippers and his socks," Alison corrected. Then, to change the subject, she switched on the old black-and-white television crowded into a corner of the small living room. "Let's watch TV."

"Don't want to." Mandy wasn't about to be deterred.

The bond Mandy had recently formed with Cord had become strong and close, and Alison wondered for the millionth time if she'd made a mistake. Maybe she should have stayed in Seattle, married Cord and hoped that someday he would return her love.

"You're a fool," she chastised.

"What?"

"Oh, uh, nothing. Come on, I'll take you into town and buy you lunch. Mommy got paid today!" Well, that was a little bit of a lie. She'd finally received the check that closed out her savings account and it was precious little. Sooner or later she'd have to find a job and a baby-sitter and make some decisions about her future with Mandy. Her only contact with the Donahue family had been Norma, and she'd sworn the old housekeeper to secrecy when she'd called her just two days before.

"Don't want lunch."

"Oh, Mandy, sure you do," Alison said, tired of battling with her child. "We'll have fish and chips."

Mandy stuck out her tongue. "Yuck!"

"You like fish and chips."

"I hate it here!" Mandy declared, eyes fierce. "We go home, now! Bangles wants to see Lazarus."

Despite herself, Alison laughed. "First he misses Cord and now Lazarus—I don't think so."

Mandy's chin began to quiver. "But I do," she said, tears filling her eyes.

Alison melted. "Oh, honey," she whispered, wiping the tears from Mandy's eyes, "I'm sorry. Things will get better. You'll like it here."

"No!" Mandy shouted, lower lip protruding as she squirmed out of Alison's arms and ran down the short linoleum hallway to the kitchen.

Bangles yelped excitedly and Alison thought fleetingly of returning to Seattle and confronting Cord—giving in to his ridiculous demands and marrying him for the sake of their child.

But maybe it was too late. Maybe Cord had already decided that he'd rather sue her for custody than propose. And then what? She stared out the window to the gray day beyond. Even the authentic English flavor of Victoria couldn't cheer her as she heard Mandy confide to Bangles, "If Mommy won't take us back, we go alone!"

Alison dropped her forehead against the cool windowpane and fought the urge to break down completely. She couldn't bear the thought of losing Mandy—even to Cord.

CORD SAT AT the kitchen table leaning back in one chair, his boot heels propped on the seat of another as he watched Norma slipping her arms through the sleeves of her faded blue raincoat. She was acting nervously and wouldn't quite meet his eyes.

Alison had been gone over two weeks, and Cord's blind fear and desperation of the first day had slowly evolved into cold determination. He had already taken the first steps to deal with her and he'd leave no stone unturned to find her, even if he had to bribe every government official and hire every damned private investigator in the country to do it. Then, unfortunately, he'd give her up again. But this time it would be on his terms. Frowning at the emptiness deep in his soul, he tried to ease his pain in the knowledge that she'd finally get what she wanted, maybe even what she deserved.

"You know where they are," he said, eyes narrowed as he sipped the cup of coffee she'd offered him.

"I have no idea where Alison took Mandy." She shoved her glasses up her nose and adjusted her scarf.

"And you're a terrible liar."

"I've not been lyin' to you."

"And you haven't been tellin' me the truth, now, either," he mocked, using her own speech cadence.

Norma pursed her lips and tucked her handbag under her arm. "Don't you be accusin' me, Cord Donahue."

"It doesn't matter," he said with a lift of one shoulder. "Because whether you tell me or not, I'll find them."

"But I don't know—"

"Alison has to have money and a job. She's probably already requested her savings, and the bank will have her change of address—maybe even the post office. Then there's social security and the IRS. Sooner or later I'll find her."

"For cryin' in the night," Norma whispered.

"So, I'm willing to wait," he lied, gambling when he saw the doubt in her eyes. "You can tell me tonight and we can straighten this damned mess out, or I'll find out on my own. It'll cost me a little time and probably a lot of money but I'll find them both."

Norma wavered; he could see it in her face. His fingers tightened painfully over his cup but his expression never changed.

"You're blackmailin' me, that's what you're doin'!"

"And you're holding out on me. Look at it this way, if Alison didn't want me to find her, I mean if she really wanted to hide, she wouldn't have confided in you."

"But she knew I'd be worryin' about the child."

His eyes gleamed and he leaned forward. "So you do know," he whispered, forcing himself to remain seated. If he'd learned anything in the years he'd grown up under Norma's eye, it was when to push her and when to wait.

"Damn you, Cord." Then, rolling her eyes to the heavens, she sat heavily in the chair opposite him. "Of course I know where they are. Alison's rented herself a place in Victoria."

"Canada?"

"She thought she'd be safer there."

Cord's muscles slackened. "She's really afraid I'll hurt her or Mandy?" The thought made him sick inside and suddenly his coffee was bitter. He crossed to the sink and dashed the final dregs down the drain.

"I don't know what's goin' on in that mind of hers," Norma said vehemently. "This stunt is just about as bad as the one you pulled. But I'll tell you this—you two are so bullheaded and filled with pride you belong together." She reached into her pocket and handed him a wadded piece of paper.

He smoothed it on the counter, realized it was Alison's address and smiled at Norma. "Thanks."

"God help me when she finds out," Norma muttered, then left.

Cord didn't waste a minute. He yanked his jacket off

the peg, locked the door behind him and ran to his Jeep, wondering how he could stand the few hours it would take to drive to Victoria. He only hoped he'd make it to Anacortes before the last ferry left the mainland.

SHIVERING BENEATH HER umbrella, Alison clung tight to Mandy's hand as they walked along the uneven streets, peering in each shop window, delighting in the treasures displayed behind the glass. English bone china, Scottish plaids, French pastries and books from all over the world lined the windows.

After lunching on fish and chips, she had taken Mandy to an indoor park displaying exotic plants and birds. Mandy, wide-eyed and awestruck, had forgotten her pledge to run away from home—at least for a few hours.

They'd strolled along the marina, watched lovers climb into horse-drawn carriages, then ordered high tea at an elegant old hotel overlooking the bay.

By four o'clock Mandy was rubbing her eyes and Alison decided it was time to head back to the sorry little cottage on the outskirts of the city. "Let's go home now, pumpkin," she whispered to Mandy as she carried her to the car.

"Uncle Cord calls me sprite," Mandy reminded her.

"I know he does," Alison said, gently kissing Mandy's dark hair.

"I like it."

"So do I." *Here we go again.* But though Mandy obviously wanted to pursue her favorite subject, she leaned close to Alison's shoulder and began to suck her thumb quietly, the long day having taken its toll upon her. "Does he love me?" Mandy mumbled softly.

"Oh, yes, very much."

"Does he love you? Norma says he does."

If only Norma were right. "I don't know, sweetheart," she thought aloud, holding her daughter close.

Mandy was already asleep and didn't wake as Alison strapped her into her car seat.

Climbing behind the steering wheel, Alison glanced at the somber sky. A light drizzle fell from purple-tinged clouds and darkness began to cloak the streets. Snapping on her lights and wipers, Alison guided the car into the heavy evening traffic leading from the city and wondered if she had the nerve to swallow her pride and face Cord again.

Her thoughts were still as cloudy as the coming night when she wheeled into her driveway, stopped the car and promptly stepped into the middle of the largest puddle in the twin ruts. "Great," she murmured, unbuckling Mandy and hoisting her carefully to her shoulder.

The sleeping child barely stirred, even as Alison fumbled with the lock on the back door and slipped off her shoes on the porch. Rather than disturb Mandy, Alison placed her daughter on her bed, took off her shoes and socks, then wrapped her favorite blanket snugly around her tiny body. "You are precious," Alison whispered, turning off the light. *And Cord has the right to want her in his life.*

Cold inside, she started a fire, then wound her hair onto her head, stripped out of her wet clothes and stepped into a steaming hot bath. Closing her eyes, she leaned back, letting the warm water loosen her muscles.

Though she tried to concentrate on her future, her thoughts kept straying to Cord and that little twinge of guilt she'd felt ever since the night she'd driven away from Seattle. She'd left without saying goodbye, without a note or a phone call explaining that she and Mandy were fine and unhurt.

He must have been frantic when he'd discovered that Mandy was gone.

Blinking back a few stupid tears, she finished bathing then drained the tub and stepped into her terry bathrobe. She didn't bother taking down her hair but checked on Mandy. The child had barely moved and still lay under her tattered blanket.

Determined to shake off her latent sense of the blues, Alison padded to the kitchen, scrounged in the refrigerator and placed a pan of the previous night's lasagna in the oven. Then she poured herself a glass of wine and sat in front of the fire, staring at the red and gold flames.

She must have dozed because she was startled by a loud banging on her front door. Loud and insistent, the pounding kept up until she was on her feet and squinting through the tiny peephole. There on the front porch, his face angry and set, his eyes flashing with determination, was Cord.

Alison didn't know whether to laugh or cry.

CHAPTER THIRTEEN

"UNCLE CORD!" MANDY CRIED, the sleep in her eyes disappearing as Cord strode into the room.

"How are ya, sprite?" he asked, his voice catching as he kneeled down and held open his arms.

Without a second's hesitation she ran across the dull wooden floor and threw herself at him, her black hair a wild mass of curls.

"Hey, whoa," he said, but he chuckled deep in his throat and the menace in his eyes was suddenly gone. "God, I missed you," he whispered into her hair.

Alison felt tears sting her eyes but quickly dashed the betraying drops aside, hoping that Cord wouldn't guess the depths of her love. Seeing him there, bent on one knee and hugging Mandy so fiercely, made her realize she should never have left him.

"What took you so long to get here?" Mandy finally asked as Cord lifted her into his arms.

He glanced pointedly at Alison, his brown eyes accusing. "I had a little trouble finding the place."

Alison wanted to die.

"Now you know," Mandy said, glowing. "And we're all together again."

As if to add emphasis to her words, Bangles barked noisily from the kitchen, jumping up and down next to the gate. Grinning, Cord carried Mandy to the back of the house and promptly let the puppy out of his cage. In a mad dash the dog raced around the room, his toenails clicking on the hardwood, his tongue hanging out. Lamps rocked precariously as he dashed by at full gallop.

Cord tossed back his head and his rich laughter filled the rooms. "I see you haven't changed," he said with a chuckle, patting Bangles's broad head. In response the puppy licked his face and hands. "Lazarus has missed you."

"I told you," Mandy said, staring triumphantly at her mother. "Can we go home now?"

"Home?" Cord repeated.

"To Seattle," Alison clarified. "I've heard of nothing else since we got here." She heard the breathless quality in her voice and couldn't take her eyes off him. Had it only been two weeks since she'd stared into his mahogany-colored eyes or heard the warm sound of his laughter?

His hair was wet and disheveled, falling over his forehead as it had the first day she'd met him so long ago, and his features, though hard and defined, were as handsome as she remembered them.

He swallowed and set Mandy on the floor. "We can't go home tonight," he said, glancing at Alison. "Your mother and I have a few things to work out between us."

"Then we can go?"

"Maybe," he said, still watching Alison. She could feel his gaze on her neck and cheeks before his eyes slid lower—to the cleft between her breasts, a dusky hollow just peeking above the lapels of her bathrobe. Nervously she fingered her collar, hoping that the pulse at the base of her throat wasn't jumping so visibly as to betray her feelings.

"I'll go pack," Mandy decided.

"Hey, wait a minute—"

"Let her go," Alison said. "She's been waiting for this a long time." She met Cord's gaze with a faltering smile. "She's missed you. There hasn't been a day go by that she hasn't badgered me to take her home or call you."

"So why didn't you?"

"I...I needed time."

"And now?"

She blinked rapidly. "I don't know," she admitted. "I realize now that I was running away."

The buzzer rang on the oven and Alison used its insistent clamor as an excuse to leave the room. Being with Cord was dangerous and she couldn't think clearly when he was around—a symptom that hadn't changed over the years. She knew she had to return to Seattle and either marry him or fight with him over custody of Mandy. She couldn't wait any longer.

Undecided, she extracted the steaming casserole, and the warm scent of tomato paste, oregano and cheese filled the air as she set the hot platter on a breadboard.

She didn't hear Cord enter the kitchen and was surprised to feel his hands slip possessively around her waist. "I've missed you, too," he said, pulling her gently to him and burying his face in her nape. "It's been two and a half weeks of hell."

Shivering, she rubbed her arms, hoping not to fall victim all over again. "I should have called."

"You should never have left in the first place." He sighed heavily and she felt him tremble. "I know I was wrong. I overreacted after that talk with Benson. I'm sorry."

She squeezed her eyes shut tight but felt a flood of hot tears beneath her lids.

"When I first found out you left, I went out of my mind. But I've done a lot of thinking since then. I'm not about to force you into marriage, Ali," he said gently, his voice raw with unspoken emotions. "And I won't take Mandy away. But I want you to come home. I don't want my child to grow up alone. All I ask is that you let me see her."

Stunned, Alison could barely speak. Cord was giving up all his demands. She should have been happy but instead she felt a welling sense of disappointment and horrible, grieving loss. She'd hoped stupidly in the past few weeks that he would come to realize that he loved her and ask her to marry him because of that love.

"Come home, Ali. Bring Mandy. You can have the house. I'll move out. All I want is for the child to know I'm her father."

"Of course." She turned in his arms, saw the pain in his eyes and couldn't imagine living in the Donahue manor alone. The old house would seem empty and cold, and besides, it really belonged to Cord. "But you don't have to leave."

"Sure I do. It's what you've wanted all along. A lot of things have happened since you left, you know. The police are completely satisfied that I'm innocent and even the insurance company seems placated. They're still going over every piece of evidence and talking to old employees, but Jenkins called and admitted that it looks as if David was the embezzler. Smith National isn't all that pleased, but there's nothing much they can do except go after Francine Caldwell, who, upon Louise's urging, came clean and finally confessed."

"So the company is back on its feet."

He nodded, slowly dropping his arms. "It's just you and me who have the problem. And I'll leave."

Alison shook her head. "The house is yours. I don't want it."

"It's Mandy's," he corrected.

"I'm ready," Mandy sang out, running into the room and dropping her suitcase on the floor. Unlatched, the case flew open and all of Mandy's favorite toys fell out to scatter in all directions across the cracked linoleum. "Oh-ho."

"Oh-ho is right." Cord was on the floor in an instant. "I'll help you pick these up," he said, touching her nose fondly. "Then we'll let Mommy serve dinner. I'm starved!" He forced a grin but Alison could see the brackets of strain etched across his forehead and around his mouth. Giving up his child had been one of the hardest decisions of his life.

Cord helped Mandy scoop her toys back into the case, then played with her in the living room while Alison served dinner. A few minutes later they had all squeezed around the tiny Formica-topped table, and Mandy had managed to spread tomato sauce all over her face.

"Look at you," Alison chided, reaching over with her napkin to wipe Mandy's streaked chin. "You need a bath."

"I'll handle that while you do the dishes," Cord said as easily as if they all had lived together since Mandy's birth. Her heart squeezed painfully and she wondered how she could ever keep father and daughter apart—and why she would want to.

She cleared the table and listened to the water running in the bath. Cord was singing and Mandy giggled.

Torn inside, Alison went through the motions of cleaning the kitchen and heating water on the stove for instant coffee. She was reminded of the weekend she'd spent on the island with Cord. If only they'd taken Mandy with them. Perhaps things would be different between them now.

Mandy bounded out of the bathroom. Her face was pink and clean, mint-green pajamas covering her from her neck to her toes. "Those are the damnedest things to figure out," Cord muttered, shaking his head as he dropped into one of the chairs. "All those snaps."

"Cord put 'em on backward."

Laughing, Cord nodded. "Didn't know it till I tried to put Mandy's feet in and they were turned the wrong way."

"I've done that before," Alison remarked.

After searching through a pile of books, Mandy climbed onto the chair with Cord and plopped into his lap. "You read," she demanded, then her eyes brightened as she glanced at Alison. "Cord said I could call him Daddy," she announced proudly.

Alison nearly fell out of her chair. "He...he what?" she sputtered, hands shaking so badly she had to set her coffee cup on the table.

"He said it would be okay if I called him Daddy. So I will!"

"But—"

Mandy's lower lip stuck out. "I don't got a daddy no more and I want one!"

Oh dear God, Alison thought weakly. *So it's come to this.* Cord's arms were wrapped firmly around his child and Mandy was contentedly turning the pages of a picture book, one thumb in her mouth, her wet curls just under the sharp angle of Cord's chin. Cord's eyes stared straight into Alison's and she knew he was waiting for her to tell Mandy the truth.

"You can call Cord anything you want, honey," Alison said, her voice decidedly wobbly. "As long as he agrees."

"He told me."

"To call him Daddy?"

"That he is my daddy. I told him he was wrong. My daddy's dead," Mandy said matter-of-factly, then grinned up at Cord. "You read this one." She pointed emphatically to the book in her lap and Cord, after a meaningful look at Alison, began to read.

So he told her. And Mandy took it with a three-and-a-half-year-old's aplomb. Alison should have been angry but she was too tired to fight and all the pain of the past seemed such a waste.

At the steady drone of Cord's deep voice Mandy eventually nodded off. Without a word Cord lifted her gently and carried her into her bedroom. Alison's heart nearly broke at the tender way he held his daughter.

"Now," he said, returning to the living room. "What's it gonna be? Are you coming back to Seattle in the morning?"

"Yes," she decided, considering all her alternatives, which were practically none. "Mandy's been miserable ever since we left."

"And you?" he asked, eyes serious.

"It's…it's been rough," she admitted, swallowing back that peculiar lump that always formed in her throat whenever she thought of being separated from him.

"But you've managed."

"Scraped by," she said, avoiding his eyes and plunging her fists into the deep pockets of her robe. "I thought about getting a job and staying up here permanently but I don't think Mandy could adjust."

"Now she won't have to," Cord said quickly, standing and grabbing his jacket from the back of the couch. "I'll be back at ten tomorrow morning."

She watched him in despair. "You're leaving?" she whispered, disbelieving.

"As long as I have your word that you won't take off on me again."

"I...I won't." She forced a tiny smile.

"Good. Then I'll see you at ten."

Before he could change his mind, Cord walked out the front door and into the chilled night air. He took in several deep breaths, trying vainly to forget the inviting picture of Alison in her long white robe, her flushed face and the twisted knot of her dark hair pinned loosely to her crown. But her luminous hazel eyes haunted him still and he nearly turned around and strode back into the room. Instead he fished for his keys in his pocket and climbed into his Jeep.

She didn't want him—that much was plain. She was trying to be kind to him because he was Mandy's father but she wasn't interested in marrying him—not now and probably never. And he wasn't about to wait. If she wanted to raise Mandy alone, he'd live with it, as long as he could visit the child when he wanted.

Sure, his mind taunted as he jammed the Jeep into gear. *And you'll get over Alison.*

Swearing violently, he cranked hard on the steering wheel and drove toward the city, intent on stopping at the first motel he saw. It didn't take him long to spy a flickering red neon sign announcing vacancy, cable television and a pool at a run-down, two-story motel. Cord didn't care what the amenities were, just as long as he had a bed to toss and turn in the rest of the night. He would have stayed at Alison's, except that he couldn't trust himself with her. So he had to distance himself from her, just as he soon would in Seattle. Though it would be hell. Gritting his teeth, he signed the register, paid for one night and climbed the stairs to room 215.

The room was as bad as he'd expected but he didn't give a damn; he knew he wouldn't be able to sleep a wink.

ALISON HAD EVERYTHING packed by the time Cord knocked loudly on her door. She'd already talked to her landlady and written notes to the post office and phone company, and she was as nervous as a cat at the prospect of returning to Seattle.

"He's here!" Mandy announced jubilantly as she tugged open the door. "What took you so long?" she demanded, raising her arms, anxious to be lifted.

"Doesn't matter, does it, sprite? I'm here now."

Alison cleared her throat. "My car's all packed. All I have to do is drop off the key."

"I'll ride with Daddy!" Mandy decided, beaming.

"But—" Alison began to protest, then caught Cord's questioning glance.

"Not afraid I'll run off with her, are you?" he asked, lips twisting in an ironic smile.

"Of course not. Let's just transfer her car seat."

"And Bangles can come with us, too!" Mandy continued.

"Let's leave Bangles for Mommy," Cord said, chuckling despite the tension in the room. "That way you and I can talk!"

Mandy, the little traitor, seemed pacified as Cord unbuckled her car seat and placed it in his Jeep.

Bangles barked excitedly and tried to chase a cackling blue jay when Alison let him outside. He nearly bounded over the fence in his efforts to reach the taunting bird. "Come on, you," Alison ordered, snapping on his leash and waving as Cord backed out of the drive. Mandy was sitting proudly beside him, her teddy bear under one arm, waving with the other.

Wondering how she would ever be so cruel as to keep Cord from his daughter, Alison shoved her car into gear and left the little cottage in Victoria without any regrets.

She caught up with Cord on the ferry to Anacortes. He was standing near the prow of the huge boat, holding Mandy on one arm and pointing out the different islands of the San Juan chain.

The late-morning sun was pale but warm, and mist rose from the gray waters of the sound, surrounding the emerald-green islands in a transparent shroud. A stiff breeze made Mandy's nose turn red, and she whispered excitedly to her father as they passed buoys and other boats in the choppy water.

Alison wrapped her arms around her waist, standing near Cord, yet feeling miles away from him.

"Is that yours?" Mandy asked, pointing frantically toward Lopez Island.

"Mine?" he repeated, laughing. "No."

"Mama says you got an island all to yourself."

Alison rolled her eyes. "No, honey, I said Cord had a cabin on an island."

"That one?"

"No." Cord chuckled. "But someday I'll take you there."

"Today," Mandy decided.

"Not today, honey," he whispered, his voice barely audible over the steady rumble of the big ship's engines. "Today we go back to Seattle and work a few things out."

"Like what?" she wanted to know, turning her pixie-like face to his.

"Lots of things," he said gruffly, holding her close, and Alison felt her eyes burn from more than the wind.

The rest of the trip was without incident, and when Alison walked into the house, startling Lazarus from his perch in the windowsill, Norma beamed. "About time you came back here," she chastised. "I've got hot coffee in the pot and a feast fit for a king—crab and French bread and a huge salad!"

Alison's stomach quivered at the thought of food. She'd been so upset, she hadn't bothered eating anything all day. "Sounds great," she said weakly, trying to force some enthusiasm back in her voice.

"But not that great," Norma guessed. "Don't tell me, you and Cord had another row."

"Nothing so obvious as a row," Alison replied.

"Doesn't matter what you call it—it all means the same. You didn't work things out." Sighing, she turned back to the table where she was cracking the larger pieces of flame-colored Dungeness crab shells with a pair of pliers.

"We can't…" Alison said, barely able to utter the words. "Cord and I just can't seem to get along."

"Hogwash! Stubborn pride, that's what's in your way—both of you. I've said it before and I've been right." Muttering to herself, Norma kept working, cracking the crab with new fire.

Alison was too tired to argue. After returning Bangles to the utility room, Alison took her things back to her room upstairs and began unpacking. She hung up her clothes but couldn't shake the feeling that she was trespassing, turning Cord out of the home that was rightfully his.

Dinner was barely over when Cord pushed his chair away from the table. "I'm going out," he said. "If you need me, I'll be with Carl Zimmerman."

"The attorney?" Alison asked.

"A few last things to tie up for the insurance company," he explained, kissing Mandy before leaving.

"I thought that was all taken care of," Norma mused, watching the door shut behind him.

"Maybe there were some last-minute details."

"Maybe." But Norma didn't seem convinced.

Less than an hour later Mandy fell asleep on the couch. Alison carried the sleeping child upstairs and placed her teddy under her arm. Cord was right about one thing, Alison thought, glancing around the room at the pink wallpaper and curtains, clean white bookshelves and rainbow-printed toy box, Mandy did belong here with Norma and her friends. *And her father.*

Leaning against a white bureau, she knew what she had to do. She had to swallow her pride and ask Cord to marry her. Even if he didn't love her, she loved him and, in time, maybe they could capture again what they had once had. And if she spent a lifetime without his love, it was better than spending a lifetime without him. She couldn't cast him out of his own house, away from his only child.

Deciding she had to confront him, she waited in the den, watching the fire slowly smolder and die and listening as the clock chimed midnight, then one and two. With a sigh she finally gave up her vigil and climbed the stairs.

She thought she'd never fall asleep, that she was too keyed up, but the minute her head hit the pillow and she'd closed her eyes, she drifted off, her dreams vivid with Cord's image.

She awoke to the sounds of rain peppering the window and Mandy's running feet as the child hurled herself into Alison's room.

"Norma says it's about time you woke up."

Stretching, Alison glanced at the clock. "Oooh, she's right," she mumbled, realizing it was nearly ten and she still hadn't talked with Cord. "I'll be down in a minute. Is Cord up?"

"*Daddy* already left."

"*Great,*" she muttered, knowing she'd have to catch him tonight. They had so much to discuss—not only Mandy, but Alison's position at the company, when they would get married and where. "And *if,*" she told herself, frowning as she stepped into the shower.

Half an hour later she hurried downstairs to find Norma in the kitchen. Mandy was standing on a chair, helping cut out cookies.

"Good morning," Alison said, pouring herself a cup of coffee.

"Mornin'."

"Sorry I overslept."

Norma smiled. "You probably deserved it."

Alison laughed, filled with new hope. Today she would finally square things with Cord. "Look, I've got some errands to run," she said.

"I don't wanna go!" Mandy said. "I'm baking cookies for Daddy."

Norma's eyebrows quirked but she held her tongue and Alison blushed.

"I'll be back this afternoon," she said, waving as she slipped into her jacket and stepped outside. Ignoring the bad weather, she spent the day downtown, reestablishing her account with the bank and calling Celia from a nearby phone booth so they could meet for lunch.

"Tell me everything," Celia insisted, once they were seated in a small seafood restaurant in Pioneer Square.

"I thought maybe you'd heard *everything* from Cord already."

Celia shook her blond curls. "He's been a grouch of mammoth proportions since you've been gone."

"I didn't realize," Alison said, toying with her shrimp salad.

"At first he acted like a madman, but by the third day he calmed down and threw himself back into work. He managed to get back some old clients and he's refinanced the building—"

Alison's head snapped up and her heart began to pound. "You're sure about that?"

Nodding, Celia pronged a forkful of quiche. "It's kind of strange," she admitted thoughtfully. "When you first left, he was on this…this rampage. And then he turned a one-eighty and was so calm…so deliberate, it was downright scary. Weird, if you know what I mean. Like a man ready to die who was getting all his things in order."

"Such as?" Alison prodded, pushing her plate aside. She had no more interest in food and she fixed her eyes on her friend.

"Such as refinancing the building and the house."

"The house?"

"Yes, didn't you know?"

Feeling stupid, Alison shook her head.

"I think he received the money from selling his business—the cannery or whatever it was. He applied it toward the mortgage on the house and paid off the bank for the building."

"How did you find out about it?" Alison wanted to know.

"Because Cord Donahue can't type to save his soul. I found him struggling over some legal forms and offered.

He didn't look pleased to have me see what he was doing, but I think he was relieved."

"When did he do all this?"

"Just before he took off to find you. But he wasn't done."

"He wasn't?"

"Nope. But he told me he'd finish himself. That the rest was personal."

"I don't understand."

"Me either," Celia confided, tossing her napkin onto the table. "And he's been stranger ever since he brought you back. You'd think he'd be turning cartwheels. Even though his name has been cleared completely by the police and the insurance company has backed off from their claim against him, he's been as moody as an old grizzly bear!"

"I wonder why?" Alison mused, not liking the path of her thoughts.

"I was hoping you could tell me."

"Is Cord in the office?" Alison asked, suddenly anxious to talk to him. Stupidly, she had a sudden premonition of impending disaster.

Celia shook her head. "Nope. He's over at the attorney's office all day today. I think they're finalizing some of the papers I typed." She glanced at her watch and gasped. "Look, I've got to run," she said, reaching into her purse.

"This one's on me," Alison insisted.

"Okay, I don't have time to argue, but next time I'm buying." She grabbed her umbrella but stopped before walking away. "I guess I haven't said it, but I'm glad you're back. And please, consider coming back to work. That place is like a *tomb* without you, and Cord, well, he just hasn't been much company lately." Celia wended her way through groups of tables to the door, which she shouldered open before scurrying outside.

Alison leaned back in her chair and sipped the final drops of her coffee. What was Cord up to? Something wasn't right—she was certain Celia wasn't imagining things—but what?

Tonight, she decided, she'd find out by swallowing her stupid female pride, casting aside her vow of marriage only with mutual love and begging Cord to marry her.

CHAPTER FOURTEEN

DARK CLOUDS MOVED swiftly over the city, pouring rain from a leaden sky and turning day to night. Traffic was snarled, creeping past accidents on the slickened freeways. Taillights winked red on the road ahead, shimmering in the puddles.

Alison sat behind the steering wheel of her car, watching the wipers slap furiously at the sheeting rain and listening belatedly to the static-filled traffic report about the clogged conditions of the city's freeways.

By the time she reached the house it was after five and black as midnight.

Stepping through the door, she shook the rain from her hair and let a sorry-looking Lazarus into the kitchen. "Sorry I'm late," she said as Norma came bustling up.

"I heard about the traffic."

"Miserable," Alison admitted, for the first time glancing into Norma's worried face. Something had happened. Norma's usually bright expression had changed and her eyes behind her glasses were shadowed.

Mandy!

But the child was playing quietly in the corner of the kitchen with her dolls and toys. Other than offering her mother a bright smile, Mandy didn't say a word. She was too wrapped up in her world of make-believe. "What happened?"

"You tell me," Norma said. "I want to know everything that happened between you and Cord."

"Nothing—"

"Somethin' did!"

"Why? Oh God." Paralyzing fear started deep in her heart, catching her in its clammy grip. Something had happened to Cord!

"Tell me," Norma demanded. "And I want to know everything from the minute you left here for Victoria."

"But Cord—where is he?"

"I don't know! I'm hopin' you'll give me some clue," the older woman said, controlling the panic registering in her eyes.

Alison tried to stay calm. "Okay, okay. When I left here it was because Cord gave me an ultimatum," Alison admitted, lowering her voice so that Mandy couldn't hear the discussion. "You probably guessed Mandy is really Cord's child."

"I'd thought it was possible, yes. And I did hear her call him Daddy this mornin'."

Quickly, in hushed tones, Alison related the events of her relationship with Cord and subsequent marriage to David.

"And now?" Norma prodded.

"The ultimatum. Either I marry him or he threatened to take Mandy from me."

"He wouldn't!" Norma insisted. "And besides, what's to prevent you from marryin' the man?"

"Nothing, now. Because he's changed his mind. When he came to Victoria, he told me he would never take her away from me."

"But you still won't marry him?" Norma clucked her tongue. "And why not? You'll never find a better man."

"I know, and I've decided to take him up on his offer, if he'll still have me," she confided.

"Don't you love him?" Norma asked, laying a comforting hand over Alison's forearm.

"That's not the problem," Alison admitted. "He doesn't love me. And…well, after my marriage to David, I swore if I ever married again it would only be for love."

"You don't think Cord loves you?" Norma asked, clearly astounded.

"Not anymore."

"And what are ya, blind?"

"But—"

"Don't you go buttin' me. That man cares more for you than life itself! Why else do you think he took off all those years ago? You said it yourself, he was protectin' you. Didn't he take the blame for everything, risk his life and reputation to save yours? And you don't think he loves you?"

"He did then, but that was years ago."

"And love dies, then, does it?" Norma shook her head. "Think about it, Alison. Didn't that man stay away, thinkin' you were happy and safe married to David? Didn't he come back here the minute he knew you were free?"

"For revenge."

"Revenge, my eye! He loves you. Always has and always will. Open your eyes, girl," Norma said, her fingers curling over Alison's arms. "Or you just may lose him forever."

"Why? What's happened?"

"He's gone," Norma said simply.

"Gone where?"

"I don't know. But somethin's not right. Ever since he

returned from Victoria he's been moody and quiet, even with me. Last night he didn't come home till the early hours and then he took off out of here at the crack of dawn. I'm tellin' you, he's plannin' somethin', sure as I'm standin' here. And it's not good."

"Did he say something?"

"That's the trouble—didn't say a word. Just kissed the child goodbye and hung on to her as if he'd never see her again. Then he left."

"When?"

"Not more than half an hour ago."

"Maybe you're making more of this than there is."

"I raised that boy," Norma stated, her eyes filled with worry. "I know when he's upset."

Not wanting to contradict Norma and fighting her own sense of panic, Alison ran upstairs to Cord's room. His clothes were still in the closet, his personal belongings all intact. Alison breathed normally again. Norma had panicked, that was all. Surely she'd blown the entire situation out of proportion.

"Alison!" Norma called from downstairs. Her voice quavered. "Down here!"

Alison's feet barely touched the stairs as she hurried to the study. Norma was standing at the desk, reading sheet after sheet of legal forms. "I knew it," she whispered. "He's gone."

"Gone?" Alison picked up the first legal document, her eyes quickly scanning the legalese. She drew in a swift breath as she read the neatly typed pages, a stone forming in the pit of her stomach.

"He left everything to you," Norma whispered. "You and Mandy. The house, the business, everything." Tears began to slide down her weathered cheeks.

Alison didn't waste time. Crushing the damned documents in her fist, she ran to the hall closet, found her raincoat
and called over her shoulder, "Can you watch Mandy?"

"Yes, but where are you goin'?"

"I don't know." Without another word she found her
purse and ran outside to the garage. Flicking on the ignition,
she plunged the forms deep into her pocket, rammed the
car into reverse and then tore out of the driveway.

Where was he? And why was he leaving? Sick inside,
her hands clammy over the wheel, she drove toward the
city. She couldn't believe that she would find him but she
knew one place she had to look.

Her fear as great as it had been four years before on a
stormy night, she drove crazily to the marina on the slim
chance that he would try to leave by the same means he
had in the past.

"Please, God, let me find him," she prayed, slamming
the car into park and throwing open the door. The wind
was violent and rain slanted from the black sky. Cold and
wet, it drenched her hair and slid down her neck as she
ran, slipping on the wet boards of the docks.

"Cord!" she cried, her voice as lost in the wind as it
had been years before. "Cord. God, please, be here." Her
boots slid on the slick planks and the wind and rain tore
at her face, howling across the sound, tossing the tiny
boats on the reckless sea.

Ali's Dream swayed on its moorings and there, uncoil-
ing the rope, was a man. *Cord!* She'd caught him. Heart
pounding crazily, she leaped into the boat before he had
a chance to glance up and catch sight of her. The small
craft rocked and swayed beneath her.

"What the devil?" he cried, whirling around, his face
ashen when he saw her. "What're you doing here?"

"Maybe I should ask you that," she said, her eyes locked with his. "I've played this scene before, Cord, and I won't play it again." For the first time since he'd returned, she was unashamed of the love shining in her eyes.

"I think you'd better leave," he said, his jaw working, his eyes hard.

"Never," she replied, her own eyes bright with tears, her voice nearly lost with the rush of the wind.

"What?"

"I said you can't get rid of me that easily. I'm never leaving you."

He stood stock-still, unmoving as rain slid down his face and neck and the wind whipped his night-dark hair in front of his eyes. "You don't have to say anything," he whispered.

"But I will. I'm here because I love you, Cord," she said bravely, half expecting a caustic rebuff. "I always have and I always will. The only reason I wouldn't marry you before was because I was afraid you didn't love me. But now it doesn't matter. Because whether you love me or not, I want to be your wife—not because I'm Mandy's mother but because I lost you once before and I never want to take that chance again."

He dropped the rope but still the doubts lingered in his eyes. "You don't have to do this, Ali. Not for Mandy, not for me. I've left you everything—"

"To hell with what you left me," she cried, reaching into her pocket and withdrawing the damned legal forms. With strength born of anger, she ripped the documents in half and then half again.

"Wait a minute—"

But she cast the blasted pieces of paper into the blackened waters of the sound where they drifted apart on the rough water. "I don't want your money, Cord, and I don't want your social position. I don't care about the house or the investment company. All I want is you."

Standing on the rocking boat with rain lashing at her hair and face, she squared her small shoulders. "I want you to marry me, Cord. I only wish I hadn't let my pride get in my way before!"

"This is a proposal?" he asked, a smile beginning to tease the tight corners of his mouth.

"Yes."

He took a step forward. "And you didn't think I loved you."

"No."

He slowly reached her. "After everything I did?" he asked, cupping her wet chin with the palm of his hand.

"Let's not go into all that. Every time we do, it gets us into trouble."

"For once, Ali, I agree with you."

"Then you'll marry me?"

"Yes."

He considered a moment and said, "Right now?"

"Now?" Her heart was beating so fast she could hear it above the rush of the wind tangling her hair.

"There's a preacher on the island who has been waiting for years to do the honors—a friend of my dad's."

"But we just can't run off and…" Then she saw the sparkle of amusement in his eyes and she bit her tongue. "Well, sure we can," she teased, kissing his rough cheek and reveling in the touch and smell of him. "Let's go, skipper. Anywhere you say."

With a grin he wrapped his arms around her and kissed her wet lips. "Later," he promised. "First we have to go back to the house and tell Norma and Mandy. I have a feeling they would both kill us if they weren't involved in the ceremony."

Alison giggled, sliding her arms around his soggy jacket. "I can wait," she teased.

"But only a few hours."

"Whatever you say!"

He brushed his lips over hers again. "This time, Ali, nothing will keep us apart. I loved you then, I love you now, and I'll love you forever."

"And I love you," she vowed.

He tilted her chin up with his fingers and, in the shower from stormy skies, claimed her lips with his. She could feel him tremble and knew without a doubt this time would be forever.

* * * * *

HQN™

We *are* romance™

**Don't miss the second installment in the
McKettricks of Texas trilogy from *New York Times*
and *USA TODAY* bestselling author**

LINDA LAEL MILLER

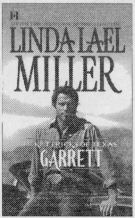

Fast track up the political ladder, fast cars, fast women—that's Garrett McKettrick. Make that *was*, as a scandal has brought him unexpectedly home to the family ranch in Blue River, Texas. Garrett doesn't think he has the land in his blood, but Blue River has other attractions—like his former high school nemesis, Julie Remington. Good thing they have nothing in common...except their undeniable attraction and a future brighter than the Texas sun.

McKETTRICKS OF TEXAS:
GARRETT

Available now wherever books are sold!

www.HQNBooks.com

PHLLM441

FROM THE MASTER OF PARANORMAL ROMANCE,
NEW YORK TIMES AND *USA TODAY*
BESTSELLING AUTHOR

GENA SHOWALTER

Dare to open Pandora's Box...again?

Available now!   Coming soon!

Don't miss these darkly sensual tales in
the *Lords of the Underworld* series—
including a brand-new bonus guide in *Into the Dark!*

We *are* romance™

www.HQNBooks.com

PHGST2010R

New York Times and USA TODAY bestselling author

Susan Andersen

is back with a classic tale of high-stakes romance.

After wagering a World Series baseball that wasn't his to lose, professional poker player Jax Gallagher will do anything to get his hands on it...including wining, dining and seducing sexy dancer Treena McCall, owner of the ball—and his heart.

Skintight

Available now!

"Bright, smart, sexy, thoroughly entertaining."
—*New York Times* bestselling author Jayne Ann Krentz

We *are* romance™

www.HQNBooks.com

PHSA457

A steamy, sexy, scintillating new romance from

VICTORIA DAHL

A magnet for wild, complicated women, treasure-hunting millionaire Max Sullivan is thrilled to have finally found his "normal" girl-next-door fantasy come to life with Chloe Turner. But when Chloe's notoriety catches up with her, will their torrid romance make it to the mainland?

Coming soon wherever books are sold!

"A smashing success, filled with a titillating combination of sexual fantasy and suspense."
—*Booklist* on *Talk Me Down*

HQN™

We *are* romance™

www.HQNBooks.com

PHVD462R

REQUEST YOUR FREE BOOKS!

2 FREE NOVELS
FROM THE ROMANCE COLLECTION
PLUS 2 FREE GIFTS!

YES! Please send me 2 FREE novels from the Romance Collection and my 2 FREE gifts (gifts are worth about $10). After receiving them, if I don't wish to receive any more books, I can return the shipping statement marked "cancel." If I don't cancel, I will receive 4 brand-new novels every month and be billed just $5.74 per book in the U.S. or $6.24 per book in Canada. That's a saving of at least 28% off the cover price. It's quite a bargain! Shipping and handling is just 50¢ per book.* I understand that accepting the 2 free books and gifts places me under no obligation to buy anything. I can always return a shipment and cancel at any time. Even if I never buy another book, the two free books and gifts are mine to keep forever.

194/394 MDN E7NZ

Name	(PLEASE PRINT)	
Address		Apt. #
City	State/Prov.	Zip/Postal Code

Signature (if under 18, a parent or guardian must sign)

Mail to The Reader Service:
IN U.S.A.: P.O. Box 1867, Buffalo, NY 14240-1867
IN CANADA: P.O. Box 609, Fort Erie, Ontario L2A 5X3

Not valid for current subscribers to the Romance Collection
or the Romance/Suspense Collection.

Want to try two free books from another line?
Call 1-800-873-8635 or visit www.morefreebooks.com.

* Terms and prices subject to change without notice. Prices do not include applicable taxes. N.Y. residents add applicable sales tax. Canadian residents will be charged applicable provincial taxes and GST. Offer not valid in Quebec. This offer is limited to one order per household. All orders subject to approval. Credit or debit balances in a customer's account(s) may be offset by any other outstanding balance owed by or to the customer. Please allow 4 to 6 weeks for delivery. Offer available while quantities last.

Your Privacy: Harlequin Books is committed to protecting your privacy. Our Privacy Policy is available online at www.eHarlequin.com or upon request from the Reader Service. From time to time we make our lists of customers available to reputable third parties who may have a product or service of interest to you. If you would prefer we not share your name and address, please check here. ☐

Help us get it right—We strive for accurate, respectful and relevant communications. To clarify or modify your communication preferences, visit us at www.ReaderService.com/consumerschoice.

MROM10R

HQN™

We *are* romance™

USA TODAY bestselling author

KASEY MICHAELS

brings you a passionate and sensual new tale in the Daughtry family series.

When her beloved dies in battle, Lady Lydia Daughtry assumes she'll never love again. Until Tanner Blake, the deliciously handsome Duke of Malvern, awakens a part of her she never knew existed. But it will take all of Tanner's powers of persuasion to convince Lydia that his love is worth risking her heart once again.

How to Beguile a Beauty

Available now wherever books are sold!

www.HQNBooks.com

PHKM433

LISA JACKSON

77409	MONTANA FIRE	___ $7.99 U.S.	___ $9.99 CAN.
77373	RISKY BUSINESS	___ $7.99 U.S.	___ $8.99 CAN.
77274	HIGH STAKES	___ $6.99 U.S.	___ $6.99 CAN.
77202	THE McCAFFERTYS: RANDI	___ $6.99 U.S.	___ $8.50 CAN.
77046	TEARS OF PRIDE	___ $6.99 U.S.	___ $8.50 CAN.

(limited quantities available)

TOTAL AMOUNT	$ _____
POSTAGE & HANDLING	$ _____
($1.00 FOR 1 BOOK, 50¢ for each additional)	
APPLICABLE TAXES*	$ _____
TOTAL PAYABLE	$ _____

(check or money order—please do not send cash)

To order, complete this form and send it, along with a check or money order for the total above, payable to HQN Books, to: **In the U.S.:** 3010 Walden Avenue, P.O. Box 9077, Buffalo, NY 14269-9077; **In Canada:** P.O. Box 636, Fort Erie, Ontario, L2A 5X3.

Name: _____
Address: _____ City: _____
State/Prov.: _____ Zip/Postal Code: _____
Account Number (if applicable): _____

075 CSAS

*New York residents remit applicable sales taxes.
*Canadian residents remit applicable GST and provincial taxes.

HQN™

We *are* romance™

www.HQNBooks.com

PHLJ0610BL